The Evo

RI

THE EVOLUTION TRILOGY

RETURN

Vanessa Wester

Kathryn

In the Game of Life,
Destiny is the winner...

Vanessa
xx

ISBN-13: 978-1492770794
ISBN-10: 1492770795

For my husband, Robert

Love at first sight.
Love that holds tight.
Love will divide,
And yet, it can last forever...

Vanessa Wester, 2013

Cast of Characters

* The Originals – First inhabitants of the community

English

Roberts Family

*Jeff Roberts, *founder of The Community, deceased*
*Judith Roberts, *his wife, deceased*

*Emily Roberts, *their daughter*

*Ian Roberts, *their son*
Carmen Roberts (nee Clausen), *Ian's wife*
Enrique Roberts, *Ian's oldest son*
Joaquin Roberts, *Ian's youngest son*

Thorn Family

Steven Thorn, *Emily Roberts' son*

Paul Thorn, *his father*
Clara Thorn, *his step-mother, deceased*

Other

Caitlin Chance, *Steven's girlfriend*

German

Abel Family

*Isaac Abel
*Catherine Abel (nee Roberts), *his wife*

Benjamin Abel, *his son*
Lina Abel (nee Santos), *Benjamin's wife*

Susanna Abel, *Benjamin's daughter*
Gideon Abel, *Benjamin's son*

Jan Abel, *his son*
Beatrice Abel (nee Santos), *Jan's wife*
Tobias Abel, *Jan's son*

Else Abel, *his daughter*

Spanish

Santos Family

*Franco Santos
*Elena Santos, *his wife*

*Juan Santos, *his son*
*Anna Santos (nee Roberts), *Juan's wife*
Francis Santos, *Juan's son*

Lucy Santos, *his daughter*

Swedish

Clausen Family

*Morten Clausen
*Arla Clausen, *his wife*

Eilif Clausen, *his son*
*Lana Clausen (nee Santos), *Eilif's wife*
Ingrid Clausen, *Eilif's daughter*
Tomas Clausen, *Eilif's son*

Doctor Johannes Clausen, *his son*
*Hortensia Clausen (nee Santos), *Doctor Johannes wife*
Jenson Clausen, *Johannes' son*

Prologue

Southampton, England, September 2011

Caitlin turned as she stuffed the numerous leaflets into her bag. Her curly, red hair was in the way again. She really hated it, one day she would go short. Her cheeks burned as she got flustered. It was no surprise she was on edge. It was the first time she had lived away from home. Finally, she had become a student. Not to forget the fact she had her own place, away from her parents. She gave a sly smile at the thought.

Distracted, she bumped into the person behind her and a dull thud followed. She watched in horror as her bag, and all its contents, scattered on the floor like a wave. Frazzled, she leant down to pick everything up.

A deep male voice caught her off guard as it apologised. It was followed by a pair of toned masculine hands that reached out to help. They looked interesting.

Caitlin looked up to see who it was and time seemed to stop. Transfixed, she gawped with a slightly open mouth.

Conscious of the fact he had spoken, she snapped out of the trance and focused. She could feel the heat radiating off her cheeks.

'Hello.' His expression was one of amusement.

'Erm, err, yeah, hello,' she stuttered.

Mesmerised, she stared. It was probably rude but she didn't care. His hair was thick, wavy and practically black in colour, and he towered above her by quite a few inches. But it was the eyes that intrigued her the most. She had never seen amber coloured eyes with such exquisite detail. They looked like cats eyes, framed by dark, thick lashes and a perfect face.

'Are you a swimmer?' he asked, as he handed over the swimming club leaflet.

His received pronunciation gave away his upbringing. It was polished and refined, as expected of someone from a posh background. It wouldn't surprise her if he had attended something poncy like boarding school.

9

'I–I guess so, but I'm considering my options,' she said, holding up the water polo flyer. Nervous, she looked to the right, unable to maintain eye contact.

'Interesting.' He took a step forward and moved towards the swimming stand. 'Well, I might see you around. Sorry to make your things fall like that.'

She could not believe *he* was apologizing.

Her jaw dropped as she saw him picking up the same leaflet she had only just been browsing. If he was a swimmer, hell would freeze over before anyone stopped her joining. Paranoid, she re-joined her flatmate Georgina and casually glanced in his direction. She muttered under her breath, 'I didn't even say sorry for being such a klutz.'

Deep down she knew it didn't matter if she did come across him again. There was a zero chance someone like that would be interested in someone like her.

Chapter 1

Restless Minds

Caitlin hadn't said a word to Steven in hours. She had to admit she was worried his mother, Emily, would hear. She glanced over her shoulder and stared at the misshapen body slumped on the back seat. It was a sorry sight, twisted at an odd angle. Emily's face retained an angelic expression as she slept.

Steven refused to sit next to Emily, and had taken the wheel. It was obvious she was not going anywhere in a hurry. She wondered if it was cruel to let Emily suffer, frankly she was past caring. That woman was evil and she scared Caitlin.

Caitlin struggled to understand how Emily could have killed Steven's stepmother, the mother who had loved and raised him. With murder, Emily had ensured that her only son would never, ever care about her. She was convinced the only reason he kept her alive was because he had a conscience.

Caitlin had no idea what they were planning to do, but she suspected Steven would leave Emily in the capable hands of the community.

The community.

Caitlin struggled to come to terms with everything that had happened over the past few weeks. Her life had been turned upside down when Steven changed her. A new life waited, the old one no longer accessible to someone like her – a killer, freak of nature, or even, a *vampire*. She struggled to understand why she had allowed Steven to change her, to make her like him. What had she been thinking?

The signs for Southampton Airport Parkway meant they were getting close, so she broke the silence. 'Are we going back to the house?'

'I don't think we have any choice,' Steven replied. His hand covered hers for a second and he gave a worried smile. 'You okay?'

Caitlin wanted to laugh, but she refrained herself. 'I'm as good as could be expected.'

'Right.' He pursed his lips.

'Steven,' she sighed, 'you know what I mean.'

'It's okay, you don't have to be nice. This situation is, well, just a disaster. A man is supposed to protect the woman he loves not destroy her life.'

Caitlin put her hand on his leg, 'Steven, you were never meant to be my protector. This is not a fairy-tale. There is no way to ever determine what life throws at us. This could be fate, you never know. Ever thought of that?'

'Fate?' he scowled. 'In that case, I hate fate. Fate took the only mother I have ever known away,' he sounded choked, 'the fact it was via the hand of my real mother makes me think fate is a real joker.'

Caitlin withdrew her hand. He was right of course.

In his rage, Steven had nearly strangled Emily.

Caitlin knew they were very strong, almost superhuman. It felt wrong to think it now, but a part of her could not wait to explore the facets of what she had become. Steven had made her as close to an immortal as any human was ever likely to get. Of course, they knew they were not immortal, death would come to get them one day.

Saying that, from what she knew, they did not change appearance for a long time, had inhuman strength, were all extremely smart, and had certain extra gifts thrown in. She wondered what her something special would be. Steven could use echolocation to track things down from a great distance. It was a nifty skill. She did hope whatever she was good at would be really, *really* clever.

'Sorry,' Caitlin apologised. She did not want to say sorry, but she thought she should. 'It was wrong of me to say fate could make this all happen. I'm really sorry about your mum.'

Steven rubbed her hand gently. 'It's okay. Maybe fate has its hand on some, but not all, of it.'

'Maybe,' Caitlin gave a half-smile. 'We should go out tonight and just have a good time.'

Steven put his hand back on the steering wheel. 'Caitlin, do you get that we have some serious problems. We can't just go out. What if…?' he trailed, lost in thought.

'What if…?' Caitlin repeated. She needed to know where he was going with this.

Steven gave her a quick glance, she loved his amber eyes. She could look at those forever. She was glad he wouldn't age. It would be a shame for a face that perfect to get lost through old age.

'Please remember. What if you get tempted, what if I get tempted? I don't think we want to kill near home, do you?'

Caitlin sighed again, 'Steven, if we need to drink blood, we need to drink blood. Stop apologising for what we are. You changed me into what I am. I have to live with this for the rest of my life, as do you. No point feeling bad about it. Why do you feel bad about what you are?'

Steven became deep in thought and stared ahead for a few minutes. Caitlin looked away, not knowing what to say. She was not going to spend the rest of her life feeling sorry for herself. She had been there, done that. She was ready to be a new person, a person who did not wallow in self-pity and worry about everything. In fact, she was not going to worry at all. She would let the wind take her.

She was a free spirit – within reason of course.

***

Steven did not know what to say. When he had been taken away the previous year and forced to leave everyone he loved behind so that he could make the change, he hated everything about the community he supposedly belonged to. He did not want to have to drink blood, animal or human. He did not want to kill. Yet, he had killed and he was stronger for it. He had learned to hunt, share, and survive when he lived in the Amazon jungle. He had found out about his ancestors, about the accident that made them what they had become.

He still struggled to believe his kind had evolved after mutated bats bit them and changed them into a new type of humanity. It was a fantasy, and now he knew they could also change humans. He was the hybrid child. Caitlin was the second ever changed human, his grandmother the first. He could not understand why his grandparents had chosen to share the secret with him. Either way, he regretted having changed Caitlin. It had been a reckless act, a moment of insanity.

Worst of all, he had no idea what the community would make of them.

They had accepted him when he lived there, but he sensed a lot of suspicion and he knew some resented him. They were both mongrels, not pure breeds. His real mother, sat on the back seat, was pure. She was one of the first to be bitten by the bats. She was one of the originals. Yet, she was crazy. It seemed to him like she was the reason all the safeguards were implemented in the community. She had been out of control from the start. She had made the originals scared that more would be just like her, ruthless killers.

'You know Emily killed many people, don't you?' He had to try to explain.

'I guess, but why does it matter what she did? You can't live your life based on someone else's mistakes.'

Caitlin seemed to see the world in black or white, she used to see things in grey. 'No, true,' he paused, 'but, there's no need to repeat them. Emily killed many humans for her survival, and most of it happened when she was amongst humans. She has no control. We have to be different. I don't think we can live in a world where we can kill at will.'

'It sounds to me like the community has everything we need. Why would we want to live in the open when we can live there?'

'It's not that simple, the community is designed well, but it is also designed to keep people in. It's a community where people are self-sufficient, but in a cage nonetheless,' he bit his lower lip. 'Do you want to lose your freedom?'

'When you put it like that, no. Why would anyone want to lose their freedom?'

Steven could tell he was finally putting his point across. The sound of her voice alone told him she did not like the idea of living in a cage. 'So, you have to learn control. Otherwise, we'll end up like her.' He thumbed towards the back seat, glanced in the rear-view mirror and grimaced as he saw she was awake.

***

A muffled sound in the back made Caitlin turn. She jumped back in the seat when she saw Emily's eyes open, glaring at her. The strangest thing was they were the same colour as Steven's. Now she came to think of it, Steven looked a lot like his mother.

'My son has a valid point,' the hoarse, muffled voice of Emily was disturbing. 'I certainly never wanted to live in a cage, because that is exactly what the community is.'

Steven narrowed his eyes. Caitlin flinched as she looked from Steven to Emily, she did not like where this was going.

Steven spoke slowly, 'But if you break the rules and threaten to expose the community then you don't deserve to leave, especially when you're a cold, calculating and ruthless murderer.'

'Perhaps,' there was amusement in her tone, 'but, I'm not the one who told a human about us. I'm not the one that actually threatens to expose us. Who is this girl, Steven? Who are you, my dear?'

Caitlin's jaw dropped, she had no idea what to reply.

Steven saved her. 'She's not your concern, and we don't have to explain anything to you. You're nothing to me, nothing.'

Caitlin could not help noticing the way Emily's eyes drooped – she did care what he thought. She stared at Caitlin, gave a small smile and then closed her eyes.

Caitlin put her hand behind Steven's neck and gave it a slow rub, then ran her hand down the base of his skull and gave him a gentle massage.

Steven eased back into her hand, turned to the left and kissed her arm, 'Thank you. I needed that.'

'I know.' Caitlin smiled. 'What are we going to do?' She knew it was a loaded question. She wanted to add, 'With Emily.' But she knew she didn't have to.

'The only thing we can,' his eyes expressed a sadness his voice hid.

Emily was outraged. It was bad enough she had allowed herself to get overpowered by Steven. For a moment she actually considered giving up on life, but death was not waiting for her yet. She needed more time, there was more she had to achieve in this life. The problem was she had become immobile, there was nothing she could do. She needed to get some human blood, it was the only way she would heal.

The question was how.

Her foolish son and that girl had and gone and left her alone, she could not believe they had done that. She had yelled, but her voice could not carry at all and eventually she gave up. She knew there was no-one in the house but her.

Something told her she was paralysed, and the thirst was killing her.

They had left her to die.

Even though she knew that by killing Steven's beloved stepmother she had stooped to a new low, she never expected this. She never expected his hatred.

The girl knew too much.

It was strange they planned to move to the community, impossible even. The girl would never survive there, unless... unless, Steven had done something. Her mind clicked and whirred as all the facts aligned.

Her mother, Judith, had chosen to die. Her father, Jeff, had chosen to die. She wondered, cursing aloud, if her mother had lied. Could it be true that her mother had never been bitten by the bats? Emily remembered a vague admission, followed by a denial when Emily had pressed the point later on.

The thing was if her mother had not been bitten by the bats, then someone must have changed her, made her like one of them. The only person capable of doing that was her dad. He was the only one that would have wanted it.

If this was true, they must have told Steven how to do it. The girl could have been changed. Her eyes narrowed as anger took over. She failed to understand why her parents had trusted her son, when they had not trusted her. She could have had a life with Steven's dad if they had told her there was a way.

It was not fair. Nothing in her life was ever fair. There had to be a way to get to the girl.

Chapter 2

A Community Meeting

For someone like Ian, to admit defeat or even to acknowledge he was to blame for anything was a hard pill to swallow. But, swallow it he would. It did not matter he had not done anything personally, his family had. Now, he had to account for their actions. He had to represent them and take the heat. The situation sucked – big time. If it wasn't for his principles, he would have disowned his parents. He shuddered at the thought. Even he could not do that.

It seemed unreal that as the youngest son he bore the weight of responsibility for the Roberts family on his shoulders. His father, Jeff, the founder of the community was dead. His mother, Judith, was also dead. His sister, Emily, was missing and his two older sisters were traumatised at the loss of their parents.

As an Englishman, he had to maintain his composure. He would not fall to pieces so easily. He squeezed his wife's hand, Carmen, who offered him a constant sanctuary. His beautiful and patient Spanish wife was his soul mate. He could not imagine life without her. He had to admit he was just like his dad in that regard, which was why deep down he could not resent his dad for giving up on life when his mum died. Regardless, it did not make the situation any easier to handle.

He watched the faces of the others as they arrived and noted the fact no-one made eye contact. This was unchartered territory after all. It was inevitable that a meeting would be called, but it still unnerved him. If anyone had a problem in the past, his father always had the solution and his mother became the mediator when disagreements broke out. Neither of them would be there anymore. Their absence left a gaping hole in the proceedings.

He looked around the table as the original members of the community waited. At the head of the table, he now assumed the role of chairperson. It felt natural to take over from his dad.

He clasped his hands together and began, 'Before I begin, Lana will not be joining us, and has passed her vote to Carmen?'

A few nods acknowledged the arrangement.

He continued, 'As you all now know, my parents, Jeff and Judith, have passed on. It is a huge blow to the entire community. When my father made his decision to stay in England he wanted to keep an eye on Steven, but he also wanted to stay with my mother. I'm sure you can understand. Apparently, when she died he also gave up on life. We only know that he's dead. As far as we can tell, Steven buried him as he promised. We believe he's telling the truth.'

The Spanish contingent shuffled in their seats and the oldest, Franco, frowned and interrupted. His thick, Spanish accent still enveloped his speech, 'If you choose to believe Steven, so be it, we do not have any reason to believe him. For all we know, he could have murdered them both. It is possible.'

Ian shook his head. He might have his doubts about his nephew, but even he would not go there. Through pursed lips, he replied, 'Steven did *not* kill them.'

Franco narrowed his deep set eyebrows and scowled, 'We've never been given the luxury of choice. Ever since 1943 all we've ever done has been in the interests of our *united* future. I thought the idea back then was to create a community we would protect. Going back to live within normal humanity was never an option,' he raised his eyebrows, as though he wanted to add effect to his pause, 'and yet, both Jeff and Judith went back and gave up on the life they envisaged. You really expect me to believe that?'

Ian maintained eye contact and faced Franco. Franco's stern expression, thick bushy eyebrows, clean shaven face and slicked black hair gave him an air of sophistication. He was always in control. Ian glanced at Franco's wife, Elena. She was so timid in comparison, petite in stature, with a mop of curly brown hair and childish features. He could not think of anyone more complacent.

Ian had to keep calm. 'Granted, but I'm sure that if

something happened to Elena you would want to have your final resting place next to her.'

Franco chuckled, 'But, of course – in an ideal world, we all know that our situation has always been far from *ideal*.'

'Your point is valid Franco, but let's hear what Ian has to say before we make judgement,' Morten interceded. The Swede had always been the diplomat in any negotiations. With wavy bleach blond hair and an athletic build to match Thor, he was equally intimidating and yet alluring in his countenance. 'We're sorry for your loss, Ian. We all miss Jeff and Judith. Please continue.'

Franco huffed. Elena squirmed in her seat.

Ian tried to ignore them and continued, 'Emily's disappearance was unfortunate…'

It was the turn of another Spaniard to speak. This time it was his sister Anna's husband, Juan, who put his oar in with a sarcastic cough. He glared at Ian. 'Careless if you ask me, *not* unfortunate.' He looked and acted like Franco, he was just a younger version.

'Fair enough, careless then, but if I can finish my sentence. Steven has found Emily and managed to restrain her. We'll bring Emily back here, have no doubt about that. The point is,' he paused, before he continued, 'I acknowledge it has been my family that has caused the problems, therefore, it is us that will have to lead the way to fix the situation. We can't change the past, but we sure can face the future.'

'So, what do you propose we do then to explain the fact that *your* family is allowed to do what they want?' Franco snapped.

They were getting a rise out of him. As much as Ian fought to stay in control, he could not stand their impatience. His tone increased in volume. 'We don't all do what we want. The things that have happened stem from the mistake that Emily made years ago. We've been trying to make amends for her lack of judgement. I guess we failed. If you all think it best the Roberts family leave the community then…we shall. We can set up a new stronghold elsewhere. We all knew that eventually something would have to be done. We're running out of space as it is.'

They had not expected that. Their facial expressions spoke volumes.

'Hold on a minute Ian. That's a hasty proposition. If you leave, what'll stop anyone else from joining you?' Arla intervened, her eyes narrowed. She had always been outspoken like her husband, Morten. Her emerald eyes sparkled. She was shrewd, with an innate ability to flush out the crux of the issue.

Anna had been quiet so far, now she laid her cards on the table. 'The split in the community had to happen. It's been coming for years. Too many children are born and we have no way to accommodate everyone comfortably. Why don't we let people choose for themselves? Why not involve everyone in the decision. To make it fair, I suggest that anyone interested in moving to a new location state their intent and then we select a number to make the move.'

Ian could not avoid feeling uncomfortable as she spoke. Emily was her identical twin and yet they were like chalk and cheese, polar opposites in character not features. The way she tucked her black hair behind her ears made her look insecure.

Arla continued to probe, her hands beseeching, 'But where will they go and who will decide who goes and who stays?'

'We will decide,' Ian added firmly. 'Anna, I agree with you. That is a fair way to make the selection. As for location, there is only one obvious place I can think of where we could live.'

Everyone raised their eyebrows. Even Franco seemed interested now.

'Borneo,' he announced. He could not resist a smirk.

A lot of faces dropped.

Franco shook his head and Juan frowned at Anna. It was clear from his face she had kept her promise and not told him before the meeting.

'Borneo? You have given this some thought. Why?' Morten asked.

'It's a huge country with areas that are still uninhabited. We can easily find somewhere to hide. It offers huge possibilities.'

'Isn't it easier to just find another area in the Amazon to

live in?' Ian's oldest sister, Catherine, said. Her husband, Isaac, squeezed her hand in support.

'I don't think so,' Ian shook his head, 'a fresh start is what some need.'

Franco thumped his fist on the table. 'Why? It's important to stay together. We'd probably never see you again.'

'And why would that be a bad thing?' Ian had to smile.

Morten was not amused. 'We're all a family. Even though some of your family members are not here, that doesn't mean we want to go our separate ways,' he said, whilst looking directly at Franco and gesturing for him to calm down. 'What we have not talked about yet is why Judith and Jeff died. That is what I think we need to discuss. Personally, I never hoped to be immortal, but I never actually thought about death much either. The fact that we don't age seemed to quell the thought. But now, things have changed. Let me get this straight. From what I understand, it appears that without human blood we will start to deteriorate quickly and then eventually die. Is that right?'

Ian leaned back on his chair. He spoke slowly, lethargy seeping in, 'The only thing we know is that my mother aged quickly and then died of natural causes. We don't know if human blood would have saved her. But, my father has been suffering similar symptoms and when he had human blood he was rejuvenated. That does not mean that'll happen indefinitely. It's obvious that eventually we'll all die, as we should.'

'So, Jeff chose to restart the aging process so that he could *die*?' Franco's eyes widened.

Catherine leaned forward, her red hair flowing over her shoulders. 'Exactly, and it looks like all of us could do the same thing at any time. My mother was happy to go. She did not want to kill anymore and she was home.'

'So, what if we want to go home too?' Franco flippantly threw in. 'Would any of you stop us going back to our homeland to die?'

The room went silent.

Morten spoke first. 'I for one would not have an issue with

it. I would want to go back to Sweden too, if I had the choice.'

'So all of a sudden everyone wants to go their own way?' Ian said, as his hands rose.

'It appears so.' Franco folded his arms.

Isaac broke the impasse. 'I don't want to go back to where I was born. It brings back no good memories.'

Ian was grateful for the interruption, whenever Isaac spoke people tended to listen. With his long face, pensive eyes and pointed beard that reached his chest he still retained his Jewish traditions. His immaculate attire and impeccable manners always gained him respect. 'Germany is no longer my home. I'm sure Catherine and I would be more than happy to start the new community. That would be our new home and our final place of rest. It would give us a reason to live longer.'

Catherine smiled at him, hand still in his, and added, 'I think we're the right choice too.'

'I would support that decision,' Juan added, his voice raised.

The room went silent for a minute as everyone considered the turn of events.

Finally, Ian resumed the discussion. 'Let's take a vote then. The proposal is that Catherine, Isaac, Carmen, and I will take our families to start a new community. We will ask who would like to join us and decide on the right number collectively. Then I propose that we start afresh and leave for Borneo. Does anyone have a counter to that?'

'I do,' Franco intervened. 'I think you should stay. Carmen should be with her family.'

'Carmen, how do you feel about this?' Ian asked.

Carmen fidgeted with her hands and bit her lip before she replied, 'If I'm honest, I would like to stay. We can always visit.'

Ian was slightly deflated, he expected her to follow his lead.

Franco smiled, pleased, before he added in a gruff voice, 'And you're sure it is not easier to create a new community in South America?'

Morten ignored the suggestion. 'Let's vote. Those in favour

of a new colony in Borneo?'

Everyone apart from Franco, Elena and Juan raised their hands.

'Agreed,' Morten concluded. 'So now we have to decide upon the next contentious issue. When we are coming to the end of our lives can we choose to die where we wish? Those in favour?'

At that, everyone raised their hand.

Morton nodded. 'Done, so the issue now is who will lead the meeting to tell everyone in the community what we have decided?'

Ian did not hesitate. 'I will.'

'Good for you, you're a chip off the old block,' Morten joked. 'Anyone got a problem with that?'

No one raised any objection and the mood seemed to lift.

Ian could not believe he had just agreed to let his big sister and her husband move to Borneo. The number of Roberts in the community dwindled by the minute.

Chapter 3

A New Start

Even though the prospect of moving was daunting, Catherine was exhilarated for the first time in years. A fresh start, a new life, a different dream, she could barely contain her excitement. She felt sorry for Ian. He would have wanted to be a part of it.

Ian clasped his hands behind his back, his brow narrowed in concentration. He reminded her of her dad. She still found it hard to believe her dad was dead. Yet he was, there was no way to bring him back.

Ian was nervous. She could tell by the way he searched out into the crowd, looking at no-one and at everyone all at once.

The members of the community waited.

Obviously satisfied, Ian raised his hands and lowered them gently. Immediately, the crowd hushed.

'Thank you everyone for coming today, my family appreciates it.' He placed his hand in front of his lips and gave a short cough.

Catherine could understand he did not want to mess it up. She could not blame him for his uncertainty.

He continued, 'I also want to thank you for your support. My mother's death has not been easy for any of us. It is a loss that hits the heart of the community we built together. Unfortunately, Judith's death is not the reason I stand before you now. I am sorry to have to inform you that our founder, my father, has also passed on.'

A few members in the crowd gasped, others broke down and held on to each other, and Catherine felt a lump grow in her throat. It was hard to hear the truth. She was also moved by the reaction. Her father was loved and respected – of course he was. The only thing that worried her was the look of utter horror in a lot of people's faces.

Was it fear? She could not tell.

Ian tried to ignore them as he ploughed through his speech

amidst the intermittent sobs. 'We need to figure out how their deaths can lead to a new way of living. A way we never considered. It was my mother's final wish that her grandson, Steven, should lead the life he chose, not the one we imposed.'

Now everyone listened.

The Spanish contingent glared. They did not like this development.

Ian kept his eyes fixed on the centre of the crowd. 'For that reason alone, my father Jeff stayed in England to help Steven. I know many of you think this is unfair, but I hope you will try to understand. I have to admit this has been hard for me too.' His eyes wavered; he was not lying about that. 'We need to remain strong. We cannot let our guard down because of what my parents decided to do. The survival of our kind needs to be preserved. Isaac will explain more.'

A few nods of appreciation followed Isaac, partly in wonderment. She knew they had no idea what he could possibly add. Catherine moved to the side of Isaac and their eyes briefly met. Ian had done his job, now it was their turn.

'Thank you Ian. We're all sorry for your loss. Both of your parents will be mourned by all. The reason I am addressing you now is to tackle the issue of overcrowding. We have outgrown our home. For this reason alone, it is time for some of us to move and start a new community elsewhere.'

Another set of audible gasps ricochet off the cavern walls, followed by a series of mumbles. The tide was turning from sadness to anger.

Isaac continued. His voiced unchanged, still strong. Catherine was so proud of him. 'My friends and family, listen. I know this will come as a shock to some of you – this is your home. But, for others this is an opportunity to create a new life elsewhere. However, let me make this clear, this is not a holiday. It's going to be hard work and we will have to stay away from normal civilisation. This is not integration, its segregation. We cannot live with humans. So, what we propose is…'

A loud voice broke the moment as it forced its way to the front. It was Francis, Anna's son. 'What do you mean? Your sister and nephew still live amongst humans – they are integrated. And yet, you're telling us that we can't. Why exactly is that? Don't you trust us?'

As he spoke, Catherine noted Franco nodding sagely. She imagined his grandfather eagerly fanned the flames of his fury.

Isaac did not face Francis. He pursed his lips and waited.

Ian shook his head and glanced at Anna briefly before he replied, 'What has happened with them is not an example to the rest of us. My father died by my mother's side after he promised to help Steven. As for my sister, well, there's nothing I can say about her. She was always a rebel. But, both Steven and Emily are to return to the community soon. They have agreed to come back.'

Francis shook his head and flicked his hand. 'Isn't that good of them?! Double standards! You impose rules on us that your own family willingly break.'

A lot of cheers seemed to side with Francis.

'I agree,' Ian nodded, 'and for that reason I must be the one to lead the members of the community into a new start. I am ashamed by the mistakes we have made and to atone, I will put all my efforts to enable our existence elsewhere.'

Catherine clenched her teeth. That was not what they had agreed. 'No Ian,' she interrupted. She walked up next to him. 'Ian cannot be held accountable. The council has agreed that Isaac and I will lead the new community.' She held Isaac's hand.

'See they can't even agree amongst themselves,' Francis scoffed.

More jeers erupted, before Anna stepped forward. 'That will be enough from you, son.'

Francis shrugged his shoulders and melted back into the crowd.

A new voice in the crowd changed the tone. It was Lucy of all people. 'So how will we decide who goes and who stays?'

Catherine could not believe Lucy was putting herself out there. She was normally a recluse.

Isaac replied, 'We will lead our families and anyone willing to join us to the island of Borneo. It's the ideal place to build a new community.'

'Borneo,' a lot of voices in the crowd murmured.

Isaac raised his voice again and squeezed Catherine's hand. 'The island offers us a very similar climate to this one and has a range of species that we can survive upon. The jungle is dense and uninhabited. We will find somewhere to hide.'

Even Ian looked bemused.

'Anyone that would like to join us has until the end of the week to submit their names. Then the council members will decide who will get to leave with us. Before this starts we need to know that people agree. To keep it simple, raise your hands if you think it is a good idea to start a new community in Borneo.'

Over half of the people raised their hands and a wave of relief washed over Catherine.

'Thank you,' Isaac nodded, before he tensed. 'Can we be clear on one thing? If you're not selected now, it doesn't mean that you will not get the chance in the future. We have to start small. Once we are established we will be able to expand the numbers. Good luck everyone and thanks for coming.'

Just as they thought they had finished Lucy spoke again. 'You still have not explained why *they* died. Will we all die?'

A lot of people glanced at each other in surprise. She rarely spoke up – in fact she was rarely seen. She preferred a life with plants not people.

Catherine answered. 'They chose to die, they refused to kill humans and we suspect monkeys are the reason we stay healthy here. But the truth is that we now think in time we all will die. We are not immortal.'

A stony silence followed. A lot of wide eyes confirmed this was quite a revelation.

Ian stepped forward again. 'Either way I want to reassure you all that Steven and Emily will return to the community. Once they are here we can plan for the future with more certainty. I will choose the reconnaissance team shortly. For now, just live as normal and enjoy what we have here. We can thank my parents for what they achieved. No-one can take that away from them.'

The hushed atmosphere spoke in volumes.

***

Lucy wandered down the corridor, eager to get back to her sanctuary. She was beginning to get odd looks from some of the others. She suspected they knew something was up with her. Luckily, she had always worn loose clothing, it was easy to hide what she was desperate to conceal. Once inside her beloved greenhouse, she quickly made her way to her room and went to the toilet. Recently, she spent half her day needing to pee, to usually find that the effort was greater than the result. It had been bad enough with the constant sickness up to twenty weeks, she had never been so ill in her life.

She rubbed her now rounded belly affectionately and felt a light kick as her baby protested. It amazed her that something so small could be so strong already. Soon she would find it harder to hide. Perhaps, a new start in Borneo was what she needed, a new place where she could raise her baby

Lucy could not suppress her huge grin, she loved the fact she was pregnant. It did not matter that the father would never know it was his. All she had ever wanted was a child of her own and now by a sure miracle her wish had been granted. In a way, she was glad it had happened with Steven. There was no way anyone would suspect it was his. And even if he did return, she would not stay long enough for him to find out. Her independent streak made her relish the thought of raising a baby alone. She would make all the decisions without the need to answer to anyone.

It was still too early to decide but she wondered what name she would use. Would it be a girl or a boy? She did not care either way. The main thing was if she moved to Borneo, no-one would need to find out until after they arrived. She could avoid the looks and accusations from most of the community. That would be a welcome relief! She would confide in Catherine, she could not do it all alone.

***

Ian clenched his teeth as he saw his sister Anna approach. Her scowl was never-ending. He took a large bite from his slice of bread and chewed, she would have to speak first.

'Can I come with you to get Emily?' she asked, her tone impatient. Ever since the decision had been made, Anna had been really snappy. He suspected she was jealous. Her husband Juan had no intention of moving and her son, Francis, sided with him.

'No,' he finished his mouthful and continued, 'I'm not sure that's such a good idea. Catherine has it under control and Steven knows her.'

'Why?' She sat down opposite him, deflated.

Something was really shaking her up at the moment. The chances were that her husband Juan was seething at the plans and venting.

'Emily has a way of getting what she wants with you. You helped Steven before, give Catherine a chance now. She knows what she's doing. I think she's the only one that has always kept a level head.' He continued to chew.

'I kept a level head,' Anna snapped.

Ian raised his eyebrows. 'Maybe, at times, but Emily has been known to be persuasive.'

Anna leant on her hands and pouted. 'I hate being a twin.'

'It doesn't change anything. Emily and you have a connection. A connection that has been helpful at times, but, you must admit, has also caused many problems. What does Juan think?' He rubbed his hands and finished the remains of his juice.

'You know what he thinks,' she huffed, 'fine.' She got up to leave. 'Let me know if you need anything.'

Ian nodded. He would need things, just not from her. As much as Anna was not to blame, he would never forget the time she let Emily leave. Anna always had a soft spot for her twin sister.

Chapter 4

Phone Call

Ian continued to eat. Food helped to ignore the multitude of problems that seemed to grow like weeds of late.

'Anna's not happy,' Carmen noted, following his gaze.

Ian glanced at his wife. Talk about stating the obvious. 'It's not my problem your dad has riled Juan and Francis up. You're happy with the situation, aren't you?' He had not asked her directly yet.

Carmen's eyes flinched, but he knew she would not lie. 'It's not what I would prefer but it is what it is. It's time for some of us to move on. Perhaps the problem is many people see this as an opportunity. There are going to be some very disappointed members of the community at the end who will have to stay behind.'

'A lot of them want to stay too. Some people don't like the thought of change,' Ian grunted.

'We'll have to wait and see. I can't imagine it's going to be fun to decide who gets to stay and who gets to go. Luckily, you'll be there to guide us.' She squeezed his arm.

'Your help is just as valuable. You will help me?' His eyes narrowed. He hoped she would want to help even if she did not approve.

'You men could do nothing without us to guide you. Of course, I'll be there.'

He could not help his sigh of relief. 'You proud Spanish woman, give your man a kiss,' he teased and leant in.

She turned her head away and spoke candidly, 'You English men don't understand about passion. Romance me, then I'll kiss you.'

'Are you blackmailing me, Mrs Roberts?'

'Of course, Mr Roberts.'

'Alright then,' he sighed, with exaggerated disapproval. He knew this was a game they'd been playing for years. 'You are the most beautiful woman in the world, I am honoured that you chose to marry me, and I would be the happiest man alive if you kissed me.'

With a slow, seductive smile she beamed, victorious, 'It would have been better without the hint of sarcasm, but that'll do.' She leant in and gave him a kiss. Not of the lingering variety, no more than a peck.

Ian longed for more. It didn't seem like she was going to play at the moment.

Breakfast over, they got up to leave just as they saw Catherine come in and make her way towards them.

Catherine nodded at Carmen and then looked at Ian. She kept a straight face. 'We need to call Steven.'

'What about this afternoon?' Ian countered.

'Nothing like the present.' Catherine turned to face Carmen. 'Carmen, you don't mind?'

Carmen shrugged her shoulders. 'No. Do what you have to.'

That was his wife, practical to the core.

***

Catherine was apprehensive about calling Steven. The last conversation they had was difficult, to say the least. It was not easy for her to find out from Steven that her dad was dead, as well as knowing he had her sister, Emily. It was such a mess, all of it. Ian did not help, but she knew that to not involve him would be a mistake. He would only force himself on the situation. She would keep him sweet, let him come along for the conversations, and make sure he did *not* tag along when she went back to England.

'Does he know we are calling?' Ian asked, irritated.

'I texted him an hour ago, he knows.' She really hoped Ian would control his temper this time.

They entered the metallic, grey lift and Ian inserted the key into the control panel. They made their way up to the secure upper level. Once the doors opened they made their way towards the control room, hardly anyone knew it existed. Ian placed the key in the keypad and an automated voice reacted.

'What is your name?' the robotic voice asked.

Ian replied in monotone, 'Ian Roberts.'

A second passed before the automated voice reacted. 'Access granted.'

The door opened automatically and they made their way in. A long narrow corridor greeted them, the lighting subdued. The same low lit conduit piping ran through the entire facility. Catherine loved the natural rock walls; she had helped to carve out the passages many years earlier. At the end of the corridor, they turned to the right and made their way into a decent sized room. Computers and gadgets littered the room. A lot of them were now broken or defunct. Her dad had collected a lot of rubbish in his time, now it was their rubbish. She could not wait to have a clear out, even though she suspected she'd act like a sentimental fool.

Ian took a seat by the large wooden table against the wall. A speaker phone waited.

Catherine moved the chair back, which scraped the floor as she did, and sat next to him. She tucked her red hair behind her ears and adopted a business-like stance. She could do this. She dialled the number and put it on loudspeaker.

After a few rings, Steven replied, 'Catherine.'

'And Ian.'

Catherine faced Ian, and widened her eyes. She really, really hoped he would behave. They needed some answers. 'Steven, are you at the house?'

'Yes, we got back last night. Emily is lying down. It seems I damaged her spine when I attacked her. She's not in good shape, not that I care, but the good thing is she's not going anywhere,' Steven chuckled.

'Why did you attack her Steven? What did Emily do now?' She dreaded to think.

There was a long pause.

Catherine glanced at Ian, who shrugged his shoulders and slouched slightly on the chair. He folded his arms over his chest.

Finally, Steven spoke, 'She killed my mother.'

Catherine's jaw dropped. She never thought Emily could stoop any lower, she guessed she was wrong. 'I'm sorry, Steven. I really am.'

'It's not your fault Emily is a psychopath.' There an element of humour in his tone.

Ian kept silent, at least he was behaving.

Catherine fidgeted. 'Steven, we could not come over as quickly as I had hoped. Things are changing here. I'll talk to you when I get to England. I'm coming over with Isaac. Is that okay?'

'Yes, that's fine. Isaac is a decent guy.'

Catherine noticed Ian flinch at the remark. She continued, 'Can you contain Emily until we get there?'

'No problem.'

'Who else is there with you, Steven?' Ian leaned forward.

'That is not your concern, Ian. I'll talk to Catherine and Isaac when they arrive. I have to go.'

Catherine was concerned about Steven's attitude. Time would tell what he was brewing. 'Steven, we'll be there in a few days. See you then.'

'Yeah, see you then.'

The phone line went dead.

Ian shook his head. 'I don't like it. I just don't like it.' He got up and paced the room, his eyes drifted to the surveillance screens.

'No-one is asking you to like it, Ian. You just have to get over it. I'm going with Isaac. Decision made.'

She hoped, somehow, she would know what to do.

Ian turned to the screen of the entrance. 'Eilif is coming.'

'He must be doing his usual checks,' Catherine said. She stared at the screens; they mainly focused on the exits and open areas. It was their best way of checking for predators. Now, it was also a way to check no-one tried to leave. Sometimes she felt like they were monitoring a prison, not a society.

Eilif ambled through the door and stopped, he looked from Ian to Catherine. He frowned and then smiled. 'I wasn't expecting to see you two here today.'

Catherine liked Eilif. She remembered the day he was born. He was the miracle child, the first baby born in the community. All blond and blue eyed. Still was, just older, but then again when most of them looked as though they were only twenty years old, *old* was a relative term. She was one of the few in the community that was slightly older, even though it was only by two years. Her age was fixed the day the vampire bats bit her.

'We were just going,' Ian said. 'Everything looks good to me, so I don't think you have to worry, Eilif.'

'Sure. I'll just have a look at the internet search I started earlier. We have to see if Steven is up to anything in Southampton. You did tell me to check?' Eilif looked at Ian.

Ian's face froze.

Catherine fumed, 'I knew it was too much to ask for you not to interfere. But, actually what did you find? It could be useful.'

***

'Not much yet,' Eilif said. He took a seat in front of the screen and got on with business. He had known Catherine and Ian too long to get bothered by their sibling banter. He focused on the newspaper reports and scrolled through, there had to be a connection. From his earlier search he sensed something was going on in England, he had always been able to pick things up. Everyone called it his *extra* sense.

A part of him felt partially responsible for Steven. After all, he had helped to erase his existence.

'Anything?' Ian was looking over his shoulder, there was nothing like a bit of pressure.

'Patience.'

The internet had made things a lot easier, it meant a lot less phone calls, but it still took time. He huffed aloud and continued to search, desperate to nudge his memory. Eilif was sure he had seen something – he just could not think what it was. In a bid to retrace his steps, he resumed his last search and scrolled through the options to see if whatever it had been appeared again.

He froze and stopped clicking as he read the article.

'What is it?' Catherine asked, she got closer to the screen.

It documented a suspicious death in Hampshire. It did not give many details but the police did not sound happy about the condition of the body, it apparently had unidentified markings and an unexplained loss of blood. The police were appealing for more witnesses to step forward.

Even though they had no suspects or leads the story had made it onto a local television channel. The only witness they had found was an old lady who claimed to have seen a couple wondering around the neighbourhood on the night of the death. The only reason it had been raised was that they were seen to leave the building where the suicide took place at one o'clock in the morning, a strange hour to be leaving unless invited.

Eilif had read enough. 'This does not make sense, a couple? I would not have thought that Steven would kill with Emily. Would you?'

'No.' Catherine's jaw had dropped. 'But who else would be with him?'

'That's it, I'm coming with you,' Ian exclaimed, he held his finger up in the air.

Catherine took a deep breath, 'Ian, no, I'll go with Isaac.'

'I could come with you, Catherine. Steven knows me and I could also help to smooth over any loose edges that have been left by whatever he's been up to. I'd be happy to help.' Eilif glanced from Catherine to Ian.

'That's a good idea. If I can't go, then Eilif goes instead. I'm happy with that. Are you?' Ian glared at Catherine.

'You know, it is actually a good idea,' Catherine admitted. 'But, we won't tell Steven. You stay in the shadows.'

'Fine. When do we leave?' Eilif took a final glance at the screen.

Catherine started to make her way to the door. 'Tomorrow, I'd better go pack.'

Once Catherine had gone, Ian faced Eilif, 'Bring them back, whatever you do, bring them back.'

'Don't worry Ian. I'll do what I have to. I've never let you down before, have I?'

'I know.' Ian paced up and down the room. 'I need to get a grip. I don't think I've ever felt so out of control.'

'Things have a way of working out, don't stress about it. It's not your fault.'

Ian stopped, his eyed widened. 'Isn't it? I brought Steven back here. It was when he arrived that everything started to go wrong.'

Eilif shook his head. 'You know we had no choice. Besides, Steven was just one catalyst. There would have been another eventually. There has been some unrest for years.'

Ian gave a half-smile. 'You're right, I know. You're right. Shall we go back, or do you have to do anything else?'

Eilif smiled. 'I have a few things to do. You go, I'll see you later. Go for a swim, that'll help.'

'Yeah, I'll do that. Thanks.'

Eilif was glad he was not in Ian's shoes. He did not want the responsibility of the community on his shoulders.

Chapter 5

Search Party

Eilif focused on the screen. He was sure he had seen something else. He started to scroll back. On impulse he typed in "Thorn" and did a search. Nothing relevant came up. Then he typed in "Thorn, death." A few entries down he saw what he was looking for. A Clara Thorn, living in Ilfracombe, had been found dead in her home a few days earlier. She was noted to have been the wife of Paul Thorn, Steven's dad. He wondered if Steven knew, he could not help thinking Emily had something to do with it. Was that why they were together? He just could not understand why Steven would hunt with Emily, if she had killed his mother. It did not make any sense.

He logged off, locked up and made his way back.

As he approached the main dining hall, he bumped into his daughter, Ingrid. He would do anything to see her smile like she used to, her carefree days were a thing of the past since she met Steven.

Ingrid gave him the same half-baked smile. 'You alright?'

'Not really,' he said, and then laughed. At times like these, Eilif found it hard to believe she had been his child not that long ago. He tossed the thought aside. 'Can I trust you?'

'Of course,' she replied, eyes wide.

'I'm pretty sure Steven's up to no good.' He narrowed his eyes. 'Don't tell anyone you know, but I'm going with Catherine and Isaac to England tomorrow. We're going to bring Steven and Emily home.'

'Can I help at all?'

The request was innocent enough. It made him wonder. 'I wish you could,' he mused. His mind wrestled to come up with a plan. 'Actually, maybe you can.'

'What are you thinking?'

'Do you think you could convince Catherine to let you come?'

'I can try.' Her eyes fell to the floor. 'It would mean I'd get to see Steven again.'

Eilif knew there was a glitch. 'I'd forgotten about that, you're not still pining for him are you?'

Ingrid flicked her long blonde hair back, and raised her chin. 'It's in the past.'

'When did you grow up so fast? It doesn't seem that long ago that you were a baby,' he said, as he put his arm over her shoulders and gave a squeeze. 'You're sure you can handle it?'

'Promise. Now, let me go and convince Catherine that I am indispensable.'

'Clever girl.'

As he watched her leave he was overwhelmed with a sense of pride. The only thing she needed was a nice man to settle with. It was a shame Ingrid had not made a connection yet. The thing was men were short on the ground. It was a problem. Either way, Steven had been a fool to disregard his daughter so easily.

***

The remnants of dessert remained on the table. Musicians played a Spanish flamenco song to the enjoyment of the crowd in the middle of the room. Some of the Spanish women had taken to the dance floor, as expected. A lot of children ran around playing chase or hiding under tables. Everyone seemed to be having a good time. In the corner, Ingrid spotted the Spanish male contingent huddled in deep conversation. A puff of smoke rose in the air from the group. They loved their tobacco. They had to be discussing the latest developments.

Ingrid paused, surveyed the room, and found her target. Food could give her the excuse she needed to mingle with the right people. She made her way over and smiled at friends and family. It had to look casual.

'Can I join you?' she asked, her voice sweet as honey.

Ian glanced up, he looked deep in thought. He just nodded, as he ate a mouthful of chocolate cake. His wife, Carmen, looked at her curiously, as though she suspected she was up to no good. Ingrid observed that women were always more perceptive than men.

'They look yummy,' Ingrid said, as she helped herself to a

slice of meringue and fruit. The sugar rush was instant when she ate the first mouthful.

'Jenson and Susanna are so in love,' Carmen said, her eyes on the couple on dance floor.

They were the lucky ones. Rumour had it they would be getting married soon.

Carmen turned to Ingrid. 'You haven't found anyone yet, have you, Ingrid? I would have thought that with your looks and personality you would have been snatched a long time ago.'

Even though she knew that Carmen meant well, it was still hard to listen to the usual *advice*. In a small place like this, married women were always on a mission to match up the single ones. What really stung was the condescending way in which they always reminded her that in time she would find the right one, as if they would know. The saddest part was that there was nothing she wished more than to know they were right. It would remove a huge weight off her shoulders when she could put Steven out of her mind for good.

She put on a brave face and replied, 'I'm just enjoying the life of a single woman.'

'But, surely you must want to settle down?' Carmen insisted, her dark brown eyes serious, insistent.

'Eventually, I've got a lot of time on my hands.'

'I guess you're right,' Carmen replied, as she sipped her water. 'Although we might not have *as much* time as we thought since Jeff and Judith passed away.'

Ian gave her an annoyed glance.

'I'm sorry for your loss. I always admired your parents.' Ingrid met Ian's eyes. 'Is someone going to go to check they were buried properly? You really should see whether the house has been left in a good condition.'

'We are dealing with it.'

'I loved spending time there with my family last year. It was such a lovely place. Just think what would have happened if I had not told you about Steven.' Ingrid left the sentence hanging.

'Hmmm,' he murmured.

'It was difficult to know what to do, but I'm glad I told you the truth. We really did love it there,' she hinted, more aggressive this time.

His eyes met hers.

'Did you want to go and check on the house, Ingrid? It would give us peace of mind to know that everything at the house was left accordingly,' Carmen said.

Carmen was going with the suggestion, perhaps she felt sorry for her after all.

Ian raised his eyebrows and glanced at Carmen as if she had spoken out of line. 'One of us is already going,' he snapped.

'Of course, but Ingrid could be a great help.' Carmen insisted.

'Maybe,' he paused. Turning to Ingrid, he asked, 'Would you go back to England again?'

'If you need me to,' she said, as she withheld a smile.

'I'll think about it. Talk to your father, if he says he needs you then you can go. He's leaving tomorrow.'

It took everything she had to restrain the smug feeling that threatened to burst free. It was time to tell her dad she was coming along for the ride.

***

Ian picked up the clothes from the floor and threw them on the bed. At the corner of the room, he sat on a chair and read the monthly bulletin for the tenth time. His parent's death had shaken him to the core and all the latest developments were unsettling. Steven was with someone else and he had Emily. How could his family, one that was so united, be broken to pieces? It was all Emily's fault. The deep resentment that had slowly built up towards her was taking a grip. He doubted he would be able to stop himself from killing her when he saw her again. He did not want to think it, but he felt let down. His parents had let him down, just when he needed them the most.

The move was something to be excited about. Regardless, it was a huge responsibility. A lot of decisions still had to be made. Who would go, when they would go, how they would go? The whole thing was giving him a bad headache. Worst of it all, he was convinced someone would expose them. It was all too much. The cherry on the cake was the acidic response to the idea by most of the Santos Family, apart from his wife, Carmen, who tried her best to support him.

As if sensing his unease, Carmen came in with their toddler, Joaquin. She half-smiled and tilted her head to the side. 'Are you still fretting? Come here.' She made her way over and started to massage his shoulder and neck muscles.

Ian let himself go, his wife had magic hands. 'Thank you.'

At that, Joaquin toddled up to him and called out one of the only words he knew, 'Dada.'

Ian looked into his angelic deep brown eyes, picked him up and tossed him up in the air. Immediately, his son squealed with joy. He held him up in the air for a minute, then cuddled him and gave him several kisses on his head before his son protested and called out his favourite word, 'Mama.' With a sigh, Ian handed him to Carmen and broke into a smile. There was something the young would never have to understand, responsibility – to be a child again.

***

The journey was long and tedious. It was always difficult to be confined to the cramped space provided by a plane, and the food proved short of diabolical. Relief washed over Catherine as the plane came to a standstill – they had reached English soil. As soon as the seat belt fastening sign was switched off the people came to life, as everyone reached for coats, jackets, hand luggage, books and any relevant children. Finally, the slow exit began and like rats they scuttled out.

The queue for passport control was long and winding. Catherine glanced at Isaac and raised her eyebrows. They would have to be just a little bit more patient. Eilif was the first to reach the counter. The man aged in his fifties looked completely bored. He scrutinised the passport and went to scan it. Just before he did, Eilif leant over and whispered something. Catherine knew he was using his persuasion.

Immediately, the man handed back the passport and waved him through.

The man smiled at Ingrid, who followed Eilif. He glanced

at her passport and handed it back.

Catherine was not sure she had made the right decision in letting Ingrid come. Eilif was a good idea – he was capable of manipulating the human mind in a way neither Isaac nor she had mastered. The fact Ingrid knew the lay of the land meant she could help Eilif, but Catherine remained suspicious. There had to be a reason why Ian approved. She had a feeling he owed her for something she had done. If her memory was correct, she thought Ingrid had told Ian about Steven. It could be the reason.

When Catherine saw the sun shining through the huge glass windows she nodded in approval. The sky was blue, with not a cloud in sight. She did not think the sun existed in England.

Once in the rental car, Ingrid handed over one of the CD's she'd purchased in the airport to Catherine. A minute later, the sound of Whitney Houston filled the car.

'This was always one of my favourites,' Catherine contemplated, she glanced back at Ingrid.

Ingrid smiled. 'It's also one of mine.'

'Lucky, we bought a few different ones. We have to drive for a few hours yet.'

'Yes,' Ingrid replied. She looked as though she'd remembered something.

'Anything wrong?'

'No, no, just wondering what we're going to find. I'm sure Steven buried Jeff correctly. I just can't help thinking about the fact there might be two of them.'

Eilif interrupted, 'And I'm pretty sure Emily and Steven don't get on. It's strange don't you think?'

'We'll find out soon enough.'

The sight of green pastures dotted with sheep seemed to distract Ingrid, as she closed her eyes and dozed off.

Chapter 6

The House

An image of Steven floated through Ingrid's head. She remembered the first time she had kissed him and smiled. It was the only moment she ever stood a chance and it would stay with her forever. The memory was quickly clouded by his rejection, *'I'm not available, and even if I was, I would not want to be with you.'* The words still stung and her lower lip wobbled. She instinctively tried to curl up into a ball.

'Ingrid? Ingrid, wake up.'

It was her dad. It was just another pathetic dream. She opened her eyes and yawned, feigning ignorance.

'Bad dream?' he asked.

'I think so, I can't remember.' She was a bad liar.

It took everything she had to ignore how she felt, even though it hurt. There was nothing she could do about it. She still wanted to be with Steven. The idea was foolish –Steven hated her.

The drive back into Southampton brought back mixed memories. The last trip had not taught her anything useful. Heartache was not her favourite lesson. Ingrid wished she could change so many things. Perhaps, if Steven had been brought back when they first found him everything would have been different. He would not have rejected her so easily since he had not fallen in love yet. But then, she had got so close to seducing him back in the community until Kayla, her stupid cousin, put a stop to it. Another opportunity missed.

Hindsight – a bitter pill to swallow or a way to remember the way fate plays its hand.

As Eilif pulled into the service station, Ingrid welcomed the opportunity to refuel.

Catherine and Isaac made their way to the restaurant, whilst Ingrid convinced her dad to join her for an unhealthy burger. They found a small table and tucked in. It was an indulgence they could afford.

Eilif opened his burger box. 'You know, it's nice to spend time with my daughter. How are you feeling about being back here? You've barely talked to me about what happened with Steven,' Eilif paused. He always did that before broaching a tricky subject. 'Did you fall in love with him?' He picked up the burger and took a bite.

Ingrid fiddled with the chicken burger wrapper, then started to unfold it. 'I love you, Dad, you know I do. But, sharing my private thoughts is not something I'm about to do.' Honesty had to count for something. She took a bite and relished the taste. Sometimes processed food was exactly what she needed and, right now, this was one of those times.

Eilif picked up his drink. As he put it down, he shook his head. 'Why not?' I'm offended. You forget that I saw the way you were with Steven when you met. Do you think I've never suffered a broken heart?' He took another bite, ketchup staining the side of his mouth.

'Have you?' This was a revelation. Ingrid passed him a napkin.

Eilif wiped his mouth and then chuckled. 'Of course, before I got to know your mother.'

'Too much information,' Ingrid scoffed. She grabbed a handful of chips, dipped them in the ketchup pot and chewed.

Eilif picked up his burger again. 'When I met your mum I discovered the real thing. It'll happen to you one day.'

'Spare me.'

Eilif laughed as he chewed. After another sip of Coke, he continued, 'Anyway, we've diverged, talk to me. Recently, I don't know…you look lost. I worry about you. So does your mother.'

The change in his tone started to break down her defences. 'I know,' she paused, 'but, look, we're here to help. I promise I'll do everything I can to do just that, but you know how I felt about Steven.' She had to make it sound like it was in the past. 'I don't know why I fell in love with him. It was not a rational or, should I say, conscious choice. I know I have to put it behind me. It doesn't even matter anyway, he hates me.'

'Love never makes sense,' Eilif huffed, 'besides, he *can't*

45

hate you.'

'Yes he can. Nothing helps. I can't help how I felt?' She fought to keep it together.

'I can't understand why he would reject you, my beautiful girl,' Eilif held out his hand and placed it on her shoulder. 'You'll see. Your Mr Right is out there somewhere. I promise.'

Ingrid nodded. 'The problem is I thought Steven was my Mr Right.'

'We don't always get who we think are the right one. You're stronger than this. I never took you for the type to fall so hard.'

'I'm strong, nothing could be worse than how he's rejected me already.' She continued to eat her burger. That conversation was over.

***

An hour later, as they took the turn into the road that led back to the house Catherine started to get apprehensive. Steven was not expecting Eilif and Ingrid. She wondered if he would mind.

When the car came to a standstill, Catherine got out. 'We should look for the gravestones.'

'Now?' Ingrid glanced in the direction of the house.

Isaac held Catherine's hand. 'It's as good a time as any. It might not be easy when we talk to Steven. He must know we're here anyway. He can come out.'

They walked to the back of the house, and up the hill. As the hill seemed to plateau the trees formed a natural wall around the site. On the ground, two simple memorials lay side by side. A cross made out of wood and an inscribed stone marked the spots. Jeff's was not as neatly written as Judith's.

'Steven did bury Jeff,' Catherine said, she knelt down on the floor. She made the sign of the cross over her chest and leant her head on her clasped hands in prayer. Eilif knelt down beside her.

The others followed suit.

Catherine felt a light drizzle on her head. She looked up and saw black, dense clouds overhead. She knew the blue sky could not possibly last.

A few minutes later, they all started to make their way towards the house.

Catherine moved to open the door, but it was locked. She took out her key, unlocked the door and stepped in. It was dark, but her vision adapted immediately. 'Hello. Is anyone home?'

Eilif turned on the lights, the sight was an improvement on their less effective night vision, and Ingrid helped Isaac bring in the bags.

'What do you think?' Isaac looked at Eilif.

Eilif concentrated, his eyes followed the staircase. 'Someone's upstairs.'

'I'll go,' Catherine said. 'Let me go alone, please?'

'If you're sure,' Isaac said. He put his hand on her shoulder. She appreciated the sentiment.

On the walk up the stairs, she glanced at the photos on the wall. Her family, her past. What they had become was crazy, which reminded her. They would need to feed soon. The irrational hunger developed and it had been a long journey. She listened once she reached the top step. A faint sound at the end of the corridor drew her towards it. She turned on the hall light.

'Anyone there?'

A faint voice replied.

She walked faster and opened the door.

The scene shocked her. Emily lay flat on the bed. Her skin was pale, practically translucent. Her black hair lacklustre, it had started to grey. Her face was gaunt and shrivelled, her eyes shut. Even after everything Emily had done, she did not deserve this. It broke Catherine's heart. She rushed to her side and held her hand. It felt paper thin, fragile – she was scared to put any pressure on it. 'Emily.'

Catherine felt a little pressure on her hand, and then saw Emily's eyes flutter.

Emily groaned, and her amber eyes came into view. She turned her head slightly and her lips turned up just a little. A croaky voice acknowledged Catherine, 'It's you.'

Catherine picked up the glass of water on the bedside table, put her hand behind Emily's head and gently eased it up.

Emily drank, and then spluttered, 'It doesn't help. There is only one thing that can help me. I'm paralysed, by my own son.' She gave a throaty chuckle. 'I deserved it.'

'What happened? Did you kill Steven's stepmother?'

Emily nodded.

Catherine let go of her hand. 'Why? Why would you do such a thing? You know Steven loved her. What were you thinking?'

Emily stared at the ceiling. 'The woman had my Paul.'

'Paul?'

'Steven's dad,' Emily snapped, she flashed Catherine a set of sharp canine teeth.

Emily looked like a vampire, one that had been dead for a long time.

'Why are your teeth extended?' Catherine asked. She knew the answer, but she just wanted to hear it.

'I'm thirsty,' Emily rasped, 'really, really thirsty. I need blood. Bring me blood, Catherine. Please?' Her voice now angelic, it was always the same when she wanted something.

'I'm not sure that's a good idea. I'll speak to Steven first. Where is he?'

'With his bitch!'

The malice in Emily's tone, and evil laugh that followed, made Catherine wince. Emily sounded deranged.

'He changed the girl, Catherine! After all these years I found out the truth. I knew Mum and Dad lied. Mum was changed! They never admitted it to any of us, but they told Steven how to do it. They lied to us. Steven changed the girl – it is possible. I could have changed Paul, I could have been happy...' Emily's anger was replaced by a tormented grimace.

Catherine was confused, none of it made sense and yet, maybe it did. 'What are you saying Emily? You must be mistaken. Mum was not changed, she never...' she said, the thought left hanging in the air.

Yet, it all made sense. Her mum had been so scared. She never shared their confused excitement, and her bite was different to everyone else's. Catherine did not want to acknowledge the truth, but now she could not ignore what had been obvious from the beginning. It explained why Mum never wanted to leave the community or became sad when someone changed. 'Oh, Emily, I'm so sorry.'

Emily coughed. 'Sorry! Not half as sorry as me, get me some blood. I have suffered enough.'

Catherine nodded, 'I'll bring you some food.'

'Can't stomach it, although, maybe some soup? Emily closed her eyes again.

Catherine made her way down the stairs with a heavy heart. Emily was probably more dangerous than she had ever been in her entire life, and that was saying something. Blood was the last thing they would give her.

***

Isaac watched Catherine falter for a moment before she moved to the suitcase, now on a mission. She talked quickly, 'First, we'll unpack, and then we'll check out the university. We might find a lead there. You know, he might be staying at the apartment. At this time of day, the university is our best bet. It would be nice to catch him unawares.'

Isaac nodded, experience told him it was best to remain calm.

Over the years, Catherine had occasionally lapsed into an irrational state under duress. It was his job, as her husband, to ensure she stayed focused. He would not allow Steven to ruin what they had spent years protecting. Saying that, he was sympathetic, he did understand Steven's dilemma. If Emily was telling the truth, which he had trouble believing, Steven had actually changed someone. He had become just like a fictional vampire. Funny, he had never considered his kind to be vampires. This development led to a grey, obscured future. In the wrong hands, this knowledge could be very dangerous indeed.

'What do you think?'

Isaac knew the silent treatment would not keep Catherine happy for long. 'That's a great idea. We'll head for the university.'

Catherine stopped unpacking and stood up straight. 'What's on your mind? I know you too well, Isaac. You're telling me what I want to hear.'

Isaac had been busted. Catherine was far too shrewd. 'I'm just thinking about what Emily said. I never considered any of us to be vampires. But, if we can actually change humans with blood, it changes things.'

Catherine sat down on the edge of the bed. 'It certainly does.'

Isaac took a seat next to her and held her hand. 'You're sure Emily is telling the truth?'

'She's not lying, I wish she was. But, it's all true. I think Mum tried to tell me once. I remember now. She told me she was different to the rest of us, I just never thought much of it,' Catherine said, as she leant her head on Isaac's shoulder.

Isaac cuddled her and kissed her head. 'We'll sort it out. Try not to worry, my love.'

'You know me.' Catherine nuzzled for a minute, before she eased out of his arms, stood up again and continued to unpack.

Isaac gave a half-smile. He knew she found it hard to keep still when she had something on her mind. 'Tell you what, I'll go and find Eilif and bounce off ideas.'

Catherine gave him an absentminded glance, and mumbled, 'Good idea.'

Chapter 7

Confrontation

Isaac ran his hand along the banister as he made his way down the stairs. He loved the house. It had a certain quality about it, something indefinable. And he loved the pictures that remained on the walls. His wife's interesting past, a fragment of who she was. Over the years she had born him many children, their youngest was now eighteen years old. It was interesting she had not got pregnant since. They had twelve children; it was enough by anyone's standard.

Since the recent developments, Isaac was beginning to wonder if Catherine was unable to conceive, regardless of her youthful features. He had realised that some of the older women had stopped having children, but they never thought the women were actually aging. Not until Judith died, and death became a sudden possibility. By the sounds of things, they were all ageing. As natural as it was, the thought made him apprehensive. He was nearly 100 years old, would he be next to die? Would Catherine die first? It was not a thought he wanted to consider.

Isaac made his way into the lounge and found Eilif, who appeared to be perusing the books on display. 'Anything of interest?'

Eilif turned around. 'Plenty, actually. But, take a look at this. I found this copy of Dracula on the table. Someone has been reading it recently.'

'Doing some research then?' Isaac could not help adopting a sarcastic tone.

'Would not exactly help now, would it?' Eilif smiled. 'Anyway, what's the plan? What do you want me to do, I'm here to help.'

'Catherine wants to go to the university to look for them, although she suspects they might be in the apartment. We could just call Steven, but Catherine would like to see if we can catch them unawares. To find out whether he is with someone else.'

'Well, there I can help. Remember, we abducted Caitlin the first place. I can find out about her recent developments. Why don't I head to the university with Ingrid, and you head for the apartment. Works better that way. Ingrid knows where things are at the university. She can help me.'

Isaac did not like the idea of Eilif and Ingrid meeting Steven first, but he could not deny the logic of the argument. 'Sounds like a great plan.'

'What does?' Ingrid casually walked into the room.

'Fancy a trip into the university with me?' Eilif asked. 'I need you to do some research.'

Ingrid smiled, as the words tripped out of her mouth, 'You know me. I'm always up for research.'

'I'll go and tell Catherine and let you both head off.' Isaac tried to ignore the feeling of unease. 'Remember, keep a low profile. Watch, but don't be seen.'

Ingrid grinned, 'Of course.'

Isaac had always liked Ingrid, but he suspected her interest in Steven went a lot deeper than to help the community. The question was how much deeper?

***

As the university came into view, Eilif stopped the car to allow some students to cross at the pelican crossing.

Ingrid tensed, and grasped the edge of her seat.

It was Steven – with a redhead, besotted by the looks of it. Their proximity, the way they held hands.

Her mind raced as a flashback reminded her she had seen the girl before, *with* Steven. It had been the second time she had ever set eyes on him. When they were searching for a victim in Southampton. The first time she had glanced at Steven had been in the students union and he had ignored her, which surprised her at the time.

She breathed deeply as the realisation hit her. Steven had probably met the girl already. She had been wrong all along. She had not got to him first, someone else had. *That* girl.

She did everything she could to suppress her emotions.

Eilif nodded. 'It's Steven.'

'Let me go after them.' Ingrid had to see him up close.

Eilif frowned. 'Let's go together.'

'No, I'm going.' Before Eilif had a chance to move the car forward Ingrid opened the door. 'Meet me inside the library – that's where they're headed.'

In a flash, she was concealed behind the bushes. She watched Eilif drive off and panicked, she had made a rash decision. Without time to consider her options, she walked in the direction they had gone.

She remembered the library did not allow access unless you had a student card, but luckily the entrance was empty. She walked towards the guard and gave him her most alluring smile.

The guard looked bored and unimpressed, but he approached her anyway. 'Can I help you?'

'I left my card behind at home. Can you let me in?' She kept her eyes fixed on his and concentrated.

'No problem, come on in,' he replied, his expression robotic, as he swiped his card to let her in.

'Thank you.'

She smiled as she heard a boy come up behind her giving the same line.

The guard replied sternly, 'You'll have to sign in.'

The boy complained, 'You let that girl in without her having to sign in.'

'No I didn't,' the guard replied, confused.

Ingrid moved away quickly before the guard called her back. The opportunity to see Steven again beckoned.

The library was huge with many areas to choose from so it was difficult to decide where they could have gone. Hedging her bets, she made her way towards the mathematics area. Catherine had mentioned the subject he had decided to study. The area was quiet with many students working either independently or in groups around neatly organised tables. She scanned the nearby vicinity. He was nowhere in sight.

In a bid to remain inconspicuous, she disappeared into one of the long corridors stacked with books. She glanced over a shelf, pulled out a book and pretended to look interested. Book in hand, she made her way back to an empty seat and sat down to peruse it whilst keeping a lookout. After five minutes, she contemplated getting up to look elsewhere.

She closed the book and nearly jumped out of her seat as a bitter voice whispered behind her ear, 'What're *you* doing here?'

Ingrid turned around to face him and held her breath. He left her giddy just by staring at her, even if his expression was one of loathing. She miraculously made a comeback, 'What do you mean? I'm just reading.' She held up the book.

'Right,' he replied, his tone sarcastic. 'So, why are you really here?'

Ingrid shrugged her shoulders. 'Can we talk?'

'Do I have a choice?' he huffed, 'so much for Catherine coming alone.'

The extent of his aversion towards her stung, but she would not let him see it. She folded her arms over her chest, and then gave a confident stare. 'Catherine needed help.'

Steven arched an eyebrow. 'Your help? Something tells me you volunteered.'

'It's none of your business why I choose to do things. Look, I haven't come here to argue, you have some explaining to do. I mean, it looked to us like you left Emily to die.'

'Us? Who else is here?'

Ingrid's shoulders slumped. 'It's easier to meet up. You don't have to be so defensive. We only want to help you.'

'Whatever, I'll meet you back at the house. I'll be there tonight.' He turned and walked away at a brisk pace.

It was tempting to follow him but she decided to be patient. If he meant it, they would get answers very soon.

***

Eilif debated whether to go into the library. The last thing he wanted to do was draw any unnecessary attention. In the end, it seemed like a better idea to wait in hiding.

As he checked the exit, he saw Steven coming out.

His jaw dropped as he saw Caitlin, the girl whose memory he had erased, next to him. He could recognise that pretty redhead anywhere. She had her hand entwined in his arm, carefree.

Steven's face looked sombre. Eilif suspected Ingrid had crossed his path.

As they walked away, hand in hand, a simple explanation revealed itself. They were a couple, a pair.

A newspaper article he had read flashed across his mind. A couple had been seen leaving the scene of the suicide in Southampton. He had discounted it at the time because Steven was supposed to be alone. But now, he wondered if Caitlin had been with him. Why would she do that? Unless, and this seemed unbelievable, she knew what he was.

It seemed impossible that Caitlin would accept Steven for what he was, or even that she would remember him. The options swirled in his mind. Steven might have got to know her again, or, and this seemed impossible, he might have found a way to get her memory back. He remembered Steven was a good student when it came to mind manipulation and control.

But, either way, the idea that any human could act that normal around one of them was mind-boggling. And yet, Emily had managed to deceive a human, so it was not impossible for Steven to do the same.

The solitary figure lingering at the entrance to the library caught his attention. Ingrid's face said it all.

Eilif made his way over and put his arm around her shoulders. Ingrid thrust her face into his chest and started to cry. As her gasps eased, Eilif coaxed her towards the main pavement and they headed away from the university. Eilif figured she would want to talk, he wished her mother, Lana, was here. She was better than him at dealing with emotions.

After a few minutes, Eilif asked, 'Shall we go and get something to eat?'

'So long as it contains chocolate,' Ingrid sighed.

'That can easily be arranged.'

Ingrid straightened up and wiped the tears away from her eyes. 'I don't get it, what's he *doing* with that girl?'

'I don't know, but I don't like it,' Eilif replied, 'something's not right, and we're going to find out what it is.'

Chapter 8

Revelation

Caitlin stroked the underside of Steven's hand in a slow caress as they walked. Something was on his mind. She could be patient. The past week had been surreal, she had adapted too easily.

Once they got back to the apartment, Caitlin removed her long burgundy coat and shook out her curly red hair. Then she made her way over to the kettle, checked it had enough water, and flicked the switch. As it started to boil, she turned to face Steven. 'Are you alright?'

Steven had taken a seat. He glanced up and gave her a fleeting smile. It was unconvincing.

'You're not, are you?' She sat next to him on the sofa. 'What's up? You can tell me anything. You know you can.'

'They're here.'

Caitlin leant her elbows on her knees and pursed her lips. 'Right.'

'The girl I told you about, the one who found me, Ingrid, she was in the library just now.'

'Now?' Caitlin stood up, surprised at her unexpected resentment. 'Why didn't you tell me?' She had no reason to hate the girl. She actually felt sorry for her after Steven had told her how he had rejected her advances.

'I don't know,' he murmured.

Silence ensued, as they both considered the implications of the visitors.

A moment later, Steven eased his hand into Caitlin's and gave it a squeeze. 'We have to go to see them tonight.'

'Tonight?' It seemed too soon. She knew they would arrive but now it all seemed too fast.

Steven leant in and kissed her nose.

'That tickles,' Caitlin said, as she broke out into a broad smile.

'Just wanted to see you smile.'

'What are we going to tell them?' Caitlin could not help being scared. A part of her wondered if they would be angry with them.

Steven ran a hand over his hair. 'We can only tell them the truth, no point trying to make anything up. Can you handle it? Otherwise, you can stay here if you like. I'll break the ice first.'

Caitlin shook her head and then tucked her hair behind her ears. 'No, I'll come with you. The sooner we get this out of the way, the better.'

'You're sure?'

'Absolutely, let's get some things together and head back to the house.' A part of her felt guilty for the way they'd left his mother. But, Steven had insisted he did not care what happened to Emily. Caitlin could not blame him after what Emily had done. She would never forgive anyone who killed someone from her family.

'I'm sorry, Caitlin.'

Caitlin frowned. 'Sorry for what?'

'For this mess I've got you into. I don't think I've made you a better person at all. I mean, don't you feel bad about what we did the other night?'

'You mean, Adam?'

Steven nodded and avoided eye contact.

Caitlin knew she should feel bad about killing Adam, but she just didn't. Adam had made her friend, Sally, miserable. From the moment Caitlin had met Adam he had made lecherous advances and showered her with inappropriate comments. He deserved what he got.

'I'm sorry about Adam,' she lied.

She was sorry for Steven, Adam had been his friend. But, she was not sorry they had killed him. In fact, it had been really satisfying to lure him into a false sense of security. The idiot probably thought he finally stood a chance with her. It was laughable. It was ironic Steven seemed to feel bad about her killing Adam, and yet, he could not be bothered about his own mother.

'It's okay, you needed to feed. And after I saw how he

57

looked at you, he seemed like a good choice. I wish you could have resisted human blood, I guess we really need to talk to the others. They might be able to help you control your thirst.'

'You worry too much about my need for control. We are what we are, accept it – I have.' It surprised her that she accepted what she had become so easily, but she did. It made her feel powerful. She loved everything that came with the change. Intelligence, speed, extra strength, and youth. What was there not to like? She didn't think it was that much of a sacrifice to have to drink blood, human or otherwise.

'I know you accept it. That's what worries me. I don't accept what we are. I don't want to kill anyone else to ensure my survival.' Steven clenched his hands into fists and pursed his lips.

Caitlin bridged the gap between them and wrapped her arms around him, then stroked his hair, 'We'll look after each other. Stop worrying.' She let her hands wander along the curve of his spine as her nails lightly caressed his body. She loved the fact he reacted to her touch every time. She pulled away and found his lips. There was still enough time for close contact before they had to face the others. She knew just what to do to make him relax.

***

Steven did not know what to make of this new, empowered Caitlin. Ever since he had changed her she had lost all of her insecurities. She seemed so sure of herself, assertive even. And she was firmly in control, even when they made love. She was still Caitlin, but there was something about her that unnerved him. It was probably the fact she appeared to have lost her conscience where certain issues where concerned. He still could not believe she had killed Adam. He had watched her do it and done nothing. He had never considered himself to be a coward since he had never had trouble in the past standing up to people. He just could not go against Caitlin. He narrowed his eyes and shook his head slightly. He wanted to make her happy at whatever cost.

'We're nearly there. You're sure we should go in together?'

He blinked a couple of times, then turned to face Caitlin

and gave the best smile he could muster. 'We go in together.'

The sight of the house on top of the hill made him wince slightly. He wondered if Emily was still alive. He was loath to admit he hoped her dead. He had never hated anyone as much.

'Time to face the music, I've got to admit I'm curious about Ingrid, the girl you resisted.' Caitlin gave a confident chuckle.

'Yes, well, you don't have to worry about her. She means nothing.'

Caitlin flicked her hair off her face. 'I know that.'

Even with that comment Steven internally groaned. The old Caitlin would worry about any girl Steven even looked at. The old Caitlin always thought she was not good enough for him. It seemed the old Caitlin had gone, vanished without a trace. It made him even more wary about introducing her, but it was too late to back down now.

Once out of the car, Steven held Caitlin's hand and they knocked on the door. Almost immediately, the door opened.

'Steven, nice to see you again,' Eilif said, he held the door open and stayed back, 'and this is?'

'Caitlin,' she held out her hand, 'we've met before under more strained circumstances.'

Steven was taken aback by the confidence in her tone. Even Eilif raised his eyebrows.

Eilif shook her hand and then waved his hand in the direction of the house. 'Please, come in.'

Steven kept his hand on Caitlin's lower back as he guided her into the corridor.

Eilif directed them further, 'Make your way into the lounge.'

Steven was relieved to see that no-one else was in the lounge. 'Let's sit down.'

Caitlin shrugged her shoulders. 'Sure.'

'Can I make some tea or coffee?' Eilif asked, 'Catherine will be down in a minute.'

Steven asked for a coffee, Caitlin a tea and they waited in near enough silence. He could not remember a time when he had felt so awkward.

When Catherine and Isaac graced the doorway he felt a sense of relief and fear simultaneously. Isaac had the same stern look about him, he could not remember ever seeing him smile. Catherine's eyes showed the concern she was trying to hide.

'Steven, and I believe this is Caitlin. Nice to meet you,' Catherine said, before she gave a weak smile. She did not move closer. 'We have much to discuss.'

'Yes, we do,' Steven replied.

'Emily is very sick, she's dying. Did you realise?' Catherine's face was sad, she had to know the answer to that.

'I thought it was a possibility. She killed my mother, I don't really care what happens to her,' Steven tried to sound matter of fact but it came across bitter.

Isaac shook his head slowly. 'She's still your mother. You should always show respect, no matter what.'

Steven scoffed. It was best not to reply to that one. It was lucky Eilif walked in with the hot drinks on a tray.

After a polite passing around of drinks and a few subdued slurps, Catherine took her cue, 'Why is Caitlin here? No offence dear, but what do you know?'

Caitlin drew the mug towards her smug face, as she replied, 'Everything.' She took a long slurp of the tea which drowned out the sound of three heavy gasps.

Eilif narrowed his eyes. 'Then the question is *why* do you know and yet come here with no fear? I know you're not scared of us. I know how to read fear.'

All eyes focused on Caitlin, even Steven was curious about what she would say.

Caitlin sipped her tea again. She took her time, before she gave a broad smile. Her eyes sparkled, her hair glistened and her red curls fell perfectly at the side of her face. She was so beautiful. 'I have nothing to fear,' she said, as she exposed her fangs.

'What?' Eilif sprang to his feet. 'How is this possible?'

Catherine put her head in her hands, Isaac said nothing.

As Ingrid raced into the room all hell broke loose. She lunged at Caitlin, her hands in the shape of claws and screeched like an animal. Steven managed to block Caitlin and took the brunt of Ingrid's anger. He felt the scratch on his face, and a trickle oozed off his skin. He pushed Ingrid away, but said nothing.

Ingrid hit the wall and remained still, her face to the wall, only the sound of her heavy breathing echoed in the room.

'Eilif, take Ingrid away,' Catherine said, her voice calm, kind even.

When Eilif put his hand on her shoulder she shook it off, but then after what sounded like a whimper they left. Steven was mortified. He could not believe Ingrid was so upset. He never meant her any harm.

Once they had gone, he noticed Isaac held Catherine's hand. Caitlin had slouched back on the couch after finishing her tea, a bored, restless expression on her face.

He gripped the couch, on edge. What Caitlin had done made things easier, but it had not exactly made for a smoother transition.

The sound of the door made everyone turn to it, as Eilif came back in. 'Ingrid will not come back for a while, she's gone for a walk.'

Steven broke the tense atmosphere. 'There's no easy way to explain this so I'll just come out with it. Catherine, your mother was never bitten by the bats.'

'Emily suspected it and told us. I didn't want to believe her, but I guess it must be true and it explains a lot,' Catherine was subdued, pensive.

'You knew?' Eilif asked.

Catherine gazed in his eyes, 'No, I didn't *know*, but I knew something was different about her. I always did.'

'You never said anything to Ian,' Eilif sounded hurt, 'he would have said something.'

Catherine half-smiled. 'There was not much to say Mum always said things that made me think that she was different, but it never added up and she never explained so it was best left alone. I mean, we had so much to deal with when we set up the community. We did not have time to dwell on a lot anyone said, we worked day and night at times.'

Isaac nodded. 'True. So, Steven, or Caitlin actually, how did you become like us?'

Steven glanced at Caitlin, who smiled before she looked in the direction of the bookcase with an expression of utter boredom. He gave a deep sigh, 'Jeff told me what to do.'

Catherine's eyes widened, 'My father told you how to change Caitlin? But that goes against everything he ever believed in, it goes against everything he told us, it goes… oh.' Her hands fell limp on her lap, her lip wobbled. 'Of course, if my mum wasn't bitten by the bats then someone had to change her. And that someone could only have been…,' she fought to get the words out, 'my father.'

'This is very dangerous, in the wrong hands this information could lead to further problems. You must not tell anyone how to do it. It has to be your secret.' Isaac narrowed his eyes and stared at Caitlin. 'Do you know?'

When Caitlin nodded slowly, his nostrils flared.

Catherine sighed, 'Steven, why did you tell her?'

Steven shrugged his shoulders.

Isaac's cheeks reddened. 'For years we have protected what we are and now both of you know how to do something none of us knew was possible. You must both come with us, and yet, do we want you in the community, exposing the truth?' Isaac stood up and paced, as he held his hands in the air. 'This will not do.'

Chapter 9

Suggestions

Caitlin had been taken aback by Catherine's vibrant red hair, she was nothing like Steven. Isaac's beard and general countenance did nothing to appease her, if she remembered correctly he was Jewish. It explained why he thought Steven should respect his mother, even though she was, in her opinion, a witch. The Ten Commandments took humanity to the limits, even though she had to admit they actually made a lot of sense. Yet, when her parents had driven her crazy she really could not just honour her father and mother, it was draconian. The thought made her pause for a moment; the chances were she would never see them again. She never, ever expected it to be an issue, but all of a sudden it was.

She would never see any of her family or friends again.

She swallowed involuntarily as she thought of little sister, Jeanie, and her older brother, Mark. She could not imagine a life where she never saw them again. They had grown up together, they shared memories. None of them had to leave any of their family behind. Steven had. She glanced at him, and for the first time considered just how tough the last year must have been for him. He had lost his life. It was not a surprise he was willing to do whatever he could to hold on to it. She could understand why he would try to suppress the urge to kill.

Then she considered Emily. Again, Emily had been forced to lead a life she did not want, and when she finally found love she had to leave her only son behind. She could not even begin to imagine what she had gone through, it was too hard to even contemplate. It made the fact she was so twisted, almost, understandable. She wanted to talk to Emily, she wanted to know more about her past. She just had no idea how she would get the time alone with her. Steven was always by her side, she doubted they would leave her alone.

'Are you going to stay here now? You're not planning to go back to the apartment are you?' Catherine asked, breaking the stilted silence.

Steven glanced at Caitlin for a moment, 'I'm not sure it's best for us to stay here. Besides, what are you planning to do with Emily?'

Catherine looked away, distant.

Isaac answered, 'We will have to take her back to the community.'

'Has she fed?' Steven asked. His eyes darted from Catherine to Isaac.

'Not yet,' Catherine answered, as she got off the chair and made her way over to the large sash windows and gazed out. 'She will have to. We can't take her back as she is. We can always sedate her. I will make sure she poses no other threat.'

Caitlin raised an eyebrow. It was a bold statement.

'Catherine, why don't you go with Steven to the apartment to get their things? Caitlin you stay here,' Isaac said, his tone authoritative.

Caitlin wanted to protest, but she held it back. He did not trust her, yet he had also given her the chance she needed. 'That's fine, Steven, you go, I'll stay. I can look after myself for a while, lucky there's Wi-Fi. I can easily kill a few hours.'

She could see them all flinch as she used the word kill, they were an oversensitive bunch.

'Are you sure?' Steven placed his hand over hers and gave a slight squeeze.

Caitlin smiled, 'Of course.'

Steven got up, whilst Catherine moved away from the window and stood by his side, 'I could do with some fresh air.'

'Then it's settled,' Isaac said.

Once Steven and Catherine left, Isaac made to leave the room, 'Caitlin, I don't suggest you go anywhere without telling us first.'

'I wouldn't leave,' she replied, her tone dry.

'Good to know.'

Finally, she was left alone. She picked up the iPad from the table and checked her Facebook page. Her friends were up to their usual antics, she did not dare reply, like or comment. She browsed her Wattpad account and found a few good stories online. She had always fancied herself as a bit of a writer. She could certainly write a good true life story now.

She wondered if anyone would know if she went upstairs, she did not want to bump into crazy Ingrid. Head in hands, she closed her eyes and tried to think. As she did the strangest thing happened. She could hear them. In her mind, she could visualise their rough positions and map out almost a 3D visual of the house. It was bizarre, yet exciting. Isaac was in the front room, which had to be a study of sorts. At the back of the house, she could sense a smaller more feminine body, Ingrid. And at the top of the house there was someone else, someone weak, Emily.

If she went out of the window she could get to the top quickly, without alerting them. Then again, Isaac would hear the window open and think she was running away. She would just go up the stairs, and say she was looking around if anyone asked. If she had to stay she would have to find a room anyway, she could bluff it.

As she went up her eyes were drawn to the old pictures. Even though she had seen them before, there was something about black and white photos that made her feel nostalgic. She carried on up the stairs, conscious of the fact that at any moment someone might come to challenge her. But, as it turned out no-one did.

Hand on the door handle she hesitated for a split second. She knew Steven would have serious issues with what she was about to do. Either way, she did not really care, she wanted to talk to Emily so she would. She gave a half-smile, she had never been able to do anything selfish or singular in her life. There always had to be a first for everything. Her hand pushed the handle down and she eased in slowly.

The stench hit her hard. It had only been less than a week since she last saw Emily, but from the look of it she had deteriorated badly. It was hard to think the skeletal figure on the bed was the woman she had first seen. Her hair was completely white, her face shrivelled, eyes depressed, and her arms looked like brittle bones. It scared her to think she might look like that one day. She pushed the thought aside and moved closer.

She sat on the chair next to Emily and whispered, 'Are you awake?'

Emily's eyes opened quickly. A hoarse, whispery voice replied, 'I knew you would come.'

'You did?' Caitlin gave a slight huff.

Emily's lips curled slightly at the edges, 'Of course, you want to know about the life you are about to lead. And you figured I was the only one who could give you an insane, but honest, answer.'

Caitlin was impressed, she couldn't have said it better herself.

'So, listen carefully. They'll figure out that you're here soon enough. It's lucky for you Steven is not, his hearing is outstanding. The others have better things to do at the moment,' she chuckled.

'I'm listening,' Caitlin said.

'The community is a jail. It might sound fantastic to you, don't bother denying it, I can tell you think it is where you want to go, but they'll not let you leave it. If you want that life then go, but if you do make sure you keep your eyes and ears open. Don't give them any reason to doubt you. It took me too long to hide my true feelings, you must hide yours. I can see the hunger in you, I heard it. Be good to my son, but don't let men rule your life. Make your own choices, make your own destiny. Then help my son do the same, please. I never wanted to hurt him.'

'Why did you kill his mother?' Caitlin fiddled with her nails, 'I need to understand what could make you do something like that. I'm worried I might do something just as stupid one day.'

Emily grimaced. 'It wasn't stupid. That woman was not his mother and she was in my way. I only wanted my true love. Shouldn't you do everything in your power to have your true love?'

'Within reason,' Caitlin said, she knew Emily was a nutcase but she could not deny that love had made many people kill. Deaths of passion – what a way to go!

'I had every reason to do what I did,' Emily hissed, 'I'm not as crazy as everyone thinks I am. I'm just prepared to go to extremes to get what I want, are you?'

Caitlin stared at the antique lamp, the glass moulded like a tulip bulb on a brass stand. 'I have to go.'

Emily's eyes glared, 'Don't leave me like this. If you help me when we get back to the Amazon, I will help you too. Do we have an agreement?'

Caitlin flicked her hair off her face and raised her eyebrows, 'Why would I want to help you?'

'For the same reason you're here, I'm the only one who'll give you an honest answer. You know it's true, and you know you feel sorry for me. I have to make amends to Steven. I will find a way to help you both. But first, I need to get better. Think of a way to help me and I will help you.'

'I'll think about it.' Caitlin left without another glance. She was stupid to think someone like Emily could do anything to help them. But, at least she had some answers. It was possible to get just as crazy as Emily, she had to be careful. She needed to start listening to Steven, and the others. They were the ones she should trust. They were the ones that knew what was best for her, not Emily.

*****

Emily allowed herself a slow smile. The seed had been planted, she had given it some water and now it would start to grow. The girl, Caitlin, was weak. She was no match for her. She would make her do exactly what she wanted, with some carefully planned manoeuvres. It would help her son in the long term – she did not want him to become as righteous as Ian. He needed to live a full life, not a life full of restrictions. She did not know why she knew Caitlin would come to see her, it was strange.

The girl wanted to know what she could become. Emily could have shown her the full monster, but she did not want to scare her. It had taken every last bit of control she had to keep her teeth from extending. She needed Caitlin to feel sorry for her, and if she played her cards right again, she stood a chance. Emily knew she had a habit of ruining every fresh chance she got – she did not want to get it wrong again.

It was her son's future as well as her own that was at stake.

Chapter 10

Explanations

After all the bags had been packed and stowed away in the car, Steven sat on the passenger side and fiddled with the radio. If he found something good to listen to he could suppress the need for much conversation. Catherine had barely said anything so far, it was promising. He settled on Heart, a station he had grown to enjoy whilst at university. The idle chatter of the presenter was perfect background material, before the music started.

'Steven, I have to ask you something. Can you give me an honest answer please?'

He knew the lack of conversation was too good to be true.

'I can't promise anything, but you can try me. I reserve the right to stay silent,' he chuckled.

Catherine could not suppress her smile, she had to like his dry sense of humour. 'Okay then. Do you trust Caitlin?'

'Why do you ask?' Steven did not want to sound defensive, but he could not help it.

Catherine nodded, 'As I suspected. You don't know what she has become, any more than you know what you are. I am guessing it was not a calculated decision. I am guessing that you acted before you had time to consider the implications of your actions.'

There was no reply to that, it was true after all.

A minute later, Catherine continued, 'It's not a mistake, you can't change it and it must have happened for a reason. But, Caitlin is volatile. I'm good at sensing these things. She reminds me of your mother.'

'She is nothing like my mother, anything but that,' Steven blurted, his anger surprised him.

'Don't get me wrong, I just think she might be reckless at the moment. She is wild, you were not like that.' She tapped her finger on the steering wheel.

He knew she was right. He might have wanted to escape,

but he never wanted to kill. Caitlin was different, he could not deny it. 'How do I help her?'

'We take her back with us, we teach her to maintain control. In time, she'll learn. But, at least she has you. Remember, the community is supportive. Emily had no-one, it did not help her. She never allowed anyone in, not even Anna.'

Steven found the fact Anna was Emily's twin fascinating. Their personalities were so different.

'I do have something to tell you though. There has been a development,' she paused.

'What do you mean?' Steven eyed her through the corner of his eye. He did not like the sound of that.

'The community is going to split, and I'm leaving with a select group to make a new start in Borneo. It could be an option for you. It's not going to be easy, we need hard workers. You could come with us, have a fresh start.'

Steven's jaw slackened, it sounded too good to be true, 'Really?'

Catherine's face broke out into a broad smile, 'Well, I wouldn't have told you if I didn't mean it. Interested?'

'Of course, it could be just what we need. A new life, a new place, we could help with anything you need. You think the others would mind?'

'It would be for the best. In fact, a part of me wonders if you should really come back at all. We could keep Caitlin a secret for a while,' she paused. 'Then again, it would be foolish. She has so much to learn, as do you for that matter – what were my parents thinking? No, you'll have to come back. You need to learn as much as possible so that we can replicate the community in Borneo.'

Steven focused ahead, his hands clasped together. It was a lifeline. At last, something to be excited about. Something he could work towards. He hoped Caitlin would also be up for the challenge, the old Caitlin would have been. The newer version could not be that different from the Caitlin he knew.

***

Ingrid stared at the gravestones with Isaac and Eilif at her side. 'Why do you think they gave up on life?'

Eilif shrugged his shoulders. 'Rumour says they would've died anyway. Is that true, Isaac?'

'Apparently, Judith had not been well for a while.' Isaac turned to face Eilif, 'Human blood might have healed her, but we think she was dying anyway. I think it was the same for Jeff, even though he died after Judith. I have to admit that I don't feel any different, but then I was much younger than they were.'

'Or is it just because they were different – Judith was changed by Jeff, the bats changed Jeff. Was she weaker maybe?' Ingrid hoped she was right. If she was it meant Caitlin would also be weaker, and that could only be a good thing as far as she was concerned.

'Another puzzle for us to solve and investigate,' Eilif mused.

'We can trust you, Ingrid, I hope,' Isaac said, he glanced at her, his eyes narrowed.

Ingrid was offended at the suggestion, but she knew she had acted irrationally earlier with her crazy outburst. 'You have always been able to trust me. I will not let you down now.'

Eilif smiled, and nodded in Isaac's direction, 'My daughter has never let us down. She is one of our best. Love has a habit of bringing out the worst in people.'

'It certainly does that,' Ingrid said, she was amused yet annoyed. She could not believe she had fallen for the one man that was not interested in her. She had rejected so many in the past, she was not used to being on the receiving end. It hurt.

'Look, even though we know Caitlin is still in the house I don't like leaving her. I need you both to erase Caitlin's existence. Can you do that?' Isaac asked.

Ingrid watched her dad agree, and looked forward to delving into Caitlin's past as they made her disappear. She wondered what she would find, with luck something would make her seem not as perfect as Steven obviously thought she was. She could hope.

With one final glance at the gravestones, Ingrid felt a shiver run down her spine. She had never thought much about death, and now it was a possibility. Either way, she still had many years ahead of her, and she would not refuse human blood to heal – ever. As she walked back to the house, she mulled over the fact that Steven had made her feel guilty for a time. She was sure she was over it now. She was not going to apologise for what she was. It was stupid to feel remorse over something she could not really control.

'I'm going to go do some research and use that iPad device, it looked interesting,' Isaac said, there was a definite glint in his eye.

Ingrid was used to the fascination by now. Gadgets and scientists went hand in hand.

'I'll go and get the car ready,' Eilif said.

Ingrid nodded and went upstairs to get her bag. She liked having her things with her. Even though her bag mainly consisted of rubbish, it was her rubbish.

As she got to the landing, she saw the door at the end of the hallway open and Caitlin walked out.

She was pretty, Ingrid had to give her that. She was shorter than Ingrid, with a slim, petite build. It was the hair that made her stand out. A vibrant red, curls that hung everywhere. As she got closer, Ingrid noticed her eyes were deep blue, the colour of the ocean. She fought hard to find something she did not like about her. But even when Caitlin smiled at her, she melted. There was something about Caitlin that compelled her to like her. She resented the fact and did her best to come across hostile. She would not smile back.

'Ingrid, right?' Caitlin asked, her smile broader – if that were possible.

'Yes.' A curt reply, Ingrid convinced herself she could do this.

'I love your hair, I've always been jealous of blonde girls with straight hair.' Caitlin picked a strand of her hair up and frowned. 'I have this! I hate it, you're so lucky.'

And with that Ingrid smiled, annoyed at herself for doing so. 'Thanks.' She cursed inwardly again, she was not meant to be nice to her.

'I know you probably hate me and all, but it really isn't my fault... you know, about Steven. Why he would like me over... err... I mean. Oh, you know what I mean... you know you're gorgeous, right?' Caitlin laughed again, it was of the infectious variety.

Ingrid grinned, she could not stop herself. 'You're not like I expected, I wanted to hate you.'

'Sorry about that, I tend to say what comes to my head,' Caitlin sighed, 'I blame my parents.'

Ingrid nodded, 'It's always a good call. So, if you have any questions, I guess I can help.' She could not believe she was being won over so easily.

'Thanks for the offer. I think I'd like to learn as I go. Steven is so uptight at the moment. I think I am happier about *us* than he is.' She laughed again.

'That doesn't surprise me somehow,' Ingrid mused. She ran a hand through her hair and cradled the tips with her hand. 'I have to grab my things and then I'm going out with my dad. Isaac will be downstairs. It was nice chatting to you. By that way, stay away from the top floor, Emily is sick. No-one can help her.'

'I gathered,' Caitlin said. Her eyes glanced up.

Ingrid wondered how much she knew, probably everything. She was not surprised Steven had fallen in love with Caitlin. That was annoying.

Ingrid went into her room, grabbed her bag and sprayed some of her favourite scent on, she found it comforting. Then she made her way downstairs. The door to the room was shut now, she wondered what Caitlin was doing, either way she could not exactly tell Caitlin what they were planning to do. She might like her, but she was not going to tell her everything.

Once downstairs, she found the garage. Eilif was already in the car, the engine running. She eased into the seat and dumped the bag by her feet.

'Ready?' Eilif asked, he glanced at the bag.

'Yes,' Ingrid replied.

After five minutes of driving, Ingrid said, 'I talked to Caitlin.'

Eilif sounded surprised, as he replied, 'And?'

'She's really nice. We should help her settle in. She has not done anything wrong,' she paused. 'I'm really sorry about my reaction. It was stupid. It won't happen again. I'll just get over Steven. I have to, right?'

'Right, I knew you'd find a way to overcome your emotions. You were never the type to be led by the whimsical world of *feelings*,' he chuckled.

Ingrid shook her head, her lips, like traitors, curled up. 'No, feelings never used to trouble me in the past. I guess they find a way to get to everyone in the end. Whatever happens, at least I know I'm capable of falling in love.'

'Yes,' Eilif nodded. 'I'm happy about that. I don't want you to lead a lonely life, Ingrid. Your mother has been worried about you.'

'Mum always worries, no matter what any of us do. It's inbuilt.'

Eilif grinned, 'Someday, when you become a mother you'll understand. It's so easy to judge when you have no experience.'

'I guess,' Ingrid shrugged her shoulders. 'Where do we start?'

'The university, it's time to erase Caitlin.'

Ingrid felt sorry for Caitlin. She would never want to leave her family. It surprised her that Caitlin seemed so relaxed. She would miss her family if she was never able to see them again.

Chapter 11

Unexpected Friendship

Steven did not know what to make of it. At first, he wondered if they were having a joke, but then he realised he wasn't so lucky. From the way Caitlin and Ingrid were chatting, he realised they had become friends. They even giggled. In fact, he was beginning to feel like the outcast. Caitlin had barely spoken to him on the journey back, and then on the plane she had opted to watch movies or listen to music. Yet, as soon as they left the plane she hooked up next to Ingrid and they resumed their chatter as if they had been the best of friends all their lives.

It made him uncomfortable, and as far as he could see, neither of them seemed to care what he thought. It was strange. He had convinced himself he hated Ingrid. Yet now, as he saw her with the girl he loved, he realised perhaps he had misjudged her. After all, if Caitlin liked her, he guessed he might have been too harsh. The honest truth was he was jealous. He didn't like the fact Caitlin paid less attention to him, and she seemed so excited about the community.

He just did not get it.

Now they had landed in Manaus, the wait was nearly over – the Amazon jungle waited. Soon Caitlin would be introduced. He could not help a sense of wariness overcoming him. Caitlin was acting all giddy, and Ingrid did not help matters as she described the community as some sort of utopia. He kept a straight face and hid his disgust.

Isaac had bundled Emily up in the wheelchair and was pushing her to the exit as fast as he could, without adopting an impossible pace. It was lucky Emily could not attack anyone. A few times she made some very loud and embarrassing hissing noises, it was lucky people were so stupid. Catherine would fob them off, and tell them she was mad. People are scared off easily.

Steven followed alongside Caitlin, Ingrid on the other side.

They seemed to talk and talk, about what he had no idea. He had switched off ages ago.

When they finally got the luggage, they eased out of the arrivals lounge. It was no surprise when Steven saw Ian waiting. He gave Catherine an embrace and glanced in the direction of Caitlin. It was obvious he was thrown by the fact she was near enough glued to Ingrid's side. He nodded in Steven's direction, a twinkle in his eye.

Steven frowned, even Ian thought it was funny.

Ian extended his hand in Caitlin's direction and gave her the biggest smile Steven had ever seen from the likes of Ian. 'Caitlin, we meet again.'

Caitlin stretched out her hand and gave what looked like a firm handshake, 'I remember you, but only just. You scared the hell out of me the first time we met.' She let go of his hand and smirked, 'I'm not scared of you anymore.'

Ian chuckled, 'Really?'

'Really.' She stood her ground and raised her head in what looked like a definite challenge.

Ian blinked, did a double take, and then relaxed, 'Good to know. Let's get a move on.' He lifted the blanket hiding Emily, and then grimaced, 'We should get her back.'

A barely audible grunt muttered.

Ian had brought a minibus to greet them. Catherine lifted Emily up and placed her on the back seat, everyone else found a space and they were on the move again. The hustle and bustle of Manaus did not interest Steven anymore, Caitlin did. He reached out for her hand and held it. Caitlin stopped chatting to Ingrid, turned to face him and squeezed his hand back.

'You okay?' he asked.

'Why wouldn't I be?' Caitlin replied. 'This is going to be great.'

Her smile was infectious, and he found his eyes relaxing as his lips naturally eased up. He nodded, as he replied, 'I hope so.'

She tilted her head to the side, bit her lip slightly, and then turned back to Ingrid to resume the conversation.

At least she kept her hand in his.

When the port came into view a sense of déjà vu overcame him. All around people went about their frantic business. A series of fishing boats were scattered around the area and some makeshift shacks seemed to be selling the fresh catch of the day.

Ian dropped them off at the start of the right pontoon. Once everyone and everything was offloaded he mentioned he was going to take the minibus back. Steven guessed it was a rental. Isaac took charge and started directing people. Caitlin immediately offered to help and was busy grabbing bags. Steven followed suit and gave a hand. It was all too easy so far. He saw the way Caitlin glanced at people, but did not get distracted as Ingrid whispered something in her ear and Caitlin nodded and looked away. She was doing an amazing job at controlling her instinct. Whatever Ingrid said worked.

Steven could not help a feeling of inadequacy coming over him. It was supposed to be his help she turned to. Not once did he ever imagine she would turn to someone like Ingrid. He felt deflated. He lugged the bags towards the river cruise ship, which still looked as old and outdated as he remembered, and pushed the thoughts out of his mind.

Carmen greeted them with her usual flamboyancy. Caitlin immediately smiled and Carmen greeted her warmly. When Caitlin spoke to her in Spanish, Carmen melted even more. That was Caitlin – she had a way with people. She knew what to say all the time. After a series of disjointed conversations they got busy, and loaded everything on the ship. Catherine agreed to take responsibility for Emily, and disappeared, sister in tow, in search of a cabin.

Steven could not understand how it had been so easy for Caitlin to be accepted. He was happy about it, obviously. Yet, a part of him could not help being suspicious, or perhaps it was just plain old jealousy.

Once they set off, he eased up next to Caitlin, who had leaned over the edge of the barrier to look at the river, 'Are you alright?' Ingrid was not by her side for once, he was glad.

Caitlin replied in a sing song laugh, 'Of course I am. Why

do you keep asking?' She gave a stern, but playful smirk.

Steven shook his head slightly, his cheeks flushed, 'It's stupid of me to worry, right?'

'It IS, you catch on fast,' Caitlin scoffed, a sneaky smirk on her face.

Steven pushed her hair off her face, and cupped her face, 'I only want the best for you.'

Caitlin eased into his hand, and gave what he would class as her cute smile. He wanted to kiss her. Truth, it felt like years since they had been intimate. He hesitated.

'I know,' her voice softened.

'I'm not interrupting anything, am I?' Ingrid chirped.

Steven wanted to tell her she had, but he did not get the chance as Caitlin cried out, 'No, join us. So, tell me where we're going?'

Steven felt affronted now, she could have asked him. But she didn't, she asked Ingrid, her new buddy. 'I'll go find a cabin and chill out for a bit. See you later...' he trailed, as he saw Caitlin was already in deep conversation, the brief time they shared a moment of the past. She laughed and waved him off dismissively.

Steven shuffled off and sulked. He could not figure out if she was playing hard to get, had genuinely become best friends with Ingrid, or she had just gone off him. Sometimes being a man was really tough, he had never understood girls. He thought Caitlin was different. He thought she was not like the *others*. Then again he was starting to realise he did not really know this Caitlin at all.

***

Ingrid noticed the way Steven's shoulders slumped and her heart jumped for joy. She could not believe Caitlin actually ignored Steven in order to talk to her. It was a mystery. Ingrid would never choose someone else over Steven, ever. It took everything she had to resist the urge to run after him. Yet, she knew she had to play the game right. She could not let Caitlin see how much Steven meant to her. The truth was she really did like Caitlin, she liked her a lot, and she was not about to try to steal her boyfriend away when they had only just become friends.

Saying that, if Caitlin didn't want to be with Steven, that was a different matter. Then he was open season, and there was no way Ingrid would let anyone in on him before she got her chance. It was all about timing.

Caitlin continued to ogle at everything, she reminded Ingrid of the children back in the community. Questions, they always had so many questions. Caitlin was no different. She wanted to know everything, and Ingrid was happy to oblige.

When the Solimões River and Rio Negro met, Caitlin got even more excited as the dark and light green colours eased alongside each other, stubborn in their quest to remain independent. When the colours finally merged she seemed to settle down. She stared into the distance, as she said, 'Do you think I should go see Steven? I've got a feeling he was upset.'

'Really? I didn't think he was fussed, tired maybe,' Ingrid said, quite pleased with her tiny lie.

'Oh, you didn't notice the way he slouched off,' she laughed, 'it's so typical of Steven. He tends to mope if things don't go his way.'

Ingrid remembered the way Steven had become withdrawn when Jenson, his best friend, had been taken away for his change whilst at the community. Not to forget, the way he had berated her for the way she had acted, it was embarrassing now to think back to the way she had thrown herself at him. She would not act desperate again. She had to act aloof, indifferent, it might work. 'I never noticed,' the lies came easy enough.

'Hey, I think I'll go check on him. Speak to you later,' Caitlin smiled, 'it really has been great to get to know you. I never thought I'd make a friend so easily.'

Ingrid beamed and waved her off. It killed her to think of what they might get up to, she hoped not much. It was a lot to ask for.

She made her way to the front of the ship, her hand running over the wooden banister. At the entrance, she climbed the stairs leading up to the cockpit. Carmen was there, she was one of the best navigators they had.

'Ingrid,' Carmen smiled, and put her book down.

Ingrid gave her a hug and sat next to her.

Carmen resumed her position in front of the wheel. The river was quite wide, but you still had to watch it. 'New girl seems to have settled in alright. Ian says you've become friends.'

Ingrid felt herself blush, 'She's nice.'

'So I hear. It sounds like it's going to be hard for anyone to actually dislike her,' Carmen mused. 'Of course, the fact she's so normal will give fuel to the fire for those that think that a life with humans is the way to go.'

Ingrid had considered that already, 'It's not difficult to see why. Do you think maybe we have been wrong all these years? Do you think what we have been trying to protect was just something that was meant to happen? I don't know what to think.'

'I don't know either, Ian is beside himself,' Carmen sighed, 'he tries to act like it doesn't matter, but he's scared. He knows he's holding on to control by thin tenterhooks as it is.'

Ingrid got up and made her way over to the window. 'I'm starting to think that maybe we should be amongst normal humans. Perhaps, we were meant to co-exist. It was not a fluke. The world needs a way to suppress humanity?'

Carmen laughed, scornful, 'What by creating us, a species capable of outliving every human in existence, capable of reproduction on a much grander scale, capable of feats that should be impossible?'

Ingrid knew what she was saying, but she had considered this too. 'But, we don't age and we can heal with blood. Think about it. Natural diseases, old age, cancer, all those horrible afflictions normal humans succumb too. We would make people stronger and take away the need for suffering.'

'And slowly irradiate a species in the process,' Ian said, as he came into the room. 'I don't think any creature has ever consciously wiped out another, do you want to be the first?'

Ingrid huffed, 'Actually, humans make animals extinct all the time. They don't care, so why should we? And also, we would not be eradicating it, don't be so melodramatic. We would be making it different. You can't tell me change doesn't happen all the time. It would take thousands of years for our small group to dominate in a world this big. Our kind is but a drop in the ocean.'

Ian dropped his eyes to the floor for a moment. Slowly, he raised his head, 'We would start the chain reaction.'

Carmen broke her silence, 'And so what if we did?'

'I'll let you ladies chat, I have things to do,' Ian said, as he turned on his heel.

It was the first time Ingrid had seen the fight taken out of him. If Ian did not want to fight, it looked like it was game over. It made her giddy to think that soon they might plan a life out in the open. There was no point going to Borneo, when they could just go back to their homelands. Ingrid had no idea what that would be like. Her home had always been amongst the community, some had never left the Amazon. She had no idea what people would choose to do if given the choice.

Chapter 12

Truth

Caitlin could not believe what she was seeing. She was actually on a ship, currently sailing on the Amazon River, that is, the *actual* Amazon River in Brazil, not the make pretend one in her dream. She remembered when Steven had shown her the vision in the dream, the dream that revealed the truth about Steven, the truth about their relationship. It seemed like months ago when she had found out that Eilif had erased her memory. She still resented the fact she had been so embarrassed in front of Daniel. She blushed at the thought – how was she supposed to know she was not a virgin?

It was all forgotten now though.

Steven had changed her and she was one of them, only the second human to have ever been changed. It was an interesting development, it was a shame neither of Steven's grandparents were there to shed any light on what she would be. They had both chosen to die. She found it hard to understand why they would have done that. She knew his grandmother had chosen to die first.

Since his grandmother was the only other human to have been changed before, she wondered if there had been something else wrong with her. She wondered if she was actually like the others. She hoped someone might have some answers, and so far the only one who seemed to know something was Steven's mum, Emily, and she was not exactly trustworthy.

She did not think she could trust Emily, but if she wanted answers she might just have to listen regardless of the fact she was unstable. It was obvious Ingrid still wanted to be with Steven, yet Caitlin did not feel threatened in any way. She almost wanted Ingrid to have him. She knew she was a fool. Steven was a kind, gorgeous, intelligent man who had done everything in his power to get her back. And yet, something else had changed. Caitlin was amazed by her reaction. When they had made love it had been amazing, but she did not feel overwhelmed by him anymore.

She did not know if it was just a phase, or whether there was more to it. Either way, she had to find out. She had to go and see him. By giving him a cold shoulder, she was only delaying the inevitable.

She did not know where he had gone, so she had to go and investigate. She opened the door and eased past the cabin doors. They were all shut, this was not going to be easy. She started to walk down the corridor and the door at the far end opened. Steven stuck out his head and smiled, it was a tired smile. She suspected he had actually been having a rest.

She made her way over, and stopped outside the door. 'Hey.'

'Do you want to come in?' he asked, his eyes blinked slowly.

'Sure, as long as I'm not disturbing you. Am I?' She gave a half-smile.

'Not at all, please come in.' He made way for her and backed into the room.

It was a small cabin, barely over a few metres squared. A small single bed was nestled on the side on the room, one of those that could be pulled back up after use. There was a small sink opposite, and a pull-out table. It was a basic, but functional, room for one.

She sat down on the bed, head low, and said, 'So?'

Steven sat next to her. He took her hand and held it on his. He turned it round and with his other hand traced her vein from her hand up to her elbow. Before he had got very far she pulled it away and chuckled.

'I knew that would make you laugh,' Steven said, his voice low, almost tempting.

She gazed up into his eyes and was entranced once again by the pool of amber. She could not look away, but neither moved closer. Caitlin wondered if he *needed* her to make the move. She narrowed the gap and gave him a small peck on his lips before she fell back, watching him. Steven did not kiss her back, but his thumb glided up and down on her wrist. It was a very sensual experience.

Caitlin placed her other hand behind his head and leaned in towards him so that their foreheads were touching. 'Steven, I...' she did not know what to say.

'It's okay...' he said, neither could finish.

The both raised their heads and came in for another kiss. This time is was slow, steady, as though they were having a first kiss all over again. The kiss became deeper, more desperate, as they sought out the connection which she knew had been partially severed. She started to feel lightheaded, as every nerve ending in her body stood to attention. She raised her other hand and played with his hair. His hands sat on the curve of her lower back, their warmth creating a small furnace.

Even though she wanted to carry on kissing, the position was not the most comfortable. A supposedly 'better' human could still get a sore neck. She pulled back. 'Can we lie down? I would like to kiss you some more, but my neck is at an awkward angle.'

Steven laughed, 'I thought you'd never ask.'

Caitlin lay down and Steven eased on his side alongside her, it was a bit of a squeeze but they made it work. He put his arm under her head and she nestled into his shoulder. It was nice to just lie together. She was not bothered if it did not develop into anything else. It was just comfortable to be with him. She closed her eyes as Steven ran his finger along her cheek, and she let herself relax.

*

Caitlin opened her eyes and noticed Steven had stopped caressing her cheek, her mouth felt dry and she had a slight saliva trail on the corner of her mouth. She wiped it off quickly and sat up. She was alone.

She got up, made her way over to the basin and turned on the tap to splash water on her face. Her stomach growled since it had been a while since they last ate. She had no idea how long she had been asleep for, or how long the journey would take. Since Steven had disappeared it was probably a good idea to go see where everyone had gone. She could not believe she had fallen asleep when she should have been trying to figure out what was going on between them.

As she made for the door, it opened and Steven walked in. He held a plate with some thick slices of bread and two mugs of what looked and smelled like coffee in his other hand.

'I can't believe I fell asleep?' Her shoulders slumped.

'Yes,' he smiled, 'and you looked very cute.'

'Cute? Urgh, how embarrassing,' Caitlin sighed, 'I'm starving. Can I have one?'

'I thought you might be, help yourself.' He held out the plate and Caitlin took a piece. 'They only had coffee, but I figured it was better than nothing.'

'Thanks.' Caitlin took the mug and had a sip. With the buttered bread the combination was heavenly. Hunger made anything taste good.

She ate the slice quickly and downed the rest of the coffee, Steven watched, as though amused.

Caitlin smiled, 'Told you I was hungry.'

Steven chuckled, 'I believe you.' He finished his own bread and put the plate on the side table, then he looked out of the small, round window, 'We'll be there soon. Are you nervous?'

Caitlin replied, 'No, not nervous, uncertain really. So far, it's been too easy. I expect something will happen to complicate things.'

He turned back to face her, nodded, a sad expression in his eyes, and then looked away again.

Caitlin swallowed involuntarily. She could hear every sound they made, her gulp magnified. She thought of sitting down, but then decided against it. 'Steven, I…' she trailed.

'I know, Caitlin, I know,' he turned to face her. 'Something has changed for you. You don't feel the same way you used to. Love is a fickle thing sometimes. All I can do is hope that you'll feel the same way you used to about me, but if you don't I'm not going to begrudge you forever. We can both move on, and I'll always be here for you as a friend if you need me.'

Caitlin raised an eyebrow and frowned. 'It almost sounds like a breaking up speech.'

Steven walked towards her and held her in his arms, his

head on hers. For a minute they just embraced, it felt right. When he pulled back, he put his arms on her shoulders and looked her in the eyes. 'You're not in love with me anymore, are you?'

Caitlin did not know what to say, she opened and closed her mouth, unable to engage her brain.

'You don't have to say another word, it is what it is.' Steven let her go and made to leave.

Caitlin stood frozen on the spot for a second, unable to move, unable to react. As the door was about to close, she rushed towards it and managed to put her hand on his arm, 'Steven, don't tell anyone yet, please.'

He nodded, his eyes devoid of all emotion, and then walked away.

Caitlin eased back into the room and leant against the wall. It took her a few minutes to breathe properly. As she did, her breaths got louder and louder, as the constriction at the back of her throat erupted, and she broke down. She sat on the bed, head in hands, and wept. She could not believe it was over. Was that all it took?

After she had calmed down, she wiped her face with the back of her hands. She missed Gemma. She would do anything to have her best friend there. To talk over the situation and try to figure out what, if anything, could be done. Her chest ached, it was a dull pain. She could not understand how it was possible to be completely infatuated with someone one minute and then feel nothing the next. Well, not nothing exactly, but Steven was right she was not in love with him anymore. He had known it before she had acknowledged what had happened.

If she was honest, she wished she could lie better. It would have been easier to pretend she was still in love. She was just not the sort to play with someone's emotions. You either loved them or you didn't, it should be simple. But, the truth was it was far from simple.

What she most feared was the reaction of the community. Steven had changed her because she was supposedly his true love. If she actually wasn't, it made things a nightmare for them to explain. She figured the community would understand love more than irrational lust. Either way, maybe she should talk to Steven, so they could get their story straight. She would do that for him.

Caitlin cursed and made her way back to the sink. After she had ensured her eyes were less puffy, she made her way out. She had to find Steven, she had to find a way to make things right.

She opened the door and stopped, as her ears picked up a faint whispering, calling her name. She followed the sound to a cabin door and opened it. Inside, Emily was waiting. Her eyes open, staring at Caitlin.

'Where's Catherine?' Caitlin asked.

Emily whispered back, 'She went to get some food. Come closer.'

Caitlin moved closer the bed, but remained an arm's length away.

'We're not that different, you and I. We both want freedom, to see the world, to taste everything on offer. My son, he's not for you, is he?'

Caitlin narrowed her eyes. 'Did you hear us?'

'My hearing has always been short of remarkable. Yes, I heard. I can help you escape this place. I can help you find happiness,' her soft voice pleaded, 'let me help you.'

'What do you want me to do?' Caitlin asked, she could not help it. Her defences were low and she would take any lifeline offered.

'Hold out your hand, give me your wrist,' Emily said.

Caitlin bridged the distance and held out her hand, she had stopped thinking.

'Closer,' Emily whispered.

Caitlin put her wrist in front of Emily's face. When Emily bit into her wrist and started to feed, Caitlin watched with mild curiosity as her eyes drooped. She knelt down on the floor and barely noticed the fact she had dozed off.

Chapter 13

Blood

Steven needed to clear his head, to get some air. He had no idea why he had done that. He had just made it easy for Caitlin, he had let her go. He could not understand why he had been compelled to take the conversation there. It hurt like hell, and he fought the urge to cry. He never cried, it was stupid, and yet he wanted to. It was him that had made the break, not Caitlin. And yet, he didn't think he had any choice. He could not carry on with the charade if she did not want him.

Once on the side of the ship, he took a gulp of air and focused on the muddy green river water. He was tempted to jump in and go for a swim, to explore, to get away. But, he had to protect Caitlin and she was right, they should not tell anyone. He could not let the others know they were not together, not yet.

'Penny for your thoughts? That's what you say in England, isn't it?'

Ingrid.

'Trust me a penny will not be enough. Seriously though, thanks for being a good friend to Caitlin. I misjudged you. I'm sorry for the way I've been with you in the past.' He held out his hand, it was better to start afresh, 'Friends?'

Ingrid smiled, her eyes alight, as she held out her hand, 'Friends.'

Steven gave her hand a squeeze, he noticed her grip was firm but casual. 'Caitlin was a bit tired. Maybe you can check on her later on?'

'Sure, do you want me to go now?' Her reply was eager, she was willing to please.

'No, give her some time.'

'Is everything okay?' Ingrid eased up alongside him.

He needed to think about something else, fast. 'Talk to me, what's been going on since I left? How's Jenson, Susanna, Gideon?'

Ingrid laughed, 'Slow down. They're all doing great. In fact, I think Jenson and Susanna are going to be tying the knot soon.'

'They're getting married?' Steven gave a half-smile, 'that's great.'

'It is. They'll be very happy together. Sometimes, you see a couple and you just know they are meant to be together,' Ingrid flicked her hair out of her face, 'You know what I mean?'

Steven faced the River, deep in thought, his hands clasped over the edge of the wooden barrier. 'Yes, I think I do.'

Ingrid had her back to the water, her arms folded over her chest.

For a moment, they just stood side by side listening to the sounds around them. Steven relished the fractured peace, the sound of nature. Not silence, it was never silent in the jungle, just peaceful.

After a few minutes, Steven turned his head to face Ingrid. She had not moved, her face basking in the full sun, her eyes closed. As though she sensed his movement, she opened them and in that glance Steven felt a jolt of something he had forgotten. A flashback of the first moment he had stared into her eyes. He had convinced himself that she had seduced him, but now as he stared into a sea of emerald he became momentarily transfixed and wondered.

'Anyway, maybe you should go check on Caitlin?' He needed some space. It had been a while since Caitlin showed him any real affection.

Ingrid blinked, her cheeks now a slight shade of pink, 'Yes, of course. I'll go see if she's, err, okay.' She gave an awkward smile and rushed off.

Steven lowered his head, elbows on the barrier, and gripped his hands behind his head. He gritted his teeth and made a low guttural sound.

'Steven?' Catherine asked, as she came up alongside.

Steven rubbed his eyes with the back of his palms and raised his head, 'Catherine.'

'Are you ready to face the community?'

Steven laughed, 'No.'

Catherine chuckled, 'You'll be fine, what will be will be. We've always been open about the outside world in the community, we teach our young well. So now we also have to teach about other possibilities. The community will adapt to this new development. We have much to learn from Caitlin and you. I see this as an opportunity, not a failure. Everything happens for a reason.'

Steven was not sure what the reason for Caitlin to fall out of love with him was, but he was not in the mood to argue the toss. He nodded instead. He wanted to get away, but on a ship he did not have many choices. Soon he would be confined within the community. At least he would have Jenson to talk to. Then again, from what Ingrid said he was likely to be all loved up. It was all starting to get to him.

He wanted to swim fast, to escape from everything by immersing himself in a world where all he wanted was speed.

'You know Steven, I know it's hard for you, but I think you should know by now that I'll look out for you. I promised my mum and dad, and I always keep my promise. And seeing as Caitlin is with you, I'll protect her too.'

Steven did everything he could to stop himself from screaming at her. Caitlin did not love him anymore. He could not understand why it not as obvious to everyone else as it was to him. A distant shout for help brought him out of his melancholy state.

They both turned to face the direction it had come from, the cabins.

Without another word they both ran towards the door, Steven pulled it open and Catherine rushed through. The sound was coming from Emily's room, Steven was sure it was Ingrid shouting. He stood behind Catherine as she peered in.

The sight of a pale, lifeless, Caitlin on the floor made him want to gag. He pushed past Catherine and knelt on the floor next to her, her hand now in his. He felt a weak pulse, she was not dead.

'Where's Emily?' Catherine shrieked.

'I don't know,' Ingrid said, 'The door was open. Caitlin

was on the floor, Emily's gone.'

'Not again,' Catherine shook her head, confusion in her tone. 'I need to find her before she escapes. Ingrid you know what to do.'

Steven watched Catherine leave and Ingrid knelt next to him.

'She needs blood, since you changed her I imagine your blood will work,' Ingrid seemed hesitant.

'Okay,' Steven pierced his vein with his fingernail, and held out his arms towards Caitlin's mouth. As soon as the blood started to trickle into her mouth, Caitlin's eyes flickered open, her mouth latched on to his wrist and she started to feed.

A few minutes passed as Caitlin sucked, Steven started to feel weak.

'Stop Caitlin, stop,' Ingrid said, her tone firm and insistent.

Caitlin's eyes flickered over to Ingrid then to Steven, but she continued. Steven tried to pull away but she was firmly latched on. His shoulders drooped and his eyes started to roll back. The last thing he heard was Ingrid shout, 'Caitlin, STOP.'

***

Ingrid could see what was happening and everything inside her screamed to protect Steven. She did the only thing she could. She put her hands around Caitlin's neck and squeezed, not hard enough to break her neck but enough to make it difficult for her to swallow. As soon as she did Caitlin let go and gave a pained screech, before she scampered back. Her eyes darted from left to right frantically, confused.

Ingrid cradled Steven in her arms. He had gone limp. She needed Emily, only her blood could help. 'CATHERINE,' she screamed over and over.

The next minutes seemed to go by really slowly until finally Catherine appeared, flustered, 'What is it now?'

The sound of Caitlin whimpering in the corner was hard to ignore, but she did, 'Did you find Emily?'

'Yes, we found her,' Catherine sighed, she knelt down next to Steven. 'What happened? What's wrong with Steven?'

'Bring Emily here, NOW,' Ingrid pleaded.

'No, we take Steven to her. Caitlin, can you get up, can you follow us.'

Caitlin looked up, her cheeks glistening with fresh tears, and nodded.

Catherine scooped a lifeless Steven up into her arms and Ingrid followed, the sound of sniffling continued behind them.

They ran to the cockpit, where they found Emily tied up next to Ian.

'I hope you're happy sister, this is what you've done,' Catherine scowled, 'Untie her wrists, we need them.'

Ian grunted, 'Eilif stay on her other side.'

Ingrid was proud of Eilif as he held Emily's shoulders whilst Ian undid the knots. Then he held her right arm behind her back, as Ian extended the other. Catherine lowered Steven to the floor next to Emily. It was lucky Emily's legs were tied up. When Catherine made Emily's blood flow into Steven's mouth, he latched on and started to suck.

Emily hurled abuse at everyone. She had gained some youth, but her eyes were crazed and her body trembled. As Steven sucked the blood, her hair started to turn white again and her cheeks shrivelled. 'I save my son and I die,' she screamed.

'So be it,' Catherine said.

Ian nodded.

Ingrid could not believe what she was seeing, as Steven continued to take her blood and Emily aged and withered before them.

No-one stopped Steven, or said a word, as Emily shut her eyes.

Ingrid was poised to say something, but she couldn't. Emily would have rather saved herself than her son, it made her sick.

It took a while for Steven to stop, and when he did there was no doubt in anyone's mind that he had sucked Emily dry.

Steven fell asleep, so Catherine picked him up and took him back to his room. She nodded at Caitlin as she did, 'Come with me.'

Ingrid watched as Ian felt for a pulse, and then shook his head. It appeared Emily was dead, hard to believe but it was true.

'She can't be, is she really, I mean, *can* she be dead?' Ingrid had to say something.

'She can be dead,' Ian said, 'She is dead. All of us have a pulse, she doesn't have one. It's over,' he rubbed his forehead with his hand and lowered his eyes to the floor.

'Ingrid, help me,' Eilif said. 'Let's take her back to the cabin.' He picked Emily's withered and empty frame in his arms. Ingrid watched Carmen put her arm over Ian's shoulders, before she opened the door and let Eilif pass.

Ingrid followed with a heavy heart, her thoughts now in complete disarray. She could not understand why Caitlin had healed Emily, or why they had allowed Steven to kill Emily. She knew Emily had crossed the line again, but she doubted she was so dangerous she had to die. Yet, they had always killed for survival and this was no different. Emily had saved her son and Ingrid was glad Steven had survived.

Once Emily was laid to rest on the bed and a white sheet covered her body, Ingrid gave her father a hug. She refused to cry.

'You go with Catherine,' Eilif kissed her head, 'I'll watch the body.'

Ingrid flinched at the word body. It hurt more when their own died, regardless of who they were.

She did not want to argue, so she eased out of the room, glad to be away from the cadaver, and found her way to Steven's cabin.

Catherine sat by the edge of the bed. Caitlin was hunched on the floor, head in hands, her body shaking.

'How is he?' Ingrid asked, it seemed to be the only thing she could say.

'When he wakes up he'll be as good as new,' Catherine said, 'Caitlin, you need to rest. You've been through a lot of trauma. Ingrid, she's obviously in shock. Take her to my cabin and watch over her, please.'

'Of course,' Ingrid said, before she made her way over to Caitlin and helped her to get up. Sleep and more blood would enable a speedy recovery, the fact they had stopped Caitlin feeding had left her in no-man's land.

Slowly, Caitlin shuffled next to Ingrid until they made it to the cabin and Ingrid helped Caitlin lie down. Just as Caitlin was about to close her eyes, she gripped Ingrid's hand, 'I nearly killed him, I nearly killed him, didn't I?'

Ingrid could not answer, 'Go to sleep Caitlin, Steven's alive and well. It's not your fault.'

Caitlin lost her fight with sleep and closed her eyes. Ingrid sat in the corner chair and stared out of the tiny circular window. She knew Caitlin did not intend to kill Steven, but she did wonder why Caitlin had gone to see Emily. She could not understand what could have compelled her, or why Emily knew Caitlin's blood would heal her.

Yet more questions that needed answers.

Chapter 14

Back In The Community

When the ship docked and jolted to a standstill Caitlin came out of her exhausted sleep. Dread overcame, as the excitement and euphoria of the journey was eclipsed by Emily's death. She could not believe what had happened, or what she had nearly done. Steven had done so much for her, and he was handsome and sexy and everything she ever thought she wanted. Yet, it was all not good enough for her. Not only had she convinced herself Steven was not *the one*, she had nearly killed him. It made her sick. She loathed the person she had become. Self-centred, egotistical, vain. All qualities she had never possessed. She owed it to Steven to find Caitlin again, to find the girl he fell in love with, the girl who fell in love with him. She had to try.

Caitlin rose onto her elbows and noticed Ingrid watching her from the corner of the room. It dawned on her that she might be keeping guard, not watching out for her.

'Caitlin, we've arrived,' Ingrid eased up alongside the bed. 'Freshen up, I'll wait outside, okay?' Ingrid put her hand on Caitlin's shoulder and gave a light squeeze.

Once Ingrid had left, Caitlin sat up on the bed. Apart from the trauma of the day, she felt great. It was a real pain in the neck she still got emotional. It was a shame evolution didn't make her stronger in that respect.

Once freshened up, she opened the door and braced herself for whatever else she would have to face. Ingrid was outside. She was starting to resemble a guard dog. 'You know, I'm not going to run away.'

Ingrid burst into giggles, 'Never thought you would, honest. But, I was told to stay with you, so I will.'

'Okay, I just never had a guard before,' Caitlin gave a nervous smile, 'it's a bit creepy.'

'Don't see me as a guard. See me as a friend looking out for you.'

Caitlin gave a half-smile. Even though she had clicked with Ingrid and liked her she was wary for the first time. She could not help wondering if Ingrid had an ulterior motive. 'Do you know if Steven is okay, I should go see him?'

'As far as I know he also made a full recovery, you'll be together soon enough, be patient,' Ingrid laughed.

Caitlin bit her lip. She could not exactly tell Ingrid they were not actually together. There was no point telling anyone. The truth was, she still loved him even though she was not in love with him. She had no idea what she was doing. Confusion ruled.

'Let's go, Caitlin, there's no need to worry, honest,' Ingrid put her hand on Caitlin's shoulder, 'I'll look out for you.'

Caitlin tried as hard as she could to return a confident expression. Somehow, she doubted she had pulled it off.

Outside, Caitlin searched for Steven. She could see the others unloading, but she could not see him. The scene took her breath away as she forgot Steven for a moment and focused on where they were. Colossal trees towered above them, and giant shrubs were haphazardly scattered here and there with leaves the size of people. The sound was intense. A chattering, playful sound came from high above in the trees, and there was a lot of buzzing. She smacked the back of her neck, she guessed some insects wanted to suck her blood too.

A dark, green jeep waited to be loaded up, there appeared to be a makeshift road easing through the trees. Someone had arrived in the car but Caitlin had not been able to see who it was.

'Can I help?' she asked Ingrid, there was no point just watching.

'Sure, just take some of those bags to the car. Then I'll walk you to your new home, I'm sure you're going to love it,' Ingrid beamed.

Caitlin picked up a few bags and balanced them on her arms. They were not heavy, just cumbersome. She made her way to the car and passed them to Carmen who was loading up the jeep.

Carmen nodded, 'Thanks for your help.'

Caitlin passed them over and went back, if she kept busy she would stop thinking about the fact she really needed to know where Steven was. Back on the ship she set about grouping together as many bags as possible. As she was about to set off, she looked up and her jaw dropped. It was Emily with Steven. The bags fell out of her hands and she stared. She could not understand, she had seen Emily dead, she was sure of it. Her lower lip wobbled.

She glanced at Emily and then back at Steven, both wore forlorn expressions. It did not make sense.

Steven seemed to register her look of confusion and rushed over, all the time glancing nervously towards Emily. 'Caitlin, this is Anna, Emily's *sister*.'

Caitlin mouthed the word 'oh' and then closed her mouth shut. Emily's sister, no wonder she looked upset. She could not help noticing how much Steven looked like Anna – Emily had changed so much when she was ill.

'Caitlin, it's nice to meet you,' Anna said, she extended her hand.

Caitlin wanted to give a firm handshake but she was too shaken so it ended up limp as she let go almost immediately.

'Anna, is it okay if we take Caitlin to the community?' Steven asked.

Anna gave a deep sigh, her eyes tearful. 'Yes, it's a good idea. Sorry, excuse me,' she seemed to fight to keep in control. 'My sister, Emily, was a nightmare. But, I always loved her, I'll miss her.'

Steven gave a slight nod. 'It's a shame it had to happen like it did. I'm sorry.'

'Don't apologise, it's not your fault. You did what you could to survive, as we have all done in the past. My sister made her choice, we must make ours.' With the back of her hand she wiped the lone tear that escaped, held her head high and led the way.

Caitlin walked next to Steven, Anna made off at a cracking pace. 'So, you're feeling okay?'

He glanced at her, 'Better than ever, you?'

'Yep, I'm fine, just fine.'

The awkward silence created a gulf between them. She hoped this polite conversation would not be an indication of the way things would be like in the future. She just didn't know what to say. Instead she concentrated on not tripping over the bracken and ample hazards on the floor. She was sure the view from the top of the trees had to be amazing, somehow she didn't think now would be a good time to go see.

'Caitlin, I...' Steven hesitated.

'Yes?' Caitlin encouraged.

'I hope you like the community.' Steven recovered.

She had the feeling he was going to say something else, but he didn't.

'I'm sure I will,' she replied.

The way her hand hung within reaching distance of his made Caitlin uneasy. It could have been straightforward, she would just reach out and take his hand, and they would smile at each other like they used to. She would feel his love, let his warmth engulf her and she would be complete. Yet, she had broken the link, she had destroyed the love they had. To want or even desire it would be foolish, she had to look forward and stop messing with Steven. It was wrong to hurt him.

***

Steven swallowed and forced back the words he was desperate to say. Even though he knew it had been the right thing to do, the fact he was not with Caitlin caused him physical pain. He just could not let her see how he really felt. He had to maintain a positive front so that the others would not suspect, he could not let Caitlin down. Whatever the reason for her change of heart he had to try to understand it, even if his own heart broke into pieces in the process.

As Anna led the way to the entrance Steven glanced to the side. He wanted to see Caitlin's reaction and he was not disappointed as her eyes widened and a broad smile graced her face, the former discomfort momentarily blurred.

'The community is in *there*?' Caitlin gasped.

Anna turned round, her eyes still blotchy but somehow she held it together. 'Well, at least you're more excited than Steven was when he first came here. I thought I'd have to drag him in.'

Steven frowned. He didn't like being the brunt of anyone's joke. 'That's not exactly fair, my life had been erased, and I was more or less abducted. Caitlin chose to be here.'

Anna stopped, stood straight, and stared at Caitlin. 'Really? You chose this life?'

Caitlin faltered for a moment, but then matched Anna's pose, head held high. 'Yes, I wanted to be here, I wanted to be one of you.'

Anna shook her head and sighed, 'Well, I sincerely hope you're not as foolish as you just claimed to be. No-one would choose to be like us if they really understood,' she looked from Caitlin to Steven, 'I hope you both know what you've done, because we are at a complete and utter loss.' Then Anna turned and strode off.

'Well that sure told me,' Caitlin gave an enthused mumble.

Steven knew Anna was right, Caitlin had no idea what she had let herself in for, and he knew he was to blame.

As they passed the electric lighting, Steven tried not to find Caitlin cute as her eyes surveyed everything around her. He did not want to find her so attractive, he did not want to see her as anything other than a friend, yet he had to be honest. She meant far too much to him, there was no way he could simply shut down his emotions. He would not let her see them, but remain they did.

When they got to the lift and Anna gained access, they stood in silence. It was clear to Steven that Anna was not sure what to say. He had a feeling Anna knew something was not right, Anna had always been able to connect with Emily's feelings, he wondered if she could also sense his.

When the doors opened to the first floor and Steven faced the familiar long corridor of rooms he felt a pang of regret. They looked even more like prison cells now than when he had first seen them. Ashamed, he hung his head low, he did not want to see Caitlin's reaction.

Her eager voice surprised him, 'Wow, this is a much cooler version of student halls. And there are no doors, just curtains. I hope no-one snores too loud,' she giggled.

Anna raised her eyebrows, 'Hmmm.'

Steven could tell she was warming to Caitlin. It was impossible for anyone not to. Caitlin was that kind of girl. Caitlin steered away from arguments from what he knew, other than the ones she mentioned with her family. Even when they broke up they hadn't even argued. It was an amicable break-up, too amicable probably.

When they reached the end of the corridor, Anna stopped by one of the only rooms with a real door, and lock.

'This is your room, you're both staying together, right?' Anna looked to Steven.

Steven averted his eyes, and heard Caitlin reply, 'Of course, we want to be together.' Caitlin slid her hand in his and every nerve ending flinched. He longed for her touch, but this way it was like getting thin shards of ice piercing his skin.

Somehow, he managed to look at Anna, 'Yes, of course. Thank you.'

'I'm sorry, but for now you both need to stay in hiding. We need to introduce Caitlin to the community, we need to explain. It's not going to be easy. You understand, right?'

Steven licked his lower lip, and then replied, 'Of course we do.'

'Great,' Anna unlocked the door. 'You have a bathroom, and we have provided food for you. We thought you'd be hungry. All of your things are here. Anyway, I'll leave you both to it. Someone will come to check on you later.' She started to head out of the door, but then turned, 'Steven, it really is good to have you home. Caitlin, we will try our best to make you feel welcome.' And then she was gone, the door locked again.

This really was a jail cell now.

Chapter 15

What to do?

Anna hesitated for a split second as she locked the door, it felt wrong. She did not think either of them would be a danger to anyone, but she was worried about what people would think of Caitlin. Her arrival changed everything. When Steven had arrived on the scene that was bad enough, but the fact a normal human could really be changed made everything different. The fictional vampire really existed in their form. They could actually do what they always thought was impossible. She needed to talk to Catherine to get some answers.

Anna made her way back to the lift, and headed out into the jungle. She could see Catherine, Isaac, Ingrid, and Eilif arriving with some of the gear. Carmen and Ian were not there, they usually took care of the ship. They were all in on the secret now, and she wanted to know what they were planning to do.

'Anna,' Catherine smiled, and then embraced her. 'Are they secure?'

'Yes, they're locked away. It feels wrong Catherine, but what choice do we have.'

'None,' Isaac replied, 'They have to stay away for now, until we figure out what we should do.'

Catherine turned to Ingrid. 'I need you to keep a close eye on Caitlin. I gather you became friends?'

'Yes, we did,' Ingrid said.

'Really?' Anna raised her eyebrows.

Eilif laughed, 'Don't be so surprised, my daughter can be a good friend.'

'Sorry,' Anna gave an apologetic smile. 'No offence Ingrid, I just remembered you also got close to Steven in the past. Is that not a problem?' It was best to be direct.

'Not a problem at all, the thing with Steven is long gone,' Ingrid gave a light shrug of the shoulders.

'Anyway, maybe you can check on them tomorrow,' Anna

said, 'they have everything they need for the rest of the day. Let's meet tonight, we'll all discuss this then. We need to think of the best way forward,' she paused, the words hard to say, 'with Emily also gone we have a lot to consider.'

'You can say that again,' Catherine stared at the ground for a moment, 'Let's get inside. We all need food.

'Great idea,' Eilif beamed.

Anna made her way back in, her thoughts in complete disarray. A part of her felt broken, she had sensed the moment Emily had gone. A weight had lifted and another had fallen over her. The loss of her mother and father was hard enough to bear, but losing her twin sister left a gaping hole in her heart. She doubted it would ever be filled again.

The conversation was stilted and awkward as everyone, apart from Anna, got out on the first floor. Anna continued to the upper level, it was always busy by the shops, and she needed to blend in to the crowd. As she made her way past the stalls and watched the children playing games in the open area her eyes glazed over. The community they had built was a sound foundation for a society, her father's vision had been a good one. Yet, she also knew there would be those that wanted to leave it, to create their own niche in the world, human nature could not be suppressed.

Anna cruised past the multitude of basic shops and arrived at the tables of groups playing chess, ludo, or jenga. It made her smile. It was such a simple thing, a board game, yet it provided hours of entertainment and was a source of major rivalry. It brought them together and it taught the children about fairness and pushed them to try their best, regardless of a win. Saying that, some remained bad losers, which was why they came back for more, she called them the sadistic lot. Her husband, Juan, happened to be one of them.

She eased up behind him and slid her arms over her shoulders and gave him a squeeze.

Juan raised one hand, placed it on her arm and gave her a light caress. Then he turned to face her, and gave a half-smile, 'Querida, you okay, shall I quit the game?'

Anna nodded, the tears would break free any moment.

Juan got up and opened his arms, 'I'm afraid that today I lose willingly, my wife needs me.'

The other men seated by the ludo board gave grunts of discontent and rolled their eyes – they had heard it all before.

Juan put his arm around her shoulder and gave her a hug, she loved the fact he was so protective. He kissed her forehead. 'Let's go where we can talk.'

They walked off holding hands and Anna did everything in her power to keep her emotions in check.

Finally, once they had reached the lower level, they sat down to talk. It was always quiet in the produce and livestock area.

They sat facing each other on the floor, Juan still held her hand.

Anna loved the feel of his hand – no-one would ever make her feel the way he did. He might irritate her incessantly, but he was hers and she was his. No relationship was perfect and he loved her, she knew from the way he always looked at her. It made her feel complete, like nothing else mattered. She held out her hand and stroked his face, 'I love you.'

He eased his face into her hand, then asked, 'Querida, tell me what is bothering you.'

She dropped her hand, 'Emily is dead.'

Juan immediately bridged the gap between them and held her tight in his arms.

Anna let her guard down and broke down. The tears cascaded down her cheeks, and her throat burned as it constricted. She could not stop her body from shaking. As she let everything out, Juan rocked her gently and stroked her hair, all the time whispering sweet nothings in her ear.

Anna closed her eyes, as her tears started to subside, until eventually she simply whimpered and allowed herself to rest for a moment. It felt so good to be within his protective embrace, there was no-one like her Juan.

She had no idea how much time had gone by before she opened her eyes. She eased off Juan, and looked up into his dark, chocolate eyes. Juan smiled and eased in to kiss her, it was deep, full of passion.

Anna relished his kiss, which always sent shivers down her spine. She matched him and their lips moved in unison. Finally, they broke apart, Anna felt slightly out of breath.

Juan gave a sly smile. 'Now that your heart has momentarily stopped grieving, tell me what you know.'

Anna chuckled, 'You always know how to distract me.'

'But, of course.' He gave a content smile.

He was right, the kiss had made her stop and push thoughts aside. Now, they came rushing to the surface. 'Emily is dead. She nearly killed Steven.'

'Why would she do that?'

Anna looked around, she knew no-one was there, but it still made her uneasy, 'Steven had to save Caitlin, a human girl who is now one of us, after Emily attacked her.'

'How can a human be like us?' he interrupted.

'I don't know, we'll get more answers tonight,' she rubbed her thumbs together, 'apparently, the girl drained Steven and they had to let him feed off my sister to survive. They had no choice.'

Juan narrowed his eyes. He stared up into the sky for a moment. 'I see.'

'It was either him or Emily.'

Juan pressed his lips together, his voice rising in anger, 'This *human* girl put his life in jeopardy. It led to Emily's death. The girl could only be like us via another reckless act, just like Steven's birth. This situation is a mess.'

'I know,' Anna trailed.

'So, what's going to happen?'

'We need to get everyone together, tonight, to discuss the future.'

Juan sighed, 'Again.'

'Again.'

Anna got up, 'There's only one thing that worries me, but let's keep it to ourselves for now.'

Juan followed suit and stood next to her, 'What now?'

'You know how close I was to Emily, how I could feel her emotions?'

Juan nodded.

'I think I have a weaker connection with Steven,' Anna paused, 'and something tells me that things between him and the girl are not as they should be.'

'How so?' Juan cocked his head to the side.

'Steven felt really sad, heartbroken almost. I remembered Emily being the same when she returned. I believe he changed the girl because they were madly in love, it seems strange that he should now feel like a wreck, don't you think?'

Juan put his arm around her shoulder again. 'Anna, your senses are unparalleled. It is indeed interesting, and I think you're right, let's keep this to ourselves for now.'

Anna was struggling to understand why it felt important, but somehow she just knew that if Steven and Caitlin were not in love it changed things, it changed things a lot.'

***

Lucy had kept perfectly still from the moment she heard Anna and Juan enter her sanctuary. They should have thought about the fact she might be there, but then her obscurity had its advantages. It was handy being a recluse. It was useful to hide, to go unnoticed. It enabled her to hear and see things others failed to notice, like the conversation she had just heard. It was hard to believe even so.

She could scarcely believe Steven had changed a normal human, and this girl had been changed because they were in love. There was no other way the girl could be like them, as hard as it was to believe. Yet, now it seemed the love that had led to the change had faltered, and it was Steven who was heartbroken. Lucy did not want that for him. He was not a bad person. And what they had done, that moment when they had given in to each other, had resulted in the child she now carried. A child she had to protect.

Whatever the situation it was not her place to get involved, or to feel sorry for Steven. There was not much she could actually do. The thing was, as much as she wanted to keep her pregnancy hidden from him she could not change the fact he was the father of her unborn child. Yet, it sounded like he had more than enough to handle at the moment.

Whatever happened, she had to stay away from him.

This latest development could be a problem for her if it held off the plans for a new start in Borneo. She needed that new start, she deserved it.

With a new found conviction, she raised her head high and started to plan, to think of a contingency. If they did not leave for Borneo then she would have to find another way. She had to talk to Catherine. With Emily gone, Catherine would have to help her. After all, the baby she carried was family and she knew family was at the heart of every decision Catherine ever made.

As for Steven, she did not want to see him or his new girlfriend, if that was what she actually was. From what Anna had said, it sounded like someone had a change of heart, and it didn't sound like it was Steven. She still remembered Steven's features, and the attraction. She considered him good looking from the moment they met, but when they talked, when they shared time, she had felt a connection. It just seemed wrong. It was not possible for someone like Steven to be with someone like her, and yet, everything had happened so naturally. They had fit perfectly just like a lock and key, and it had led to the baby she now carried and loved.

Logically, she knew it was not enough to just fit with someone else – there was more to it. She was realistic. What had brought them together was a short lived fling, nothing more. Either way, she had no intention of finding out if the connection they had once shared still existed. It was best to leave him to his own devices, a baby was the last thing he needed right now. And she was more than capable of looking after the baby on her own. She had never been, nor intended to become, the sentimental type. She had only been in love once, and that had been the biggest waste of emotion ever. Ian had broken her heart, and she was not about to let his nephew have a stab at breaking it again.

Chapter 16

Claustrophobia

Caitlin stared at the small indentation in the ceiling for what felt like the millionth time. It was hard to remember she had been really excited to live in the community two days earlier. But what with the break up, Emily's death, the sombre arrival and apparent incarceration, this was not really living up to her expectations. She would actually give anything to be back in her student house, chatting to Gemma over a cup of tea and a packet of custard creams. They would be talking about annoying students, or boys they fancied, or the particular man in Gemma's life, or complaining about the amount of work they had to do. An average student conversation.

Of one thing she was certain, sitting in a confined space with an ex was not up there on her list of top things to do. In fact, it lay at the bottom of the pile. For the first time since Steven had changed her, she was worried about what would become of her. She actually wondered if they planned to let her live, she was a threat to their misconceived existence. The fact she had been created was a problem, and perhaps the best way to solve the problem was to eliminate it. She gave a deep sigh, placed her forehead on her knees and wrapped her arms around her bent legs.

'Caitlin, are you alright?' Steven walked towards her and took a seat on the floor next to her.

She lifted her head and met his eyes, she still loved the amber colour. 'No, not really. This really sucks. I was looking forward to being here, now I feel like I've been jailed. I wish I'd listened to you, I wish I'd heard what you were saying.'

'Honestly, it wasn't like this when I came here. Sure I hated it, but I was not locked up. They're obviously scared of something,' he hesitated for a moment, 'I doubt it's us, seriously.'

Caitlin looked away, and stared at the TV, the computer games, the books. They all looked out of place in a room carved out of rock with no natural light. 'Did you think this would happen? Did you imagine they would do this?'

Steven sounded choked, 'No, I never imagined this. I'm sorry, for everything.'

Caitlin placed her hand over his, and he faced her, his eyes weary, 'It's not your fault, Steven. None of it is.'

He removed his hand and stood up. 'It is my fault. I should have left you alone. You would have led a happy, normal life if I had not come back for you. My grandparents would still be alive. I have caused unnecessary pain and death.'

Caitlin got up, her hands clasped together now. 'Steven, stop it. Things just happen sometimes, for no reason, not due to cause and effect. Destiny has a way of steering life sometimes.'

Steven turned, his eyes narrowed, his hand clenched, 'NO, this is not destiny. This is a bloody nightmare, and I hope I wake up soon. I want this to end.'

The way he shouted surprised her, Steven always stayed so calm, so composed. She gave a small smile. 'Is this because of the way things are with us?'

Steven huffed, 'Caitlin, for goodness sake, just get over yourself. My stepmother is DEAD, my mum is DEAD, my grandparents are DEAD, Adam is DEAD – so many have died because of me. The last thing on my mind is what you think of me, besides you have made it clear it's over. I'm not going to mull any more. This situation is about more than our stupid romance.' He made his way over to the TV, turned it on and then proceeded to play an Xbox game.

Caitlin closed her mouth, it had opened and she had not even noticed. The venom is his tone hurt her to the core. There was a possibility that she had pushed him away so far that now he didn't actually love her. Her chest constricted, but she held back the tears. Instead, she said, 'I'm sorry you feel that way,' and made her way into the bathroom. She closed the curtain, it was better than nothing, slunk to the floor and closed her eyes.

**

Steven blanked out the sound of Caitlin's sniffles. He did not want to care about her, he did not want to think about her.

He needed to move on, to think of his life for a change. Ever since he had found out about his identity, his mind had been clouded by the idealistic view of Caitlin and what he had lost. He had made so many bad decisions because of love, a love that now spat in his face and laughed. He was glad she was crying, he didn't care, well, he did, he just didn't *want* to. He focused on the strategy game and ignored the sound.

After a while, he noticed the sound had stopped but she had not come out. He paused the game, put the controller down and went to look for her. He found her lying in a foetal position on the floor fast asleep, her cheeks still slightly wet. She was so beautiful. It hurt to look at her like this, so vulnerable, innocent even. He put his arms under her legs and shoulders and lifted her up as she nestled into his chest and gave a deep sigh.

He carried her out and lay her down on the bed, then covered her in a blanket. He stared at her again, shook his head lightly, and could not help lowering his hand and stroking her forehead. He leant down and kissed it, then stared at her perfect lips, the lower one fuller than the top. He could not resist and he kissed her lips softly. Caitlin's eyelids fluttered open.

'Steven?'

Steven backed off, but Caitlin grabbed his hand and pulled him on to the bed. Steven managed to fall next to her, not on top – he was not ready for that proximity.

Caitlin turned to face him, 'You kissed me.'

'Sorry,' he turned away to face the wall.

Caitlin gave a muted sigh, 'Steven, look at me, please.'

Steven kept his resolve.

Caitlin moved over and faced him, her mouth but inches from his. 'Steven, *you* kissed me.'

'Yeah, so?' He refused to make eye contact.

Caitlin smiled, and narrowed the gap.

He wanted to refuse the kiss, he wanted to stop and say no, but he just couldn't. His hand ran through her hair and pulled her face closer to his. He kissed her with a passion that surprised him, he needed her so much. Luckily, Caitlin reciprocated and their bodies became tangled, meshed together. He needed her, but he would not give in so easily. He kissed her lips, her face, her eyes, yet kept his hand firmly on her back. He wanted Caitlin to want him as much as he wanted her, and it gave him great satisfaction when he heard her give a low moan.

When her hands moved to his belt, he held her hand and managed to say, 'No.'

'No?' Caitlin gave a cheeky smile.

'No, not yet, I don't want this to *just* be about lust. I can't do this if that's all *this* is.'

Caitlin got off him and sat next to him on the bed. She smoothed down her hair and pursed her lips. 'Sorry, I shouldn't have kissed you.'

Steven did not know what to say. He really enjoyed that kiss, and he really did want to take things further but she had hurt him, bad. He was not about to let her use sex to get back together again. It would have been the easy option, but he just couldn't do it. He got off the bed and made his way over to the game controller lying on the floor. He put it back next to the TV, and turned the machine off. They needed to talk, even if he did not want to. Some things had to be said.

He wandered back to the bed, made his way over to her side, and sat down next to her. He picked up her hand, and rubbed the top of her hand with his thumb. 'I still love you, Caitlin.'

'You do?' Her eyes alighted.

He gave a half-smile, she really had no idea sometimes. 'Of course I do. I was just angry. It happens.'

'Steven, I still love you. You must know that, I just feel so confused, so lost. Since you changed me, I've felt different, more distant, I can't explain it,' her voice started to get croaky. Caitlin always got so emotional.

'I know you feel different about me, but I really think I can help you,' he held both of her hands in his. 'I don't think you should give up on *us* just yet. Do you?'

She gazed at him, eyes wide, as though she was seeing him again for the first time. He remembered that *look*. When she looked at him like that she made him feel like he was the most important person in the world. He narrowed the gap this time and leant in. The kiss was slow this time, more sensual. He released her hands and cupped her face. When they stopped kissing he nestled her in his chest and they just held one another. Steven wanted to protect her. He guessed that was what his instinct told him to do.

He did not want it to be all serious between them either, he wanted to have fun like they used to and he knew just the thing to cheer them both up, to change the mood.

'Caitlin, tell you what. Why don't you just thrash me at a game of tennis, virtual of course...' he gave an easy smile, 'I'll even let you win.'

'HA!' she backed up from him and grinned, 'I don't need you to let me win. I can beat you – easy!'

'Well, I wouldn't count on it, but you never know,' he smirked.

Caitlin growled, amused, 'Give it your best, I don't need your charity.'

'Doubt it,' he shrugged his shoulders, 'besides, I'm in a charitable mood.'

Caitlin huffed, 'You are a very, very, very annoying man. But, as you well know, I'm game! Play on, MR!'

Steven chuckled, and set up the game. It was nice to relax, to stop thinking, to just be a couple. 'Shall we eat something whilst we play? We need energy, right?'

'Now you mention it, I'm starved.' She got off the bed and browsed the selection of items on the table. She came back with a plate heaped with bread, some sweet looking pastries, and a couple of drinks. 'These drinks look a bit dubious, but they must be alright if they're here for us.'

Steven looked at the bottled drinks. The glass was dark, so you could not make out the colour of the drink. He had an inkling on what it might be. He took one of them, unscrewed the lid and took a slug. 'Enjoy.'

Caitlin followed suit and before long their bottles were empty.

'Nice,' she said, before she took a bread roll and took a

bite. 'Now, about that tennis match?'

'Game on,' Steven replied, as he gave a broad grin.

When there was a knock on the door an hour later, Steven nodded in Caitlin's direction and whispered, 'Ignore it.' He did not care what they wanted anymore.

As they heard the sound of the door unlock, and the door open, they both remained focused on the game.

When it finished Caitlin whooped for joy, 'Finally, I knew I would beat you at least once.'

Steven smirked, and then turned to face the door. When he saw who it was he quickly made his way over. 'Jenson!' He held out his hand.

Jenson shook hands warmly, his expression amused, 'I knew you'd find a girl that would beat you. You're Caitlin, right?'

Caitlin lowered her eyes, her cheeks had turned a shade of pink. 'Yes. I've heard about you.'

'All good I hope,' Jenson laughed, his body leaned forward.

'Of course,' Steven rolled his eyes, and then looked behind Jenson. He doubted he was alone.

Anna waited behind him. Her eyes widened expectantly, 'I hoped bringing Jenson here would sweeten this experience. By tonight, we'll have told everyone what happened. Then hopefully you'll be able to join us. Jenson wanted to see you, I hope this is okay.'

'It's great, thank you, Anna,' Steven said.

'I'll come back later,' Anna closed the door and locked it again.

'Weird, never been locked in before,' Jenson said, 'you must be precious cargo, Caitlin. This VIP treatment is only reserved for the best.'

'Sure it is,' Caitlin drawled.

'Serious,' Jenson repeated, 'anyway, I have something to ask you, Steven.'

Steven shook his head, he had no idea what his friend was up to now, 'Go for it.'

Jenson gave a broad smile, 'Will you be my best man?'

Steven's jaw dropped. He had no words. A wedding was the last thing he wanted to think about.

Chapter 17

Best Man

Caitlin chuckled, 'That's a great idea, Steven as best man. It's just what we need as a distraction.'

'I figured it might be a way to melt the ice with you two,' Jenson flicked his blonde fringe off his face. 'But seriously Steven, I'd appreciate it if you'd consider it. I helped you out when you got here. Maybe, you'll consider returning the favour.'

'Don't know that I'd be much help,' Steven raised an eyebrow.

Caitlin tried to suppress the grin, but could not help being amused. She clapped her hands together as she came up with an idea, 'Jenson, do you know how to ballroom dance?'

'Oh no,' Steven frowned, and held out his hand to cover her mouth.

Caitlin jumped back, and continued, 'Steven here is an expert dancer – or so he told me – and I have yet to see his moves. I think he should teach the wedding couple a waltz or two.'

'Really?' Jenson mused, 'And what's this ballroom dancing?'

'Oh, you'll both love it,' Caitlin kept a straight face, and refused to meet Steven's glare.

Steven grabbed her from behind, and wrapped his arms around her waist, 'Tell you what sweetheart, you can be my partner.'

As Steven spun her out, Caitlin giggled, and then groaned, 'What have I let myself in for?'

'Sounds like fun. I'll introduce you to Susanna as soon as possible. She's keen to meet you. Anyway, good to see you again, Steven, pleasure to meet you Caitlin, we'll catch up properly soon, but seeing as the wedding is in a week you can imagine I'm kept busy. I've been waiting for your return so that we could plan. Somehow, Susanna knew you'd be here for it.' Jenson raised his eyebrows, and then knocked on the door. It opened immediately. He gave a half-smile and left.

As soon as the door shut, Steven pinned Caitlin against the wall and pursed his lips, a faint smile lingered. 'Ballroom dancing? You want to dance with *me*?'

Caitlin gave a slow nod, as she felt her stomach muscles contract at the proximity. Ever since they had got the chance to spend time together alone, and she had seen what it was like to be shunned by Steven, her feelings had started to change. It was like she was getting to know him all over again.

Steven took a step back, and held out his right hand. 'All you had to do was ask?'

She placed her hand in his, and he placed his other hand on her waist. She put her other hand on his shoulder and allowed him to lead her into a slow dance. She felt a bit uncertain, clumsy even, but Steven held her tight and showed her how to move. Before long they swayed to an unspoken rhythm. Caitlin relaxed and placed her head on his chest, she could hear his strong heartbeat. With just the sound of their shuffling feet, it was strange and yet comfortable. They danced for a while, until finally Caitlin stopped, unable to hold back the words any longer, 'Steven, I'm sorry.'

Steven kept her firmly against him, 'Sorry for what?'

'I hurt you, I'm sorry. I...'

Steven cut her off and kissed her, she had to kiss him back, desperate to be close to him again. She loved the taste of him, the feel of his strong body against hers. They fumbled with their clothes and collapsed on the bed.

Suddenly, Steven stopped and sat on the edge of the bed.

'Steven,' Caitlin whispered, 'why do you stop?'

'I'd love to be with you, I really would, but it feels wrong,' he hesitated for a moment, and then recovered, 'I'm also worried about getting you pregnant. We don't have any protection, and once we start I don't think I'll be able to stop.'

Caitlin gave a sly smile, 'You know. I think that we have to start again, find each other again. And I think between us, maybe, we can think of ways to have fun, without getting me pregnant. Don't you?'

Steven gave a cheeky smile, 'Miss Chance, you never cease to amaze me. Come here.'

Steven pulled her hand towards him and kissed her.

Caitlin had not felt so liberated in a long time, she allowed herself to let go, to enjoy this man she loved, to stop thinking about why she loved him and just let it happen. She just hoped no-one would interrupt their game.

As luck would have it, no-one did. The *game* had ended in the shower, it was fun. Caitlin rubbed her hair down with a towel, glad to be in a new set of clothes and refreshed. It was lucky they had stocked her size. The clothes were pretty boring, a khaki colour pair of shorts and t-shirt. Steven was wearing the same colour trousers and t-shirt – it could almost pass for a uniform.

'So, does everyone wear this type of clothing?' Caitlin asked.

'Pretty much,' Steven replied, 'Although, I wore this when we were going out to hunt in the Amazon.'

'Oh, I get it, *camouflage*,' Caitlin said, impressed. 'Hang on. Do you think they're going to let us out?'

Steven shrugged his shoulders, 'I have no idea, but I have to say I don't really mind this solitary confinement. Do you?'

Caitlin gave a sexy smile. 'No, funnily enough, I don't have a problem with it either.'

Steven bridged the gap between them. As their lips met, her body leaned against him, eager for more. When the kiss came to a natural end, Caitlin sighed, 'You drive me crazy. I hope they have protection here, because if they don't I can see this is going to be a challenge for us.'

Steven smirked, 'Not for me, I can hold out.'

'Really?' Caitlin placed her hand on his stomach and felt him flinch.

He eased her hand off, 'Really.'

The sound of the key saved them. Caitlin moved to the chair in the corner of the room and sat down.

Anna came in carrying a tray with a covered metal platter. Whatever was in there smelled good. Caitlin smiled at her.

Anna placed the platter on the table, 'I thought you might

both like some hot food.' She put it down and looked from Steven to Caitlin, her features relaxed. Caitlin sensed she was more at ease.

'Anna, do you have any news for us? As much as we don't mind being left alone,' he glanced in Caitlin's direction and gave her a knowing glance, 'I would love to show Caitlin around her new home.'

Anna broke into a broad smile. 'That's great, Steven. I'm glad to see you've both had a good rest. The journey must have worn you out. I'm afraid you'll have to wait until the originals have met. We are going to discuss the situation in an hour. As soon as I know anything I will come to let you know what has been decided. Anyway, enjoy your meal. Jenson said it was one of your favourites.'

Steven peaked under the cover of the platter, 'Toad in the hole, perfect.'

Anna's gave Caitlin an uncertain glance. 'Hope you like it, Caitlin.'

'I'm sure I will,' Caitlin said, glad to have been acknowledged.

Caitlin met Steven's eyes as Anna left. His look intense, yet loving, she could not help melting even more under his glare. Steven had to be the most attractive man she had ever met. She had no idea why she doubted their relationship or why her emotions had gone topsy turvy. Either way, she had it under control now, Steven was *her* man – period.

***

Anna closed the door, hesitant for the first time. They seemed happy enough. Perhaps there confinement had helped them to sort out their differences – the atmosphere between them had changed completely. She knew that Emily would have wanted Steven to be happy, and her parents had definitely wanted him to have a future with this girl. She could not make Caitlin love Steven, but if she could ease their transition into the community it might make things easier for Steven.

She was convinced Steven and Caitlin were important to the future of the entire community. Their existence changed everything, it opened up doors. She could not help wondering what doors would open. The unknown, even though exciting, could make life worse. The biblical story of Adam and Eve came to mind. The apple, even though sweet, was best left on the tree. Temptation, in whatever guise, changed everything. And she did not think they were any different just because they had evolved. They were just as open to being seduced by a different way of life as any other human.

Anna stopped by Ingrid's room and called out her name, 'Ingrid, can I come in?'

She heard Ingrid reply, 'Of course.'

She made her way in and found Ingrid sat on a chocolate tub chair, a book in hand.

Ingrid looked up, and placed the open book on her lap. 'Anna, nice to see you. Can I help?'

'Ingrid, I don't mean to interrupt.' Anna felt sorry for Ingrid for some reason.

Ingrid closed the book and placed it on the small wooden table next to her. Then she stood up and smiled, 'You are not interrupting.'

Anna moved over to the other tub chair and sat down. 'Please sit, Ingrid. We need to talk.'

Ingrid nodded, serious now, and sat down.

Anna clasped her hands together. 'I know you have feelings for Steven, it's been obvious for a while. And Catherine told me you became friends with Caitlin.'

Ingrid nodded.

'We need them to stay together, to be a unit. We do not need any,' she paused, 'distractions for either of them.'

Ingrid kept her eyes to the floor.

'Ingrid, if you want to be friends with Caitlin then that's fine. But, let's be clear on something, you will *not* try to take Steven away from her. Not now. Once the dust has settled, *if* they break up, then go for it. You know what I'm saying?'

Ingrid moved her head up, her eyes set, a slight crease in the middle of her brow. 'I understand.'

'Anyway, now that's out of the way I can get on to the real reason for the visit. We feel it is wise to include you in the meeting tonight. You've shown that you can be trusted and we believe you might be able to help. Will you join us when we discuss the future of the community? Your dad believes you have an insightful nature. And I actually think it is a clever thing to get Caitlin on our side. I like her and don't see her as a threat.'

Ingrid jumped in, 'I don't see her as a threat either. Becoming her friend was not a tactic – it just happened.'

'I know, Catherine told me,' Anna smiled. She did not really think Ingrid could have caused the rift between Caitlin and Steven even if she had tried, Anna sensed something else had happened. 'The point is you became her friend even though she's the reason Steven remains indifferent to you. Ingrid, I'm being as direct as I can, we need you. The originals will listen to what you think.'

Ingrid's lips curled up as though embarrassed, her cheeks glowed a shade of pink, 'The originals want me? In that case, I would be honoured to attend the meeting.'

'Great, let's go and find your dad. We need to make sure you coordinate with Catherine and Isaac. The four of you have to fill in the gaps.'

'We can try, but I don't know what I can add.' Ingrid bit her lower lip.

'And that's why you're important. It was you who found Steven, it was you who knew to tell Ian, it was you who immediately befriended Caitlin. Too many coincidences,' Anna put her hand on Ingrid's shoulder, 'don't worry about it, it might be your skill, you never know.'

'A skill,' Ingrid laughed. 'I never thought I had one.'

Anna smiled, 'I believe you do, and I'm not alone.'

Chapter 18

The Originals Meet Again

Catherine brushed her hair slowly and watched her reflection in the mirror. She could see Isaac making notes behind her – he'd been at it for a while. She loved the fact he was so methodical, nothing passed him by. Ever since they had returned he had been withdrawn, lost in his thoughts, she was sure he was on to something. But, she knew what he was like. He was not going to say anything until he had it all figured out. To ask, or even to try to talk to him, was a futile task when he was like this. She had been with him for too long to even try to go there.

She was apprehensive about the meeting, too many hot heads with opinions, especially the Spanish contingent. Her dad's absence created a void, Ian could not fill his footsteps. But, they needed a leader, someone needed to step up. She wondered if she should. In many ways, she was more sympathetic than Ian to the needs of others. Isaac had always kept her grounded, she never assumed or expected, and she was the only one that could have in depth discussions with her father. The thought of her father brought a lump to her throat, she still missed him. She fought back the urge to cry and put the brush down.

She clenched her teeth, got up and turned to face Isaac. 'Are you ready to go?'

Isaac nodded slightly in acknowledgement, but he did not look up.

She hoped whatever he had come up with worked. They were a great team, and if they planned to head the move to Borneo, *if* it was still going to happen, they needed to think everything through.

Catherine made her way to the door. Isaac stepped in her path and put his hand on her waist. She faced him and he kissed her nose and smiled with a distinct twinkle in his eye.

She held out her hand and slipped it in his. 'Are you

ready?'

Isaac nodded. She loved the fact he was so calm and collected, it kept her together.

'Let's go and face the others then, it's time to see what the future holds for Caitlin and Steven.'

'And the rest of us,' Isaac added.

Catherine pursed her lips, she found it hard to remain positive. 'And the rest of us.'

When they arrived only Ian and Carmen were there. Early, they had much to discuss. The large wooden table was bare, but soon it would be surrounded, and she knew they would all have a lot of questions.

'Ian, Carmen,' Isaac said.

'Isaac, you're ready?' Ian asked, his eyes bloodshot, Catherine doubted he slept much these days.

'Yes, Ian, I have come up with a plausible way forward, one that will not disrupt the existing plans.' Isaac gave a half-smile in Carmen's direction, 'Carmen and you are needed here, we will move on.'

'And by we you mean?' Carmen asked.

Isaac kept a straight face. 'I will make a suggestion, everyone else will decide. It is not my choice who stays and goes, it is ours.'

Carmen gave a sigh, 'That is the only way.'

'The only way for what?' Franco asked, he strode in with a slight swagger. His dark, practically black, eyes narrowed.

His wife, Elena, hid behind him like she always did. Juan came up alongside his father, a younger but practically identical version.

'Franco, we have a lot to discuss,' Isaac said, his voice relaxed yet exerting some control.

'I'm sure we do,' he said, his tone impatient. 'We'll sit down and wait for the others.'

A minute later, Morten and Arla arrived and took a seat.

No-one was late for this meeting.

When Catherine saw Eilif come in with Anna and Ingrid she was slightly surprised. Ingrid was not one of the originals, but she had a feeling she knew why she was there.

'Ingrid cannot attend,' Franco huffed, standing up.

Anna glanced at her husband, Juan. 'She has important information for the rest of us.'

Franco slumped back in his chair and folded his arms over his chest, 'I'm sure she does. You might as well send the girl in, let everyone join in!'

Ingrid waited at the entrance, and stared at the floor.

Eilif went next to her and whispered in her ear. Then he lightly grabbed her upper arm and led her to a seat.

As everyone sat down there was a momentary pause. They were all there, the remaining few, short of three originals.

At the head of the table, Ian cleared his throat, 'Friends, we have much to discuss. And Isaac has stepped up to lead the proceedings. I feel I am ill-disposed to lead any more, unless I have everyone's vote of confidence.'

Franco guffawed slightly, Catherine scowled at him. Ian was right – he did not have Franco's support.

No-one ever questioned Isaac. She was glad he had stepped up to the role.

From the other end of the table, Isaac spoke, 'Thank you Ian. We all appreciate what you do. It has not been easy on you. The loss of a father is difficult, not a day goes by that I do not think of my own. Family is very important,' he paused, and looked around the table, 'to all of us.'

Franco shrugged his shoulders, aloof. Sometimes Catherine really wanted to thump him. He was such an arrogant and self-centred man. It was lucky Elena was so docile, she suspected few woman would tolerate him.

Isaac ignored Franco, and continued, 'A new dawn is upon us. I will cut to the chase, Steven turned his girlfriend, Caitlin, into one of us and,' the protestations started, but he held his hands out firmly, 'and, it appears that she was *not* the first.'

Around the table those that did not know glanced at each other, concerned yet curious.

'Let me explain,' Isaac said. 'It appears that Judith was not bitten by bats, she was turned by Jeff. They kept it a secret from all of us, and for some strange reason decided to share the knowledge on how to change humans with Steven. We believe this was because they felt guilty for never having shared it with Emily. They believed,' he glanced at Franco and Juan, 'perhaps incorrectly, that she would have led a better life if she would have been given the choice.'

Franco could not hold back, 'Emily should never have had *that* choice.'

Isaac gave a curt nod, 'I agree with you, my friend, I do agree with you. But, if you remember Steven at all you will acknowledge, as we all must, he is not like his mother. This is why, I think at least, his grandparents gave him the choice.'

'And so, this girl, this *child*, is one of us?' Franco spluttered the words.

'It appears so,' Isaac added. 'We have only just got to know her, but Ingrid became friends with her straight away. Ingrid, can you please tell us about Caitlin?'

Ingrid sat a bit straighter. 'Of course. She's a very nice person. I don't think she'll have any problems settling into our way of life. She seems keen to learn, to adapt. Very different to Steven,' she said, raising her eyebrows.

Juan frowned. 'In what way is she different?'

Ingrid dropped the smile. 'She's friendly. Steven was very hostile at first.'

Morton spoke for the first time, 'Does anything about her strike you as different from us in any way?'

Ingrid cocked her head slightly to the side. 'Not really. Then again, no-one ever suspected Judith was different, did they?'

Catherine gave a little cough, 'I did.'

Franco gave her a venomous stare. 'And why have you never said anything?'

'She was my mother,' Catherine said, 'I suspected from the beginning she was different, but I did not dwell on it. Emily suspected something too, and it made her angry – she did not like the fact something was held back.'

Anna sheepishly joined in, 'I also thought my mother was different.'

Ian raised his hands, 'I didn't, honest.'

Catherine held back a smile, she was not surprised. Ian was

only ten when the attack happened. He was too young to notice then, and when he was old enough to realise he was not looking for anything.

'So, the question is – different *how*?' Isaac asked, he looked around the room. It seemed he did not want an answer as such. 'I have given this a lot of thought, and I believe Caitlin may reveal a lot of possibilities and their disadvantages to our race.'

'How so?' Morten asked.

'Ingrid, thank you for your time,' Isaac deviated for a moment. 'I only have one more question for you?'

Ingrid made to stand, but then waited, 'Yes.'

Isaac continued, 'When you drank Steven's blood you were repulsed, correct? Any other side effects?'

Ingrid looked straight ahead as she considered, 'I was repulsed, yes, but I still drank from him. I stopped when I realised how weak I felt. I knew then something was very wrong.'

'Thank you, Ingrid. We have things to discuss that it is best you do not hear for now, it might change the way you look at Caitlin.'

'Oh,' Ingrid narrowed her eyes, then got up and hastily left the room.

Once the room was secure again, Isaac turned back to face everyone. 'I have a suspicion, and we would have to carry out tests of course, that Caitlin is barren. Judith was considered too old to have children, but it was still possible and yet she never conceived. I believe that normal humans that are changed cannot reproduce.'

'That would simplify things,' Franco said, a smug look on his face.

'Possibly,' Isaac said. 'The question is what about Steven? Can he father children? We would need more tests.'

Catherine gritted her teeth. She did not want Steven and Caitlin to be treated like lab rats, but she did not want to interrupt her husband.

'The interesting thing is that Ingrid was repulsed by Steven's blood, in the same way we're all repulsed by the blood of our kind. Saying this, we know from the journey that Emily fed from Caitlin and recovered. Then Caitlin fed from Steven and recovered, and then Steven fed from Emily and recovered. The point is Caitlin's blood was not bad for Emily, and then Emily's blood healed Steven. Do you not see the implications?'

A lot of faces paled.

Anna spoke slowly, 'Caitlin is capable of feeding us, but can regenerate herself when she has blood,' she glanced around uneasily. 'Any human changed could help us survive. We would not have to die if we had a steady source of human blood that would not kill the human involved. This would have saved my mother. There would be no more guilt, if any of you felt any. Think about it, we would have no more bodies to conceal.'

Ian gave a low whistle. 'It would change everything. But, if you're right, how do you think Caitlin will feel when she finds out she can't have any children when all of us have them like rabbits?'

'That I don't know,' his expression became forlorn, 'first, we find out.'

'What about the plans for the move to Borneo?' Carmen asked.

'Nothing has changed,' Isaac replied. 'We stick to the plan. Catherine and I will lead the move to Borneo, Ian and Carmen will lead the community here. Ian, Carmen, are you still happy to do this?'

Ian looked around the table. 'Only if I have everyone's backing.'

Franco's features relaxed. 'We do not want to lead.'

'Neither do we,' Morten smiled, his hand firmly in his wife's.

'Then it is agreed, 'Isaac said, 'Nothing changes, but until we find out more about Caitlin I suggest we keep her in solitary confinement. It would be dangerous for her if any of our kind found her appealing, so to speak.'

'What about Steven?' Catherine asked. She doubted he would leave Caitlin, but wondered if he should be given the choice.

Anna stretched out her arms. 'I have a feeling Steven is happy to stay where he is. Let's leave them together until we decide to introduce Caitlin.'

'Is it wise to introduce Caitlin at all?' Juan asked, his face quizzical.

Anna placed her hand over his, 'She is not an animal. We have to let her out eventually. After this, what will be, will be.'

Catherine glanced at Isaac, her eyes pleading.

Isaac caught her stare and gave a low nod. 'Caitlin will be introduced after the tests. Everyone in favour?'

All of the hands shot up.

Catherine relaxed. At least Caitlin would have a chance in the long run. It was a chance, nothing more. It was not a big surprise her father was so overly-protective of her mother. It also explained the bite marks her mother had fought to conceal over the years, Catherine had seen them though. She knew someone bit her, and now she knew who it must have been and why her father was always so strong when her mother was so weak. It made her sick. She just hoped her mother had never suffered, and yet, somehow she knew the answer to that. It explained why her mother had chosen to die.

Chapter 19

Testing

Steven did not know what to think. Caitlin seemed to be back, the old Caitlin, the girl he fell in love with. He was worried about her though, there was no denying it. She seemed so unstable, hot and cold. Yet, she seemed to have calmed down, to have come to terms with what she was and, if he was lucky, to have fallen for him again. He could not bear to lose her, he loved her too much. He just knew she was the one he was meant to be with, she had to be, otherwise none of it made any sense.

They had decided to watch a film in the end, to pass the time. There was not a lot they could really do whilst confined to four walls. Steven squeezed his hand against her shoulder; he loved the feel of her body against his. To hold her again, to be comfortable together, it was a luxury.

At his squeeze, Caitlin moved slightly and said, 'You okay.'

'Yes, I'm fine.'

Caitlin eased off his body and sat to face him. 'Do you think they'll be long? This suspense is killing, and I'm looking forward to seeing that waterfall you all talked about.'

'You'll see it,' Steven smiled. 'Don't fret. Let's watch the end of the film.'

Caitlin slumped back into his chest and gave a loud sigh, 'I was never the patient type. I wish they'd hurry up.'

An hour later, as the end credits for the film started to scroll down, they heard the sound of the key in the door. When it opened they saw Catherine at the door, Isaac behind her.

'Caitlin, Steven, good film?'

Steven sensed her voice was strained, as though she was trying really hard to sound friendly. It was not like Catherine.

'Yes, we're fine,' Steven said, 'bored, but fine.'

Isaac stood alongside Catherine. 'We've explained your presence to the others and we do not see that you pose any threats, however we would like to take blood from both of you and carry out some routine tests before you join the community. We need to make sure you do not carry any diseases, even if inadvertently.'

'Neither of us have diseases,' Steven frowned. 'You didn't do any testing on me when I arrived.'

Catherine bit her lip. Steven knew he was on to something.

'Things have changed since you arrived. We have to be more cautious, for the sake of the community.'

It sounded like a plausible excuse, but Steven still did not like it. 'Can we stay together for the testing?'

'As much as possible,' Isaac said, a smile on his face.

Steven looked at Caitlin. She looked resigned to the fate, as though she had no fight left. He did not like what they were doing. He knew they wanted to test Caitlin, not him. It was easier to say they needed to do both of them, but he could see through the lie.

'Caitlin, are you okay with this?' Steven asked.

Caitlin put on a brave face, he knew it well. 'If it's in the interest of the community how can I refuse? When do we go? The sooner we get this over with the better, as far as I'm concerned.'

'In that case, come with us,' Isaac said, 'a team is ready and waiting, it should not take long. When it's all done, we will introduce you to the community and your new life.'

Caitlin took hold of Steven's hand and pressed hard, 'I'm ready.'

Steven held her hand securely. 'We're ready.'

He could see Catherine's shoulders relax. She had been tense from the moment she walked in. He suspected she thought they would say no. He could not think why, he did not think they planned to hurt them in any way, at least he hoped so. It would be strange if they did. He tried to remain at ease, convinced it was just his macho instinct out to protect Caitlin again.

***

Caitlin followed Catherine and Isaac, her hand in Steven's – she did not want to let go. The corridor had an austere quality, nothing felt welcoming anymore and she did not like the sound of this testing. She was not going to let them in on it though, she had to rise above it, and she would be brave. Ever since she had changed she had vowed that she would never fret again. These people knew what they were doing, they had her best interests at heart. It was easy to tell herself this fact, even though doubt lingered at the back of her mind. She fought the urge to run and just gripped Steven's hand harder.

When they made their way out of the lift and faced a very clinical corridor further alarm bells rang, but she kept her composure. She would do as they said. She would conform.

At a set of metallic double doors, Catherine turned to face them. 'Steven, you can go with Isaac now. I'll stay with Caitlin.'

'You said we would stay together,' Steven retorted.

'I did,' Catherine replied, 'as much as possible. We need to separate you for a moment, it won't last long.'

Steven gave Caitlin a fleeting kiss on the lips, his hands on her face. 'We'll be together again soon.'

Caitlin nodded and followed Catherine through an electric door, which sealed shut as soon as they walked through. The room was a small box shape in clinical white, and properly formed, there was no sign of rock anywhere. She imagined it was soundproof. A round table in the centre of the room housed a small laptop. Catherine flipped it open, typed for a while and almost instantly another set of metallic, double door opened. They had been constructed to blend into the décor, she had not even realised they were there.

Catherine glanced in her direction and smiled. 'Let's go. It might seem weird but this security is necessary, we carry out a lot of research in here. Have done for many years.'

Caitlin did not even want to think about the kind of research she was talking about. She followed, her hands clenched into fists.

A large expanse greeted them. A lot of people worked on a range of tables. It had the feel of a scientific research laboratory.

Caitlin could not help checking it all out, her mouth

hanging slightly open. She could see the men and women were using what she recalled were pipettes to create new mixtures in large glass containers, some over Bunsen burners, others being swirled around to give a mixture of colours. A lot of them were a red colour, ranging from a deeper to a clearer colour. They were all so busy, and none of them looked up, they worked like robots. It was bizarre.

They crossed the room and walked into a smaller office.

Inside, a lady wearing a lab coat greeted them and stood up, 'There you are.'

Catherine made her way over and gave her a hug, 'Else, this is Caitlin. Caitlin, this is my daughter, Else.'

'Your daughter?' Caitlin nodded and bridged the gap to shake her hand.

She was slightly shocked when Else gave her a hug, 'It's so nice to meet you. Steven has given us a few scares in the past, but this one tops the lot,' she chuckled, 'he brought a human back with him.'

'I'm not a *normal* human,' Caitlin smiled.

Else seemed to consider this, and glanced at Catherine, 'No, I know that. But, you are different.'

'Anyway, I'll leave you with Else. She has a lot to talk to you about,' Catherine smiled at her daughter and walked out, the room sealed immediately.

'So?' Else said.

Caitlin gave a slight frown, uneasy. 'So?'

'Caitlin, I'll be honest with you. I have to carry out some tests to check if you are like us. We have reason to believe you might be different.'

'Would that be a bad thing?' Caitlin blurted out.

Else gave a half-smile, 'No need to think like that.'

Caitlin noticed she did not answer the question, she started to worry.

Else sat down, and asked her to take a seat. 'This might take some time, can I get you a glass of water?'

'No, but some of what you are brewing outside would be great,' she smirked.

'Ahhh, yes, you know what we're creating then? You're

quick.'

'We had some in the room, I think. Is it blood?' Caitlin asked.

Else nodded, 'It has the properties of blood that we require. We are still trying to create the perfect blend. It takes time.'

Caitlin leaned back on the chair, and said, 'I guess.'

Else leant back and took a bottle out of what looked like a small fridge. 'Enjoy.'

Caitlin un-swirled the cap and took a slug. She felt instantly refreshed, more relaxed, ready for the inquisition.

'Caitlin, the questions are going to be very personal,' Else hesitated slightly, 'are you okay about this?'

Caitlin took another slug. 'Sure.'

Else pursed her lips, her eyes narrowed. 'Okay, so first obvious question, you are in a relationship after all. Are you sexually active?'

'Wow,' Caitlin exclaimed, 'straight at the jugular!'

'I'm sorry, you said you didn't mind,' Else ran her hair through her wavy brown hair, her hazel eyes darted for the first time.

'It's okay.' Caitlin got comfortable and put one of her feet under her leg. 'To answer your question, I have been sexually active, but we've held off whilst we settle in. Don't want to end up pregnant now do I?' she scoffed.

Else looked down at the table and mumbled, 'Indeed.'

Caitlin had no idea where this was going. She hoped it would end soon.

'So when did you have your last period?'

'Jeez, again?' Caitlin sighed aloud, 'I can't remember.'

'Interesting,' Else clasped her hands together.

Caitlin thought about this and sat up, both feet now on the floor. She placed her arms on the table, 'Hang on a minute. Do you think I'm pregnant already?' Her eyes widened, this was not a good thing.

'No, we don't think you're pregnant,' Else was abrupt.

Caitlin mentally counted back the weeks. At a rough estimate, she had a period before Steven changed her. But, she had taken the morning after pill when they had unprotected sex. It would explain why she had not had a period since. She did not want to voice her thoughts aloud, but Else seemed pretty convinced.

'Why don't you think I'm pregnant?' Caitlin asked, wary.

'We need to do some tests,' Else said, 'I need to take some blood and we have to do some x-ray scans. None of it will hurt, and you can have as much of this stuff as you like.'

Caitlin nodded and finished the bottle. A knot had formed in the pit of her stomach, she felt sick.

'Other than this, you feed from blood, eat food and are the same as you were before the change, right?' Else asked, mechanical now, as she got up and made her way around the table.

'Right,' Caitlin answered, her voice whispery. She felt sleepy.

Else's face seemed to blur in front of her and Caitlin struggled to stay upright. 'I feel so tired all of a sudden,' she slurred.

'Then have a rest,' Else said, 'let me help you.'

She felt Else's arms pick her up and she nestled into her shoulder, and said, 'Yes, I need to sleep.' She closed her eyes and thought nothing more of the fact she had just been carried away like a baby by a near stranger.

The image of a little boy with Steven's features flickered in front of her, he was laughing and being tickled. She had always pushed the image of any child they might have away, even though at times it resurfaced. As her mind moved to the subconscious state, she wondered why she would be dreaming of a baby boy again. It made no sense.

Chapter 20

Barren

Steven was bored, really bored. He had been led by Isaac to a small room and met up with Dr Johannes, who had not changed one bit since he last saw him. Although this time he wasn't fretting as much as he had when Steven was attacked by the tapir, for obvious reasons. Dr Johannes had checked out his foot, made light conversation and then taken some blood and it had all been over in the space of ten minutes. Then he had been asked to wait and they had left him alone in a clinical room, to twiddle his thumbs.

He hoped Caitlin was okay. He had no idea why her testing was taking so long. A part of him wished he had asked more questions, made sure she was looked after properly. It was all a bit surreal. It made him think of a time when Ingrid had implied that if they were ever discovered by humans they would be tested on like lab rats. He was starting to feel like a lab rat, and it was their doing. He could not pinpoint what they were all so afraid of, but he knew there was something that had got them all hot and bothered, and not in a nice way either.

He had just about started to doze when the door opened and Catherine walked in. 'Steven.'

Steven quickly rubbed his eyes and stood up. 'What's going on? Why's this taking so long?'

'Sit down, Steven, we need to talk.'

It sounded serious. Catherine sat down next to him.

'Go on then, I'm listening,' he folded his arms over his chest.

'It's about Caitlin,' Catherine paused, as though she was having difficulty finding the right words.

'What about Caitlin?' He edged out of his seat.

'This is complicated.'

'As complicated as you make it,' he sighed.

'Okay, hear me out. When I finish you can talk, okay?'

'Sure.'

Catherine looked away from him as she spoke, 'My mother could not have more children after the change. Of course she was nearly fifty so everyone assumed it was because she was older. It probably was.'

Steven watched her, focused now, his hands clasped together.

'We wanted to know if Caitlin could still conceive. Isaac had a suspicion that she wouldn't be able to have children, since she was *changed* not naturally born.'

'And?' he could not help getting impatient.

'It turns out Isaac was right. Caitlin is barren, her age is frozen and her reproductive organs have stopped working. She cannot have children.'

Steven's first thought, and it made him ashamed to think it, was that they could have had sex after all. He pushed the thought aside, this was bad. Defensive, he blurted out, 'Caitlin never said she wanted children, it might not be something that bothers her.'

'Yes,' Catherine looked at him now, her eyes sad, withdrawn.

'How can you be so sure?'

'We x-rayed her internal organs, her ovaries and fallopian tubes have shrivelled up, her uterus has collapsed. She does not produce any eggs anymore and never will. But, there is more.'

Steven could feel the blood drain from his face. 'More?'

'Yes, I'm sorry,' she paused again. 'Caitlin's blood remains human-like. We think this is why Emily attacked her. It appears any of us could drink her blood and regenerate. Do you understand what I'm saying?'

'You mean, she's in danger here? She could be attacked?'

'Well not exactly, we don't know for definite. We don't think we can entrance or manipulate her. She's just appealing to us in a way none of us are appealing to each other. Do you remember how Ingrid was repulsed by you when she first met you?'

'Yes, well, I heard about it,' he said.

'Caitlin doesn't repulse us. It seems that when a human is

changed, they lose the ability to reproduce, but remain human enough for us to feed from them whilst keeping them alive.'

Steven closed his eyes and placed his head in his hands, then he whispered, 'I created a blood donor, one that would not die.'

'You understand then,' Catherine sighed. 'Judith was also a donor for my father. It explains why he kept her away from everyone, why he was so protective.'

'This is impossible. Caitlin will hate me again.'

'Again?' Catherine asked, her tone surprised.

'Yes,' Steven raised his head, 'She distanced herself from me. She was not in love, but then she was. Oh, I don't know what to think.'

'Interesting,' Catherine mused, 'perhaps her natural defences were kicking in, protecting her. But now, you are both in love again?'

'I guess, but not for much longer,' Steven grunted, he got up and paced. 'What the hell have I done?'

'You might have inadvertently stumbled on our future. A future where we don't have to kill any more, a symbiotic relationship with humans.'

Steven stopped pacing and fought to control his anger, 'What do they gain from this bargain?'

'A longer, youthful life. It's not a bad thing.'

'I'm sure Caitlin will be grateful,' he retorted, his voice laced with sarcasm.

Catherine stood up, 'I'm here to ask if you want to explain it to her.'

'Are you crazy? Of course I don't want to tell her,' he shouted, before he managed to calm down. Eyes narrowed, he continued, 'But I guess I have to, or I should,' his shoulders slumped in defeat.

'I can come with you. You need to put a positive spin on it, for her sake,' Catherine stressed, 'besides, we have plenty of children here. She will always be able to help with ours.'

'I'm sure she'll be happy to hear that,' he snapped, bitter.

'You didn't want to have children, is that the problem?' Catherine studied him.

For the first time he really loathed Catherine, so clinical in her approach. 'No, I don't need to have children. I've never given it much thought.'

'Caitlin needs you, and you'd be wise to do what you can to hold on to her. She's a great asset.'

Steven could not believe she had called Caitlin an *asset*, as though she was an object, an item to be bought and sold. Then again, if what they were saying was true, she was just like a walking blood bank for any of them. And she would regenerate him if he ever got sick or injured. He could see the advantage she referred to, he just did not like to think of himself as a bloody leech attached to the woman he loved.

***

Caitlin rubbed her eyes as she awoke. For once she could not remember a dream, nothing. Her mind was completely blank, erased even. She tried to remember what had happened before she fell asleep and came up empty. Her finger traced the vein on her right arm, it was itchy, and she realised a plaster was over it. Strange. She made to get up and realised she was slightly light headed, but she forced herself to sit.

Almost immediately, there was someone by her side. 'Caitlin, you don't have to sit, lie down.'

Caitlin frowned and noticed she was only wearing a flimsy gown, with no underwear. She pushed the gown as low as it would go, then looked up and remembered. The woman in front of her was Else, she had been talking to her and then, well, she had no idea. 'What on earth is going on?'

'We are looking after you. We needed to run some tests.'

'Tests?' Caitlin's eyes widened, she repeated the question as the realisation hit her, 'What tests?' She slid her legs over the side of the bed and made to stand.

Else stood in front of her and prevented her from getting up. 'Don't worry about that now, rest. Steven is coming to see you soon.'

Caitlin hesitated, but she did not have any fight left. She remained seated, her hands limp on her lap, and closed her eyes. Steven. She loved him, she really did. She wanted to be with him, and yet a part of her wished she was in a dream. She wanted to wake up and be back at university leading a normal life. She could not believe they had run *tests* on her. She was doing everything she could to stop freaking out.

Slowly, she opened her eyes again. Else had gone, but a covered plate sat on a tray on the bedside unit. She was hungry. She leant over, placed the tray on her lap and lifted the silver dome off the top. Immediately, she got wafted with the smell of garlic. It was what looked like a fish stew, with tomatoes and herbs. Her mouth watered, she was ravenous now. She picked up the metal spoon and scooped some in her mouth. Her taste buds exploded as she savoured the first mouthful. Whoever had cooked the dish knew what he was doing. She wanted the recipe.

A few minutes later, the large bowl was empty and her mouth was on fire, there was some serious chilli in the dish. She loved the burn, not enough to hurt but enough to stimulate her taste buds.

She picked up the glass of water and downed it in one. She remembered the red stuff she drank in Else's office, but could not remember what happened next. She had a feeling she had been drugged. In fact, she was certain she had been. She lay her head back on the pillow as tiredness overcame her again. As she dozed off, she wondered if they had put anything in the food, or the drink. She doubted they would have done that, and yet the thought remained.

*

The sound of Steven's voice made her stir. She was under the covers again, still practically naked. She fought to open her eyelids, they were still so heavy. It reminded her of the worst flu she had ever had. Her entire body was in agony, and she was exhausted even though she knew she had slept for hours. Even so, the fact Steven was there brought some consolation. She stretched slightly and then lay on her side to face him, her eyes now open.

'You're awake at last,' Steven said, his hand reaching out to stroke her cheek. His thumb gently rubbed her cheek as his fingers gently caressed her lower jaw.

She closed her eyes for a second, enjoying the feel of his

hand. When she opened her eyes again, her voice sounded hazy. She still felt half asleep. 'Steven, why am I being drugged?'

'Drugged?' Steven removed his hand, a guilty expression plastered on his face. His eyes never lied.

'You know it's true, look at me,' she gave a half-smile.

'They needed to run some tests,' Steven looked away, 'they needed to check a few things out.'

Caitlin stared right at him, her eyes locked on his, 'Else said. What tests did they run?'

He stood up and paced. She knew he only did that when he was worried, this was bad. She tried to stay focused, and stretched out her hand to get the glass of water.

Steven rushed to her side and helped her lift her head to drink.

'Thank you,' she said.

Steven knelt next to her, his eyes watery. She was shocked to see him so distraught.

Now she was getting worried. She could not tell for definite, but she was sure those looked like tears, and Steven never cried. She did not even want to think about what could have happened to make him so upset, or more to the point, what could be *wrong* with her. Either way, it was pretty damn obvious it was something bad.

Chapter 21

Motherhood

Lucy sucked the blood of the capybara, disappointed it was dry within minutes. In the last hour, she had already fed from three medium sized capybaras and yet she was sure she had space for more. Her hunger seemed insatiable and her figure had ballooned. The weird thing was her fixation with mango juice, she just couldn't get enough of it. She had done a great job so far of keeping her condition a secret, but she knew time was running out. Catherine had helped her and made it easier for her to hide. Rarely did she have to speak to anyone and when she did they just assumed she had got fat. It was lucky that everyone was not slim, even though they were on the whole outwardly young.

The problem was there was fat, and then there was *fat*. She was sure she looked pregnant now. Even though her face, arms and legs had swollen beyond recognition the unmistakable pregnancy bump was clearly visible. At least, she thought so.

The fact Steven was back complicated things. She had hoped to be in Borneo by now, wishful thinking she knew, but the delay in the immigration meant she was likely to have the baby at the community after all. She could hide and pretend nothing was going on, but she could not hide a physical baby. She knew for a fact they cried a lot.

The sound of rustling in the distance made her turn defensively, even though she knew who it was. She had taken her time. 'Finally, if you hadn't come soon I would have been forced to hunt again!'

Catherine tilted her head to the side as she studied her crouched form, 'Let's see you then?'

Lucy stood up, a timid smile now on her face. She was proud of her bump.

'You've grown bigger again. We're going to have to do a scan you know. I know you've been against it, but it's best to check everything is as expected,' Catherine sighed, 'lie down and I'll check for the heartbeat.'

Lucy lay down on the ground, her arms by her side. She lifted her top and lowered her bottom so that her bump was fully exposed.

Catherine gave a low gasp, 'Wow, it's grown a *lot*, not just a bit. And you're now only six months, right? Mine were never this big. Seriously, we have to do a scan,' she said, then lowered her head to her belly, took the foetal doppler out of her bag and got it ready. Catherine squeezed some gel out of the tube, placed it on the probe and then pressed it against her belly.

Lucy flinched slightly, it was always so cold.

The slow, pumping sound started straight away. The steady beat a relief every time. Her baby sounded healthy to hear anyway. The sound died away as she felt her stomach lurch. Catherine moved around the belly and locked on the heartbeat again.

'A healthy heart,' Catherine chuckled, and then she stopped, her face serious as she moved the probe to the other side of the belly. Again the heartbeat came up loud and fast. Catherine swiftly moved it again to the other side and the sound came up again. Catherine took the probe off and stared into Lucy's eyes. 'I'm pretty sure you have two babies.'

Lucy sat up abruptly, and frowned, as she said, 'Two?'

'Definitely two.'

Lucy mulled the thought over in her head. Two babies. She was ready for one, but two seemed like a lot of work. Saying that she could not stop a huge silly grin spreading across her face, 'Two!'

'At least...' Catherine's eyes widened, unamused.

'What do you mean...?' Lucy paused, as she wondered if Catherine was saying what she thought she was saying.

Catherine nodded. The realisation must have been plain on her face.

'I could have *more* than two?!' Lucy slumped on the ground. There was nothing she could do. They would have to do a scan. 'So, when should we go?'

'You know what,' Catherine paused, 'we have to go *now*.

Lucy, you're pregnant. I know you want to keep the identity of the father a secret, and that's fine, but you can trust me. Besides, people will be okay about your pregnancy once they get used to the idea.'

'Oh, I don't know about that. There are many who still consider children out of wedlock a sin, in fact more than many,' Lucy gave a slight eye roll. 'Most people think it, you have to be honest, and my dad will kill me when he finds out.'

Catherine sighed, 'Franco will not kill you. He might be opinionated and a pain in the backside over a lot of things but he wouldn't go that far. Either way, recent events mean we all have to adapt to a different way of life. Lucy, I'll look out for you. I promised I would help you and I stand by that.'

'Thanks Catherine, really,' Lucy smiled. 'So, how do you suggest we sneak in?'

'We're not sneaking in, Lucy. We'll just go to the labs and have some tests done. I'll keep the questions at bay.'

Lucy bit her lip, hesitant. 'Okay.'

She shuffled alongside Catherine. Even though her hunger had been partially abated she was beginning to find it hard to walk. Her pelvis had started to throb, and every now and again a sharp stab made it hard to move. She didn't want to sound weak, so she kept on going and endured it. The last thing Catherine needed, after everything she was doing for her, was to hear any more of her woes.

After a few minutes of walking, when they had nearly reached the entrance, Catherine stopped and put her hands on her shoulders, 'Lucy, you know you can tell me anything, right? You know that I will not judge you?'

Lucy nodded lightly. 'I know.'

She knew Catherine hoped she would share who the father was, but there was no way she was going to tell her that. Even Catherine would find it hard to believe Lucy had had a one-night stand with Steven. After all, he had barely just changed when it happened. No, it was a secret she intended to keep.

After they had made their way back in, Lucy remained behind Catherine and flapped her loose clothing around her, she could still try to look fat. They made their way past the laboratory entrance and continued to the medical centre. She hoped Else would be there, where pregnancy was concerned she preferred to speak to a woman than a man.

They rounded the corner and the hallway split into two different directions. They turned to the right to see if they could find Else. The emergency area was empty, accidents were rare.

Catherine motioned to one of the empty wooden chairs. 'Sit here, Lucy, I'll go and look for Else.'

Lucy sat down and stared at her hands. They looked so podgy, she barely remembered what they used to look like. She stood up and walked around, if she stayed seated she would get restless and she was already nervous about what they would find.

She made her way past the empty rooms and slowly ambled towards the other side, she doubted there were many patients. She carried on walking and had a peek through the window to see if anyone she knew was around. This was probably one of the only areas that had doors and windows. Sickness was confined in the community when it happened, which was not very often. All that trouble for nothing. It was unlikely anyone was around yet something compelled her to check.

She stopped as she heard some voices, or was it crying? She listened intently. It was definitely crying and a male voice. A male voice that sounded like someone she knew. She nervously edged towards the window of the room the sound was coming from. The sight made her flinch and she backed away immediately. It was Steven with a girl she did not know, a redhead by the looks of it. He was holding the girl's hand. Whatever they were talking about was not good. She needed to get away quickly or Steven would hear her, if he had not already.

The sight of Catherine walking towards her brought some temporary relief. 'Lucy, what are you doing here? I told you to wait.'

Lucy flinched at the sound of her own name – she did not want Steven to know she was there. 'I heard voices, I just…' Her eyes darted from Catherine to the window.

'Go back and wait for me there, Else is coming,' Catherine snapped. She opened the door of the room where Steven was, went inside, and shut it quickly.

Lucy shuffled back as quickly as she could. The last person she wanted to see her was Steven.

***

Catherine could not believe that Lucy had come so close to Caitlin, the last thing the poor girl needed to see was a pregnant woman. She had no idea what Steven had told her, but after speaking to Else she knew the discussion was not going to be an easy one. She tried to appear outwardly calm and kept her smile sincere as she spoke, 'Caitlin, Steven, I just came in to check you were both okay. That you did not need anything.'

Steven wore a haunted expression, his eyes glazed. He gave her a fleeting glance and shook his head.

Caitlin looked away and stared at the floor, lost.

Catherine knew Steven must have told Caitlin what they knew. 'Right, well, I'll let you both talk then. I have to lock the door, for your own safety.'

Caitlin's face flicked back to glare at her. She snarled, her eyes narrowed, 'I'm not safe here now, am I?'

'Of course you're safe,' she replied, slightly hasty, 'no-one will hurt you, Caitlin.'

'No, no-one will *hurt* me,' Caitlin said, tears now springing from her eyes. 'No-one can hurt me anymore, I am beyond it. You have destroyed me.'

'You have me, Caitlin, you'll always have me,' Steven stressed, his hands still holding hers like a vice.

Caitlin shook her hands out of his, and leapt out of the bed, her frame shaking as she leant against the wall. 'Leave me alone, both of you, LEAVE ME ALONE.'

Her shout echoed in the near empty room.

Steven turned to Catherine, 'Please go.'

Catherine made for the door.

'GO AWAY, TAKE HIM WITH YOU,' Caitlin screamed, out of her mind now. She curled into a ball and rocked on the floor, her head tucked into her chest.

'Stay here,' Catherine said, 'I'll be back.'

Steven watched Caitlin, dumbstruck, his face had paled.

Catherine made for the door, opened it quickly and then locked it from the other side. She looked in the window and saw that Steven had not moved, Caitlin still rocked back and forth on the floor. She hated what they had done to the poor girl.

Else came up alongside, 'I was afraid this would happen. I'll come and see Lucy in a minute, first I'll arrange to have Caitlin sedated.'

'Of course,' Catherine nodded, then handed her the key, 'I'll wait for you there.'

As she made her way towards Lucy, Catherine heard the key turn again as Else went in. She had no idea what they were planning to do. How did anyone come to terms with the fact they would never be a mother, and yet always be at someone else's beck and call? Caitlin did not gain anything from the arrangement. She might view herself as nothing more than a blood bank. Yet, Catherine could not help thinking there was more to this development than met the eye. She wanted to think that Caitlin would benefit too in some way. It would make her sleep better if she knew there would be a future for someone like Caitlin.

She owed it to her parents to find out why they encouraged Steven to change Caitlin if it was only going to ruin the poor girl's life.

Chapter 22

A Surprise

Lucy fidgeted as she sat on the solitary chair. The piercing scream she heard as she walked away still rang in her head, something had happened to that girl. She had no idea what it was but it didn't sound good. Either way, she was curious about what the scan would show. The fact Steven was there had only made her predicament all the more precarious. She focused on the smooth, white wall in front of her and hoped they would hurry up. She needed to lie down soon.

After waiting another ten minutes, she finally saw Catherine and Else approach.

Else gave her a half-smile, 'Lucy, come on then, let's see what, or who I should say, is in your belly. Do you mind if Mum stays?'

'Of course not, Catherine has been so helpful. I need a few friends,' she could not help smiling. It felt good to share her pregnancy. She got up and waddled after them. At times, she wondered if she was on water.

They made their way into a small room with a lot of different gadgets on the side board. A monitor sat on a table with wheels, her ticket to seeing what was inside her. A reclining, padded chair waited in the centre of the room.

'Take a seat,' Else instructed.

Catherine drew a chair next to her and sat by her side.

Else wheeled the monitor over, and prepared the equipment. Lucy started to feel butterflies swarming through her stomach, aided by the disco party her unborn children seemed to be having. She flinched slightly at the thought of *babies* – she never dreamed there would be more than one. Although thinking about it, Steven's mum, Emily, was a twin.

'Right then, let's have a look. Can you expose your belly, please?'

'Sure,' Lucy said, as she lifted her top and unbuttoned her trousers, then lowered them just past her pelvis.

A second later, she felt the ice-cold gel on her stomach again and flinched. 'Does it always have to be so cold?'

'Afraid so,' Else chuckled. 'Right, let's see who we have.' She focused on the screen, and then started to smile. She turned the screen so that Lucy could see it. Lucy could tell that Catherine was also eagerly watching.

She could see what looked like two heads side by side, a foot stuck out beneath their chins.

'How did that foot get there?' Lucy tilted her head, she scrunched her nose.

'Interesting question,' Else said, she moved the probe to the other side of her belly.

Lucy's jaw dropped as she saw two sets of feet and a head this time. She tried to convince herself she was not seeing what she thought she was seeing. 'Is that what I think it is?'

'I believe you are going to have triplets, Lucy, congratulations,' Else said, as she continued to probe, now searching the entire belly.

'Triplets?' Lucy's jaw dropped.

'It's quite common for older women,' Else continued, 'but you are the first in the community. We have had some twins, but not triplets. It's quite exciting really.'

'Oh Lucy,' Catherine grabbed her hand and gave her a heart-warming smile, 'it's so exciting.'

The last thing on Lucy's mind was the excitement of it. Three babies: not one, not two, but three. Some things should not happen in real life, this was one of them. She could have coped in Borneo with one baby, maybe even with two, but three was a different matter. She had no idea what she was going to do.

'Who's the father, Lucy?' Else asked, 'he should be involved, you'll need help.' She carried on making observations as she talked, she looked like she was measuring the heads, and checking the length of their spines.

Lucy shook her head, and replied, 'I can't tell you that.'

'Fair enough,' Else said, 'but he should be involved.'

Lucy and Catherine both focused on the screen, intrigued by Else's ongoing study.

A few minutes later, Else turned to face Lucy, 'you're about 22 to 24 weeks in gestation. For a triplet birth, I do not expect you to go to full term. With luck you'll get to 34 weeks. Have you had any abnormal pain, any problems?'

Lucy thought about that, in ten weeks she could be a mother to three children. She focused on answering, 'I was really sick for a while, but in the past few weeks I started to feel better. They just kick a lot. No wonder it felt like a party in there, there was obviously one going on,' she tried to keep her laugh light, it sounded tense.

Else nodded. 'Hmm. It's best if you stay here, under observation.'

'I can't leave my babies unattended, who will look after my greenhouse?' she said, whilst staring at Catherine, beseeching.

Catherine held her hand again. 'Lucy, do as Else says, it's for the best. And maybe think about telling us who the father is?'

Lucy looked away, she felt her cheeks flush. In her mind, the words 'your nephew' popped out.

**

Catherine found it hard to come to terms with what she was seeing. Three foetuses, Lucy was going to have *three* babies. She could not force Lucy to tell her, but she wished she knew who the father was. It would be better for the community if Lucy was in a relationship. There had never been a single parent in the community, with all children being born within wedlock. It would be another thing for the community to deal with. The fact that someone had got pregnant, outside of a relationship, within the community was likely to cause a stir. The fact that she was expecting three babies could be seen as a bad omen, or a punishment. She knew Else wanted to keep Lucy hidden for her safety, not just for that of the babies.

'I have to go and check on Steven, Else will look after you,' Catherine said, 'and don't worry, I'll make sure your other babies are tended well.

'Thanks,' Lucy smiled, her face still focused on the fixed screen in front of her.

Catherine nodded at Else, and made her way out. Else knew

what to do since she had briefed her before the scan, Lucy was not to be seen by anyone else. The pregnancy would be kept a secret.

Catherine walked quickly down the corridor and looked through the window. Caitlin was back on the bed, fast asleep, sedated no doubt. Steven sat by her side, he held her hand in his. She turned the key to the door and made her way in. Steven did not look up as his eyes remained focused on Caitlin's face.

'Steven, this is not your fault. You know this, right?'

He did not acknowledge her.

'Steven,' she stood next to him, 'I guess she didn't take the news well. What exactly did you say to her? I need to know what she fears.'

Steven still did not acknowledge her.

'Steven, please talk to me.'

In a muffled voice, he said, 'I have nothing to say. Leave us alone.'

Catherine pursed her lips, this was worse than she thought. If he clammed up too, there would be no hope for either of them. 'Steven,' she sighed, 'Steven, you have to talk to me.'

Steven turned his head to face her for a brief moment, his eyes glazed, as said bluntly, 'No, I don't.'

She was slightly overcome by the hatred in his tone. He lowered his forehead to Caitlin's hand and dug his head into the bed. It hurt Catherine to see him in so much pain. She swallowed involuntarily and held back her emotions. 'I'll come and see you later then.'

She eased back out of the room and locked the door. Then she leant against the door for a split second, before she stood straight. She needed to see Anna. She rushed down the corridor, her thoughts in disarray. There was a lot to consider. Steven, Caitlin, now Lucy. Lucy, the thought lingered. Lucy was just over twenty weeks gone. Steven had last been in the community about the same time. Surely, there couldn't be a link, it would be madness. And yet, something told her it was not a coincidence, her instincts had never been wrong.

Lucy seemed too cagey about the father. She also seemed

nervous about Steven's return. Catherine wondered if it was her imagination, but she could not think of any other man that would have had the opportunity to be with Lucy. No other man would have actually *been* with Lucy. They all avoided her. If she was right, if it was Steven that was the father, this whole situation had just got a lot worse.

Catherine headed towards the hall where Lucy was staying and found her alone, settling into her new room. Else was nowhere in sight. Catherine locked the door behind her. 'Is my nephew the father?' She could not say his name aloud.

'What?' Lucy's jaw dropped, a guilty expression clouding her face.

'Oh no, no, tell me this isn't happening?' Catherine took a seat, her head in her hands.

She heard Lucy sigh.

Catherine lifted her head, and stared at Lucy's rounded form. 'You're about to bring three babies into the community, whose father is a hybrid. God help us, what have you done?'

'I didn't mean for it to happen, it was just the one time,' Lucy's lower lip started to quiver.

'It only takes the one time,' Catherine said, she did not want to get Lucy upset but she was angry, 'Lucy, what were you thinking?'

Lucy's voice wobbled, 'I didn't think, I was lonely. I had been for such a long time. Steven was the first man to show me attention.'

Catherine raised her voice, 'He's not a man; he's a boy. You should've known better.'

Lucy let out a low gasp, as a stifled cry filled the room. She cupped her face in her hands, her shoulders shaking.

Catherine stood up and embraced her. 'I'm sorry, don't cry. I don't mean to upset you. It's just this is all a big mess. The future of the community hangs in the balance and yet everything's against us. I'm scared, Lucy. I'm scared.'

'I'm scared too,' the sobs continued, 'I'm so…'

'It's okay, we'll figure it out,' Catherine stroked her hair, 'there has to be a reason for all of this, somehow we'll find out what it all means.'

'We will?' Lucy stopped crying and stepped back, her eyes wide, hopeful.

'Of course we will.'

Catherine wished her conviction matched her confidence. At the moment, it fell well short.

She waited until Lucy had calmed down and then rubbed her chin slowly. 'Lucy, we've got to keep you a secret. Steven must not know about the children.'

'Now you understand why I couldn't tell you about the father,' Lucy smiled.

'Yes,' Catherine said, and then took a deep breath. 'Can you let me figure this out? Will you trust me and know that I'll only do what's best for you?'

'Of course,' Lucy's eyes brightened, 'I trust you. I always have.'

Catherine nodded and tried to look nonplussed. She hoped the trust was well placed. She had no idea how she was going to ensure that everyone's best interests were maintained, at the moment it was an impossible task.

Chapter 23

Experimental

Ingrid dived down and sat on a rock double her size, covered entirely by lush underwater plants. Her hands ran through the tangled mess. It was easy to think there with no other sounds or distractions. It was one of her favourite places. The fact she could be under for a long time helped. She wished she could go to see Caitlin and Steven. As much as she knew she was still very much in love with Steven, she actually cared a lot for Caitlin. She guessed she sympathised with Caitlin for also being caught in Steven's net. In addition, she could not imagine it was much fun to be cooped up.

Either way, when they came out she planned to be a good tour guide. She reluctantly accepted Steven was never going to be hers. A small part of her held on, but other than via some sort of miracle she doubted she ever stood a chance. It was a shame her faith had never been as extensive as her mother hoped. Miracles just did not happen to her.

She pushed off the rock and swam breaststroke along the sea floor, then she kicked off the ground and pushed up so that she was just below the waterfall. Bubbles gushed all around her and she forced her way through so she surfaced behind the waterfall. She sat on the rocks and watched the powerful water descend, relentless.

'Ingrid, are you there?' It was the sound of her mother's voice.

'I'm here. I'll come out and get changed.' She never enjoyed having chats when she was naked. She still found it hard to believe she had been so brazen when Steven had first come to the community. She actually swam naked next to him, it was the bravest thing she had ever done. It didn't make any difference though, nothing ever came of it. Steven had made it obvious he didn't like to be forced into things. She should have realised all along that being pushy would not work; then again she had never fallen in love before.

Love made people do irrational things.

She walked out and saw her mum standing next to her clothes, towel in hand. Her mum's darker skin colouring, brown hair and hazel eyes were so different to her own.

'Thanks,' Ingrid slipped it over her shoulders and rubbed her body down.

'It looks like there's going to be a delay,' Lana spoke slowly, 'there will be no introduction to the community after all. Only Steven will join us soon. Did you know?'

'*Only* Steven,' Ingrid faced her, and bit her inner cheek. She started to put her clothes on, another ensemble of green.

'Yes.'

Now clothed, Ingrid made to leave. 'Tell me what's going on then.'

'Well, we have to keep quiet about this,' she looked around uneasily, 'I got most of it from Catherine; she thought you should know what was going on. She knew you would *want* to know.'

Ingrid gave a half-smile, 'I'm grateful. So can you tell me what's happened?'

'It seems that *she* is not doing very well, she's in isolation,' Lana held Ingrid's hand and pressed it gently, 'it's for her own good, but Steven might need a friend.'

Ingrid chuckled, 'I doubt he'll want to talk to me, but I guess at least I know Caitlin. He can talk to me if it helps.'

'That's what we were thinking,' Lana let go of Ingrid's hand, 'Jenson's also there for him, but it doesn't hurt for him to have another friend.'

'How's Caitlin?' Ingrid could not help being concerned.

'I don't know what's happened, but something's not right. But, that isn't important. It's been a week since we got back. Steven has to join us, regardless. The community needs to be kept informed.'

'Can you go and see Catherine?' Lana glanced over quickly, as they walked, 'Jenson has convinced Steven to join us. He's been trying for a few days now, but Steven is likely to be even more miserable than he was the first time he came to the community. I wanted to warn you.'

'I don't think he could be worse, is it possible?' Ingrid gave a nervous chuckle. She hoped he did not hate her as much as he did back then. She could not bear to think about the way he had looked at her, the way he had told her to *stop dreaming*. She had never felt as insignificant in her entire life as she had when he rejected her.

Lana nodded, her eyes had a sadness Ingrid rarely saw, 'I'm afraid it's a lot worse than last time.'

Ingrid's mouth opened to say something but then closed. Even though she resented the fact Caitlin was Steven's she did not want anything bad to happen.

'You'll find Catherine in her classroom,' Lana said, she gave Ingrid a hug as they came to the junction. 'I have to go help in the produce area. Lucy's not very well at the moment. It's strange, I've never known Lucy to be ill either.'

Ingrid mulled over the thought. Lucy was such a recluse, the lifeblood of the produce area. She did not know why anyone would be happy to be alone all the time. All she did was look after the animals and talk to her plants – she was a bit strange. And now she was sick, it did not add up. She bet Catherine knew what was going on. It would be worth asking.

***

'Well done everyone, you're making real progress,' Catherine smiled, as the mental agility class came to a close. She watched the students amble out and followed. Everything seemed to carry on as normal but she could feel something was amiss, everyone did. She hoped that when Steven re-joined them the gossip would stop, or at least stop getting out of hand. New rumours flew around every day, it was hard to suppress them. Caitlin was best left in the dark, introducing her to the community now could result in a catalyst of self-destruction.

At the doorway, she came across Ingrid.

'You wanted to see me?' Ingrid stopped in front of her, one hand on her hip.

Catherine was momentarily lost in her thoughts, her eyes flickered and then she did everything she could to put across her most convincing smile. 'Ingrid, did your mother send you?'

'Yes,' Ingrid nodded slowly, and then dropped her hand from her hip to her side.

'Walk with me, please,' Catherine began, 'Steven's joining the community today. I would appreciate it if you kept an eye on him. I know you became friends with Caitlin. You might want to go and see her, it might help.' Catherine stopped walking, and checked to make sure no-one else was around, then carried on, 'on another note, I know you've been working on the cure. Can you tell me about your progress?'

Ingrid beamed, 'Of course, I'd love to.'

'Do you mind if Steven hears this too?'

'Is that wise?' Ingrid shifted her posture, uneasy.

'If he knows we're trying to find a way for Caitlin it might help,' Catherine gave a small sigh, 'anything is worth a try.'

Ingrid licked her lower lip. 'Is he really as bad as my mother said he was?'

'Probably worse.' Catherine walked on, determined now. If Steven knew as much as possible then he would accept the transition. At least, she hoped he would.

Once in the lift, Catherine's shoulders relaxed. 'Let's find Steven first, then we can talk.'

Ingrid gave a small nod, and then looked straight ahead. Even though Catherine had reservations about Ingrid, she knew she could be trusted.

They made their way to Steven's accommodation, knocked and waited. When Steven's gruff voice told them to come in, Catherine unlocked the door.

The smell was overpowering, but Catherine fought to keep calm. She could see Ingrid flinch, her nose crumpled. Steven sat in a chair, staring straight ahead, lost. He looked rough, really rough. He had not shaved, his hair was dishevelled and unkempt, his clothes looked dirty and crumpled, and his head slumped low. She knew he had refused to wash, barely eaten a thing, and drank minimal blood. His new look did not do him any favours.

'Steven, we have some news to share with you,' Catherine began, 'we think you'll find what Ingrid has to say interesting.'

Only his lips moved as he mumbled, 'I doubt that.'

'Ingrid, can you please tell Steven about the program. It's time he realises we're not monsters.'

'Of course,' Ingrid moved closer, placed a chair in front of Steven and sat down. 'Steven, when I met you I realised that there had to be a better way of life for us, a way without killing normal humans. As much as you might think us heartless animals for killing humans for blood, the truth is we've been trying to find a way around this for years.'

Steven raised his head slowly and met her stare. 'You have?' The tone of his voice betrayed his interest.

'We have,' Catherine added, and then moved alongside Ingrid.

Steven shrugged his shoulders, 'Fine, carry on. I'm listening, for whatever its worth.'

'I've been working with a team for a long time now,' Ingrid began, 'This is the reason I was in Southampton when I found you. The research trips are invaluable. We've been trying to find out if anything at all makes a difference. We studied different blood groups, race, and genetic background. The university was a great place to carry out the research over the years. The range of nationalities that attend is staggering. It made it easier to have a base. We have collected many samples, and yet, nothing seemed to make any difference, that is, until you came along.'

'Me?' Steven glared, interested now. Catherine was glad to see a reaction.

Ingrid gave a half-smile, and continued, 'When your blood repulsed me, I knew you were different. And yet you didn't make me ill. If we drink the blood of each other we get very ill. So, when you came here and were attacked by the tapir we managed to get a blood sample. When you left for England, we worked with your blood. By mixing it with animal blood we made artificial blood. It was our best yet.'

'The bottles? Those were manufactured, not real?'

'Yes, we did not kill for those,' Ingrid's smile broadened. 'We've figured out how to create the samples, but it was still not perfect, not strong enough to enable the change. However, we believe we have managed to make the perfect strain now.'

Steven's eyes narrowed, in a stern voice, he said, 'Caitlin's blood. Did you use Caitlin's blood?'

Catherine knelt down beside him. 'Steven, even if we did, do you understand what this could mean?'

'Did you use her blood?' His hands clenched into fists.

Ingrid stood up and paced for a moment. Catherine ran one of her hands through her hair. She could not understand why he would be annoyed over a little blood.

Steven got up from his chair and spat, 'You used her blood. Now tell me why this is good for *her*.'

Ingrid stopped in front of him. 'It means her blood is not the only blood that can heal us, we can now create a synthetic blood that can heal and change all of us. At least, we think so.'

'You *think* so,' Steven huffed, as he turned away from them.

Catherine stood up and walked towards him. 'The blood has not been tested yet, but we wanted you to know that we're doing everything we can to allow Caitlin to be safe amongst us. She will be safe with us.'

Steven turned to face Catherine and scratched his lower jaw as he said, 'In that case, I hope your tests are conclusive. When will you know?'

'In the next few weeks,' Catherine said, 'but the community cannot wait to see you for another few weeks. There's a lot of unrest. With Caitlin still not being well, she'll have to stay in the medical suite. The community doesn't need to know about Caitlin yet, but we need you to join us. We need you to show everyone that you are normal, unchanged. Many are beginning to think you are dead.'

'I wish I was dead sometimes, I wish I had died the day you met me,' he glared at Ingrid.

Catherine gritted her teeth, then breathed in and relaxed. 'Steven, we cannot change the past. We must look to the future. Things happen in life for a reason, it is not up to us to question that reason.'

'I can question it if I bloody well want to,' he shouted, and then slumped back in the chair.

Ingrid walked over to Steven and put her hand on his

shoulder, 'Steven, you're not helping Caitlin by letting yourself go. She needs you to be strong, to be there for her.'

In a sharp motion Steven stood up, his face but an inch away from Ingrid's, and snarled, 'Do you know about Caitlin? Have they told you what *I* did to her?'

Catherine intervened, 'No, she doesn't know.'

Steven moved towards Catherine. 'Then stop telling me what to do. Caitlin doesn't even want to see me. She hates me.' His voice choked, as his body crumpled.

'She doesn't hate you. She needs you now more than ever. The sooner you realise it, the better,' Catherine said, 'you have an hour, after that Jenson's coming to help you sort yourself out. The next time I see you it'll be in the main hall for dinner, I hope you'll make an effort. Let's go, Ingrid.'

She could sense Ingrid's reluctance to leave. Steven was lucky to have Ingrid watching over him. It was a shame he did not see it that way.

Chapter 24

Cleaned up

Steven stared at the door for a few minutes after it closed, his head full of irrational thought. If the cure worked then Caitlin would be safe, no-one would ever need to know about what her blood could do. He would never have to use her, not that he would have taken her blood without her consent. At least, he liked to think so.

The fact Caitlin could drink his blood and heal made him wonder if the same would apply to any human changed. He wondered if Caitlin, and Judith for that matter, could be more like the myth of vampires. They could not reproduce, drank blood, and remained frozen in time with the ability to regenerate.

He felt stupid for thinking it. They had a heartbeat and ate normal food. They were not creatures of the night.

He wished he could talk to Judith, he wished he could find out more about her life. He tried to remember more about their last conversation. It was hours before she died. Judith had talked about Charleston, about *talkies*, about love. He could not help smiling as he remembered her animated eyes. He shook his head, his lips drooping down again. The situation was hopeless. She had told him nothing.

The fact remained – Caitlin hated him.

He lowered his head into his hands. He had told her about the fact she could not have children and Caitlin had gone crazy. Her eyes had nearly exploded out of her sockets. He would never forget that look of horror, of sheer distress. She had held on to her stomach and rubbed it slowly, as though she was trying to fix her broken reproductive system. They had never spoken about children. They had never even discussed the idea, it was an assumption. He realised everyone thought they would be able to have children.

They had been so careful.

A part of him wished now they hadn't been. If she had

fallen pregnant before the change, Caitlin would not have to face the rest of her life without knowing what it would be like to have her own children. He hated what he had done to her. He could only hope that she would come around one day. That she would realise that a life without children might not be such a bad thing. He had never considered children, being an only child he had never sought the company of others.

The way he saw it, his feelings were irrelevant. He wanted Caitlin to be happy. He just did not know if it was the fact she could not have children, or the fact she was different, or whether she was still shocked after Emily attacked her.

He did not know a lot.

It was easier to hide his head in the sand, to pretend his life was over.

He needed to buck up his ideas. He needed to act normal, or as much as was possible. The concept of *normal* had never been so blurred.

He turned on the TV and the Xbox and got ready to play his favourite warfare game to clear his head. Then he would do what was necessary. When Jenson came, he would be ready. It was time to join the land of the living.

*

An hour later, he heard steps approaching and faced the door as he heard the lock click open.

Jenson walked in and grinned. 'You look the same to me.'

'Yeah, well, I decided to wake up,' Steven said, his face serious, 'it's amazing how a man's face changes with a shave.'

'If I were you I would have stuck to the dodgy look. From what Catherine told me, even Ingrid looked like she was put off by you,' he laughed raucously.

Steven made for his friend and gave him a friendly punch on the shoulder, 'If you were a real friend, you would stop laughing at me. But hey, I'm nothing special.'

Jenson stood up straight, 'Okay, okay.' Serious, he continued, 'I agree with you, you're nothing *special*, but…' a slight grin surfaced as he paused dramatically, and held up his thumb in the direction of the door, 'every single female out there thinks you're unattached and available. And now they know you have changed, it's open season. So, good luck blending in,' he smirked, and started for the door.

'Oh great, just what I needed. For your information, I am *attached* and *unavailable*.' Steven began to wonder whether the shower, shave and change of clothes had been a good idea after all.

'Oh, I know that, the problem is they *don't*,' Jenson chuckled again, and then called over his shoulder, 'You coming?'

'I guess I am,' Steven said. He took a deep breath, resigned to whatever fate lay ahead.

As they walked, Jenson talked, 'So, anyway, I know that no-one is talking about Caitlin, and I'm not going to ask what's going on. I've been *told* not to talk about it. So, if you want to talk we'll go somewhere we can't be heard, okay?'

Steven rolled his eyes. 'I'm all talked out.'

Jenson nodded. 'Lucky. Just so you know, given the circumstances, we have postponed the wedding. It'll happen, just not until the dust settles.'

Steven swallowed, 'You sure you want to wait?'

'It's no big deal. We can wait a few more weeks. We do have the rest of our lives together.'

Jenson sounded so matter of fact. It caught Steven off guard. He blinked a few times and wished he had shown the same restraint. 'It's a very nice gesture. I just don't know how long it'll take before Caitlin,' he hesitated, 'gets better.'

'It'll take what it takes, we'll wait. You've agreed to be my best man, and we're both really grateful. The least we can do is wait.'

Steven was lost for words. Jenson really was a true friend. It was hard to believe.

Jenson continued, 'Anyway, the community has been told that you're back. They know that Jeff, Judith and Emily are dead. You know about Emily's funeral, right?'

'Yes, I chose not to attend,' Steven pursed his lips.

'I can understand,' Jenson nodded, 'anyway, people understand you don't pose a threat to any of us,' he winked, 'some are suspicious, as usual, but they never got to you in the past so why start now, right?' he chuckled again. 'Besides, I actually think a lot of them are glad Emily's gone. She was never the heart and soul of the party. I felt sorry for her actually. Did you know she asked me to look out for you when you arrived?'

Steven glanced over. 'Is that why you became my friend?'

Jenson slapped his shoulder. 'At first, but I got your dry sense of humour straight away. I knew you were alright.'

'I'll take that as a compliment,' Steven rolled his eyes, and then changed tack, 'how's Anna?'

'Anna, hmmm,' Jenson said, and then rubbed his rough chin. It looked to Steven like he was trying to grow a beard. 'I've not seen much of her, but she looked distraught at the funeral if I'm honest. I saw her briefly the next day, and she seemed to lack her usual bounce. It's no surprise. Everyone knew she had some strange link with her sister. I guess being a twin is not an easy thing.'

Steven nodded, and then saw the familiar sign up ahead for the dining hall. It had been a while. The last time he had arrived unannounced in the community they had all pretended he did not exist, he had no idea what it would be like now.

As soon as they walked in the hall his question was answered. The room froze and practically everyone looked his way, on their faces a mixture of anger, confusion, pity and sadness. He looked away, focused on the ground and kept walking.

Jenson made idle chit chat and greeted them as they walked past. He got mumbled replies, until Steven heard a familiar voice. He moved his head up just before he was crushed by a massive hug.

Susanna beamed, 'Steven, great to see you.' She let him go, still smiling as she linked arms with Jenson and kissed his cheek.

Steven gave a half-smile. Susanna knew how to put him at ease. Jenson was a lucky man. Susanna looked more confident, glowing. The change suited her. Her hair was slightly longer, a more vibrant sandy brown, and her eyes had an extra sparkle to them. Brown never looked so good. And he knew just by the way they looked at each other, they were madly in love. He could not help clenching his jaw as a jealous pang hit him.

The atmosphere around them seemed to have changed as everyone went about their business and resumed conversations. Susanna had broken the ice, he was grateful.

'Time for food, I think,' Jenson said, as he made for the serving counters.

Steven followed. His mouth salivated, as his senses of sight and smell took in what was in front of him – Spanish cuisine. Spanish omelettes, meatballs in a thick tomato sauce, prawns in a chilli dip, assorted fish, a range of mixed salads and his favourite, paella. His mouth watered and he took a deep breath. If there was one thing he had always liked about this place it was the food.

After piling up a plate with a selection, he picked up some cutlery and followed Jenson to the familiar table. He gave a low chuckle, they still sat at the same place and a seat remained for him.

Another pair of familiar brown eyes glanced up at him. Susanna's brother, Gideon, swallowed his mouthful, got up and gave Steven a firm handshake, 'It's good to have you home.'

Steven glanced up at Gideon, who had shot up since they last met. He had lost some of his gangly youth and looked more like a man with broader shoulders and a more chiselled face. His words also showed added wisdom.

Home – Gideon was right, this was his home now.

He sat down and started to tuck into his food. Susanna and Jenson held hands and closed their eyes in a silent prayer for a minute. He guessed Jenson was going to get married the traditional way, he knew Susanna had been raised with Catholic traditions. It was sweet to see them so united. He stopped eating out of respect for them, his stepmother would have been proud. With her Catholic upbringing, she had brought him up to thank the Lord before he ate. His dad had always followed suit even though before he had met her they had never followed the tradition.

He had got out of the habit easily once away from home. It

was easier to ignore religion, to pretend it did not matter. Yet, now as he watched them he realised that perhaps a bit of faith never hurt anyone. He could do with some guidance now.

As they opened their eyes and started to eat, he tucked into the meatballs and relished the flavour. They were just like his stepmother made them. The thought made him choke. He still found it hard to believe Clara was dead, especially since his own, now dead, mother had killed her. He did not miss his real mother at all, but he would always remember the woman who raised him. Genetics could never compensate for real love. His biological mother had fallen short of the mark. She had never given him any sense that she really loved him. Emily might have claimed to love him, but her actions said otherwise. In a way, he thought her incapable of love. It hurt him to admit that he was glad she had died.

'Sorry about Emily,' Gideon said.

Steven was surprised at the remark. It was as though Gideon had tapped into his thoughts. Either way, he had not said *his mum*. He wanted to reply *I'm not*. Instead, he suppressed a smile and swallowed another meatball. With a full mouth, no-one would expect him to talk.

'It's been hard to understand everything that's been going on. We still can't believe Jeff and Judith are also gone. No one ever talked much about death until now,' Gideon continued, then ploughed another huge helping into his mouth.

If he was expecting Steven to say much he would have a long wait. Steven ate, and diverted his eyes.

Jenson stepped in, 'It's been hard for everyone to understand. We still have a lot to learn.'

'You can say that again,' Gideon scoffed, as he wiped his mouth with the back of his hand.

Susanna scowled at Gideon. 'Give Steven a chance to settle in at least.'

'It's okay,' Steven said, 'You don't need to pretend everything's okay, but I appreciate the thought. Thanks, Susanna.'

Susanna beamed at him. Steven had been harsh with her in the past. After what Jenson had told him, he had no intention of being mean to Susanna again. He was still reeling from the news they would wait.

'It's not a problem, Steven. We all want you to fit in now.'

'I know,' Steven gave a half-smile. He could not help thinking how they felt about him was irrelevant. He was not the only one they had to make welcome.

Chapter 25

Reality

Caitlin ran her hand through her auburn hair. It nearly reached her elbows now, it had grown so long and she had not exactly had time to visit a hairdressers. It all seemed so pointless now. None of it mattered. She hated what she was, who she was. It would be so much easier to end it all, to find a way out. She gritted her teeth and dropped her hands to her sides, then clenched them into fists and started to punch the wall. It hurt, but she carried on until her knuckles were bleeding. She stopped and stared at her hands, then brought them to her face and licked the blood off. The wound would heal.

She stared at the food they had brought in, a mixture of Spanish cuisine, her favourite. She would not eat it, regardless. The prawns alone brought back a memory. They were Steven's signature dish. He had seduced her and then made her fall in love with him again. If only he had left her alone. She was starting to get her life back, she had met Daniel, and everything was going great. She shook her head convinced Daniel would have dumped her anyway. Daniel had *known* she was not a virgin, even though she had forgotten all about Steven. Well, not exactly forgotten, her memory had been erased.

Then Steven brought it all back. She did not know how to feel about that.

She started to pace up and down the room, the smell of the food taunting her as she thought. The first time she met Steven she *had* felt an undeniable connection, she tried to argue that she had *not* fallen in love at first sight, but she knew the truth. Steven was the most attractive and compelling man she had ever met. She had loved everything about him. His amazing hypnotic amber eyes, his intellect and uncanny humour, his swimmer's physique, his embrace, the way he listened, and the way he made her feel. Her stomach lurched at the thought. She loved how they connected.

When she had become like Steven, when she had changed, she thought it was all amazing. She felt fantastic. She was fitter, stronger, faster, smarter, *better* than before. She accepted it all without any hesitation. She found it hard now to understand why she would think it was acceptable to kill another human being. She was not proud of killing Adam, even though she could not stand him. No-one deserved to die. She could not understand what had happened to her.

And now, karma had happened.

Her selfish thoughts, her haste to be better than she should have been, her lust had all come at a price. She would never have children. She would never know the feeling of carrying a child, or holding *her* baby in her arms. She swallowed, her throat felt like sandpaper. She had never thought about children a lot. In fact, she had grown up wishing her parents had only had her. She had always pulled a face of disgust at the thought of being a parent. She loathed the responsibility, the thought of tantrums, and the commitment. Now, she was spared all that. She could not help thinking it was all for the best.

And yet, she was empty, her heart had been eaten whole. She did not know how to love. She wanted to love, badly. She wanted to be held by Steven and to know that everything was going to be alright, that nothing mattered. But, it did. It mattered a lot.

She wrapped her arms around herself. They could not make her eat and they could not make her drink. It was easier to let go of her life. It had ended. She had become a killer and now she deserved what was coming to her. Her vision clouded over and she wiped the tears off her face. Her eyes flickered over to the food as her treacherous brain forced her to look. Her stomach contorted now, angry.

She grimaced. Her nostrils flared, and she ran over and toppled the plate on to the floor. The wooden bowl made a loud bang as it landed and the contents whooshed out. Red tomato sauce splattered all over, it could have been blood. She fell on to her knees and banged the floor, then smeared the food into the ground, crushing it. She wanted it to disappear.

With the scent all over her hands she gave a primal scream, and then scurried over to the corner of the room. In a ball, she rocked back and forth, all the time resisting the urge to lick her hands.

After a few minutes, the door opened.

It was Catherine. 'We'll have to clean this up. Come with me, Caitlin. We'll take you to another room.'

'No,' Caitlin screeched. She buried her head in her knees and started to cry. Her body shook as she let her guard down.

She was vaguely aware of the fact the door had closed. After a few minutes, she managed to stop the tears and she peeked out to see if Catherine was still there. When she saw Catherine still standing on the same spot, she flinched slightly. 'Why are you watching me?'

'I was just waiting for you to finish. Do you feel better now?' Catherine moved her head to the side, she was not smiling but she was not serious either. It was not a look of sympathy.

Caitlin brushed her tears aside with her hand and stood up straight. She kept her voice steady, even though she had to sniffle first. 'I do feel *better*.'

'Good,' Catherine said. She walked closer to Caitlin, her eyes on the ground as though she did not want to stain her leather sandals. She adopted a teacher tone, 'It's time for you to snap out of this. You need to eat. You need to focus. Your life has not ended, you have a lot to live for.'

Caitlin could have shared a lot of thoughts with her, but she restrained herself and bit her inner cheeks instead. She bit too hard and tasted blood. Immediately, her canines extended. She was a monster. She opened her mouth slightly, exposed them, and snarled, 'I am normal, right? I am NORMAL.'

'You are normal to us, yes. And here you'll be safe. Caitlin, I need to explain a few things. You've actually given us all a brighter future. I would like to share this with you. But first, you need to wash, you need to eat, and you *need* to trust us. Look, everyone's eating at the moment. I have ensured that we have safe passage, we can leave here. It'll help if you see the beauty of this place.'

Caitlin wanted to give a smart reply, but she was desperate to leave this place. She needed a change of scene. Her head hung low as she contemplated her erratic thoughts. None of this was really Steven's fault. She had been willing, she had wanted the change. She had to remind herself to stay positive, hard as it was. 'I'll do as you suggest.'

Catherine gave a broad smile, 'Okay, well you can start by drinking this.'

Caitlin looked at the dark brown bottle. It reminded her of the old style Coca Cola glass bottles. 'What is it?'

'Just drink it,' Catherine reassured, 'please.'

Caitlin took the bottle and sniffed the edge. It smelled really good, but it was not a smell she could place. The smell was earthy. It reminded her of her grandfather and his collection of old copper coins. The nostalgia alone made it appealing. She could not believe she would never see her grandfather again. He had always made her feel special. She did not know if it was the way he always had time for her, or whether it was his infectious enthusiasm. Either way, she would miss him. She focused on the bottle and drew it up to her lips. As soon as she started drinking she could not stop and she downed it in one.

She could almost feel it working its way through her system, giving her an instant kick. She handed the empty bottle back and gave a wary smile. As she did, she looked at her hands and noticed that the cuts she had made when she punched the wall were healing rapidly. She watched in awe as her hands became smooth. The lethargy she had felt for days also seemed to lift. She had so much more energy, and now she was really hungry. She could murder a pizza.

Catherine had a stash in a bag she had not even noticed her bring in, as she handed her another bottle. This time she paused when she was halfway, smiled, and then downed the rest. The depression that had weighed her down lessened. Thoughts of Steven came to mind. She was not proud of the way she had acted, she had shouted at him. She dreaded to think what he thought of her. She wouldn't be surprised if he gave her a wide berth the next time they met.

Caitlin handed back the other bottle. She grimaced as she took a whiff. It dawned on her she was filthy. She was still covered in the remnants of tomato sauce. She could not remember the last time she bathed. Her hair felt so greasy and her armpits were sticky. She would do anything for waxing and decent deodorant.

'You know you mentioned that I should have a wash,' Caitlin paused, 'I could really do with one.' She gave an uneasy smile.

Catherine nodded. Her eyes were bright, reassuring, as she spoke, 'Let's go take a walk. I'll explain as much as I can.'

Caitlin was eager to start again. Depression did not suit her – not one bit.

They walked out and started to make their way down the hall. Everything seemed to be in better focus now. She could not remember much about her arrival. The lighting was subdued, it looked like outdoor lights used during Christmas time, a long spaghetti of light. At the end of the corridor, they followed the path to the right. She wondered what was down the left. It also had a clinical edge to it. She could not see anyone around, but the walls were white, minimalistic.

At the end of the corridor they were faced with a set of lift doors and some stairs.

'We should walk, to make sure we don't inadvertently see anyone,' Catherine said, as she made for the stairs.

Caitlin followed, she did not want to come across anyone either.

It seemed like ages before they reached the bottom. The walls were made from rough rock now. When the stairs ended they walked through a tunnel. It looked as though it had been carved out, it was impressive. The sound of water made her curious and then she remembered what it might be – the waterfall. As the whooshing sound intensified she started to get excited. She could not help a smile spreading across her face when the huge cavern revealed itself. The waterfall was beautiful. The river's murky, mottled brown water came out of an opening high up in the cavern and landed on a large expanse of water. They had installed a range of coloured lighting. She had a feeling of déjà vu. She remembered seeing the same effect in St Michael's Cave, when she lived in Gibraltar as a child.

'No-one will disturb you here. Here are a few things that might come in handy. I know you must be used to a different way,' Catherine handed over a toiletry bag, 'I'll come back in half an hour, then we'll go get some food. Have fun.'

'It's not going to be difficult.'

Caitlin watched Catherine walk away. She unzipped the bag. Her face lit up as she saw a shaver, shower gel, shampoo and conditioner. She took the bag and its contents to the water's edge. Metal rungs had been attached to the side, and on the other side she could see smaller rock pools, behind the waterfall. She considered whether to dive in or use the rungs. As she mulled it over, she stripped off. Decision made, she dived in. If the water was shallow she could handle it, she had done many shallow dives as a competitive swimmer.

When she entered the water she felt every nerve ending relax. The water was lukewarm. She swam breaststroke underwater, before she surfaced. She turned on her back and swam backstroke at her leisure. It was strange to swim naked, she had never done that before. It was strangely liberating.

Chapter 26

Blood

Ingrid had never walked so slowly. Catherine made it clear she *had* to go see Caitlin, she had this idea that Caitlin would tell Ingrid why she was not well. Ingrid did not hold high hopes for that. Even though they had become friends, she doubted Caitlin would open up to her. Either way, Catherine was convinced Ingrid would bridge the gap. She also wanted Ingrid to explain about the new blood. Ingrid pursed her lips, and paused at the entrance to the cavern. She took a deep breath, and straightened up, she could do this. She could be the best friend to the man she was in love with. She could.

There was no splashing sound when she entered, which was a bit strange. She made her way over to the water's edge and looked at the expanse of water, then turned to face the waterfall. She fidgeted with the clothes and towel in her hands and scrunched up her nose. She could not see any sign of Caitlin anywhere.

She turned to leave, but something caught the corner of her eye. She turned and saw Caitlin's face poking out from behind the rock pools.

Caitlin's eyed widened, before she broke out into a smile. 'It's you.'

Ingrid walked in her direction, more at ease. Caitlin sounded relaxed, it was a start.

Caitlin raised her voice, 'Don't come too close,' then she lowered her voice to a whisper, 'I'm *naked*.'

Ingrid had to chuckle. 'So?'

'You can't see me naked, I don't like it. I…oh, I don't have any excuse. I just don't like it,' Caitlin gave an uneasy laugh.

'It's okay. I have some clothes for you to wear. And some other things Catherine thought you might need. We make our own deodorant here.'

'Really?' Caitlin's eyes widened again, but she still remained behind the rock. 'Okay, I'll get changed first. Can

171

you turn around, please?'

'No problem.' Ingrid faced the opposite direction. She found Caitlin's insecurity reassuring. She talked to make the situation easier, 'What did you think of the waterfall?'

She heard Caitlin's voice closer up this time, 'It's amazing. I feel so much better now that I'm clean. Can I ask you something?'

'Sure.'

Ingrid could hear hesitation in Caitlin's voice as she asked, 'Do you also remove your hair?

Ingrid's lips curled up and she flicked her hair to the side as she said, 'I have my hair cut every now and again, but I like it long.'

After a slight pause, Caitlin continued, 'No, I didn't mean your head hair. Erm, I meant your *underarm* hair. I have not had any since I was twelve. I hate it, it makes me smell and it's uncomfortable. Do you remove it here?'

'Oh, underarm hair,' Ingrid feigned surprise, 'no, we don't remove it actually. But, we know women do where you come from. A search of the web reveals all sorts of interesting habits. There is something called waxing, I believe – it looks extremely painful. None of us understand why anyone would do such a thing.'

'I have had waxing in the past, it doesn't hurt that much once you get used to it.' Caitlin stood next to Ingrid. 'I couldn't afford it as a student, so I just shaved.'

'Oh yes, you have to pay for everything there,' Ingrid mused, glad to see Caitlin clothed again. 'Maybe you could teach us about this waxing. It could be your skill. If it's worth it, I'm sure you'll have people interested.'

'As much as I could teach you, I really doubt it would be my skill. I am not a sadist. Besides, what do you mean exactly by *skill*?'

'Well, we don't have money here, but everyone has to pull their weight. So, we all focus on the things we are best at,' Ingrid paused slightly, she could not believe her luck. This line of questioning was taking her exactly where she wanted to go. She tried to sound casual, 'I am scientific, so I work in the laboratories.'

'Really? I liked Science, but I am more mathematical and enjoy learning Spanish. Even though I grew up next to Spain it was only when I left Gibraltar at the age of twelve that I really got to find out about the culture, the food, and way of life.'

'Gibraltar? The Rock of Gibraltar? Interesting place... from what I have heard. It doesn't have the best relationship with Spain though, does it?' Ingrid arched an eyebrow.

'No, that's an understatement,' Caitlin laughed, 'I never missed waiting in a queue for over 2 hours at the frontier to get into Spain – don't know why we bothered most of the time. And I never embraced the Spaniards' love of bull fighting.'

'They kill for sport and prestige. It's not a good thing, right?'

'No, not for those reasons, but then again who are we to argue with tradition? It brings people together. Many cultures do things that we consider strange. Take for example the use of ivory in China. There's no way to know if some of the ivory was bought via the black market, and don't get me started on shark fin soup. I have always had a fascination with sharks...' Caitlin trailed, her cheeks flushed pink, 'I'm rambling again. I have a habit of doing that.'

'It's okay,' Ingrid smiled, 'I'm interested. Your upbringing makes you a different person. It's good for all of us to learn from each other. I've learnt a lot from you. In fact,' she bit her lip slightly, 'you've given us all the potential for a new future.'

'Me? What have I done? I have nothing to offer the community,' her shoulders drooped.

'Let's walk and I'll tell you about it, you're probably hungry anyway.'

Caitlin put her hand on her stomach. 'I'm starving now. Whatever Catherine gave me to drink made me feel better, that's for sure.'

'That's actually where you've helped us,' Ingrid said.

'The drink, what do you mean?' Caitlin stopped walking.

'Okay,' Ingrid paused, her eyes shifted uneasily, 'basically for years we've been testing different varieties of blood. We've been trying to create blood that could heal us, that could enable the change.' Ingrid glanced over at Caitlin. She was looking ahead, serious. She continued, 'Steven's blood was slightly different, but it still was not what we needed. But, and I'm sorry we did this without asking you first, we tested your blood and we believe it's a perfect match. We found a way to use its genetic code, to sequence it. And the drink you had is the product. Catherine said it healed your hand.'

Caitlin nodded. 'It did.'

'Are you angry with us?'

Caitlin sighed, 'No, how can I be. There had to be something good out of what I've become.' She fidgeted with her hands, and then asked, 'So, will it enable the change?'

'We have to test it, we'll know soon. I just wanted you to know that you have enabled something amazing. It could change everything.' Ingrid tried to restrain her excitement, 'We would not have to kill if we can mass produce the drink for the entire community. It is an incredible outcome.'

'I'm happy for you, really,' Caitlin said.

Ingrid stopped and put her hand on Caitlin's shoulder. 'We're all indebted to you. I know the decision to be one of us can't have been an easy one.'

Caitlin brushed off her hand. 'The decision to change was very easy, it just happened. It's what I am now that's hard to handle,' her frame tensed, 'I've lost a lot.'

'Yes, you've left behind your life, your friends, and family. It's not easy to...'

Caitlin interrupted, 'I have lost a lot more than that, but I'm sure you know this already. Catherine told you, didn't she?'

Ingrid shook her head from side to side. 'She hoped you'd tell me. If you do, I promise I won't tell anyone. I trust you with everything I've said.'

'Okay then,' Caitlin walked on, then stopped at the entrance and looked back, her eyes brimming with tears. In a choked voice, she said, 'I'll never have children of my own.' Then she carried on walking, her shoulders visibly shaking.

Ingrid's jaw slackened, she never imagined that. She had not had any yet, but she always imagined she would someday. The option was always there.

She rushed to catch up with Caitlin, who had come to a standstill, now in floods of tears.

She threw her arms around her and held her tight. Caitlin put her arms around her and cried really hard. For the first time ever, Ingrid actually felt like someone needed her friendship. It was nice, even though Caitlin was the last person she would ever have thought she would empathise with. There had to be some irony in that.

It took a few minutes for Caitlin to calm down before she backed away and said, 'I'm sorry, I didn't mean to break down like that. I thought I could handle it, I-I...' her lower lip wobbled again.

'It's okay, no-one needs to know. I'll take you back. When you're ready then we'll talk about letting everyone know about you. I think Catherine wanted you to know you would be safe.'

'Safe?' Caitlin licked her lower lip, her brow furrowed.

Ingrid hesitated slightly before she replied, 'Of course. You realise your blood is, well, different to ours?'

'Different?' The furrow deepened.

'Yes, as I explained. Your blood can heal us, it was the missing link. I thought you realised when Emily attacked you,' she tried to sound matter of fact, 'our blood has never healed anyone before, it was the reason I knew Steven was not normal.'

She saw Caitlin's mouth form a circle, her face now one of astonishment not bemusement. 'I see.'

They continued to walk up the stairs, Caitlin deep in thought. Ingrid did not want to say anything else, she had assumed Caitlin had realised the consequences of what she'd said earlier.

Ingrid led Caitlin to Else's office. They had to pass the laboratories and she could see Caitlin's face harden as she observed those at work.

When they got to the door, Ingrid faced Caitlin before she knocked. 'You'll be safe, you know that, right?'

Caitlin pursed her lips. 'If you say so.'

Ingrid knocked, and then opened the door. Else was waiting as anticipated.

'Caitlin, you look much better,' Else said, as she stood up to greet them. 'Ingrid, are you staying?'

'I'll be in the lab, let me know if I can be of any help. Can I speak to you outside a minute?'

'Sure, please sit down, Caitlin,' Else smiled.

Once outside, Ingrid switched to their unique language. It was rarely used, but in these circumstances was useful, 'I have explained what we have been able to do with her blood, but she's still worried that she might not be safe. Can you reassure her?'

'Of course,' Else nodded and went back in.

Ingrid made her way to the prep room. Once there she found her long, white jacket. Then she tied up her hair in a band, placed a white cap over it and covered her mouth with a mask. Then she slipped on a pair of skin tight, transparent gloves. She pressed the code into the keypad and the automated door swung inwards. She walked through and flicked through the chart. The cell count was steady. The blood was perfect so far. Caitlin was the first person to drink it, and heal from it. Catherine had noted the success.

She put the chart back and went to find Eilif. She found him by the centrifuge.

'What are you working on?'

'I'm trying to find out if there are any more properties about Caitlin's blood we can use. It's going to take a while to test them all, but I think it'll be worth it,' he smiled, 'how is she?'

'She's doing okay,' she changed the conversation, 'who's going to change soon? Who'll be trialling the blood?'

'There are a few. Kayla, Tobias and Lisbeth are due their change. Tobias is first.'

'Can I be there to help?' Ingrid asked.

'Of course,' Eilif replied, 'he's coming in tomorrow. The timing is just about perfect.'

'Tomorrow it is then. Is everything ready?'

'Do you know me at all, daughter?'

Ingrid grinned. 'Of course.'

Chapter 27

Breakthrough

Caitlin knew she was not stupid, she was supposedly extremely intelligent, and yet she found it hard to believe what Ingrid, and now Else, claimed.

'You understand that unless we tell people, no-one will ever know that your blood can heal us,' Else clasped her hands in front of her, 'the few of us that know will never tell anyone.'

'And how are you going to explain the new discovery, the new blood?' Caitlin slouched back against the chair.

'We've been working on the cure for a long time, but I see your concern. We need to explain how you came to be here. That alone will raise questions,' she nodded.

'Exactly, you have to explain who I am,' Caitlin said, as she sat up slightly.

'Let *us* worry about that, you just have to decide when you want to meet everyone. Do you want to join our community?'

Caitlin stared at the stone floor for a long minute. She looked up, and answered, 'Not yet. I'd like some more time.'

Else leaned forward as she spoke, 'Steven would like to see you. He comes to check on you every day. Are you ready to speak to him now?'

She hesitated slightly before she replied, 'Yes, I'd like to talk to him.'

'I'll take you back to Steven's room then, you'll be more comfortable there I think. And I think you still need to eat?'

'Yes,' she knew she sounded defeated. Caitlin had tried to ignore the hunger, but she could not stand it any longer. 'I'm really hungry.'

'Okay, let's get you some food then,' Else pressed a button on her desk and spoke, 'please send food to room C35, urgent. Thank you.' She got up and ushered Caitlin out.

As Caitlin passed the laboratories again, she saw Ingrid leaning over a microscope. She was completely kitted out, just like a proper scientist. She did not know why that surprised her. Once they were out of the main corridor, Caitlin expected to bump into someone. She wanted to see what they all looked like if she was honest. And yet, they saw no-one.

'How come there's no-one around?'

Else laughed. 'Where you come from people stop a lot. Here we're always working during the day, but it's a social thing. Most of us would class work as a hobby. So, you will not see anyone in their accommodation until bedtime. There's no need to be in your room until you are planning to sleep, is there?'

'No, I guess not.' Caitlin was sure they'd all be shocked at the amount of times she had just relaxed on her bed during the day listening to music, doing nothing. Lazy, but hey, she quite liked that. She remembered Steven enjoying her lazy days too.

When they got to the room Caitlin was relieved to see some familiar items again.

Else held out her hand. 'Take the key. Only unlock the door for someone you know, although, anyone who's supposed to be here will have a key. You're not a prisoner here, but if you leave you'll bump into people. It's your choice.'

'Thanks.' Caitlin took the key and put it in her shorts pocket. Her mouth watered as she smelled her food. She turned around and saw the same Spanish selection she had discarded earlier on the table. 'Do you mind if I go eat?'

'No, I'll see you soon. We're all indebted to you, Caitlin. You have changed our future.'

Caitlin headed for the food, broke a piece of bread off the roll and dipped it in the chilli sauce, then stuffed it in her mouth. She nodded, but her focus was elsewhere. She sat down and pierced the prawn with her fork then relished the taste as she chewed.

She barely saw Else make her way out. She found it funny that they were supposedly indebted to her. She did not see what the big deal was anyway. It wasn't like they were going anywhere in a hurry, and the odd person they killed to enable the change was hardly going to be missed. She did not get why this *new blood* changed anything. There was something they were not telling her. She did not know why she thought it, but it would make more sense if it were true.

It shocked her to see the empty plates in front of her after ten minutes had passed. There had been enough food to feed at least two, if not more people. She put her hands on her stomach and sat back, well and truly stuffed. She loosened the top button of her shorts and stood up. Then she browsed the CD collection, placed one in the CD player and started to sway as the music started. She missed her iPod. It seemed ancient to listen to just one CD. She normally had a playlist with loads of tracks. She called it her mixed allsorts, part of the fun was seeing what track would come on.

As the bass intensified, she turned up the sound and closed her eyes. She wanted to get lost in the music. She needed to escape.

As a pair of hands slipped over her waist she spun around in shock, only to come face to face with Steven. The familiar half-smile pasted on his face, his amber eyes wide, amused.

She did not want to hold him just yet, so she ducked under his arms and slipped out, then lowered the music. 'Sorry, I was just…'

'It's great to see you dancing, really great.' His look intensified, she felt like he was burning a hole through her.

Caitlin's stomach twitched. She tried to relax, but the fact he was there made her nervous.

Steven got closer, his hand cupped her cheek and she had to face him. His proximity made her even more on edge. She stared into his eyes and got lost as he leaned closer and their lips touched. He gave her a light peck, and then kissed her cheek and her forehead, his arms now wrapped around her. She could not stop her arms going around his. He hugged her tighter, and she nuzzled into his chest. She felt protected.

'I missed you so much, I've been so worried. I love you Caitlin, I always will.'

The words melted her completely and she found herself swallowing back tears again, she was annoyed. She had never cried at the drop of a hat, yet over the past 12 hours all she did was cry. It was pathetic. She could not bear to let him see her watery eyes so she kept her face firmly on his chest and took deep breaths to calm down.

She was sure he sensed her unease because he did not let go. He just held her, one hand lightly stroking the back of her neck, the other rubbing her lower back. It was soothing. She knew that to kiss him again, to really kiss him, would only lead in one direction. She wanted to, really badly, and she guessed nothing stopped them. There was no more *risk*.

When Caitlin eased her head back she found his face was but an inch away as he leant down towards her. She bridged the gap and rubbed her nose gently against his, before she got even closer and kissed him. This time the kiss deepened and intensified.

It was Steven who paused, 'Caitlin, we don't have to do anything. We don't have to rush. I ...'

Caitlin pressed her fingers to his lips, and smiled. She did not want to think, or talk, or cry. She just wanted to love him, and to let him love her in return.

***

Steven had never been the type to cry, but now he was actually emotional. He could not believe he was lucky enough to have Caitlin's love. He could tell something had changed in her, the events of the past week had broken down her defences, had allowed her to follow her heart, not her head. He wanted to jump around and scream at the top of his voice, 'she loves me'. Instead, he was choked. They were lying side by side, her sweat still lingered on his naked form, and he was spent. They had never made love like that before. It had been so intimate, and yet desperate.

Out of breath, he whispered, 'You complete me.'

Caitlin rolled onto her side and flung her arm over his torso. 'And you me.'

Again the words melted him further. He squeezed his eyes tight and felt a small dribble of water run out of the sides. He blinked a few times and kept it together as he held her body against his with one hand, and grabbed the loose sheet with the other. The sheet gave some needed cover as their sweat cooled.

A few minutes later, he heard Caitlin's deep breathing and her body twitched, before it went limp.

He kissed the top of her head and eased out from under her.

He was not surprised she was tired. As far as he knew, it was the first time she'd had a proper meal in days. She had had a lot to deal with, he knew the feeling. He remembered how horrified he had been when his life had been determined for him and he had been forced to leave everything behind in England.

Right now, after being so close to Caitlin, he could not regret having gone back to find her. They were meant to be together, and if they weren't going to have children together then so be it. He wanted Caitlin, not her children. It had always been about Caitlin. He wanted to spend the rest of his life with her, to see the world with her. The last thought pulled him up short. In the community they would be stuck. Their fate bound by those around them. Yet, he doubted they would let them leave even though it made sense. A life of seclusion was not what Caitlin needed, at least he doubted it.

He would talk to Catherine. There had to be a solution. They could not expect Caitlin to live surrounded by women who could reproduce indefinitely, he imagined that life would be like having salt rubbed in a wound every day of your life.

He sat by Caitlin and moved her hair off her face. She looked so peaceful, childlike in her sleep. She had no idea how beautiful she was. Her alabaster skin, speckled with tiny freckles and her vibrant, curls of red hair were his idea of perfection. He knew she had never considered herself to be special. His could not help breaking out into a smile. She was right, she was not *just* special. She was extraordinary, unique – his soul mate. Destiny was playing a game of chess against them.

He would go and talk to Catherine. Now he had Caitlin back he wanted to know what they were planning to do. He wanted to be prepared, to have something good to tell Caitlin, and have something to look forward to. A future in the community was not likely to satisfy either of them, not anymore. Caitlin deserved more and they owed her. If her blood led to the ultimate discovery, the least they could do was ensure a secure and happy future for her.

It was the least any of them could do.

Chapter 28

Preparations

Ian checked the list again. His eyes darted over the names. It seemed like he had gone over it a million times already and yet he was still not convinced the right decision had been made.

Carmen put a mug of coffee in front of him. 'It's going to be fine.'

Ian put his hands around the mug, then lifted it up to his mouth and breathed in. The smell alone had a calming effect. He took a sip, relished the bitter taste, and stared at the list again. 'What do you really think? Is this madness?'

Carmen put her hand on his shoulder and squeezed. He turned to face her, and stared into her dark brown eyes as she spoke, 'The history of mankind is no different to our own. It is time for some of us to start anew somewhere else, to create a new way of life. Those that have put their names forward to go are the adventure seekers, the pioneers. If we didn't let them go now, they would find a way eventually. I don't think this will destroy our community, it'll make it stronger. It gives us more options.'

Ian gave a slight nod and smiled. 'When did you become so wise?'

'Hah,' Carmen mock frowned, 'you men would be lost without us women around to bring some sense into your lives.'

'Of course, how stupid of me to forget,' Ian rolled his eyes, then reached out and grabbed her, forcing her unto his lap. He held her tightly around the waist. Their jokey expressions became more serious as his hand slid up her back and made its way to her face. He eased in and kissed her softly.

She pulled away. 'I can help you relax.'

'Can you now?' his lips curled up.

'Hmm hmm.' She got off his lap, held his hand and led him to the bed, her eyes never leaving his.

Ian still found it hard to believe this magnificent woman

had chosen to be his wife and the mother of his children. Time did not change a thing. He still regarded her as he had the first day they had kissed.

An hour later, as Ian was about to doze off, he made the decision to meet with the originals. It was time to move on with the plans. What had happened with Steven should not change anything at all. Besides, after speaking to Catherine he was convinced the discovery of the latest strain of new blood would made things easier.

*

Ian surveyed the group. These meetings, now a regular occurrence, took their toll.

He began, 'The list has now been finalised. After much consideration, it's been decided to start the colony in Borneo with a modest sized group of 30. More can move over with time, as the site is developed. It will take time. Isaac, Catherine, are you happy with the progress made to date?'

Isaac rubbed his chin, 'We've surveyed the island and identified areas where we could settle and build the community. We had to tap in to several satellites, but,' he chuckled, 'this was not a problem.'

'What we are most interested in knowing is *who* will join us?' Catherine asked, leaning forward.

Franco huffed, 'I would hope that a lot of my family have shown common sense.' He glanced over at Juan and gave a slight nod of the head.

Ian had no doubt that some gentle persuasion had convinced many of their family to exclude their names from the list. 'You have nothing to fear. The only member of your family that has requested to move is Lucy.'

Franco scowled, 'Lucy? Why would my daughter want to leave? She's happy here and does a good job in produce. Who would replace her? She can't go. I hope you refused her request.'

'She will be coming with us,' Catherine added, her eyes narrowed, 'Lucy has as much of a right to excitement in her life as any of us.'

'What do you mean *excitement*?' Franco spluttered, 'she's

my daughter. I know what's best for her.'

Catherine pursed her lips and met his glare.

Ian intervened, even though he really didn't want to. 'Lucy's on the list.'

Juan banged his fist on the table. 'I've not seen Lucy in days, where is she anyway?'

'What do you mean?' Franco asked, his right eyebrow arched.

Catherine made eye contact with Ian before she spoke, 'Lucy has gone to Borneo already. She's gone to investigate.'

'On whose authority?' Franco snapped.

Catherine glanced at him again. Ian wondered what was going on. He would ask later. He held up his hands. 'Look, we need to get back on track. I'm sure Lucy is capable and went on her own authority,' Franco and Juan did not look happy, but he continued, 'as you all know, the testing for the new blood is going to happen in the next few days. Tobias is due his change and Eilif is confident that it'll work. Catherine has agreed to go with Eilif and Tobias into the jungle, close to a native tribe, just in case the blood fails.'

Morten, who had chosen to keep quiet up to that point, stepped in, 'That is wise. And the girl, Caitlin isn't it, she is better?'

Ian turned to Catherine, 'I'll let my sister explain.'

Catherine faced Morten, 'She's stable and back with Steven. We'll introduce her to the community soon. Even though there will be questions, we cannot keep her away from everyone indefinitely.'

'Indeed, and Steven? He's settled in?' Morten asked.

'As much as he ever was,' Catherine said. 'I have seen the list for Borneo and neither Steven nor Caitlin are on it. I believe, as does Isaac, they should be allowed to go. A new start for them would be wise.'

'Perhaps?' Ian said, 'But, they'll not be of much use in building the site and harnessing its potential. They should be left here until the site is established.'

'At last, we agree on something,' Franco sneered.

'I disagree,' Catherine continued, 'If they're allowed to

help create the site, it will make it their home. Caitlin, in particular, needs to get away. As you all know the change has made her different.'

Anna's face tensed. She held Juan's hand as she spoke, her voice unsteady, 'Caitlin's choice came at a price. We are all very sorry that she will never conceive, but at least she is alive and well.'

Ian had barely heard his sister talk since Emily's funeral. It was like a part of her had broken when her twin died. It hurt Ian to see Anna in such obvious distress. The death of their parents had come as a shock to all of them, but the added impact of Emily's death had sent Anna over the edge.

Catherine bit her lower lip. 'We all know she's lucky to be alive, Anna. But, we do owe her a decent life. Her blood…'

'*Might*,' Juan interrupted, 'help us. But, then again it might not. She is no more entitled to a good life than the rest of us. They are many youngsters that are keen to leave. That does not mean we will let them. If they go, others will want to join them.'

'Perhaps, no-one should know about Caitlin then?' Isaac suggested.

They all turned to face him.

Ian asked, 'What do you mean?'

'If she leaves for Borneo immediately, or as soon as she is able, then no-one needs to know about her, do they?' he clasped his hands together, 'it would make things easier. How would introducing her benefit this community?'

'And what about Steven?' Franco narrowed his eyes.

'It's easier to explain the need for Steven to go. A lot of people have found it hard to accept him. A problem gone is a problem forgotten.'

Ian nodded. 'It might be a good solution. If we allow Steven and Caitlin to leave with Catherine and Isaac, they might have a shot at a decent life. However, if we feel Caitlin should be introduced then we will. This process might take months. We cannot keep her confined for that long.'

'Yes, it wouldn't be fair on the girl. We'll leave the decision to Catherine,' Morten said.

'Anyone not in favour?' Ian asked. When he saw no-one raise their hand he relaxed. He guessed Franco would be happy to see the back of him. It was obvious he still considered Steven's existence to be an aberration. 'Good, well in that case, we'll meet again in a few days' time. Then we'll have a better idea on what the future holds. I'm sure we'll all be glad to not have to kill for blood.'

Even though he firmly believed this, he worried some people would miss the need to kill. Then again, if they did not kill for the change there would be no justification to kill for survival anymore.

As they all got up to leave, Ian glanced at Catherine. She indicated Isaac leave without her with a wave of her hand and then gave Anna a quick hug as she walked past. Ian was saddened again by the fact Anna barely returned the embrace. Her enthusiasm had been zapped. Juan held Anna's hand and led her out. If there was something that reassured him it was the fact Juan loved Anna. It was the only reason he had tolerated his brother-in-law over the years. No matter how misconstrued and easily led he was by his father, Franco.

Once they had all left, Catherine closed the door again. The room was soundproof, it was lucky. 'Lucy's under my care. As far as everyone should be concerned she's left and might never come back.'

'Is she alright?' Ian could not help but be concerned. A part of him still felt guilty for rejecting her all those years earlier. She was a lovely woman, but he had fallen in love with Carmen. It was not his fault.

'I can't tell you what the problem is, but we're doing what we can to help her. She's got herself into a tricky situation.'

Ian had no idea of what that could be. 'Do I need to know what it is?'

'No, you don't need to know. Not right now, anyway.'

'In that case, I leave her under your care. I'm sure you know what you're doing. Is Tobias ready, does he know he's our guinea pig, so as to speak?'

'We've explained it to him, he's happy to try,' Catherine blinked a few times, 'we know what to do if it fails.'

'Success could change everything.'

Catherine smiled. 'It could indeed. What a life we could lead then. It's a shame there's no Noble prize in the community, I've always fancied having a few accolades' behind my name.'

'Vanity,' Ian sighed, with a cheeky grin.

'You know Ingrid has been a big help. She's exceptional really. She explained the test to Tobias. I believe it would help me if she came, just in case Tobias decides to run. She can calm him down.'

Ian shrugged his shoulders. 'Talk to Eilif, if he wants her to go I don't have a problem with it.'

'In that case I will.'

'Thanks for everything, sis, Dad would be proud of you,' Ian smiled.

'Both of them were proud of you, little brother. Sis, huh,' she shook her head. 'I am your elder, *wiser* sister, I'll have you know.'

'If it makes you feel better, then fine. We all know the truth,' he smirked.

Catherine laughed. She stopped, on another thought, 'Do you think Anna will be back to her normal self soon?'

'I don't know,' Ian squirmed, 'she seems lost. I don't know what any of us can do. You would have thought that with Emily gone she would be free. She always said that she hated their connection, whatever that was. It's almost as though something else is affecting her. But, I can't imagine what that would be?'

'No, neither can I?' Catherine agreed, her eyes focused now.

'You look like something has come to your mind?' he could tell she was lost on another thought.

Catherine moved towards the door. 'No, nothing at all. Best get on. Keep up the good work, little bro.' She gave a little giggle and made her way out.

Ian shook his head and chuckled as locked the door. He was glad he had a big sister, he could not imagine coping with any of this without her.

Chapter 29

New Blood

Catherine hurried back to the laboratory. She wanted to talk to Ingrid and Eilif first, and then catch up with Else and Lucy. The past few days had gone by in a whirlwind. She had neglected her teaching and assigned other leaders to take her place. Her decision to leave the community impacted her role as mental agility coordinator. If she was honest, she missed it. There was beauty in using the mind. Numbers fascinated her. And yet, over the past few months she had learnt a lot about herself. Things she never knew she would enjoy.

The fact was she liked taking charge. Even Isaac seemed to enjoy his newfound position of power. Things were going to change for them as they took on the role of leaders in Borneo. She strangely relished the challenge. In the community, they had opted to raise their family and work hard. They never wanted to lead. In a way, she hoped they would be good leaders because of the fact they didn't necessarily want the job. She doubted the role would go to their heads, at least she hoped it wouldn't.

Once at the lab, she tapped on the window to get their attention. When Ingrid looked up, Catherine smiled and pointed to the entrance. Ingrid held up her hand to indicate five minutes, and then spoke to Eilif, who glanced in Catherine's direction and nodded.

Catherine was glad Else was in her office. She walked through the open door, 'Can we talk?' She closed the door behind her. Once she was within reaching distance, she whispered, 'How is Lucy?'

'Bigger,' Else raised her eyebrows.

'I found a way to keep everyone from looking for her.'

'That's good,' Else said, 'No questions?'

'No. In fact, she could be gone a long time and no-one would bat an eyelid.'

'Impressive. In that case we can relax. She still has a few

more weeks before she has to deliver, at best it might be two months.'

'Would she be able to travel before then? Catherine asked.

'Travel?' Else frowned, 'No, I wouldn't encourage it.'

'Okay, so she'll have to have the babies here then.'

Else stood up, 'We've never dealt with a multiple birth. I'm making all the arrangements and have set up an incubation room. The chances are that the babies will need help when they're born. I'll need some of my staff to help. They will of course keep quiet. I only employ staff I trust, those with discretion.'

'Thank you, I know you'll do your best. I'll go and check on her later. First, I need to talk to Ingrid and Eilif. They'll leave with Tobias tomorrow.'

Else nodded. 'Are you convinced the new blood will work?'

'Are you not?'

'I have some doubts,' Else shrugged her shoulders, 'but we'll see.'

Catherine made her way to the door, glanced back and gave a small smile before she left. At least Lucy was in good hands.

She met Ingrid and Eilif at the entrance to the lab. 'Ian has given you the go ahead to come and help with Tobias.'

Ingrid beamed and lightly punched the air. 'Excellent.'

'I'm happy for you,' Eilif said, 'are you coming to see Tobias with us?'

'Sure,' Catherine said. She followed them down the corridor to the medical suites. She was relieved Lucy was well hidden. Else had made sure no-one would bump into her unless it was intentional.

They came to a small room where Tobias was housed. They did not want to risk him being in the general accommodation this time. They needed to get to their destination well on time, so that he was not comatose when he had to drink the blood.

Eilif opened the door. Tobias was lying down on the bed reading a book. He sat up and put the book aside as they walked in, he stared at Ingrid and his cheeks flushed.

'Tobias, all well?'

'Ye-Yes,' Tobias said, he peeled his eyes off Ingrid and stared at the floor.

Catherine ignored the reaction, and said, 'Good news, we're leaving in the morning.'

'W-We are?' Tobias asked.

'Yes, the three of us will be with you. Ian has agreed that it's best for Ingrid to come along. You're in good hands,' Catherine said, 'we wanted to make sure you're happy about everything.'

'Th-Thank you, I'm glad Ingrid's also coming,' Tobias hesitated, as two deep dimples formed, 'and I'm fine about the new procedure.'

The way he glanced quickly at Ingrid before he averted his eyes left Catherine in no doubt that a serious crush had developed. It amused her, yet she suppressed the smile. She sat on the chair. 'Procedure is too harsh a word. All you have to do is drink. If we do our job right you'll change and become one of us. For the first time ever, one of us will have changed without the need to kill an ordinary human. It's ground breaking.'

Tobias kept his eyes to the floor.

'Tobias, we're all really proud of you for agreeing to do this,' Ingrid added.

Tobias raised his head and smiled at her, the colour on his cheeks now a deeper red.

Eilif raised his eyebrows suggestively and gave a half-smile in Catherine's direction. This time she couldn't hold back, her lips curled and she bit her inner cheek.

'Right well, if you're happy about everything then I'll leave you with Eilif and Ingrid and see you tomorrow,' Catherine said, then made her way out of the room.

She heard Eilif get out the equipment to check Tobias blood pressure and symptoms. They were leaving nothing to chance with this one. Tobias would turn twenty in three days. Then they would find out if the new blood they had designed worked. If it did many opportunities would arise.

Catherine made her way over to Lucy's room. It was at the end of the corridor where they had converted one of the soundproofed research rooms. It was best to not think about the research that had been carried out there in the past.

She typed in the code and heard the door click as it unlocked. She opened it, and found herself in a box room, with another door on the other side. Once she had secured the main door she opened the secondary entrance. The sight of Lucy lying on the bed made her hold her breath. Lucy had got a lot bigger in the space of days. Lucy was fast asleep, perspiration dripped down her forehead.

Catherine dipped a cloth in the water basin, scrunched it, and pressed it against her forehead.

'Thank you,' Lucy whispered, as her eyelids fluttered and she slowly opened her eyes.

Catherine took the cloth off her head, immersed it in the water and repeated the process.

'Can I have some water?' Lucy asked.

Catherine filled the empty glass with water from the jug and helped Lucy sit up as she handed it over.

Lucy wiggled up and took the glass. She downed it in one, and then wiped her mouth with the back of her hand.

'Better?' Catherine asked. 'You should eat something. Your food looks untouched.'

'I know. I just felt queasy before. I might try to eat again.'

Catherine picked up the plate of food and handed it over. Lucy tentatively took a bite of the bread and chewed slowly.

'Do you need more blood?'

Lucy sighed, 'Yes.'

Catherine opened one of the bottles. Lucy held out her hand and drank it quickly. Her eyes took on a new shine, but her shoulders remained slumped.

Suddenly, Lucy gave a shriek of pain and dropped the plate on the floor as she grabbed her side. Catherine quickly held Lucy's upper body and rocked her gently. Tears saturated Catherine's top.

'Catherine, I don't know if I can handle this,' Lucy winced, 'it's so painful. The way they kick me, it really hurts.'

'Let me get a bath ready for you. It might help,' Catherine pulled back and helped Lucy on to the bed.

'Okay, thank you.'

Five minutes later, Catherine returned to help Lucy get to the bathroom. When Lucy got up her knees bent down and she grabbed her huge belly, and then groaned, 'My pelvis. It's in agony.'

'Okay, take it slow.' Catherine felt so sorry for Lucy. She had been pregnant several times, but she had never been in that amount of pain. She knew other women had difficulty, but she was one of the lucky ones.

She started to help Lucy undress.

'It's okay,' Lucy froze, 'just give me some time alone. I can do this. I'll call you if I need help.'

'I'll be outside,' Catherine eased out of the room.

Twenty minutes later, Catherine knocked on the door,' Lucy, are you okay?' When there was no reply, she gently pushed open the door. 'Lucy?'

The sight of red water made her gulp. She lifted an unconscious Lucy out of the water and quickly laid her on the bed, before she pressed the emergency button. The babies did not want to wait another minute. She raised Lucy's legs to check for dilation and was not surprised to find she was fully dilated.

Catherine shook Lucy's face slightly to try to wake her up, but had no success. She took her blood pressure and found it was really weak. She had lost too much blood.

A few minutes later, Else entered, quickly followed by Doctor Johannes and a few other assistants.

'How long has she been unconscious for?' Else fired.

'No longer than ten, maybe fifteen minutes. She was in the bath, I didn't realise,' Catherine hesitated, 'I'm sorry.'

'It's not your fault,' Doctor Johannes snapped, 'the babies need to come out now. With her unconscious, we'll have to do a C-section. Get the prep room ready now,' he barked at the assistants.

They scurried off into the adjoining room and returned to carry Lucy into the next room after no time at all.

Doctor Johannes raised his voice again, 'We're losing her. Let's hurry.'

Catherine's eyes widened. She could not understand what they meant by losing her. They could not *lose* her. All they needed was blood, she rushed out the room in search of Eilif, and tried to ignore the fact she was splattered in Lucy's blood.

As she reached Tomas's room, she found Eilif outside. At least he was alone. 'I need some of the new blood, I need it now.'

Eilif held out his hands, 'We only have a small amount, and it's for Tobias. You look a state, what's happened?'

'I need the blood, don't ask me to explain now, please.'

Eilif scrunched his eyes, 'Okay. Follow me and give me a quick explanation, it's the least you can do.'

'Okay, let's go.'

As they raced down the corridor and made their way to the lab, Catherine explained someone was injured. She could not tell him it was Lucy.

From the tone of his voice she could tell Eilif was not impressed, but he gave her the blood he had, 'I hope you know what you're doing. I'll start production and try to make more in time for Tobias. Otherwise, we'll have no choice. He will have to kill.'

'Okay, thank you. Don't follow me, please.' Catherine raced back.

Once she had got past the security doors, she raced into the room. She could see them all working quickly around Lucy. She was sure she could hear a faint whimper. She was amazed the babies might have been born already. 'Use this blood to save Lucy.'

They set up an IV quickly and the blood was put in pouches just as the monitor let off a continuous beep and Lucy flat lined. The blood started to flow into Lucy and still the heartbeat was gone. After a minute, it was obvious the blood was not working. She had been too late. And yet, she considered another way. 'Pump, her heart, please don't give up, I'll be back as soon as possible.'

Else faced her, 'Catherine, Lucy's gone.'

'No, she's not gone. I'll be back,' she shouted, 'pump her heart.'

She raced out again in search of Caitlin. It was a distant hope, but perhaps her blood could heal her. She could not bear to think that Lucy was dead.

Chapter 30

Last Hope

Caitlin was starting to get fed up of being cooped up in Steven's room. It was great to be all in love with Steven again, it really was. But, she wanted to see more than four walls and they had already watched every DVD and played every game he had. She was approaching a brain dead state, and that was saying something for her. In her past life, she always wanted to stop and do as little as possible. Somehow, she was always too busy to stop back then, but now she finally had she could not help resenting it. Boredom was a killer.

Steven came and went as he pleased; he was not hidden from the community. He tried to keep her up to date with it all. The problem was she was done with *hearing* about it. She wanted to be a part of it. The sound of the key in the door made her breathe a sigh of relief. She could do with the company even though she wondered why Steven had returned early.

When a flustered Catherine peeked through the door, Caitlin frowned as she said, 'Catherine? Nice to see you here, I think?'

'Caitlin, I need your help,' Catherine said, her tone urgent, desperate, 'it's a difficult situation and I know you'll have questions, but can you just trust me and come with me. Please?'

Caitlin was desperate to get out of the room, so it was not exactly a tough decision.

The word rolled out easily enough, 'Sure.'

As she raced after Catherine in the direction of the laboratories and the medical suites, Caitlin started to get concerned. The place didn't bring any fond memories. She was convinced she put her depression behind her, yet she knew her emotions were still brittle. She was not sure she wanted to go back there.

'Catherine?' She stopped.

Catherine turned, quickly retraced her steps and held Caitlin's hand. 'Trust me, please.'

Caitlin did not want to carry on, but she had always found it hard to say no to anyone and Catherine did look beside herself. 'Okay.' Even though the words come out she really wanted to take them back, but she couldn't. Instead, they raced on.

At a junction in the corridor, they turned in the opposite direction to where she had stayed. That gave her a small relief. Eventually, they reached a keypad activated door. She was getting more curious by the minute. She wondered what or who needed to be hidden so well.

Once inside, her jaw slackened as she saw the amount of medical staff around.

'Wait here,' Catherine said.

Caitlin stood straight and watched as people entered and left the room in a flurry. She could hear some strange muffled noises that she could not place.

Barely a minute has gone by before Catherine came back. 'Caitlin, please come with me. I'll explain all later. Try to keep calm and keep an open mind.'

Caitlin walked towards the door and entered the hive of activity. The first thing that caught her eye was the body on the bed. A woman, with a mask over her mouth and nose and a load of devices around her. She could see a heart monitor beeping away, but it seemed erratic, wrong somehow. Then she realised there were three massive incubators to the side of the room. This was where a lot of the activity centred. She focused on each one in turn and realised each housed a baby. She had not seen a new-born before but she imagined that's what they were.

Catherine's eyes darted between the body and the incubators. 'Lucy, a dear friend of mine, is dying. They have managed to resuscitate her, but only just. She is hanging on by a thin thread. The new blood might have helped, but she is still critical. Caitlin, please, can you help?'

'Me?'

'Your blood, your blood can help,' Catherine said, 'at least, we think it can.'

'Oh.' Caitlin stared at the floor. She didn't want to see herself as a blood donor, but this woman was dying and, if those were hers, she had three babies that needed a mother. 'What do you want me to do?'

'Sit here, Else will get everything ready.'

As Caitlin made her way over to sit next to Lucy, she watched them wheel out the babies. A few minutes passed and then the door to the room shut, and only Else and Catherine remained.

Else set up what looked like a blood transfusion device and before she knew what was happening she had a needle in her arm and her blood was flowing into Lucy.

They all watched the monitor to see if the heartbeat would pick up.

The silence was excruciating.

Caitlin focused on Lucy's face and noticed the colour in her cheeks return, as the sound of her heartbeat picked up. Catherine and Else smiled. Caitlin was struck by the sight of their fangs. She shuddered slightly.

'It's working,' Catherine said, 'thank God.'

'Don't worry about our fangs,' Else reassured, 'we will not attack you, we promise.'

Caitlin tried to relax and focused on the fact she could actually help someone. For the first time, she saw her condition as a gift. She had given those babies a mother.

Else stopped the blood flow. Once Caitlin had been disconnected and was holding some cloth firmly against the puncture, Else handed her a bottle full of the red blood. She assumed it was the manufactured one.

She drank half the bottle and relished the taste. 'So, this blood could not heal Lucy?'

'No, we'll find out soon if it can enable the change,' Catherine replied, 'at the moment, it looks unlikely.'

Caitlin nodded and finished the rest of the bottle off. She tried to stay calm, even though the sight of sharp teeth was slightly unnerving.

'It's a very close match for human, and your, blood. But, it's not a match. We thought we had found the cure but it looks like we've failed again. There is no denying that your blood is stronger than what we've manufactured. I mean, just look at Lucy.'

'The interesting thing is that neither of us wanted to attack you, even though our fangs extended, so there's still something about human blood that is different. Something eludes us.'

Caitlin gave a half-smile, 'So, am I in danger out in the community then? Do you think I will be attacked by one of you?'

'No,' Catherine said, 'I think Emily only knew to attack you because you were different. She guessed you might be able to heal her, and she was right. But, there's nothing about you that will draw attention. Not if you're careful.'

'Careful?' Caitlin glanced up, it was difficult to look at the pair. Their eyes had a reddish glow to them.

'Well, if you go spilling your blood around, then it's different,' Else said, 'I can smell your blood now, because we've taken some. From the smell I can tell it's different. I'm not sure anyone would attack you if they smelt your blood, but their fangs might extend involuntarily, just like ours have.'

Catherine opened her mouth slightly and showed Caitlin her normal teeth. 'They have gone away again. The smell was strong a minute ago, but as soon as it subsided the urge to attack has gone. With humans, just their scent alone can make our fangs extend. But we're reasonably good at controlling it. I think you just caught us both off guard now.'

Caitlin felt her back and shoulder muscles relax, she had not realised until she saw their fangs retract how much they had put her on edge. 'I know what that feels like. I also had the urge to attack when I was with a normal human. I admit I didn't just think about it.'

'Yes,' Catherine nodded, 'it's hard to maintain *control*. You should not have killed anyone, but if you did we do understand. We cannot change what we are.'

Caitlin caught sight of Lucy's eyelids fluttering as she opened her eyes slowly. Her head turned slightly and she stared at them. Her eyes darted from Catherine to Else and then fixed on Caitlin. Caitlin could see confusion written all over Lucy's face.

'I'll wait outside,' Caitlin said.

'No, stay,' Lucy said, in a whispery voice.

'Okay.'

Catherine started to talk and Lucy's gaze turned to her, 'Lucy, you've given birth to two boys and a girl. They're all doing remarkably well considering the premature birth and we are taking good care of them.'

Lucy started to try to get up, but Else rushed to her side and forced her down again. 'Lucy, you nearly died. Caitlin saved your life.'

'Caitlin, that's your name,' Lucy's voice was not so whispery, 'thank you. I don't know how you did it, but thank you all the same. What happened?' She faced Catherine.

Catherine sat next to Lucy and held her hand, 'I'm not totally sure, but it looks like you're making a recovery.'

Lucy made to sit up again. Before she could be pushed back, she held out her hands defensively. 'Seriously, I feel good. Let me sit up.'

'You just had major surgery. You should not be able to move. How?' Else lifted the sheet to look under. 'Lie down a minute, let me look at the scar. We had to perform an emergency caesarean.'

Lucy slid back down again as Else pulled back the sheets. Caitlin knew she should have looked away, and yet she couldn't. When Else peeled off the blood soaked dressing, she traced her fingers lightly over the skin.

'The scar has vanished, you have healed completely.'

Caitlin could not believe her blood was able to do that, to fix someone.

'Lucy, Caitlin gave you her blood. I know you understand what this means. Caitlin can heal our kind. Do you also understand what I must ask of you?' Catherine said.

Lucy nodded, a look of awe on her face, as she stared in Caitlin's direction, 'I will not tell a soul.'

Caitlin shrugged her shoulders, and smiled. 'Congratulations, I'm glad I gave those babies their mother back.'

'I'll never forget what you have done, and neither will they,' Lucy had tears in her eyes now, 'I will call my daughter Cara, in your honour. If I used your name people would wonder why. The boys will be named Julio and Ignacio, after my grandfathers. I really must get up to see them. I feel great, better than great in fact.'

'Can I come with you?' Caitlin asked.

'I'm not sure...' Catherine started to say.

Caitlin interrupted, 'I would love to.'

Catherine glanced at Else, who said, 'Caitlin, are you sure?'

Lucy's face scrunched up, as though troubled.

'Of course, why wouldn't I be?' She hoped they were not going to wrap her up in cotton wool just because she could not have children. She was over that. The sight of the babies would probably put her off for life anyway. Children were snivelling, needy and troublesome. She had a sister, she knew all about it.

'Okay, if you're sure you're well enough, Lucy, then I'll take you to the shower and get you a change of clothes, and then we'll go to see them,' Else said, 'come with me, please.'

Catherine added, 'We'll wait outside.'

Caitlin followed Catherine outside and thought about Lucy and what she had done. Three new-born babies. It should have all been too much, but it was strangely exciting.

Outside, the entrance was deserted. Everyone had to be watching over the babies. The hub of activity had moved.

Catherine turned to face her, 'Caitlin, are you sure you want to see the babies? You don't have to. Lucy will not think less of you if you choose not to go.'

'She doesn't know I can't have children, right?'

'No, she doesn't.'

Caitlin gave a half-smile. 'Well, in that case, I'll go and see them. If I start to cry I'll tell her they are tears of joy. I can do this.'

Catherine put her hand on her shoulder, 'You're stronger than I imagined. Sorry, if I'm being overly protective. You have no idea how proud I am of you at the moment. Lucy is a dear friend. I can't even begin to express enough gratitude.'

'Well, in that case, don't. I didn't help for everyone to be indebted to me. I helped because I could and I wanted to. I cannot change what I am, I made the decision. Now, I have to make the most of it.' The last thought stayed in her mind, '*In whatever way I can*'.

Chapter 31

Introduction

Catherine could not believe Caitlin had agreed to see the babies. There was nothing she could do to put her off without being too obvious. Saying that, there would be no way Caitlin would be able to know Steven was the father. It could not do any harm.

The more she got to know Caitlin, the more she respected her. Caitlin had a strength of character that engulfed those around her. She had no doubt that the community would accept her. In time, even grow to love her. Catherine had a feeling Caitlin was meant to achieve great things.

'Caitlin, when we're finished here I'm going to take you to the cafeteria. I think it's time we just let people see you. Can you handle being amongst the others?'

Caitlin gave a broad, if slightly concerned, smile as she replied, 'Yes, I'm so ready to be out in the open. I can't stay in that room forever.'

'You sure you can handle the stares? The questions?'

'If I could handle my mother I can handle anyone. Yes, I'll come with you. So what if they stare? They might even think we're related,' she chuckled.

'Yes,' Catherine smiled. Caitlin was infectious. 'The red hair could be a handy coincidence.'

'It finally came up good for something,' Caitlin said, she flicked it away from her face. 'Never liked being red.'

'Funnily enough neither did I. I'm fine with it now though,' Catherine admitted, then added, 'you're still not sure?'

'I guess I don't exactly have a choice. I'm a redhead, I have to accept it,' Caitlin laughed, 'but I was always envious of the tanned brunettes and voluptuous blondes.'

'You're a very beautiful woman, Caitlin. You have to believe that.'

Caitlin blushed. It was endearing. 'I guess. I did feel kind of empowered after my change. But, I don't know. I guess since Emily died things have changed.'

'Yes, I can understand,' Catherine nodded, and then nudged Caitlin gently on her shoulder. 'So, we just have to find a way to get the old Caitlin back?'

Caitlin gave an enthusiastic nod. 'It would be nice if that was possible.'

'Anything is possible. Look at us. If anyone thought it was possible for *us* to exist we'd be in a comic book or a fiction novel. But, it did happen. We're the next step in the evolution of mankind, whatever that means. Steven, you, you're both the subsequent outcomes.'

'More like mutations,' Caitlin said.

'That's not a bad thing necessarily.'

'I don't think my kind is meant to thrive,' Caitlin frowned.

'Nature has a way of dictating the future. We don't know what the possibilities are for any of us. We've tried to contain our species, to prevent us becoming like a virus. But, perhaps trying to contain what we are is like finding a cure for the common cold.'

Caitlin played with her hair as she joked, 'Yeah, like impossible.'

'Exactly. There might be a way for us all to live together in harmony with normal humans. We hoped the new blood we manufactured would be the solution, but seeing as it did not heal Lucy it looks unlikely.'

'So, if it does not work, what happens?'

Catherine looked straight ahead. 'We continue with the original plan.'

'Which was?'

'Segregation and a new habitat in Borneo.'

'Borneo?' Caitlin's mouth formed a small circle.

'Yes, a small group of us have decided to set up a new colony in Borneo. It was decided before the discovery of the new blood. If it fails, the plan stands firm. I think a new start could be just what you need to feel accepted. What do you think?'

'It sounds amazing. To be a part of something like that would be massive,' she smiled again. 'I would be up for the challenge.'

Just then, Lucy walked into the room. With a set of new clothes and a wash she looked fantastic. It was hard to believe she had carried triplets hours earlier. The fact she was also wearing normal clothes, and not her usual scruffy and baggy gardening clothes, made her shine even more.

'Lucy, shall we go?'

Lucy beamed, 'I can't wait.'

Catherine led the way into the other room where they had set up the incubators and had several staff maintaining constant supervision.

Lucy made her way up to the incubators and peered in. Catherine and Caitlin followed. The babies were really tiny. They had to be about the size of her hands put together. Their eyes remained shut and Catherine could tell their breathing was heavy, in deep sleep. It would take weeks before they were strong enough to leave the incubators.

Caitlin stared at the one dressed in pink. Her eyes had gone glassy as she placed her hand on the incubator. Catherine was taken aback when she gasped and stood back.

'What is it?' Catherine asked.

Caitlin looked at Lucy, and then at Catherine. 'She opened her eyes for a split second and stared right at me, the eyes are pure black.'

'All new-borns have no colour at first. The colour will appear soon.'

'You know,' Caitlin shook her head, 'strange, but, for a second there I thought I saw a twinge of amber in her eyes. I must have Steven on the brain.' She chuckled and blushed.

Lucy stared at her, opened her mouth slightly and then gave an awkward laugh.

'Caitlin, now you mention Steven, you do realise that you can't tell him about Lucy and her children. In fact, you can't tell anyone. Lucy should not have been pregnant. I know that where you come from pregnancy out of wedlock is acceptable on the whole, however, here Lucy would be shamed. We would not want to subject her to the wrath of her family. Her father, Franco, is a devout Catholic. He would not understand.'

Caitlin stared into space for a moment, and then smiled, 'But of course, I will not tell anyone. It'll be our secret. I assume everyone else here is sworn to secrecy.'

'Of course. Lucy you have nothing to fear. As far as your father is concerned you have gone on a research trip. He does not suspect anything, and no-one will think anything of the fact you are no longer within the community.'

'Really?' Lucy hugged Catherine very tight. It took Catherine by surprise. She hugged her back and could not help smiling.

When they drew apart, she noticed Caitlin was still staring at the baby girl. It was a lost, and yet yearning, look. She imagined Caitlin had not completely put aside the fact she could not have children.

As though Caitlin had read her thoughts, she gave a weak, unconvincing smile.

Catherine wished she could think of something to make it right. For now, all she could do was to try to give her some sort of life back. 'Are you ready to go meet the others, Caitlin?'

Lucy approached Caitlin and gave her a massive hug, 'Thank you for saving my life. I owe you everything. Good luck. Let them see you for who you are. Only a wonderful person would be so selfless, so giving in the midst of trauma. I don't know what you must think of this place, of us, but I hope you do not think it's all bad. There is a lot of good here. I'm sure it will find you.'

Caitlin's eyes became watery. In a tight voice, she replied, 'I appreciate it. I know anyone in my position would have done the same. Unnecessary death is not good for anyone.'

'And now you need to get your strength back,' Catherine said, 'you need food and, probably, blood.'

She watched Caitlin's eyes widen at the mention of blood. It was time to go.

***

Steven made his way back to his room, eager to be reunited with Caitlin. He hated the fact she was still confined to the room. He knew she was bored and desperately needed to be out in the open. He kept his voice bright and breezy as he opened the door, 'Caitlin, I'm back.'

When there was no reply, he made his way towards the bathroom and called out again, 'Caitlin?'

He pushed the curtain aside to find an empty bathroom. He scratched his head and paused for a moment before he resumed his search. He looked under the bed, even though he knew she was too old to play hide and seek. Boredom could do strange things to people. Either way, she was nowhere to be found. He turned around and decided to go get some food. Hopefully, he'd bump into Catherine – he suspected she would know where Caitlin was.

When he got to the hall the hushed silence hit him immediately. Everyone seemed to be watching something or someone. He followed their gaze and his eyes fell upon Caitlin. Catherine was next to her and they were helping themselves to some food. He walked through the reasonably quiet space, the sound of his footsteps making him a tad self-conscience. He could see many heads turn in his direction as got closer to Caitlin.

An arm's length away, he stopped and tapped Caitlin on the shoulder. 'Fancy meeting you here.'

Caitlin glanced over her shoulder and smiled at him. In one hand she had a plate heaped with food, and on the other she held a bread roll. 'Are you eating with us?' Her lips curled up into a cheeky smile

'Am *I* eating with you?' He matched her expression and grabbed a plate. 'So what's good here?'

'Everything, I'm spoilt for choice' she replied.

As though the fact they were talking made everyone breathe again, the hub of normality resumed as people spoke in hushed conversations. They all wondered who Caitlin was, of course, but no one was going to challenge them. Not now, anyway.

'And just like that you both became kind of invisible again,' Catherine said, 'I'm going to sit with Ian. Good luck.'

Once Steven's plate was full, he steered her towards the table where Jenson was sat with the others.

They took a seat and Jenson looked up. 'Nice to see you again, Caitlin. This is my fiancée, Susanna.'

Susanna stood up and made her way over to Caitlin. Then to Steven's surprise she gave Caitlin a huge hug, and said, 'Welcome to the community. I've been dying to meet you.'

Caitlin blushed, and spluttered, 'Thank you.'

'None of us bite,' Gideon joked.

'This is my little brother, Gideon,' Susanna said,

'He's cheeky, but nice enough,' Steven added.

'And you are?' Gideon asked.

Caitlin's answer was cut short as Ian took to the small raised stage where various musicians sometimes played and asked for everyone's attention.

Once everyone was facing him, he began, 'I'd like all of you to welcome Caitlin to the community. Caitlin, can you please stand?'

Caitlin widened her eyes, but Steven edged her on. She stood up, not letting go of his hand.

'Thank you, Caitlin. I'm sure you'd all like to know who she is and the answer to that is tricky. All I can say, at this point, is that she is a friend of Steven, and therefore a friend of ours. If you have any questions, please ask your superiors. We expect you to welcome our guest with kindness – no one needs an inquisition. Thank you.' Ian gave a quick nod in Caitlin's direction.

Caitlin took that as a signal to sit down again. She pushed her hair over her face to hide her beetroot face.

'Well, that wasn't too painful. If it works it'll all be worth it,' Steven said.

'It'll work,' Jenson said. 'We'll look out for you too, Caitlin.'

Caitlin smiled, unable to speak. She took her cutlery in her hands and focused on eating. For once, she was intimidated. Steven had not seen it happen many times since he'd known her.

'So, what happens now?' Steven looked at Jenson.

'Life goes on. Caitlin, what are you good at?'

Caitlin chewed, swallowed her food and had a quick drink,

'I'm good at maths and I enjoy speaking Spanish.'

'Well, in that case Catherine will probably have a job for you. I take it she's looking out for you too since you came here with her?' Susanna asked.

'She is,' Caitlin replied, 'what does Catherine do again?'

'She is the mental agility coordinator,' Gideon said, 'if you are good at maths, then that job would be perfect for you.'

'I'll take your word for it,' Caitlin smiled.

'Well, I'm glad that you're finally out in the open. We have a wedding to organise,' Jenson held Susanna's hand. 'Steven, are you still up for the job of best man?'

'Definitely,' Steven replied. He glanced at Caitlin and wondered if she would ever consider becoming his wife. It was the first time the thought had popped into his mind, and yet now it seemed like the most natural thing in the world. There was no point in rushing into anything. He glanced at her cute rounded face and glowing blue eyes – it took everything to resist the urge to kiss her. He had no doubt in his mind that he wanted to share everything with her, no matter what.

Chapter 32

Leadership

Caitlin did not know what to make of it all. She knew it was unlikely they could have accepted her just like that, and yet she could not sense any hostility. There were a lot of curious glances, and some odd smiles, but no outright hatred. She smothered some butter over her roll and took a bite. The food, the people, the calm environment, the lack of flash clothing and designer gear gave the place a welcoming feel. In fact, she had never felt so at ease. She could not understand why they had been so worried that she would not fit in, what it was they were trying to protect her from. A part of her was curious. She wondered if she did cut her finger whether they would all turn into bloodthirsty vampires. She doubted it, the idea made her smile.

'Want to share the thought?' Steven nudged her arm.

'I just wondered when this place was going to get scary,' Caitlin chuckled.

'It never was scary, just isolated for my taste. Too far away from you, of course,' he blushed slightly.

'He was the scary one,' Gideon blurted out.

'Gideon!' Susanna glared at her brother.

'It's true,' Gideon spluttered, defensive, 'Steven thought this place was backwards. He could not wait to leave us all... although, I can understand why,' he smiled, his expression cheeky with a slight leer.

'Gideon!' Susanna repeated, 'Excuse my younger brother, Caitlin. I never thought he was capable of being such a flirt.'

Caitlin laughed, 'It's alright, how old are you anyway?'

'I'm seventeen,' Gideon puffed his chest, 'nearly eighteen.'

'Too young to do anything,' Susanna rolled her eyes.

'They don't date here until after the change,' Steven explained.

Caitlin raised her eyebrows in disbelief, 'Well, that would be hard in our world. Most teenagers I know are like a dog on heat.'

Gideon's shoulders slumped, 'I knew there was a reason why we should live out in the open.'

'You'll get your chance, *little* brother,' Susanna ruffled his hair.

'Hey, quit with the little. I'm taller than you, you know,' Gideon snapped.

'It's your maturity I was referring to,' Susanna narrowed her eyes.

Jenson laughed out loud, 'Don't you just love siblings? Do you have any brothers of sisters, Caitlin?'

'I have an older brother and a younger sister,' Caitlin sighed, and then sat up straight, 'and I think it's fair to say we have the same kind of relationship. I guess this place is no different to the outside world,' she paused and smirked, 'other than for the fact that we're different and fashion hasn't been invented yet.'

Caitlin surveyed the room again, she felt a lot braver now. It was a sea of green and brown clothing. Yet, the complexions of the people varied from blonde, lithe girls to dark, tanned Mediterranean males. An odd redhead was scattered here and there. She found it fascinating.

She could not help asking, 'Are the redheads related to Catherine?'

Susanna replied, 'I'm pretty sure they're her children. Good guess.'

'Not difficult really, even though my parents are not redheads,' Caitlin replied, 'my grandfather had red hair.'

Caitlin focused on a brown haired male with slightly paler features. His hair was a mottled brown and he was in deep conversation with Ian and Catherine. As though he sensed she was watching, he turned to face her and smiled. After saying something to Catherine, he stood up and made his way towards them. Caitlin looked away, embarrassed to be caught watching.

A moment later, she heard him approach. 'Steven, nice to see you again.'

'Enrique, wasn't it?' Steven held out his hand.

Enrique shook his hand, 'Can I join you?'

'Sure,' Steven said.

Enrique sat in a space opposite them, 'My father, Ian, and mother, Carmen, asked me to come and say hello. My aunt Catherine talks very highly of you, Caitlin. I'm pleased to meet you.' He held out his hand.

When Caitlin extended her hand, Enrique took it and then lowered his lips to kiss it.

The act seemed intrusive, somehow and she flinched slightly.

Enrique sensed her unease. 'My Spanish roots insist I kiss the hand of a lovely lady.'

'So smooth,' Gideon muttered under his breath.

Enrique ignored the comment and turned to face Steven, 'So, you're glad to be back?'

'As much as I could be,' Steven's jaw was tense, the reply short.

'And you, Caitlin, do you like our community?'

Caitlin found it hard to hold his gaze, his eyes reminded her of melted chocolate. Somehow, she found her voice, 'I've not seen much of it, but what I have is likeable.'

Enrique laughed, 'Well, likeable is better than anything else. Is it true you speak Spanish fluently? My aunt, sorry, she told me.'

'Yes, well, I grew up in Gibraltar so my Spanish is Andalusian with a few words that are what we call llanito.' She gave an uneasy laugh.

'Gibraltar? The rock that should be Spanish?' he have a half-smile, his right eye arched.

'I keep away from the politics,' Caitlin said. The last thing she needed was a full debate on whether Gibraltar was British or Spanish, the topic bored her to death. As far as she was concerned she was British – the end.

'Wise,' Enrique smiled, 'I would love to see my homeland one day. My father, Franco, is also very curious to see what his Spain has become. Do you know anything of the Spanish Civil War?'

Caitlin nodded, 'Yes, I studied it in university. What

happened is heart-breaking. Like many of the other wars that have happened around the world.'

'Indeed, but at least here we live in relative harmony,' he said, his hands turned up. 'No point dwelling on the past even though it is a difficult thing for my parents to talk about.'

'I can imagine…' She left the last word hanging.

'*Spain* has plenty of charm and beauty,' Steven said, his remark tainted by some insinuation.

Caitlin could not help thinking Steven did not like Enrique.

'Of course, you also speak Spanish, Steven,' Enrique's eyes dropped. 'I am sorry about your stepmother, truly.'

'There is nothing anyone can do about it now. She is gone, and in a way it is only right that the person who killed her also met her death.'

'Yes, Emily's death was felt by many,' Enrique added.

'Really?' Steven snapped, 'as far as I know, most of you did not care much about her. Or, am I wrong?'

'Emily was out of control, her way did not fit our ideals,' Enrique sounded defensive, 'but I'm sure you've realised how much your aunt Anna suffers. Juan does the best he can to give her some comfort, but it's not easy.'

Caitlin glanced in the direction of Anna, who was hunched over her bowl, face forlorn, 'Maybe you should speak to her, Steven?'

'I have nothing to say,' Steven snapped.

Caitlin met Enrique's eyes again and gave an apologetic smile.

'She might like to talk to you, Steven,' Enrique continued, 'she was not to blame for your mother's nature.'

Steven nodded. His lips became taut.

'Anyway, it was a pleasure to meet you, Caitlin. Should you want to talk in Spanish any of us would be happy to oblige. We will ignore the fact you come from *the Rock*,' he chuckled, as he stood up and took his leave.

'He is oh so charming,' Susanna grinned.

Jenson rolled his eyes, 'He's not so bad. Some of his cousins are worse. It's hard to imagine how they keep their hormones in check, but the fact they're raised to be devote

Catholics might have something to do with it. Even though, I've always had my doubts.'

Steven slid his fingers through Caitlin's and squeezed. Caitlin turned to face him and was drawn in by his amber eyes and perfect face. She should not even find someone like Enrique remotely interesting when she had someone like Steven, but she knew it was hard to ignore a suave flirt, which was obviously what Enrique was.

'It's great to have you here,' Steven said.

'I know,' Caitlin said.

Even though she was scared to be out in the open amongst the others, she tried to act brave. She watched as clusters of people started to leave. Jenson, Susanna and Gideon stood up to go.

'There's work to be done,' Jenson said.

'Lessons for me,' Gideon said, he did not look enthusiastic.

'See you later,' Susanna smiled.

Caitlin was strangely excited, 'So, what does everyone do now?'

'Everyone has somewhere to go,' Steven said, 'no-one is allowed to be idle. I have a feeling you'll have somewhere to go too. I'm working with the fishing boats now. It's great to be outside.'

'Fishing?' Caitlin chuckled, and then joked, 'any piranhas?'

'Yes, actually,' Steven nudged her again. 'Well, relatives of the piranhas. We catch a lot of Pacu fish. They're massive.'

'I'll take your word for it.'

'I have to go,' Steven said, 'let's go and speak to Catherine.'

They stood up and cleared their plates and utensils in the disposals area. Then they approached Catherine.

Caitlin did not get the impression Ian or Catherine were happy. It looked like they were in disagreement over something. Yet, as they approached, Catherine looked up and put on a forced smile, 'Caitlin, can you sit with us, please?'

Steven kissed Caitlin on the cheek. 'I'll let you talk. See you later.'

'Steven, why don't you stay?' Ian suggested. It was not so

much a suggestion, as a requirement.

'I'll be late,' Steven replied.

'They can manage without you,' Catherine said.

Caitlin took a seat, Steven sat next to her.

'I hope my son was courteous,' Ian said. The bags under his eyes gave away the stress he was under.

'He was,' Caitlin smiled.

'I should apologise,' Ian said, 'the first time we met, I did not give my kind good representation. It was necessary to abduct you, for the safety of the people Steven came into contact with, but I'm sorry for any distress it caused. As you can see we're all perfectly amiable and, now that you're one of us, we will treat you like a member of our extended family. We will protect you.'

Steven's shoulder pressed against hers.

'Thank you,' Caitlin said. She could hardly berate him after that.

'Anyway,' Catherine said, 'Ian knows about the issues, he is the head of the community at the moment. Although, we don't have a fixed hierarchy, it is more of an overseeing role.'

Ian grunted, 'Trust me. Anyone else is welcome to it.'

Caitlin nodded, that explained why he was so stressed. She guessed the fact he had lost both of his parents, and his sister was also a factor. Her arrival could not help matters.

'Ian is under a lot of strain,' Catherine added, 'things have gone from complicated to near enough impossible. The community has too many people living here now to remain inconspicuous. As I told you, some are looking to break away to form a new community elsewhere. But, our research could change what people end up doing. Caitlin, you have a mathematical brain, I'd appreciate your help with logistics. Steven, you always said you missed studying the Law. Well, now we need you to help us design the parameters for our new laws, the new regime. Are you both happy to help?'

Caitlin shrugged her shoulders, 'Sure.'

Steven nodded.

'We really appreciate the fact you've taken everything so well, Caitlin. In fact, your resolve is impressive to say the least. My nephew is a fine man, I'm sure you'll both be very happy together.'

Caitlin could not help thinking it was all so nicely premeditated. She could not help wondering if she would actually enjoy her new role.

Chapter 33

Responsibility

Catherine clenched and unclenched her hands into fists as she made her way over to the laboratory. So much had happened in the past twenty-four hours. At least with Caitlin and Steven occupied, she could now focus on Tobias. The success of the new blood could change everything. She wanted to believe it would work and tried to remain positive. Regardless of the setback with Lucy, they would carry out the original plan. A slim chance remained. If it failed, another human would have to be sacrificed – there was no other alternative.

She took a deep breath, pushed down the handle and held her head high. Her outward confidence had to count for something.

'Ingrid, Eilif, Tobias,' she nodded, 'is everything ready?'

'Yes,' Eilif nodded.

An hour later, they were all paddling, sat one in front of the other in a wooden dugout. They kept a fluid rhythm as they made their way along the Amazon River. The nearest village was a few hours away.

Catherine enjoyed the exercise and the fresh air invigorated her. Out here, amongst nature, it was easy to put aside any concerns. She was glad she was sat at the back; it gave her a chance to look around. To think. Something was bothering her, it was like she'd forgotten something. It felt like it was important, but whatever it was eluded her. As she paddled, she tried to bring it to the forefront of her mind.

As the bustle from the range of primates overhead resulted in mass screeching, presumably after some disagreement or other, it hit her. She faltered for a moment as she lost pace with the others, and smiled as she regained her composure. The answer had been staring her in the face the entire time. She chuckled at its potential simplicity.

'Anything to share, Catherine,' Ingrid asked, as she glanced back from the front.

'Later, yes,' she called out, 'I just forget something important.'

'I rarely forget anything,' Ingrid retorted.

'Well, in that case you're very lucky. Must be why you make a good scientist?'

Ingrid laughed, 'Maybe. I think it's annoying actually. Sometimes life would be easier if I could forget *some* things.'

'Yes, I guess it would. But then, all memories make us who we are. Some change is for the better.'

Ingrid did not reply for a minute. 'I never thought about it like that. Yes, I guess experiences have changed me. Perhaps, made me yearn for things I never considered.'

'So there you go.'

Ingrid glanced back, smiled, and then continued to paddle.

Catherine had always liked Ingrid, recently she felt sorry for her. It could not be easy for her to deal with rejection, especially when Caitlin was around. And yet, she had befriended Caitlin. She could not help thinking that in some ways Steven had been a fool to let Ingrid slip away. And yet, she thought the same of Lucy. As much as she knew Ian was happy with Carmen, she had no doubt Lucy would have also have made Ian very happy if he had reciprocated her affections.

Steven had impacted the lives of so many in the short time they had known of him. Her parents, Ingrid, Lucy, Emily – they had all been affected by Steven. Three of them now dead, it was hard to believe.

*

A couple of hours later, they cruised towards the shore and got out of the dugout. Between them, they lifted it out of the water and covered it in branches. The rest of the journey would be done by foot. They unpacked their bags and had some water and food.

'Tobias, how are you feeling?' Catherine asked, his eyes looked slightly haggard.

Tobias gave a weak smile, 'Okay, I guess.'

'We have to walk for a few more hours. Then we can set up

a base. We need to get everything ready and be at a reasonable distance from the village,' Eilif reiterated.

They all knew what they had to do, but Catherine guessed it made Eilif feel more secure if he repeated the instructions, 'I've also come up with an alternative strategy, if the blood fails.'

'Really?' Eilif said.

Ingrid and Tobias looked in her direction.

'Yes, Steven seemed to think monkeys are the reason we did not get ill within the community. I know they tested monkey blood in the past with inconclusive results. Perhaps, a combination of the two is what we were missing. I suggest if the new blood doesn't work that Tobias feeds off a monkey, before we have to resort to a human from the village.'

'Interesting idea,' Ingrid mused, 'well there are plenty of those around here. It's worth a try.'

Catherine nodded and took a bite from her sandwich. She felt much more optimistic now.

*

After a relatively easy journey and serene setup, reality jolted them back into the reason why they were there. Tobias had been gurgling during the night, and now on the day of his twentieth Birthday, the change was upon them.

They worked quickly. Eilif made sure Tobias was comfortable, Ingrid got the blood ready, and Catherine prepared the IV.

It was all over in ten minutes.

Now, all they had to do was wait.

Tobias continued to writhe, his face was pale and covered in sweat. His blond hair was slicked onto his scalp and his arms shook involuntarily. Ingrid took hold of them and tried to hold them down. It worked, even though Ingrid's hand had a slight tremor.

After an hour, Tobias had still not calmed down.

Catherine spoke what they were all thinking, 'We have to go to plan B.'

'I'll go,' Eilif said.

'Is Tobias going to be alright? Maybe, this was too risky?'

Ingrid said.

Catherine shook her head. 'He'll be fine. We can always go to plan C.'

Ingrid nodded. She gazed at Tobias and wiped his brow with a cloth. Catherine was impressed by her dedication.

'You care about Tobias?' It was an innocent question.

Ingrid's cheeks flushed a pale pink. 'Of course, as I would anyone from the community.'

'I think Tobias cares about you too,' Catherine said.

'Really?' Ingrid's eyes widened.

'I'm sure of it, only a fool wouldn't notice. The way he stutters when you're around,' she chuckled, 'you should give him a chance, forget Steven.'

'Maybe,' Ingrid paused. She looked at Catherine through the corner of her eye, 'How are Steven and Caitlin?'

'They seem fine and now, at least, they're more settled. They have a future to look forward to. At least, we all hope they do.'

'Is Caitlin going to be happy here?' Ingrid faced Catherine.

Catherine gave a slight shake of her head. 'About as happy as Steven will be. I think they will just get on with it. We all do anyway, right?'

'Right,' Ingrid faced Tobias again. In a weak voice, she said, 'They are meant to be.'

'I believe so.'

The sound of Eilif returning broke the stilted silence, 'Let's see if this works.'

He thrust the still alive, but seriously wounded, Southern Brown Howler monkey next to Tobias and held its neck in place. Eilif punctured the monkey's vein and allowed the blood to seep into Tobias's mouth. As it did, Tobias's canines extended into fangs. Even though unconscious, he instinctively bit into the monkey and started to drink. The animal went limp, its eyes glazed over and lifeless within minutes.

Tobias stopped drinking after a few minutes and fell into a deep sleep, his limbs flopped to the ground.

Catherine picked up her sharp dagger and the Howler monkey. A hot meal was what they needed.

'I'll build a fire,' Eilif said, 'Ingrid, you watch over Tobias. He looks peaceful at least. It's a good sign. Looks like you might have been right, Catherine.'

'I think the secret is the combination of the new blood and monkey blood,' Catherine glanced up as she worked. 'We'll need to carry out more tests when we return. As much as I loath the thought we will need to capture and experiment with Howler monkeys.'

'Why the Howler in particular?' Eilif asked.

Catherine paused, 'I don't know. But, we can start with the Howler if Tobias makes a full recovery. There are many species we can test. We just have to make sure we don't cause any damage to their family groups. They have as much of a right to live as we do. In a way, I feel bad. Humans are in plentiful supply. But, if it leads to us finding a cure, I think it's worth it.'

An hour later, Catherine chewed on the fatty meat. It was not a bad taste. It was a cross between pork, duck and venison. She had always enjoyed it. She had never been one of those who considered a monkey to be any different to any other animal they killed for food.

'Do you think Tobias will wake up soon?' Ingrid asked, as she licked her fingers clean.

'Might be a few hours, or less,' Eilif replied.

'Should we head back home? He seems to be in a coma. We could be at home before he wakes?' Ingrid said.

'I'd rather stay here until he does,' Eilif replied, 'in case anything went wrong. We might need that village.'

Catherine ran a hand through her hair, 'I'd hope not.'

'I'll go get some more wood,' Ingrid suggested, then stood up. 'It'll keep the predators at bay. I don't think we want to attract unnecessary attention.'

'Good point,' Eilif sucked the rest of the meat of the bone. 'Do you want to take these bones and scatter them far away?'

'Sure,' Ingrid smiled, 'I needed a run.'

Catherine watched as Ingrid collected every last scrap of monkey and disappeared into the forest.

'You think Tobias is a match for my daughter?' Eilif asked.

Catherine fiddled with some sticks on the floor. 'Yes, I believe he could be good for Ingrid.'

'*Good*,' Eilif chuckled, 'that is a relative term. You mean, he might be a good distraction, to make her forget Steven.'

'Well, that too,' Catherine smiled. 'My nephew is blinded by Caitlin; he does not see anyone else. I'm sorry to say Ingrid will never gain his love.'

Eilif sat next to her. 'No, I imagine you're right. Tobias is a good lad.'

'Yes, he is,' Catherine paused, 'Eilif, I... I just wanted to say thank you. You've helped my family throughout,' she started to choke up.

'Don't mention it. We're family, all of us. No matter what has transpired since Steven came to light, we pledged to look out for each other, and I intend to keep my promise. I will do everything in my power to ensure the survival of our community and our species.'

'Our species – it makes us sound like aliens.'

'I guess it does,' Eilif laughed, 'you know what I mean.'

'Yes, I do,' Catherine sighed. 'I just keep wondering what we are. If we're now the most advanced human, then why shouldn't we allow our kind to dominate? Do you think it could be our destiny?'

Eilif nodded, serious. 'I know what you mean. Why should we exist at all? What is our purpose? We have all studied Darwinian theories. The survival of the fittest is plausible and would explain what we could do, what we could become. And yet, think of the study of eugenics. Is it right to exploit our strengths to dominate, to try to create a super race?'

'No, of course not, no-one has the right to kill others in the pursuit of perfection. The thing is we're not trying to achieve perfection. We had no choice – we *evolved* to become a stronger human being.'

'Yes, but we know what we are. We know we can kill other humans, we know how to exploit their weaknesses. To use our knowledge for our own gain would not be wise.'

Catherine gave a half-smile, 'You listened well to my father's teachings, and of course you're right. I'm just scared,

scared of what our future holds. I'm convinced we cannot restrain progress. It'll just happen, whether we like it or not.'

'But, it will not happen because *we* encouraged it. Think of what your father achieved when he designed the community.'

Catherine nodded slowly, she found the words hard to say, 'And think of why he left it all behind.'

'He could not live without your mother. It was nothing to do with the community.'

'Really?' Catherine wiped away a lone tear. 'He created my mother, and then lied about what he had done. He built a prison to keep us all safe, to stop others from doing what he had done. I'm not fooled. He did not do it for the greater good. He did it for selfish reasons – to protect my mother.'

Eilif put a hand on her shoulder. 'Maybe he did. The thing is he was right to be wary. Steven is an anomaly, one that might be repeated. Caitlin is an epidemic, a virus than could spread quickly if everyone knew. Can you blame him for wanting to keep your mother safe?'

'No, I can't,' she sniffled, 'I miss my parents and wish I could ask them what to do every day.

'I think you know what we must do.'

Catherine couldn't reply, her chest tight and constricted. At times like these, she really wished her parents could speak to her and give her some much needed advice.

Chapter 34

Awake

After Ingrid scattered the remains of the monkey, she made her way up a tree, perched on a thick branch and leant back. She listened to the deep, humming sounds, ignored the humidity, and focused on the beauty around. The Amazon, her home, was truly magical. She never ceased to be astonished by the depth of colour, the array of creatures, the variety and complexity of vibrations all around. It was a place to be cherished and enjoyed, and yet she knew a wider world existed.

A world full of man-made things, where nature was secondary. A world where people enjoyed material devices – not people, family, or friendship. Recently, she wanted to be a part of that world.

Since she met Steven, and then Caitlin, she had changed. Steven had made every effort to help in the community when he arrived. He was hard working, even considerate to many. Caitlin was nice, normal, regardless of all the modern gadgetry and supposed irrational upbringing. She considered her a friend.

It seemed the way humans lived did not change the essence of a person.

She doubted anyone born in a different life, in a different country, would not adapt to their new circumstances. Any child born that was naturally good would always be good regardless. People seemed, like them, to instinctively follow a certain path.

The truth was the more she knew, the more she wanted to find out. She wanted to be out there amongst humans, observing them, their cultures, habits, to be a part of it all and to learn from them.

She closed her eyes and visualised Steven. He had shown determination, a stubborn character, and loyalty. She wished he was loyal to her, not Caitlin. Yet, she could not help but respect him for his values. She could understand why a person not confined to a location or situation in life would seek out more. She never understood human nature before, but now she did. She wanted to discover. It was human nature to explore, and that side to her was now beginning to flourish.

She wanted more.

Ingrid opened her eyes, gave a deep sigh and wondered if Tobias was awake yet. She hoped they would succeed, even though she knew their work was far from over. The cure seemed within reach now, and if they obtained it she, like many others, would get her free pass to a life amongst normal humans.

She stood up, jumped off the tree and ran at full speed back to the camp, the exhilaration of speed overcoming her melancholy mood.

As she approached, she slowed down and wiped her brow with the back of her hand.

'Ingrid, you were gone a long time?' Eilif said.

'Was I?' Ingrid brushed her hand through her hair.

Catherine gave a half-smile. Ingrid noticed her eyes were slightly puffy. She wondered what was up with that.

'Have a drink,' Eilif passed her a water bottle.

Ingrid relished the taste, and said, 'Thank you.' She passed the bottle back. 'Is he still asleep?'

'Yes, no sign of movement,' Catherine replied, 'just a steady heartbeat.'

'Well, that's good at any rate.' Ingrid sat down. She did not know why she felt uncomfortable. Something about Catherine's mood unnerved her. It made her think she might not be the only one with doubts.

She walked over to the stream and washed her face and hands, then ran some cool water over her hair.

Refreshed, she sat back down next to Catherine and waited.

'Don't worry about me,' Catherine said, 'I was only thinking about my family.'

Ingrid turned to face her, 'I understand. We all have concerns.'

Catherine nodded.

Ingrid did not have much else to say. She felt on edge, restless. She was about to stand to fetch firewood when she saw Tobias shiver and his eyes flutter. 'He's waking up.'

Eilif got the dart ready with some sedative, in case Tobias tried to bolt like all the others.

Ingrid went to Tobias's side. 'Tobias, can you hear me?'

Tobias opened his eyes and stared right at Ingrid. His hands reached out for the back of her head and he pulled her towards him. Before she had time to react, Tobias's mouth was on hers as he kissed her, with a hunger that astounded her. A few seconds in, she could fight it no longer and she matched his hunger, shocked at her reaction. The hairs on the back of her head seemed to have stood on end, her body felt like it was on fire, fuelled by dormant emotions.

She barely heard the chuckle her dad gave.

It felt like seconds, even though it was more likely to have been minutes, before he released her. He stared into her eyes, smiled, and said, 'You have no idea how long I've wanted to do that.'

Ingrid was speechless. She gave a girlie giggle, then sat on the ground and took a deep breath.

'I guess there's no point asking how you feel then,' Catherine said.

It was obvious from her tone that she was just as amused as her dad. Ingrid shook her head, still finding it hard to lose the smile. She glanced at Tobias, whose eyes remained fixated on her, and gave a wary smile. Her cheeks felt like they were burning.

Tobias stood up and held out his hand. 'Will you come with me?'

'Where?' Ingrid shook her head.

'Away from here, just the two of us,' Tobias said, seemingly oblivious of Catherine and Eilif. 'What do you say?'

Ingrid's mouth drooped. 'We can't leave, Tobias. It's not that simple.'

'Why not?' his tone deeper, 'I don't want to stay here, I want to be free.'

'Freedom is not an option for us,' Ingrid replied. She held out her hand and let Tobias help her up.

'Right?' His eyes narrowed and he pursed his lips. For the first time he acknowledged Catherine and Eilif with a curt nod.

'We have to go back to the community now,' Catherine said.

A split second later, Ingrid found she had been lifted off the ground and hurled over Tobias's back in a fireman's lift. Tobias took a mere four steps before he collapsed, with Ingrid landing on her backside next to him.

'They all try to run,' Eilif said, 'let's take Casanova here back before he tries to sweep you off your feet again.'

The way Eilif laughed at Tobias made Ingrid angry. She had been swept off her feet, and she liked it. 'I'll take him.'

Eilif raised his eyebrows, and said, 'As you wish.'

Ingrid put one arm under his shoulders and the other under his knees and lifted him up. Up close, his scent engulfed her. It was a mixture of sweat, soil, and something intangible. She liked the intangible, it was *his* smell. She cradled him close and started to run in the direction of the dugout. She didn't want to think that she had gone all soft over a kiss, but the truth was she had. If fact, she felt very protective of the man who delivered the kiss.

*

Ingrid opted to focus on the task at hand as they made their way back to the community, but now they had arrived she had to decide what she was going to do about Tobias. Or more importantly how she felt about him. If, and this was a big if, Tobias liked her she wasn't sure what the right thing to do was. She was very flattered he had kissed her, it had been a while since anyone had done that. Yet, she was not sure it would lead to anything. He was just a kid. At least, that's how she saw him. Then again, Steven was also a "kid" and that hadn't stopped her falling for him.

She licked her lower lip as she lowered Tobias on to the bed. She wanted to stay to see what he would say when he woke up. She felt her cheeks flush. She had no idea what she was going to say, or worse than that what Tobias would say.

He had always seemed so shy. She assumed that his sudden post-change confidence would not last.

'I'd like to go and have a wash now, if that's okay,' Ingrid said to Catherine.

Catherine nodded, then put her hand on her shoulder. 'Thank you for your help, it's really appreciated.'

'I'll keep an eye on him,' Eilif said, 'you two might as well head off.'

'Okay then, we'll talk tomorrow and make plans,' Catherine said. 'I think we're very close to a solution now.'

'If Tobias shows no signs of an adverse reaction then it looks like you may have found the missing ingredient for the successful blood.' Eilif took a seat and clasped his hands together. 'We'll meet tomorrow.'

Ingrid started to leave. As she did she stole a final glance at Tobias. She had to admit that his curly black hair, and heart shaped face was cute. The rest of him was not bad either. She supressed a smile.

After a minute or so, Catherine asked, 'Did you think Tobias would do that?'

'No,' Ingrid spluttered.

'I thought so, you looked pretty shocked.'

Ingrid laughed, 'That's one way to describe it.'

'He's someone for you to consider anyway.' Catherine raised an eyebrow.

'Maybe.' As they got to the junction, Ingrid turned towards her accommodation. 'I have to go and get some fresh clothes, so I might see you later on.'

'Sure. Thanks again.'

Once inside her room, Ingrid grabbed a new set of clothes and walked out again. She needed to clear her head and she hadn't washed in over a day, it was time to refresh. She also hoped to see Caitlin, since it was the time of day when women bathed.

When she entered the cavern the sound of children, as well as splashing and some chatter brought the place to life. Bathing was such a social thing in the community. She always found bathrooms in the outside world so restrictive, enclosed.

She guessed people got used to their own space.

Catherine was busy talking to some new mums and their babies by the small pools, but she glanced in her direction and waved. Ingrid continued to the main lagoon. A few women were out swimming, others chatted in small groups by the side. She could not see Caitlin.

She stripped off her clothes, left them a in a bag and set out her towel and new clothes on the side for when she returned. Then she went to the water's edge and dived in, instantly refreshed as her body was engulfed by the lukewarm water.

She headed for the surface and swam front crawl at a steady pace towards the other side of the underwater lagoon. When she stopped, she ran her hands through her hair and detangled it. Then she dived down to enjoy the underwater silence. When she saw Caitlin sat on the bottom she smiled, then waved.

Caitlin saw her and nodded, then pointed to the surface.

When they broke the surface, Caitlin said, 'Ingrid, nice to see you again. I love staying underwater. Steven told me swimming would be fun,' she chuckled, 'I never expected to be able to stay under indefinitely. It's amazing.'

'I know.' Ingrid floated on the surface and adopted an eggbeater kick. 'Another perk to what we are. No-one knows why though, it's not like bats swim.'

'Oh well, I'm not complaining,' Caitlin said. 'Shall we head back?'

'Sure.' Ingrid swam a steady breaststroke, head out of the water. Caitlin followed suit. 'You're looking well.'

'Thanks, it's still weird being here. But, I think I'm getting used to it, or more importantly people are getting used to me.'

'That's good to know.' Ingrid wanted to know about Steven but she did not know how to ask.

'Where did you go?'

Ingrid decided to be upfront. 'We have a new adult member, Tobias.' She gave a nervous laugh.

Caitlin noticed. 'Tobias? Interesting, is he?'

'No, err, he's just a friend.'

'Why did you sound nervous?' Caitlin chuckled.

'I have no idea what he is, but anyway, what about you?'

Ingrid figured it was a good way to ask.

'Things with Steven are back on track, I think. He's being very sweet, thoughtful.'

'That's nice.' Ingrid fought the urge to grimace. She was happy for Caitlin.

'Anyway, they've been keeping me busy, and I love stretching my mind. I really enjoy teaching. I've been watching and helping with the younger ones. I never even thought of being a teacher before, now I can see the appeal.'

Ingrid reached out for the metal rung and started to climb out of the water. She made her way to her towel. When she turned around she saw Caitlin a few metres away, already wrapped in a towel. She knew Caitlin would probably still find the fact they were naked uncomfortable, and she didn't want to make it worse by staring at her so she got dressed quickly and got ready to leave.

They were both ready at a similar time, so they met at the entrance.

'I'm heading back now,' Caitlin said.

Ingrid smiled, 'I'm going to speak to Catherine first. I'll see you later, it was great to catch up.'

Caitlin nodded and walked off behind a group of women and some children.

Ingrid got the impression Caitlin was adjusting, but she was not convinced she was truly at ease yet.

Chapter 35

Hen Do

Caitlin did not know why she felt comfortable around Ingrid. She suspected Ingrid still harboured an interest in Steven, but somehow it did not bother her. She was not surprised Ingrid liked Steven, he was to all intents and purposes a great catch. Caitlin had no doubt as to whether she was attracted to him, and she enjoyed his company, but she could not deny the fact something was missing. For now though, she would be stupid to let him go on a feeling. Especially when Steven did everything he could to impress her.

She rubbed her hands into her hair to help it dry. It had got so long recently. She would have to find out who was a good hairdresser, there had to be someone. The last time she tried to cut her own hair it had not ended well – she had resembled a mushroom.

Once in the food hall, she relaxed as Susanna caught her eye and waved. She was glad Susanna had befriended her, it made it easy to integrate.

'How are things?' Caitlin asked.

Susanna kissed both of her cheeks. 'Very busy, I can't believe I'm getting married in a few days. It's a shocker. But, everyone is helping out and to be honest I'm not *too* stressed out.'

'That's great.'

'So, are you coming out with us tonight? It's my hen night.'

Caitlin's lips curled at the edges. 'You have those here?'

'Of course, my mum's organising it.'

Caitlin tried to keep a straight face, but found it difficult. 'Your mother?'

'Of course, it's the tradition.'

'Sure, I'll come.' It was bound to be a different hen night to any of the ones she had heard of.

'Excellent, meet us here later at around eight-ish, okay?'

Susanna glanced behind Caitlin, smiled, and said, 'see you later.'

Caitlin felt Steven's arm over her shoulder, before he kissed her cheek. They had learnt not to kiss on the lips in public. It was considered inappropriate by many since they were unmarried. In this respect, the community lacked progress.

'Nice swim?' he asked.

'Yes, thank you. Ingrid's back.'

Steven pursed his lips. 'Is she?'

'Like I said.' It was funny he seemed to have more of an issue with Ingrid than she did.

They moved in the direction of the food counters.

'Are you enjoying your mental agility training?' Steven asked.

'Yes, I am. How's your legal brain coping with things?'

Steven's nose twitched. 'Admirably.'

Caitlin raised her eyes to the ceiling, then nudged him in the ribs.

'Playful today?' he arched an eyebrow.

Caitlin widened her eyes, 'Me? Not at all. It's just nice to know you can be stretched.'

Steven gave a half-smile. 'I can be *stretched*,' he lowered his head and whispered in her ear, 'and you would know all about that.'

The feel of his breath against her neck did funny things to her stomach, and she could not help giving a slight shiver.

He noticed and whispered again, 'Sensitive today?'

Caitlin tossed her hair in his face. 'Maybe.' Then she strode purposefully towards the food. She was not going to let him distract her, and she had a hen do to attend.

The way Steven rubbed his knee against hers as they sat, and then held her hand left her in no doubt as to his intentions. She was sure her cheeks were a shade of pink throughout their meal. She did not dare look at him much, and she chatted to Susanna and Jenson about their pending nuptial. She was actually looking forward to the hen do, even though Steven had developed a puppy dog look when he heard about it. It only made his teasing harder to resist.

When they finished eating, Caitlin got up to go. She looked at Susanna, 'Guess I should get ready. I don't really have much to wear for tonight though.'

Susanna clapped her hands together. 'Oh, didn't I tell you. My mum has made special clothes for tonight. They should be in your room. Hope you like them.' Susanna winked.

Steven got up. 'This I have to see.'

Jenson shook his head, 'No chance. We have a night to look forward to, and as best man you have to come with me. No party outfits for us though.'

Caitlin shrugged her shoulders. She leaned towards Steven and kissed his cheek. 'Have a good time.'

'Hmmm, you too,' Steven gave a cheeky smile.

Caitlin's jaw dropped when she saw the outfit. There was no way she was wearing it, no way.

She lifted the offending garment off the bed with her fingertips and glared. It was a dress. She had not owned, let alone worn, a party dress since she was about twelve. She did skirts, for formal occasions, but dresses like this one were a definite no go. She walked to the full length mirror in the corner of the room and put it over her form. She was expecting to grimace, but she couldn't. The colour seemed to go with her hair, in fact it didn't just go – it looked great.

She guessed there was no harm in trying it on.

She wanted to sulk and huff about it, but with no-one listening she got on with it. When she pulled up the zip along the side of her body, surprised at the perfect fit, she stood in front of the mirror. A girl looked back. A girl dressed in a knee length, flowing auburn dress with intricate small amber beads along the edge of the shoulder length sleeve. With a plunging, but discrete, neckline and tight bodice, it seemed to accentuate all of her curves perfectly. She could not help smiling at her reflection, and swaying slightly from side to side.

Her hair even looked great, as long curls loosely hung to the sides of her face. She always loved the way her hair looked when it had been recently washed.

A small wooden box on the bed caught her attention. She

opened it to find an amber necklace and bracelet, as well as a range of make-up.

She figured she might as well go along for the ride, so she applied some subtle make-up and then put on the jewellery. She had no idea how they knew amber was her favourite stone, just like it was her favourite colour of eyes. Thinking of the eyes that had entranced her, she wondered what Steven would make of her transformation.

A pair of auburn heels, with open toes, completed the look. She was not surprised to find they were a perfect fit. In this place anything was possible.

She draped the silk auburn wrap over her shoulders and eased out of the room to search for Susanna. She could not help looking over her shoulder, completely self-conscience. An outfit like this left her exposed, open to attention. She never liked being showered with praise for looks. It was why she had given up on dresses. She hated the fact everyone complimented her when she was all dolled up, as if she were a different person. She wanted people to notice her as she was.

She could hear the sound of giggling as she approached Susanna's room. As she made to move the curtain aside, Susanna jumped out of it, and squealed, 'I knew it was you. Look at her, girls. Stunning! Mum, you're a genius.' Susanna wrapped Caitlin in her arms and then leant back. 'Caitlin, this is my mother and all of my family and friends.'

Caitlin was momentarily stunned at the amount of women in the room.

She had seen Susanna's mum from a distance, but she had yet to be introduced. She had striking Mediterranean features, with a deep tan, dark brown hair and practically black eyes. She held up her petite hand, she was so short, childlike, and said, 'Lina. It's a pleasure to meet you. I'm glad your dress fits so well, I have a knack for these things.'

Caitlin could not help swaying slightly as she spoke, 'Thank you. I haven't had anyone pick a dress for me in a long time.'

Lina nodded. She did not look surprised. 'The English, well... let's just say they do not know how to dress like the

Spanish. You should take pride in your appearance. *Eres guapisima*. Men like to look and we should enjoy being seen.'

It seemed like such an obvious, yet backwards thing to say. Caitlin could not help replying, with a hint of sarcasm, 'Are we like peacocks then?'

She gave a low chuckle, 'No, no. In the animal kingdom the men are the peacocks, *los leones*. In our world, we let them believe we are the peacocks. But, actually they're the ones that still check each other out and compete for us. We dress up, we make an effort, to feel good about ourselves, to be proud of who we are. *Entiendes*?'

'I understand.' Caitlin saw some logic to the argument. It had been some time since she had looked in the mirror and thought she looked good. Saying that she hated the reference to men being lions. In that kingdom, the lionesses did all the hunting and reared the kids. All the lions did was argue over territory and women – typical.

'Anyway,' Susanna said, 'ladies. We should go.'

It was strange to be in a room full of women who looked the age of twenty, but whose real ages ranged considerably. Caitlin kept to the side as they all piled out of the room and followed Lina. She was glad they had not bothered to introduce her, there was no way she would remember all of their names.

She was surprised to see Susanna hold back, and hold out her arm. 'Come on then. Let's have some fun.'

An hour later, Caitlin was giggling along to a bunch of stories the women recalled from their younger days. Caitlin was nervous about having a turn, she was not sure she was ready for a truth or dare.

The party was juvenile. They had a selection of snacks, ranging from olives, tapenades and bread, to an assortment of breaded meat and fish. Caitlin thought she would burst if she ate any more, she wished she had known about the food before she had eaten supper.

When everyone faced her and Lina said, 'Your turn, truth or dare,' she jumped in the seat.

Caitlin faltered for a moment, before she said, 'Truth.'

Lina turned to Susanna, 'You can think of one.'

Susanna rubbed her hands together, 'Ooooo, I know, is it true you prefer our community to your world?'

The way they all stared at her, eyes wide, expectant, threw her for a minute. She stalled for an answer, 'They are completely different. I can't answer that.'

Susanna twirled her hair in her hand, 'Does that mean we should give you a dare?'

'NO!' Caitlin snapped. She hated dares. 'I'll answer, but don't be mad.'

They all nodded, not as cheery all of a sudden.

'The answer is no, I do not prefer the community. You have a great way of life here, one I admire. But, I love the freedom of choice. I had my whole life to figure out, now it feels figured out for me, if that makes sense.'

They nodded, but some looked puzzled. It was obvious a lot of them, if not most of them, had no idea what she was talking about.

'You'll have to tell us all about it then,' Susanna smiled, 'all we hear about is the pollution, the greed, the violence.'

'Yes, all of that is out there.' Caitlin felt a lump at the back of her throat, she could not really begin to explain the difference. They had no idea. Yet, she had to try. 'The thing is, people are unpredictable. Here it seems everyone is so busy, so involved, you don't have time to think about an alternative lifestyle. It doesn't even seem like people want a different life.'

Susanna huffed, 'Appearances can be deceptive. This is our home, but we all strive to make a difference, to create, to investigate, explore the mind.'

Caitlin gave a half-smile, 'I know, it's admirable.'

'Nothing is perfection,' Lina added. 'Next!' Lina turned to another woman, all smiles.

Caitlin wished she could belong. Somehow, even though she knew they were trying, she knew she would never belong. Even if they moved, even if they started all over again somewhere else, she would never be one of them. She was beginning to realise how naïve she had been, and she also started to see what Steven had warned her about. She should have listened. Hindsight was a wonderful, even if completely unhelpful, thing.

Chapter 36

Stag Do

Steven did not know what to make of the gathering. There were a lot of young men dressed in camouflage gear with excited faces. He had no idea what he had let himself in for, but he was game – more for Jenson's sake to be honest. As best man, he had the job of sorting the teams. He had been given a bag with everyone's name, ready to be picked, and was awaiting instructions. He had no idea what was coming next, but apparently this was a community tradition.

Jenson came up alongside. 'You ready?'

Steven gave a slight shake of the head. 'Not really. It would help to know what we're doing.'

'The teams are ready, we've got the party gear on, now we wait for my grandfather, Morton, who set up the tradition. Then it's game on.'

'Is your dad coming too?'

Jenson nodded. 'Yep. It's lucky he's the doctor, accidents are known to happen.'

'Yeah, well,' Steven scoffed, 'I don't intend to go anywhere near tapirs anytime soon.'

Jenson laughed, 'Don't blame you.'

Steven gave a slight shiver at the thought of the pain he had endured when a tapir had mauled his foot. Saying that, if he hadn't been attacked by the tapir, the chances were he would never have left the community and Caitlin would have been left to her own devices. He pursed his lips. The tapir had a lot to answer for.

'Right then, settle down gentlemen,' Morton's voice boomed behind them.

Steven turned to face him. Morton was so imposing, with his huge build and muscles, wavy blond hair, and square jaw. He had to be approaching a hundred years in age, and yet his physique was that of a thirty year old. His voice was very deep, but it had warmth. It was not a tone he considered intimidating.

'Today, we're celebrating Jenson's last days as a bachelor. When he's married, he will spend the rest of his days committed to one woman. They will hopefully have a family, and then commitments and responsibilities. So, for one night we shake off those binds. We are reckless. We get to bond as men and have some fun – if only more would get married, then I'd have more nights of fun!' He gave a throaty chuckle.

Jenson's dad shouted, 'Hear, hear to that.'

Steven was encouraged by the avid nodding. Perhaps, he was in for a fun night after all.

'Anyway, for those of you who have never gone on one of these, and that includes Jenson since he recently changed, don't worry. We'll look after you. A night in the jungle awaits. Each group has a folder, you each have a mission and we have eight hours. When we meet in the morning all will be revealed. Teams should not hinder each other's progress, and it's up to you if you wish to help someone in another team. We're not up against each other, we're only trying to meet our targets. It'll be fun. Now, I've not been on the losing team for many years, so I hope Steven will not set me up for a fall.' Morton turned to face Steven.

Steven tensed as everyone looked at him. Somehow, he found his voice, 'Do I just pull out a name at a time?'

'Yes. Everyone, it's time for the big reveal. We'll start with my first group member, who will I have?' Morton grinned.

Steven took a piece of paper out of the bag and opened it. He could barely believe it when he read out, 'Steven.'

Morton gave him a forceful whack on his back, 'Teammates, eh? Hope you're a tough one.' He laughed as he shook Steven's hand.

Steven carried on picking the teams. The leaders were the older males like Morton, Franco, Isaac, Juan, Ian, and Eilif. Only the oldest members of the community could lead a team. There had to be over thirty men at the gathering.

It turned out he knew some of the members of his team. Steven nodded at his cousin Enrique, who he barely knew and yet found hard to trust. He guessed it was because he was sure

Enrique had been flirting with Caitlin. He half-smiled at Jan, who he remembered had led him to the fateful tapir attack, and Susanna's father, Benjamin. He might as well meet the father of the bride before the wedding.

Morton opened their pack, and explained out loud, 'These games are computer generated, so no-one knows the solution or point. We have to use our heads and perhaps some brute strength.' He passed around a sheet to each team, and continued, 'We each have individual goals that can only be achieved as a team. But, there are five goals so we each get to lead, and we each get to follow.'

Morton stood on top of the wooden table again to grab everyone's attention. 'Let the games begin. See you all in eight hours, good luck.'

Steven followed the group out as everyone made their way into the jungle. For one night they were allowed to leave, to get lost. He wondered if everyone came back. He assumed the women did not have a similar game, otherwise his mother would have left years earlier. Perhaps, the competitive male streak ensured they all returned. He guessed they all wanted to know who'd won. He had to admit that his competitive spirit had woken up, he was up for having some fun!

He glanced at his task sheet. It had the number five on it, so he was last. At least, it would give him the chance to get to grips with the game, whatever it was.

Morton talked as they walked, 'Once we get out of here, I'll tell you more. But, for now we need to get to some high ground. I'm the leader of the first task, I need to ease you boys in gently,' he smirked, 'well, as gently as possible.'

After about ten minutes, they were out in the Amazon and everyone disappeared, at hyper speed, in different directions. He raced after Morton, who was now climbing up a massive tree. At the rate they could all run he doubted the tasks would take very long. Then again, he didn't get the impression speed was an essential part of being successful. It couldn't be.

Perched on a thick, robust looking branch, Morton smiled as he glanced over his sheet. When they were all comfortable, he began, 'The reason we're up here is because we have to defy gravity. We need to find a way to stay suspended, moving neither up nor down, without standing on the trees. We're allowed to have *contact* with the trees twice. Now, I'm sure no-one here suffers from vertigo, right?'

Everyone nodded, Steven scrunched his forehead. He did not suffer from vertigo, but the distance was intimidating.

'The key is we need to do this together as a team. If anyone gets hurt or fails to perform we all lose. So, any ideas?'

Jan spoke up first, 'Interesting. We need to fly, but not fly. That's what you're saying.'

Morton arched his right eyebrow. 'I don't know how they come up with these.'

'Can we even do that?' Benjamin asked.

'The computer thinks we can, so it must be possible,' Morten said, 'Problem is, how do we try it without getting someone hurt inadvertently?'

'I think I know,' Enrique said, he stood and leant against the tree.

Morton lifted his eyes to Enrique, 'Tell us your idea.'

'I think it's the same as floating in water,' Enrique said. 'We have to relax completely. Let the air carry us. We're not flying, we're not moving, just suspended. Like a bridge, by two points.'

'In water we float because the human body is composed of around 60-70 % water. We're much denser than air, gravity will push us down. We *will* fall,' Jan asserted.

'The human body will fall, but we have different abilities. We all know we adapt underwater and can breathe. What if we can also adapt in the air, has anyone tried it before? I'm sure some of us could make our bodies rigid. If the tension was right, we will not fall,' Enrique continued.

'He has a point, Jan,' Morten said, with a sly smile. 'And I think we should let him prove it.'

'I will,' Enrique said. He walked to the end of the branch.

'When does team work come in?' Morten said, he faced the others.

'Let me try it first, then we'll work as a team,' Enrique said, as he sat on the ledge and started to stretch.

Morten held up his hand. 'Not so fast. I'm in charge and I think we need to work together, not alone.'

Enrique stood up again, moved away from the edge and walked back to where they sat. His face had hardened.

'Don't be disheartened,' Morten added, he placed his hand on Enrique's shoulder, 'your theory has merit, but we will not sacrifice a team member. We are either all in, or not. One thing I have learnt from my numerous victories is that those who seek to succeed alone always fail.'

'So, what do you suggest?' Benjamin asked, he stroked his long, curly beard.

'We try it together, of course. If we all fall, then we fail and move on. This is a game after all,' Morten chuckled. 'This is a question of position. Who goes where?'

'I'm the smallest, so I should go in the middle,' said Benjamin.

'I'd like to be one of the anchors,' Enrique proudly raised his chin.

'Okay,' Morten nodded. 'In that case, I'll be the other anchor and Steven and Jan will go in between to create a human, well nearly,' he chuckled, 'bridge.'

Jan looked around the trees. 'We need to find a distance between the trees that matches our size. Can everyone stand side by side?'

As everyone did he seemed to make a mental calculation. 'I know what we need. Morten, are you happy for me to find the right place?'

'Sure thing, I'll get the rest practising at being rigid,' he said, a twinkle in his eyes.

Steven was not sure he completely got the game. He did not mind failure if it meant Jenson got to win. It was the least a best man could do. Even so, he did not want to let the side down. He was not in the habit of losing and he had to admit that when it came to competitions the right thing to do rarely entered his mind.

He listened as Morten took them through the technique. Then they all stood perfectly straight, and tried to go rigid. Steven closed his eyes and listened to every sound, it helped him relax. He could hear every buzzing sound, every chirp, and every crunch as life continued around them. He focused and clenched every muscle, until he sensed he was rock hard.

A finger prodded his shoulder, before Morten spoke, 'Excellent, Steven. Completely solid.'

Steven relaxed and opened his eyes. Enrique wore a scowl.

Morten pursed his lips, 'Go on then, Enrique. You'd best close your eyes like Steven did. It seemed to work.'

Enrique shrugged his shoulders and closed his eyes. He didn't look too bothered about the fact Steven had done it first, but Steven could tell by the fleeting glance that there was some resentment. Nothing like a bit of male competition within the team.

Before long, Enrique became rigid, followed by Benjamin and finally Morten.

When Jan came back, they were ready to give it a go, after they had explained to Jan what he should do.

Steven was impressed they all seemed to give him credit for figuring it out. He didn't think it was a big deal.

They followed Jan to the spot he'd selected and assessed the task at hand.

As they did a thought niggled. 'How do we know if everyone else has completed the task?'

'We don't, but why would anyone lie? Morten winked, 'right, I'll jump over. I suggest Benjamin and Jan come over with me, we'll form a chain. Then Enrique can hold on, and Steven can attach to form the other side of the chain. Enrique, you will have to swing Steven out so that he can link with Benjamin. Since we need to connect with our hands, I'll swing with my feet.'

Steven heard his intake of breath. If they made it, he'd be amazed. He watched as Morten, Benjamin and Jan effortlessly glided in the air towards the other tree.

'Ready?' Morten shouted.

Enrique waved back. 'Ready.' Then he turned to Steven, and grinned, 'Let's do this.'

Steven felt a wave of adrenaline hit and his heart raced.

He watched as Morten held on and first Jan and then

Benjamin climbed down him and held on. Steven climbed down Enrique and held on to his ankles.

Morten's voice boomed, 'Swing!'

Enrique started to swing and Steven swung his legs back and forth to encourage the momentum. After less than a minute, he felt Benjamin's hands make a grab his ankles. But, they slipped through.

'Again,' Benjamin shouted.

They hoisted themselves up at the same time and Steven felt Benjamin's hands take hold, before Benjamin cried out, 'I'm attached.'

'Everyone, go rigid,' Jan hollered.

Steven closed his eyes and concentrated, as his body stood firm.

After a few seconds, he opened his eyes and looked down. They were very high, the view was incredible and they had done it. They had formed a human bridge.

A euphoric cry shouted, 'Time to drop.'

He felt the bridge unravel as everyone let go and they all fell, screaming in a frenzied state.

Steven held his arms out and somersaulted in the air just in time, before he landed feet first on the ground. He unbent his knees and stood straight, a crazy smile on his face. His eyes widened. That was the furthest he had ever fallen.

The others formed a circle around him and patted each other on the back.

'Job well done,' Morten said, 'one down, four to go.'

Steven was actually looking forward to the next one. He had never been a thrill seeker, but now was as good a time as any to start.

Chapter 37

The Morning After

Caitlin's hand felt the empty space next to her on the bed. It was already morning and Steven had not returned. She had no idea what he was up to, but she got the impression from the other women that the stag do was a much more athletic event. She had to admit to being jealous. It had been fun to go out with the girls, and Susanna seemed really happy, but the truth was it had been boring. She had never been to a hen do before, but from the ones she had heard of and the odd one she had seen, with women dressed in truly outrageous outfits, last night's gathering was a sombre affair.

It seemed to her that women had one place in this community, and men had another. From what she gathered, men seemed to have a lot more fun. She had never really understood what her gran talked about until now. Her gran had constantly reminded her that girls in this day did not know their place. She had always talked about the sixties with disgust. Her gran had never mixed with what she had called the *wrong* type. Caitlin got the impression, from her gran's rambling, her mum had been a rebel – short shirts, hot pants. She could still visualise her gran's icy glare, her papery skin added to the scary effect.

Even so, her mum had settled down pretty quick after she met her dad. Her dad was the golden boy, in her gran's eyes, who had set her mum on the right path. A path where the man always had the last say even though her mum worked really hard. It seemed unfair.

Caitlin could not believe she was getting choked up. She had always given her mum such a hard time. She wiped away the lone tear and sat on the edge of the bed.

She closed her eyes for a moment and remembered how much she had hated boys at school. Well, hate was perhaps too strong a word. She could never understand them, and she did not have time for love and romance, unlike a lot of her more silly girlfriends. She had ambition, drive, she wanted to be an equal, to be just as good as any man.

Her hands lay loose in her lap, and her shoulders slumped. All of her aspirations had flown out the window when she had faced Steven's hypnotic, amber eyes. She was no different to her mum in the end. She found it hard to believe that falling in love could make her lose sight of everything she had considered important. In this community, she doubted they even thought much about feminism. It was like all of them were stuck in a time warp were man was still the provider. The woman was a natural mother, carer, and teacher. The man was the head of the household. Period.

She bit her lip, there was a slim chance she had it all wrong.

Either way, with everything that had happened, she could not see how she fit into the ideology. She could not even have children. She stood up, rubbed her eyes, stretched and made her way over to freshen up. Her stomach growled in protest. With Steven nowhere in sight, she guessed she'd have breakfast alone.

Alone.

She could be independent, she had been in the past.

*

'Did you have a good time last night?' Ingrid asked, as she eased up alongside Caitlin by the hot food counter.

'It was nice.'

'Nice, hmm,' Ingrid smiled, 'yes, it usually is *nice.*'

Caitlin could sense some sarcasm. 'Did you enjoy?'

'It's alright,' she raised her eyes to the ceiling, 'tradition. We're big on tradition here.'

'So, what do the men get up to?' Caitlin could not help asking. 'Everyone seemed vague when I asked last night.'

'You'll see soon enough. I imagine they'll be back soon.' Ingrid heaped some fruit into a bowl. 'Can I sit with you for breakfast?'

'Sure.' Caitlin was touched Ingrid had asked.

They made their way over to a vacant table, and Caitlin said, 'I'm looking forward to teaching today. Working with those older children is brilliant. I find the eight- to ten-year-olds amazing. Their thirst for knowledge, enthusiasm, and ability completely blow me away.'

'You must be a natural,' Ingrid laughed, 'I have never found them amazing.'

'I guess,' Caitlin chuckled, 'it's funny, I never realised how great being a child was until now. I think when I was 10 I was convinced the world was my oyster, nothing was impossible. Why do you think self-doubt raises its head when we become teens?'

'I don't know, although to be honest I never really cared what anyone thought of me. My parents always told me to follow my path, and I did, which is why I became a scientist. I love my work, and I get on great with my dad, so it was never a problem.'

'Really?'

Ingrid nodded and popped a banana piece in her mouth.

'You're lucky then. Both of my parents had nothing much in common with me. They found it odd that I enjoyed maths. But, growing up in Gibraltar, I was lucky to have so many options.'

'Oh, yes you mentioned. Tell me exactly where Gibraltar is again?'

'South of Spain, opposite Morocco.'

Ingrid's grinned. 'Are you Spanish then?'

'No, erm… it's complicated. I mean, do I look Spanish to you?'

Ingrid laughed, 'No, not exactly.'

'Sorry, you're probably not interested in this, and I haven't lived there in ages so it doesn't matter anyway,' Caitlin sighed.

'Tell me, I'm interested,' Ingrid pleaded, her lips in a childish pout.

'Okay, the crux is, Gibraltar is a British colony.'

'A colony,' Ingrid smiled, 'oh, of course, you told me before… the Rock of Gibraltar, right?'

'That's the one. Anyway, it's British so I was taught under the British school system and stuff there, but my parents always spoke a mixture of Spanish and English socially, most people do. So, that's why I like speaking Spanish, but I'm not

Spanish.'

'I guess, it's like calling someone from Switzerland French because they speak French.'

'Exactly,' Caitlin smiled. Someone got it quickly.

'Sorry, I couldn't help overhearing,' Carmen said, as she stopped next to them. 'Can I sit down?'

Caitlin was wary, but she nodded. She had not really spoken to Ian's wife much, but she knew she was Franco's daughter and therefore very much Spanish.

'I understood Gibraltar should have been returned to Spain,' Carmen asked, her tone innocent not accusatory.

'I don't want to go into detail but, as far as I know, it doesn't say that anywhere,' Caitlin tried to keep her voice calm. She had listened to these debates via her parents all her life. 'But, look I left Gibraltar when I was twelve.'

'So, you liked living in England better than Gibraltar?' Ingrid asked.

'Yes and no,' she paused, weighing up her words carefully. 'It took some time to get used to English ways. I felt like an outsider for speaking Spanish, and having a strange accent. Not that everyone wasn't nice, they were. It's just, even though I hated being a redhead in the Mediterranean, I always felt like I had a family in Gibraltar. I felt people cared.'

'And it wasn't the same in England?' Carmen tilted her head to the side.

'It couldn't be. We lived in a house for a start, not an apartment. And we rarely saw our neighbours in England, everyone keeps to themselves. In Gibraltar, people were always around, friends were easy to meet up with.'

'So, kind of like the community?' Carmen smiled.

'Yes,' Caitlin nodded, 'kind of. The community reminds me a lot of Gibraltar. The good and the bad.'

'Bad?' Ingrid pouted, then gave a sly grin.

'Yes, claustrophobia. I loved the freedom of living in England. It's a double-edged sword. No-one can have it all. Too much space and we get lonely, too little and we become stressed. No place is perfect.'

'A place is only what you make of it,' Carmen added.

'Exactly!' Caitlin beamed, then frowned as she added, 'and yet, sometimes you need to live and experience life before you truly know what home is.'

'True,' Ingrid rubbed her chin. 'Wow, this a deep conversation for so early in the morning.'

'Yes, it is,' Carmen smiled. 'I have work to do, so I'll leave you girls to your chat. I'm glad to have met someone from Gibraltar, and am sorry for any misunderstanding. No-one has the right to tell anyone else who they should be. We live in a fragile community, we fear those outside will not accept us. I would never want you to think that you would not be accepted here for being from Gibraltar. I'm very happy you speak my native tongue. *De verdad, tengo mucho gusto de conocerte.*'

'*Igualmente,*' Caitlin replied.

'See Carmen likes you,' Ingrid said, 'I think it's all fascinating really.'

Caitlin was surprised at the exchange. She could see Carmen was a great wife for Ian. 'I do like the mix of cultures here though, and I guess it is like Gibraltar. Everyone is represented in relative harmony. The community is not a bad place at all, even if,' she paused, 'to be honest, I'm not sure it's where I can truly call home.'

'I think I know what you mean,' Ingrid said, 'I've always wanted to see more of the world.'

Caitlin stared at the table, lost for a moment, wondering why she felt so sad. It really was too early.

'Caitlin, Ingrid, you're both up early today,' Susanna chirped, as she slid next to Caitlin.

'Yep, early birds, that's us,' Ingrid said. 'So, are you all set for the big day?'

Susanna's face creased up. 'Who knows? As ready as I'll ever be.'

'You really think Jenson is the one you want to spend the rest of your life with?' Ingrid added.

Susanna grinned, 'Of course, silly. Sometimes you just *know.*'

'Sometimes, even when you think you know, you don't,' Ingrid mumbled.

Susanna's shoulders dropped, and she lowered her eyes to the table, 'I guess.' She lifted her head and looked straight at Ingrid. 'And yet, if you don't take a chance on love when it's there, you might never find it again.'

Ingrid recovered and gave a broad smile, 'Of course, just checking. You and Jenson were made for each other.'

'When are Steven and you going to announce your big date?' Susanna turned to face Caitlin.

Caitlin coughed and sprayed some of her orange juice. When she recovered, her eyes slightly watery, she added, 'I'm not getting married. Not for a long, long time. I don't know if I'll ever be ready. I mean, what's the difference really? I don't need a ring...' Caitlin stopped as she saw Susanna's eyes widen in horror. She quickly tried to backtrack. 'Not that I don't see why you would want to. It's just not what I want.'

'I understand. I think I'll go get some breakfast,' Susanna gave a weak smile, stood up and walked off.

'Oops,' Caitlin said, her hand on her mouth, 'I shouldn't have said that.'

'Hey, I've lived here all my life and I'm with you,' Ingrid giggled, 'why should we all get married? What's the point and what's the hurry?'

'Well, I think a lot of people marry because of religion. Susanna is religious, so it makes sense. Then if you plan to have kids, it also makes sense – no chance of that happening for me,' she put on a brave smile and quickly carried on, she did not want or need sympathy, 'then again, I guess it means more to get married. You make a commitment to each other. Well, supposedly.'

Ingrid looked confused. 'Why supposedly?'

'Don't you know anything about adultery and divorce? My parents are still together, which is amazing, but loads of my friends' parents are divorced, you know separated.' Ingrid nodded. 'The reason behind a lot of them were affairs. Adultery is when you sleep with someone else.'

Ingrid's jaw dropped, 'When they are *married*? That's terrible.'

Caitlin laughed out loud. When she calmed down, she

added, 'Not terrible, *normal*, where I come from. Some people are not meant for monogamy, I guess. Hasn't anyone ever strayed in the community?'

'Not that I know of,' Ingrid said, 'at least, not when married. In fact, no-one has ever had a child outside of marriage in the community.'

Caitlin nodded and thought of Lucy. Someone had now. 'What would happen if someone did?'

Ingrid shrugged her shoulders, 'No idea. But, I can imagine some would be happier than others.'

'Like who? I mean, who wouldn't like it?'

'Well, if it happened with any of Franco's family and I was the guy I would run far, far away,' Ingrid shook her head in mock amusement, 'he is one tough cookie and a devout Catholic. No *sex* before marriage.' She whispered the word sex like it was a poison. 'My family is much more liberal, but we stick to the rules. The last thing we need is to break the community harmony.'

'Sure,' Caitlin replied. She was sure Lucy was Franco's daughter. Now she understood why she was hidden.

'You seem very interested, any reason?' Ingrid asked.

'Just curious.'

'I believe there's an expression for that, curiosity killed the cat?' Ingrid said, 'what does that mean anyway?'

'Don't sneak out where you're not wanted, I guess,' Caitlin replied. 'I have to go and do some prep for my class. I'll talk to you soon. Oh, and if you talk to Susanna, please tell her I didn't mean anything.'

Ingrid smiled, 'No problem.'

Caitlin took her tray away and placed it on the disposal area.

She made her way towards the exit, but paused at the sound of raucous cheering – the men had returned.

Chapter 38

Marital Bliss

Caitlin eased towards the exit, stopped and kept her back to the wall.

The men all entered the room on mass, a group of four hoisted Jenson up in the air, then placed him down next to Susanna, who stood up and gave him a massive hug. Susanna looked ecstatic, Caitlin could not help feeling a pang of jealousy.

Steven came up alongside Jenson, and another tall, blond and muscular man, who was patting him on the shoulder.

The blond man said, in a loud booming voice, 'Well, I'm afraid Jenson's team did not win, ours did. I guess I can't help winning. But, you've a great best man, Jenson. He did you proud.'

Steven grinned.

She could not help reacting, as her lips curled up. As though Steven sensed her, he looked in her direction and caught her watching. She instinctively hid, she had no idea why. She started to walk away quickly, she would talk to Steven later. This was his moment, not hers.

When she heard his voice, she stopped and turned around slowly.

Steven was covered with dirt, but his eyes shone, full of excitement. He ran towards her, 'Caitlin, wait a minute, don't go.'

Caitlin blushed, shy for a moment.

'Hey,' his hand rubbed her cheek.

'You're covered in grime,' Caitlin gave a cheeky smile, 'I guess I don't need to know if you had a good time.'

Steven leaned in and kissed her on the lips.

He tasted salty, but his kiss was so deep she did not care. For a moment, she lost herself before she pulled back. 'Not now.'

'But no-one's watching,' Steven said, as he got closer again and put his arms around her waist.

'I have to go teach, and you desperately need to freshen up,' she raised an eyebrow, 'maybe later, we can catch up?'

'Definitely, it was amazing. I'll see you later then.' He let her go.

She made to turn, but he placed his hand on her arm, 'Are you okay?'

'Course I am,' she replied. She knew it had been too quick a reply, but Steven did not push further.

'Okay, see you later,' Steven said.

She was sure he was still watching her as she walked, so she turned around. 'Stop it.'

He laughed, 'I missed you.'

'Whatever,' she rolled her eyes, gave him a cute small wave and pursed her lips. Steven always had a way of making her smile.

***

Steven was glad Caitlin seemed settled with what she was doing. It mattered to him a lot if she was happy. And he didn't care if they would never have children, he did not have a burning desire to become a dad anyway. He was worried that she seemed to enjoy teaching children though. In time, it could be a problem. Or, on the other hand, it might make it easier for her. He had no idea.

He made his way back to the hall. A lot of them had food and were sat down. The last ten hours had been one of the most exciting of his life. He would never forget it.

As he approached, Morten hollered, 'Steven, get some food and come sit with us.'

Steven could see Jenson was back with Susanna so he guessed it was a good plan.

After loading up his plate with a bit of everything he could find, he made his way over to what looked like the winning table. His team was one of the few that had stayed together.

Benjamin's cheeks were still rosy, his pale complexion and freckles could not hide his excitement. 'Steven, what a win! That's the first time for me.'

'Yes, you did very well, Steven,' Morten said.

Even Enrique had lost the smirk. A lot could change in a few hours. Steven could even consider him a friend, and was glad to be related.

Carmen came up to her son and hugged him. 'We're very proud of you.'

Enrique turned to his teammates, and said, 'They did it. I was just along for the ride.'

'Come on, Enrique,' Jan protested. 'Your leadership in the hunting challenge was impressive for your experience.'

'You all knew what you were doing, it was no big deal.'

'Trust me, Carmen,' Morten said, 'your son did you proud. As did your nephew, Steven.'

'Glad to hear it,' Carmen smiled, 'Caitlin is an interesting girl.'

Steven saw Enrique glance at his mum at the mention of Caitlin. Steven was no fool, he knew Enrique was interested.

'Really?' Steven asked.

'Yes, she's a bright one,' Carmen nodded, 'I had a good chat with her earlier. She's a good addition to the community. She'll fit in well.'

'Glad to hear it.' He'd ask Caitlin what that was all about later.

'Anyway, congratulations.' She ruffled Enrique's hair. '*Muy bien, hijo.*'

'*Ya basta*,' Enrique wriggled in his seat.

Once she was gone, Enrique rolled his eyes and said, 'Mothers!'

They all laughed.

'I have not had to hear mine for years,' Morten added.

'I hear mine every day,' Enrique said.

Steven stopped smiling and frowned as he held his tongue and focused on eating.

'Perhaps, we should talk about something else,' Jan said.

Steven glanced up and gave him a weak smile of thanks. He was glad someone had picked up that he didn't have one.

As they all rambled on and congratulated themselves on their success, Steven noticed the way Jenson left with Susanna. There was no doubt in his mind that his friend was marrying for love.

***

Jenson held Susanna's hand, and openly admired his future wife. He was glad he did not have to conceal their relationship any more. The following day she would be his wife. Under a little duress, he had agreed to marry Susanna under the conventions of the Catholic Church. It appeased his future mother-in-law.

'Do you think we'll be chosen to go to Borneo?' Susanna asked.

'Why are you thinking about it now?'

'I don't know. I guess with us getting married and stuff, I just wanted to know what our plan was.'

'It's exciting. I mean, I do want to start a family with you, but if we went to Borneo we could have some fun first. I've only ever seen it on a map, and the only thing we know is that deadly animals live there. We could add to their numbers, don't you think?' he joked. It was better to see the move in a positive light.

'Would you want to?' she asked, with a slight shrug.

'I think so, yes. But, I don't know if they'll let us. We've only changed recently. But, there's no harm in trying, is there?'

'No, none at all.'

'We could start a family there if you like?'

Susanna immediately blushed. She squeezed his hand and leaned into his shoulder. 'You are lovely, you know that?'

'I have something for you. Will you come to see?' he asked. He thought now was as good a time as any.

'Of course, what is it?'

'If I tell you, it won't be a surprise, will it?'

Once at his room, Jenson winked at her. 'Wait here, no peeking.'

With great care he walked towards her and handed her a small parcel, the size of her hand. It was wrapped in a huge leaf interspersed with flowers.

'It's not my birthday,' she teased.

'Open it.' He could not wait to see her reaction.

Carefully, she unravelled the leaf. Inside, was a carved wooden box engraved with the initials S & J. As she lifted the top of the box from its base she disclosed a set of rings. They were obviously handmade from gold, with an embroidered leaf design on the surface. 'They're beautiful. When did you organise these?' Her eyes had moistened.

'Gideon's a clever craftsman. Shall we try them on?'

'Yes, yes,' she said, excited. Carefully, she took out the larger ring and placed it on his finger.

Then he carefully took out the smaller ring and placed it on hers.

They held out their left hands in unison and looked at the rings. A perfect match for a perfect pair.

'Let's do it for real now,' he proposed.

'Definitely.'

As they kissed and embraced, Jenson knew that marrying Susanna would make him the happiest man alive.

*

The corridor had been decorated with flowers of every shape, size and colour. The normally dismal environment was transformed into something truly spectacular. The smell in particular was overpowering. The entire community embraced a wedding. It gave them a chance to show off and put on a show. Everyone attended. The caterers did the food, the seamstresses made the dresses and embroidered any tablecloths required, children collected flowers, and the parents prepared the honeymoon suite – a room designed for the young lovers. It left the bride and groom with little to do other than to hold their nerve.

The main catering hall had been transformed for the event. In the corner, a gigantic cake decorated with iced flowers and exotic fruit created a centrepiece. In front of it was an arbour adorned with colourful leaves and flowers. Underneath, Jenson stood waiting, Steven was at his side. Jenson felt awkward in the wedding suit, it was not his usual attire to say the least. To say he was nervous could not adequately convey how he was feeling. Petrified was a better word. As if sensing his mood, Jenson saw Steven wink at him and he could not help but smile. He needed all the moral support he could get.

Behind the arbour stood Franco, who always performed the rite. He held his slightly worn and well known bible in front of him and stood tall, a calm and composed expression on his face.

Jenson wished he could feel at peace. His stomach was doing a three sixty degree turn. He did not care how nice the place looked. The fear that Susanna would not turn up remained. Even though he hoped it to be unlikely, it was a possibility. For the life of him, he could not understand why this set-up was a good idea – it must have been a woman who thought of the arrangement. To him, this was a way to torture a prospective husband on their wedding day.

At last, the band started to play the wedding march.

He faced forward, not daring to look back yet. Not until she was closer. He could hear the series of gasps and compliments exuded by the watching community. Finally, he saw her in his peripheral vision and he felt his jaw slacken. She was a vision, wearing a white lace dress with long sleeves and a white transparent veil. It gave her a pure and untouched look. The fact that she was still a virgin made the look match reality.

Finally, they arrived at the arbour and his future mother-in-law linked Susanna's arm in Jenson's. The ceremony seemed to go on for hours. Finally, after going through all the formalities, Gideon handed them the rings and they made their binding vows. His eyes fixed on hers as pure joy swept over him. He had to be the happiest man alive.

When he was given permission to kiss the bride, he stepped forward and lifted the veil. He could not help his lips twitching as he leaned in for a subtle romantic kiss. The whole congregation whooped with joy as they linked hands and faced them. A married couple at last. Franco recorded the marriage in their book of records and the deed was done. Two grand chairs had been set for them at the head of the table next to the arbour. After speaking to as many people as possible they took their seats and the festivities began.

It amazed Jenson that within minutes the hall was transformed into a reception venue, as chairs were passed around and rearranged around the tables. The ones who took responsibility for catering arrived with trays full of food and drink which they lay on the tables. No-one got served, everyone took what they wanted.

After the main meal had been eaten, his dad, Doctor Johannes stood up. He tapped his fork on his glass and the light tinkle hushed the crowd. 'Family and friends, what a lovely couple. Today I have gained another daughter, thank you, Susanna, for agreeing to marry my son. He's alright.'

A few chuckled.

'No seriously,' Doctor Johannes continued, 'I'm very proud of you, Jenson, for the way you are and have no doubt you will both make each other very happy. Please everyone, raise your glasses to Susanna and Jenson. The happy couple.'

The entire audience repeated the words.

Jenson was sure his heart would explode soon from the way it was pounding. It was his turn to speak. He smiled at Susanna, took a deep breath, and got up. 'Family and friends, thank you for celebrating this day with my lovely wife, Susanna, and me,' he paused, to watch her blush, 'we hope that you all enjoying this day as much as we are. The truth is that you could never be as happy as I am today. I am married to the most beautiful woman I have ever met, no offence to all you other ladies out there.'

'None taken,' Ingrid called out, a smirk on her face.

'Thank you cousin,' he nodded, as she winked back at him. 'Anyway, I'd like to toast to Susanna, my soul mate, my friend and life companion – Susanna.'

Everyone raised their glasses high up in the air to toast and repeated her name.

Jenson faced Steven. It was time to pass the baton to his best man.

Chapter 39

Best Man's Speech

Steven stood up and faced the large expanse. A lot of faces stared in his direction. He took a deep breath, glanced quickly at Caitlin who gave him an encouraging smile, and began, 'As best man, I suppose I should offer some insight into married life for the bride and groom,' he paused, and stared at the table. It felt like forever before he looked up again. 'Truth is, having never been married myself, I'm not sure I'm qualified to give any advice. I have no idea why Jenson thought I should be his best man.'

Steven stared into space.

He fidgeted with his hands, briefly closed his eyes, and mustered all the courage he had left to continue, 'There is only one thing I can say to Susanna – if Jenson could become friends with a mongrel like me, and can show you the loyalty and support I have had as a friend, you can look forward to a very long, happy marriage. I...' Steven faltered, now choked. He blurted out the final words, 'I know you'll both be happy. Please raise your glasses again for Susanna and Jenson.'

As the toast was done and everyone sat down again, Steven's body shuddered momentarily and he relaxed.

Caitlin ran her hand along the back of his neck. 'You did well.'

'Never again,' Steven whispered.

Caitlin smiled, 'You did great, seriously.'

'If you say so,' Steven said. He turned to face her, and melted for a moment in her deep blue eyes. Right now, all he wanted was to get away. He picked up the glass of wine and downed it in one instead.

'Thirsty? Not like you,' Caitlin chuckled.

Steven gave a half-smile. 'This once, a bit of alcohol can do no wrong.'

Caitlin sipped her wine. 'Red is my favourite.'

Steven winked at her. 'Mine too, funny that. Red is a great

colour.'

'Yes, it is,' Caitlin licked her lips.

'What do you think of marriage?' Steven said, his voice casual.

Caitlin rolled her eyes. 'Not much.'

Steven knew Caitlin never mentioned it, but now, in the middle of this wedding it was all he could think of. A life with Caitlin, a married life. He had no idea why the thought had become so powerful, it was probably the wine. Made him sentimental. He nodded and looked away. This was not the right time.

As the band started to play for the first dance, Steven watched Susanna and Jenson take centre stage. He had never seen two people look so happy, so in tune with one another. He had no idea if what he had with Caitlin was the same. He wanted it to be, he really did. He refilled his glass for the fourth time, the wine went down like water.

As the bride and groom's parents took to the floor, followed by other couples, he held out his hand. 'May I have this dance?'

Caitlin fluttered her eyelashes, and held his hand. 'Of course.'

Steven led Caitlin out to the dance floor, now woozy from the alcohol. It made him take more notice of Caitlin's figure as he imagined it under her long, sleeveless, tight brown dress. It had a range of amber beads sown into the hem and neckline, the colour was perfect on her. She was wearing some subtle makeup that kept her natural beauty, and just accentuated her eyes and lips. He found it hard to look away from her lips, he wanted to kiss them. Instead, he held her body to his and outstretched her right arm as he led her into a slow waltz, to the rhythm of the music.

The alcohol made him more brazen as he took control of the dance and spun Caitlin slowly around. She giggled and did not seem to mind. After all her jokes in the past, about his ballroom dancing lessons at school, he finally had the chance to show off his moves. He was impressed she kept up. Caitlin had not lied when she told him she was also a good dancer.

When the number finished and a slower one started, Caitlin put her hands around his waist and nestled her head into his chest. Steven leant his chin lightly on her head and wrapped his arms around her as they slowly rotated clockwise to the beat. In that precise moment, Steven felt like nothing in the world could go wrong.

After a minute, he eased off her head and whispered in her ear, 'Will you make me an honest man, Caitlin?'

Caitlin stood still. Hesitant, she said, 'You are an honest man.'

'You know what I mean,' he smirked.

'You don't mean it,' she said, all serious.

He tilted his head to the side. 'You think I don't mean it.'

Caitlin shrugged her shoulders, pursed her lips, and shook her head from side to side.

Steven liked a challenge, and right now he had something to prove. It was about time. He stood back, headed towards the band and grinned, 'Watch me.'

Caitlin's jaw dropped and she started to protest as he gave her a wicked smile.

When he got to the stand, he glanced in Caitlin's direction. As expected, her face had turned a shade of pink and her eyes had widened, her hand waving him back discretely.

Steven was not going to be put off. 'Can the music please stop? I have an announcement to make.'

The band stopped playing after Jenson nodded in their direction. At least his friend didn't mind his impromptu speech.

'Sorry everyone for interrupting. But, I think as best man I have the right to add something else on to my speech.' Steven faced the bride and groom. 'Jenson, Susanna is the most beautiful woman in the room for you, and I can appreciate why, but I forgot to add that Caitlin is the most beautiful woman in the room for me. Since I have felt the same way about her from the moment I laid eyes on her I hope you do not find it inappropriate that I make my declaration.'

Jenson shouted out, 'Not at all.'

Susanna beamed.

Steven walked back towards Caitlin, as the entire room froze, watching his every move for the second time. Fuelled by an irrational force, his knelt on one knee. He started to get concerned by the dagger stares Caitlin was giving, but he was not going to be put off. He held out his hand and lightly held Caitlin's. 'Caitlin, I have no doubt that you're the woman I want to spend the rest of life with. Please, I am begging you, make me an honest man. Caitlin, will you marry me?'

He stared up at Caitlin, who now looked away. He started to worry again, as a second became a few and still she gave no answer.

'Go on, Caitlin, give him your reply,' Gideon called out, impatient as usual.

Caitlin seemed to jump out of her trance and made eye contact.

The fact she was not smiling rang major alarm bells.

Steven continued to smile, he was desperate for the right answer.

Caitlin opened her mouth to speak but nothing came out. Her eyes became watery, she bit down on her lip, and she removed her hand from his. In the faintest whisper, she said, 'I'm sorry, Steven. I'm not ready to say yes yet. I have to go.' She turned around and walked away as the crowd parted for her in stunned silence.

Steven dropped his head to the floor, and slowly stood up. He could not meet anyone else's eyes as he walked in the direction Caitlin had gone. His romantic gesture had failed. He had been a fool to act so irrationally. It was not the right time, not *yet*.

***

Susanna could not believe what had just happened. Caitlin had walked away from Steven. She had turned her back on marriage. She could not understand why she would do such a thing. Not unless, she was not in love with Steven. She had her suspicions, as much as she had not wanted to admit it until now. To embarrass Steven in front of the community, she could not believe it.

Tears were streaming down her face at her own wedding. It

did not seem right.

Jenson cupped her face in his hand, and wiped her tears away with his thumbs. 'I love you so much, don't worry about Steven. Think about us. Thank you for marrying me.' He leaned in and kissed her.

'Can we go for a walk? I need some air.'

'Of course,' Jenson said, as he squeezed her hand and they got up. A few people looked at them and smiled, most let them be. 'Shall we go to our new room?'

Susanna blushed, 'I'd like that.'

The fact they barely spoke for the walk spoke volumes. Susanna now buzzed with a nervous anticipation that had replaced the sadness.

At the doorway, Jenson picked Susanna up and carried her into the room. Susanna could not help giggling. It was such a silly tradition really, yet it was fun to be held like a baby. It broke the seriousness of the situation. She could not believe she was now married. The scary thing was nothing held them back. They were free to do as they pleased.

Jenson put her down, held her hand and kissed it gently, a glint remained in his eye. She could not help looking away, overwhelmed.

'We can talk if you like. I don't want you to rush into anything.'

This was why she had married Jenson. He really got her. 'I'd like that. I can't help being nervous to finally be alone with you. I half expect someone to come and turf us out.'

'I know, it's great isn't it.' He wrapped his arms around her and gave her a cuddle. It was perfect. He stroked her hair and whispered, 'Do you want to know when I first fell in love with you?'

'Tell me,' she replied, as she leant back to look at him.

'When you were eleven, something about you made me curious. I'd been helping to chop some wood with my dad, when you appeared with your mum. You were laughing about something and looked so happy that I was immediately smitten. I knew there were tenuous family links between us, so I tried to forget you. But then, as we got to know each other, it became impossible to ignore the way I felt.'

Susanna knew that feeling was mutual. 'I remember the day. The way you looked at me was disconcerting – in a nice way. Then when you stood up for my brother when he was being bullied, I just knew you were looking out for me.'

'You noticed then?'

'Of course, you always let me through first, if I dropped anything you always seemed to be close by to give me a hand. It was difficult to not get to know you, and then I knew. I knew there was something else.' She dropped her gaze for a moment. Mustering her courage, she looked up again. 'And here we are.'

'Here we are,' he repeated, as he placed his hand on her jaw line. 'Thank you for becoming my wife. You have no idea how proud I was to see you walking down the aisle to join me.'

'I kept pinching myself the whole time,' she said, unable to avoid biting her lip, 'I thought I was dreaming.'

Jenson took the cue and leaned in. His lips moulded into hers perfectly for a slow and meaningful kiss. Susanna sighed, and let her head rest on his chest. She could hear his heartbeat pounding. She wondered if he was also nervous. She hoped so. Her stomach lurched in anticipation. The feel of his body against hers, even though fully clothed was making her think of *it* again. She wanted more. It was just so alien.

As if reading her mind, he started to run his fingers down her back. She could not withhold a shiver. Following his lead, she caressed his lower back working her hands up towards his shoulders in slow circles. Jenson moved his hands towards her breasts and when he cupped one gently she gasped.

Without any further hesitation, he kissed her again. This kiss was different. She could not help it and she started to let go of her inhibitions. It was as though some primeval instinct had kicked in. The shackles undone, free to discover each other at last.

Later, Susanna panted slightly. It had taken her by surprise. She was out of breath, in awe, shivering, in some pain. So many responses for one action. It was incredible. 'Now I know what all the fuss was about,' she sighed.

Jenson hummed a response. He also seemed lost for words. He held her tightly in his arms, wrapped the blanket around them and fell into a deep sleep.

As she listened, his breathing become deep and slow. She could not help wondering how he managed to fall asleep so quickly. She had a million thoughts running through her mind. A part of her felt guilty that she should be experiencing what she considered to be true love when Caitlin appeared to be so lost. She wondered what could make someone who must have been so in love, from what she had been told, now doubt it.

She hoped the same thing would never happen to her. She wanted to believe that they would be together forever. A break up was practically unheard of in the community. They knew of something called divorce. She could not even begin to imagine what that was like, especially if children were involved. She had no idea how it could work.

Nevertheless, if people could try relationships, without the binds of marriage, it might lead to love. There were a lot of single people in the community who could not find their match, they did not have the certainty, and so preferred to stay alone. Ingrid was a good example. If she had been able to try a relationship with many of the men who had sought her hand in marriage she might have been tempted. She just never wanted to marry any of them.

Susanna gave a deep sigh. It was stupid to think about this now. Now, when she was in blissful happiness.

Finally, after what felt like hours, but was probably only five minutes, she dozed off. The last thing she remembered was the look of pain on Steven's face. He had to find happiness. It was only right that he did.

Chapter 40

Eyes

A one-night stand could lead to a miracle, a miracle in a supposedly barren wasteland. It would be easier on the children to have a father, but somehow Lucy doubted anyone would ever guess who the father was, and she certainly wasn't going to tell. Lucy stroked the head of her daughter as she suckled on her breast. She found the human body incredible. The fact she could actually feed her children after everything she had been through, regardless of what she was.

'Lucy, you look so peaceful.' A voice interrupted her thoughts.

Lucy looked up, 'Caitlin? What are you doing here? I thought there was a wedding tonight…'

'There was,' Caitlin replied.

Lucy was struck by the way Caitlin's shoulders drooped, her eyes also looked red, as though she had been crying. She chose her next words carefully, 'And was it a good wedding?'

'It was a great wedding.' Caitlin made her way over to the chair next to Lucy and sat down.

The way Caitlin stared at her baby made her uncomfortable. As her daughter released her nipple, her head lolled back as she fell into a deep sleep. Lucy made herself decent, then lifted the baby to put her in her cot.

'Can I hold her?' Caitlin said.

Lucy hesitated for a spilt second, then said, 'Sure.'

She placed her daughter in Caitlin's arms and watched in a subdued silence.

Lucy picked up one of her sons and started to feed him on her other breast. Feeding was a constant job with three hungry babies. They had brought in supplementary breast milk from a community donor to appease the babies. Lucy could barely meet the demand.

As her son suckled, Caitlin stood up with her daughter and placed her in the cot. She was still fast asleep. Her other son was not.

'Shall I get him?' Caitlin asked.

'If you don't mind,' Lucy sighed. 'His milk is over there. In that blue container, you'll find a bottle waiting for him.'

'Sure,' Caitlin said.

Once Caitlin was ready with the bottle in hand, she went to pick up the now screaming baby boy. Lucy was convinced young babies sounded like animals in pain.

As Caitlin picked him up she froze. The cries intensified.

Lucy could not understand what was wrong. 'Caitlin?'

Caitlin turned to face Lucy, her face impossible to read, then sat down and started to feed the baby.

Lucy wanted to ask what was wrong, but Caitlin seemed focused. She waited for her to speak.

Once the bottle was empty, and both sons were satisfied and asleep, Lucy led Caitlin out of the room.

'Would you like a drink?' Lucy asked.

Caitlin still seemed lost in thought.

'Caitlin?'

Caitlin looked up, her expression sad, lost. 'Yes, I'd love a glass of water.'

'What about tea? I have to be honest you don't look so good.'

'Tea would be lovely.'

Lucy made herself busy, and put the kettle on to boil. 'It's nice to see you tonight, Caitlin. I was not expecting any…'

'Are you the one that slept with Steven?' Caitlin blurted.

Lucy's cheeks flushed and she remained silent.

Caitlin continued, 'When Steven came back to find me he told me he had been with someone else. He said it did not mean anything, it had just happened. So far, I have seen no-one that could have happened with, until now.'

'Why now?'

'Your son just looked at me and showed me a set of sparkling amber eyes,' Caitlin smiled, 'eyes just like his father, his mother and his aunt.'

Lucy was taken aback by the smile. 'You don't mind?'

Caitlin relaxed, 'I'm shocked to find out that Steven has

three children. Although, when he finds out he'll be speechless. But, I don't mind. Steven deserves to be a father. He'll be a great father. I'm also glad he gave you children. From what he told me you were pretty lost when it happened. You don't look lost anymore, you look radiant.'

Lucy grinned, 'Hmm, radiant. I'd like to believe that.' She handed Caitlin the mug of tea. 'Sugar?'

'No thanks,' Caitlin said. 'Steven proposed tonight.'

Lucy nearly choked on the tea she had just drank. 'Congratulations.'

'I didn't say yes,' Caitlin frowned, apologetic. 'Lucy, I know your secret and now you can know mine.'

'You don't have to tell…' Lucy began.

Caitlin pursed her lips. 'I can't have children.'

'Oh,' Lucy swallowed. 'Is that why you said no?'

'No, I do care about him a lot, but I don't want to get married, not yet,' Caitlin replied.

Lucy glanced over and said, 'Marriage is not meant to be a chore and Steven obviously doesn't mind if he asked you?'

'He says he doesn't mind, but what does he really know? In time, he might change his point of view. I don't want him to marry me and then realise it was a mistake.'

'Can I ask you something?'

Caitlin shrugged her shoulders. 'Sure.'

'How did you change? I'm very curious about how a normal human became one of us.' Lucy leaned forward, her head tilted to the side.

'I can't tell you how, I promised not to tell anyone how it happened. I can tell you Steven made me one of you, but as you can tell I am *not* like you. It appears my blood is pure, like a human. I am told I will not age, time will tell on that one. But, we know my reproductive organs no longer function. So, I'm glad I saved you. You're the mother of Steven's children,' Caitlin gulped, 'I'm proud to have been the one to save the mother of his children.'

Lucy put her mug down, and threw her arms around Caitlin. 'I'll never be able to repay the debt.'

Caitlin returned the embrace before she broke down in

tears.

Lucy could not hold back on her emotions and she followed suit. She had no idea how long they sat there, a blubbering wreck.

Finally, they both calmed down and Lucy let Caitlin go. She wiped her eyes and gave a nervous laugh.

Caitlin sniffled, 'I need a tissue.'

Lucy picked up the cloth she had used with the babies and handed it over. 'Use this.'

Caitlin blew her nose in the cloth, and then started laughing. 'It smells of milk!'

'Sorry,' Lucy said, now smiling.

'It's okay, it made me laugh.'

Lucy knew she was out of line, but she felt bad and had to ask, 'Do you love Steven?'

Caitlin shook her head, 'I think so, but it doesn't matter. I just don't want to settle down, I don't want *him* to settle for me. Not unless I really know whether what we have is the real thing. My mum and dad were never happy when I was growing up. I know they love each other, in some strange way, but I don't want to just marry Steven because he's the first man I fell in love with. I want to marry Steven because he is the only man I want to be with.'

'And right now, you just don't know for sure,' Lucy added.

'Exactly. Since he changed me, I don't know, I see things differently. I'm not blinded by love, or lust,' she giggled. 'I feel empowered by the change, stronger than I've ever been, I want more than *just* to be with Steven,' Caitlin paused. 'It sounds terrible, selfish even. When I found out I could not have children I was in complete shock. But then as the shock wore off I wondered if it was a sign. A sign telling me that there was more to my life than settling down and having a family. I'm so sorry, I'm rambling…'

'No, no, I think I understand. You want to find out who you are before you commit to being with someone else. You're a very smart girl.' Lucy was impressed by Caitlin's maturity.

'I'm glad you think so. I feel very stupid for running out on Steven right now. I mean, he is what every girl wants. A handsome, intelligent man who is apparently madly in love with me. I must be an idiot to walk away. I just don't want to be driven by love. I want, I mean, I would like to live and make mistakes of my own, to discover what I'm made of. Oh, I'm doing it again... rambling.'

Lucy chuckled. 'You know, listening to you I feel like the fool. My parents brought me up to believe that marriage was everything. I was madly in love with Ian, Steven's uncle, but as it turned out he loved someone else.'

'Carmen?'

'Yes.'

Caitlin gave an apologetic smile, 'She's very nice.'

'I know,' Lucy sighed, 'Thing is I hid away from the community, I hid away from Ian. My heart was broken. Steven was the first... I'm sorry can I tell you this?'

'Sure,' Caitlin nodded.

'Steven was the first man I ever allowed to get close to me. It was an accident, and we were both on the rebound, mine a longer-term one. He really missed you, it was obvious he was thinking of someone else when he was with me. Now I realise, I could've been happy with someone else, I just didn't let anyone else in.'

'What happened with Steven was meant to be. Look at your lovely babies,' Caitlin said.

Lucy got up, looked through the glass window in the door, and stared at the three domes keeping her babies safe. 'I know. Of course, if my family finds out they'll disown me. I am a disgrace.'

'Really?' Caitlin moved next to Lucy.

'I don't want to think about it. At the moment, Catherine has told them I'm exploring the island of Borneo. Do you know we plan to create a settlement there?'

'Yes, I heard.'

'My father has no intention of going, it's lucky.'

Caitlin gave a low gasp. 'So, you're not telling them about your children? You plan to go there without his knowledge. Wouldn't someone tell him?'

'I guess,' Lucy said, 'but once I'm there he can't do

anything about it. And I figure everyone will be too busy there to care about what I've done.'

'Steven has to know. Are you going to tell him?'

'Tell me what?' Steven said, his voice low.

Lucy turned to face the voice, then held her hand to her mouth. 'What are you doing here?'

'It took a long time to track Caitlin down, trust me. But, I managed,' Steven said. His eyes had a crazed look, his hair dishevelled. 'Lucy, it's been a while.'

'It has.' Lucy stood straight in front of the door. 'How much did you hear?'

'Enough,' Steven replied. 'Is it true? Am I a father? Is that what you were both saying?'

'It's true,' Caitlin said. 'They have your eyes.'

Steven's face was impossible to read. Lucy did not know what to do or say.

'You should see them,' Caitlin continued, 'children need their parents.'

Steven fixed her with an icy stare. 'They do.'

Lucy could tell by his expression he was hurt. 'Perhaps tonight is not the best night for this.'

'No, it's fine,' Steven said. 'I can handle this. After tonight, I can handle anything.' He walked towards Lucy.

Lucy held up her right hand, 'Steven, no, not like this. Come back tomorrow.'

'I'll leave,' Caitlin said.

Steven faced Caitlin, and snapped, 'You will stay here. You owe me that much.'

Caitlin nodded, her eyes to the floor. 'I'll wait here then.'

Steven placed his hand on Lucy's shoulder, and in a gentler voice said, 'Please. Let me see.'

The contact made Lucy shudder slightly. She had run out of options. 'Be quiet, they're sleeping.'

'Sure,' Steven whispered.

Lucy slowly turned the door handle, and held the door open for Steven. She glanced at Caitlin as she shut the door, but Caitlin had sat down, her head now in her hands.

Steven remained frozen as he looked from one incubator to

the next. 'Three?'

Lucy gave an awkward grin, and smiled, 'Congratulations.'

Steven walked over to each incubator and stared for a few moments before he moved to the next. At the last one, he turned and faced Lucy. His eyes were brimming with tears.

Chapter 41

Destiny

Caitlin had never felt as confused as she did right now. Her head was a mess. She wanted to walk away, to leave, but Steven was right she owed him. She had just walked out on him and now he had found out he had three children. It was a lot for anyone to take. She had no idea what he could be thinking.

After a few more minutes had passed, she lifted her head out of her hands and got up. She tentatively peered through the glass and saw Steven talking to Lucy as they watched over their children. The pit of her stomach sank deeper at that thought. She would never have Steven's children. Yet, here was a beautiful, really nice woman who had given Steven three children in need of a father and love. It made sense to Caitlin that they should have a go of it. Especially since she could not decide what she wanted.

She started to back away slowly. She should just leave. Steven probably hated her anyway. She had embarrassed him for sure.

She started to walk down the corridor, then upped her pace into a jog, before she started running as fast as she could. She knew where to go. She needed to swim, to pound the water as hard as she could, to lose herself in the depths. To escape. To scream.

As she neared the place, she started to unfasten her hair and let her red, curly locks hang loose. She shook out her hair, wiped furiously at her eyes and tried to ignore her moist cheeks. Once in the desolate cavern, the only sound the roaring waterfall, she stripped off her clothes quickly and dived off the edge. When she surfaced, she swam a smooth front crawl to the other side, her legs pounding as fast as she could. Once she reached the rock she stopped then let out a primeval scream.

This was not her life.

She had lost all control.

She dived down to the bottom of the water and allowed the near silence to engulf, to take over her senses. She would be happy to end it all here, in the water, the place she felt most at home. She always wanted to be a mermaid when she was younger. As the minutes stretched, she wondered why they had adapted to survive underwater. Had she really evolved into something stronger? She did not think she was special by being what she was. It had brought nothing but trauma, compared to the promise it had shown at the beginning.

She did not consider herself to be any better than her family or her friends back home, just because she had changed. She was stronger, faster, would supposedly look the same for years, and yet, it all meant nothing. What was the point? What was her purpose?

She screamed underwater, the bubbles oozing up to the surface.

As she released air, she felt the urge to breathe again and she kicked up. She did not want to die. She wanted to know why. As much as she had never been that religious, regardless of her upbringing, she did firmly believe there was a God, a power stronger than everyone. A force driving life, driving humanity to a point, a purpose. She had studied religion, she had searched for answers. Yet, she could not see them clearly. It would be so much easier if Jesus existed now, if there was someone guiding her in her life. A life where she could have a purpose.

She broke the surface and swam back to the waterfall. All the time thinking back to her youth and the times she had fought for the rights of animals by being an avid WWF member. Had her parents not instilled in her the need to consider others before herself? If she was youthful and strong could she not use her gifts for good? There had to be a way. A life where she could find her calling, find her peace and help others. There were many places in the world where someone like her could do a lot of good. She could be the perpetual student, going from place to place, helping, learning, encouraging growth.

It made sense to her.

Staying in the community did not.

The problem remained. She had to find a way to leave. It was her only hope.

As she climbed out of the water, she saw Steven sat down next to her clothes, head down. She was not embarrassed to be naked in front of him, he had seen her before, but she still tensed as she made her way over. She slipped the dress on quickly, even though she was soaking wet, and sat down.

'Sorry I left.'

Steven raised his head. 'It's okay, I would have left too. Sorry I snapped at you.'

'It's okay. I deserved it,' she gave a weak smile.

'No, you didn't. I was an idiot to ask you to marry me like that. It was not the right time or place. I just wanted to, impulsive I guess, and, as usual, you were the wise one. You make a lot of sense.'

'Do I?' Caitlin chuckled, 'that would be a first.'

'You always made sense to me,' he gave her a determined stare.

Caitlin nodded. 'So, how do you feel about being a dad?'

'I am freaking out… that's the truth. But, I don't know,' Steven paused, 'Lucy seems really happy. So, I'm glad for her sake. I just have no idea what to do about it. She explained that it has to be a secret. Truth is, I'm all out. Can I do anything else that is wrong or out of line? I think I've broken every rule so far. I should not exist, you should not exist, and those innocent babies should not exist. And yet, here we all are – existing! It's crazy.' He ran both his hands through his hair.

'I want to believe there's a point to all of this. I've been thinking about it and I just have to find a reason for all of it to make sense. You know me, my logical brain just can't help itself.'

Steven placed his hand over hers. 'For your sake, I wish there was a point. I wish there was a reason for our existence. But, as the history of mankind has shown, man is not the most useful animal on the planet and now we're here to add flavour to the party. I sometimes what destiny is all about – we must be a huge source of entertainment or disappointment.'

'And yet, here we are. I can't help thinking... oh, I don't know what I'm thinking. This is a disaster. A tragedy,' Caitlin sighed.

'It doesn't have to be. I love you, Caitlin. I have from the moment I met you. You know, don't you?'

Caitlin gave a weak nod. 'The truth is, I know you tell me this and you have shown it by everything that's happened, but I don't really get why you do. You could have anyone you want, you have lots of girls that are interested, and now you have children with another woman. I really am not that special.'

'You are to me,' Steven said, his hand reached for her chin and pulled it in his direction. 'You do not see yourself the way I do. You are kind, loving, thoughtful, considerate, beautiful... I could go on forever. There is no reason why I love you specifically. It's everything. I love you for who you are, how you make me feel. I am a better man with you in my life. But...' he dropped his hand.

'But what?' Caitlin asked.

Steven looked into the distance. After a minute of silence, he continued, 'I know I do not make you better. I have changed your life and made it worse. I'm the one who is not good enough for you. This is why I know you were right to refuse me. You should not marry me.'

Caitlin's jaw dropped. She could not say another word. It was true. It was all true.

Steven stood up. 'Caitlin, I'm going to give you a week to yourself. I'll find another place to stay. You need to think about what you want from your life. You're right, there has to be a point to all of this,' he smiled, 'I might even pray about it for a change. I'll see you around, and maybe we'll talk in a week. I never lied about the fact that I love you. I do. But, right now the right thing to do is to walk away. It's what I should've done all along. I should never have gone back for you. I'm really sorry. I just hope,' he paused, slightly choked, 'I just hope you do find a purpose. It would make me happy to know you had.'

As he walked away, Caitlin burst into tears again. It was

pathetic to cry at the drop of a hat, yet she could not help it. She knew he was right to walk away, she knew she needed some space right now. Even so, it took everything she had to stay rooted to the spot and not run after him.

It was a good five minutes before she calmed down, her breathing ragged and slow. She stood up, slightly shaky and realised she was really thirsty. She wanted blood more than she had done in days. There was only one place she could go.

When she approached the laboratory, a wave of memories engulfed her. She tried to open the door but saw it was secured. She looked for signs of anyone, but no-one was there. Of course, they were all still at the wedding. She was about to head back to the wedding, against her better judgement, when she saw Ingrid approaching.

'Ingrid, I'm so glad to see you.'

'Caitlin?' Ingrid said, 'sorry to tell you this, but you look terrible.'

'I know, look I need your help. I need blood, I need blood now. I think I'm in shock, or something. Can you help me?'

Ingrid narrowed her eyes, 'Is this about Steven?'

'Maybe, well, yes it is, but I feel so weak. Please help me.'

Ingrid nodded. 'Of course I will.'

Caitlin watched her unlock the door and followed her. The moment they entered the lab she could make out the smell. She licked her lips.

Ingrid took a bottle out of a sealed unit and handed it over.

Caitlin unscrewed the lid and drank the contents in one. Immediately she got a rush of adrenaline. 'Thank you.'

'It's our latest formula. I'll be interested to see how you feel. We are currently testing it.'

'You like to investigate, don't you?'

Ingrid smiled, 'It's in my nature. I'm a scientist. I need to find answers, or try to anyway.'

'I want answers of my own. Can I have another one?'

Ingrid fetched another bottle from a different unit. 'Try this one. It's from the old batch, but it should satiate your thirst.'

Caitlin drank it quickly. 'It doesn't have the same kick.'

'That's what we've found. Monkey blood had added an

extra something. I think we'll have found the formula very soon.'

'And what will you do then?' Caitlin asked.

Ingrid shrugged her shoulders, and laughed, 'I have no idea.'

'Ingrid, are you still in love with Steven?'

Ingrid's eyes widened. She faltered for a moment. 'I can't lie to you. Probably. Saying that, since Tobias has been paying me some attention it's helped. Do you mind?'

Caitlin smiled. 'No, not at all. We've decided to take a break. I know you would love to be with Steven, and it's not that I don't, it's just that we need some space. I need to figure out what I want.'

'Not easy,' Ingrid sighed, 'good luck with that one.'

Caitlin sat down in a chair and blurted out, 'Ingrid, don't you ever want more than this life? Don't you want to use your special qualities for good?'

'Of course,' Ingrid leaned against the unit, 'but, we are killers. Out there we do more harm than good.'

'Really? You really believe that.'

Ingrid relented, 'Okay, no I don't. I think we can do a lot of good. But, I'm not in charge and neither are you. So, we're kind of stuck here. You just have to make the most of the life you have.'

'Difficult when you're confined to one place.'

'Life here is good, we live at ease, and everyone works hard. It's not a bad place, we survive.'

Caitlin sighed, 'Yes, you survive. I am alive. So what? I want more from life than just to survive. I want to wake up every morning thinking *I love my life* not just survive. You know what I mean?'

Ingrid fidgeted. 'When you put it like that. I agree. There's more to life than just surviving. We should all want more than that. I never really looked at it that way before.'

Caitlin stared straight ahead. 'My mum always told me to make the most of my life, to stop complaining about what I didn't have.'

'Wise mum.'

Caitlin looked at Ingrid. 'Yeah, I should've listened to her more.'

Chapter 42

Space

'Steven, you have to understand that I didn't tell you for your own good,' Catherine said.

Steven had his arms folded over his chest. 'I know, but you still should've told me. I mean, seriously, I have three children?'

'I know, I know, but the plan is to take them all to Borneo when the time comes. Lucy is keen to start again there. She wants a new start with them. You don't have to go with her. She told me to make sure you understood that she doesn't need you to be involved. She's a very determined lady'

'Maybe,' Steven said. 'But, I can't just walk away from this. I've never been the kind to shirk off my responsibility. I got her pregnant. I am responsible.'

Catherine was surprised by his little speech. 'Admirable words. But still, Lucy is happy to go it alone and I have promised to help her.'

'What if I don't want her to? What if I actually want to see my children grow up? Is it that strange for a man to actually want to be involved in the upbringing of his kids? Let's face it my mum had nothing to do with me when I was growing up, my dad did it all until he remarried. And he did a great job,' he started to raise his voice, 'I'll be there for my children. I'm nothing like my mother.'

Catherine could not help but smile. 'No, you're wrong. You're just as strong as your mother was. She just lost her way. Not everyone can live this life. We didn't realise what had happened to her until it was too late.'

'If you're trying to make me feel sorry for her it's not going to work. I will always hate her. Nothing you say will ever change that.'

Catherine nodded. 'How is Caitlin?'

'I've not seen her for a few days,' Steven snapped. He seemed to collect himself, and replied in a calmer tone, 'I'm giving her some space.'

'Space? Yes, that's probably a good idea.'

'I'll go and see Lucy and my children. Look, I don't want to take it out on you. Thanks for coming to check on me, and for helping Lucy as you have, I appreciate it. I am serious though, I will be there for them. As for Caitlin, time will tell what will happen. Sometimes love just isn't enough.'

It broke Catherine's heart just a little to hear him say that. She was prouder of him now than she had ever been. She took a step closer and placed her hand on his shoulder. 'Steven, you have to do what you think is right.'

'I will,' he said. 'I've got to go.'

Catherine watched him leave. He looked so much older now, not in his physical appearance, but there was something about his eyes that haunted her. They had deepened, matured even. He was not a boy any more, he was a man.

Catherine knew she had to talk to Caitlin, to find out what she planned to do. She knew Caitlin was teaching now, so she decided to go to her classroom and wait for her.

It was only a short walk to the area where the younger children were taught. Some of her own would be there now, she could use the excuse of seeing them before they went to lunch. She chatted to a few other mums for about ten minutes as the class ended. Some of the newer mums always collected their kids.

She managed to see her youngest child, Alicia, as she walked out. After a quick chat she waved her goodbye and made her way into the classroom, 'Did Alicia behave today?'

Caitlin lifted her head and gave a half-smile, 'She's always good and very clever. Just like her mum it seems, especially with her shock of red hair. She could be related to me.'

'I know, us redheads have to stick together.'

Caitlin laughed, 'I guess.'

Catherine got within reaching distance. 'How are you?'

'You know, don't you?'

Catherine shrugged her shoulders. 'In truth, everyone knows. You didn't say yes in the wedding after all, and we haven't seen you with Steven since then. But, I also spoke to

Steven and I know about Lucy.'

Caitlin nodded.

'Difficult situation.'

Caitlin raised her hands. 'It is what it is.'

'Sure, but can I ask you something?'

'You might as well,' Caitlin said, as she slumped against the wooden table.

'What do *you* want?'

Caitlin's eyes widened. She got off the table and paced the class. She spoke softly, almost to herself, 'What do I want? Hmmm… I want my old life back.'

Catherine shook her head.

Caitlin stood still and stared at Catherine. 'But, I can't have my life back, can I? Look, I love to teach. I've found my calling. I just want more than this. I want to make a difference. I think I could help people out there. People like us can do great things. I don't think we need to hide away like criminals. We're capable of so much more than this existence.' She held up her hands.

Catherine smiled, 'So what do you suggest?'

'I think you should let me leave so I can find my way. I've got no place here.'

'Alone?' Catherine queried. 'Steven has vowed to stay with the children.'

'Yes, alone.'

Catherine shook her head vigorously. 'It's never going to happen.'

'You asked, I told you,' Caitlin scowled, then continued, 'I've got to admit that even though I can imagine a life here, I believe in time it would stifle me. I mean, look what happened to Steven's mum. I don't think this small, community life suits me. And if Steven ends up going to Borneo with Lucy then it's not a good idea for me to go there too. At least, not right now.'

Catherine nodded. In deep concentration, she asked, 'What if you did not go alone? Would you go with someone else?'

'Who did you have in mind?' Caitlin's eyes alighted.

'I have to think about it, but you might need to manufacture synthetic blood. And for that you need a scientist…'

Caitlin's lips curled up as she said, 'We might think of the same person.'

Catherine leaned against the wooden table. 'I'm all ears.'

'Ingrid?' She could not believe she was suggesting her, she doubted Steven would approve. Then again, what did it matter?

'Ingrid,' Catherine smiled, and gave a light nod. 'We should go and talk to her, but first let me talk to my brother, Ian. He needs to know what's going on. He might know what to do.'

'Okay, let me know what he thinks. Oh, and thanks.'

Catherine gave Caitlin a hug. She could tell it surprised Caitlin since she felt stiff at first, but then she returned the embrace.

Catherine had not spoken to Ian in a few days. The last time she had seen him, his shoulders had sagged like an old man. The stress of taking over from his father at short notice was taking its toll. She made her way up to his office, the secluded soundproof headquarters where he now hid away from everyone.

She typed in the key code and gained access.

She could hear him talking as she approached. 'It's not going to work, Eilif. Look, just... oh wait a minute, I'm sure that's Catherine.'

Catherine walked in, and held back her shock as she took in Ian's appearance. His hair was dishevelled, his face unshaved, and his eyes had a reddish glaze. 'Brother, you don't look too good.'

'Thanks for that, sis. You, on the other hand, look great.'

'It's called having a wash,' she grinned.

'I do keep telling him to take a break,' Eilif added.

'A break?' Ian guffawed. 'I don't have time for a break. You might think everything is as it was, you might think the community has accepted Steven and Caitlin with open arms – hey, they're doing a good job at appearing to be the perfect host – but the truth is far from it. I hear things, I know things, and I'm sure secret plotting is going on behind our backs. I don't know what they are saying exactly – I only hear rumours.'

'But, rumours are just that,' Catherine started, 'people like to talk. They did this before anything happened, and they'll do it again for many years to come.'

'No,' Ian shook his head sadly, 'this is different.'

Catherine took a seat, and glanced at Eilif who raised his hands in defeat. 'What have you heard?'

Ian gave a low chuckle. 'It's more the case of what *haven't* I heard.'

Eilif looked at Catherine. 'The numbers for Borneo are much larger than we expected. And then, the ones that want to stay have expressed an interest in changing the way things are run. Franco, and his son Enrique, want to take over. They do not believe Ian should be in control, in fact they never saw why he assumed the position in the first place.'

'I don't blame them,' Ian said. 'I've tried my best, but the truth is I'm not Dad. I do not have his authority, his desire to lead. I was happy as I was. The truth is I'm happy for them to do what they want. I don't know what will become of us though. It's like everything is falling to pieces.'

'No, it's not falling to pieces,' Catherine said, firmly. 'Ian, Dad had the right idea all along. Don't forget Franco, Morten and Isaac were involved from the beginning too. They had to segregate us – then. But now, with the discovery of synthetic blood, the ability to breed amongst the normal population, the fact we might be able to control our needs, and eventually die a normal death, everything has changed. We're not vampires, we never were. Just because we drink blood, and are stronger than normal humans does not make us monsters. You know this!'

Ian gave a slow nod.

Eilif shrugged his shoulders. 'And yet you hit the nail on the head, we *might* be able to control our needs.'

'Is it up to us to decide?' Catherine asked, 'shouldn't people have a right to vote. Should we not live in a democracy, not a dictatorship?'

'We are not dictators?' Ian snapped.

'Really?' Catherine laughed. 'We control where people

live, what they do, what they learn, what they are allowed to know.'

Ian stood and paced up and down the room. 'It's for the best.'

'No, no it's not,' Catherine stood up. 'Ian, there's other stuff you don't know. Something you must keep a secret, and you Eilif, can you do that?'

'More?' Ian growled.

'Okay, fine,' Catherine turned to leave.

'Catherine,' Ian pleaded. 'Tell me about it. Eilif, you okay to keep quiet about this?'

Eilif nodded.

Catherine sat back down. Her stomach churned. 'Lucy has become a mother.'

'Lucy?' Ian raised his eyebrows.

'Wasn't she supposed to be in Borneo now?' Eilif asked.

'Yes, it was a scam. If Franco finds out his daughter is an unmarried mother of triplets he's not going to be happy.'

'Triplets?' Ian's eyes bulged out of his sockets.

'There's more,' Catherine added.

'The father?' Eilif asked, wary.

Catherine hesitated for a moment, as both sets of eyes focused on her. 'Don't over-react now.'

Ian spoke in a calm tone, 'Tell us.'

It was now or never. 'Steven is the father,' she paused, 'and Caitlin knows.' She might as well throw it all in.

'Oh, that's just bloody fantastic!' Ian raised his hands to the sky, before he took a seat.

'Are you sure?' Eilif said.

Catherine nodded. 'Just hear me out. Steven wants to do the right thing. He wants to help Lucy raise the children. Caitlin and Steven have decided to take a break until the air has cleared. Which brings me on to the next thing.'

'More?' Ian lifted his head, his voice more of a grunt now.

'Afraid so,' Catherine smiled. She would keep a level head. 'Caitlin wants to leave the community. And,' she turned to face Eilif, 'she would like Ingrid to go with her.'

Eilif laughed aloud, and looked away for a minute as he

collected himself. 'Sure she does.'

Ian stood up again, exasperated he rambled on, 'Fine! So, let Caitlin go with Ingrid! Let them loose. In fact let's all go, shall we? Let Steven play happy families with another new breed, let Franco do whatever he wants, maybe Morten can stay here, you can go to Borneo with anyone who still wants to go, and I'll just move back to England with my family and pretend nothing ever happened. How does that sound?' He flumped back on his seat.

Silence ensued for a few minutes.

'It's not a bad idea, actually,' Eilif said, his voice quiet.

Catherine fought the urge to laugh.

'Really?' Ian shook his head, a smile now creeping into the corners of his mouth. He looked from Eilif to Catherine and burst out laughing. It was of the hysterical kind to say the least.

Catherine had to laugh with him. 'You really need to loosen up you know. Laughing is good. And yes, actually, everything you said. Let's do it.'

'Years of protection are going to be thrown down the drain just like that? It's that easy?' Ian said.

'Yes, we need to give people the choice to leave. Anyone who wants to stay can. I'm happy to start the new community in Borneo, as planned. I believe Steven and Lucy will come with me and I don't think we should tell Franco about her.'

'No,' Eilif said, 'I agree with you there. He would kill Steven.'

Chapter 43

The Future

Steven rolled out of bed, and stood up. He gave a massive yawn and stretched. It did nothing to wake him up, he was completely drained. Over the last week, he had only had a few hours' sleep every night. He worked all day, then helped Lucy with the babies at night, until sleep deprivation forced him to shuffle back to his room. Then he woke up and repeated the cycle. He was ashamed to admit he had not even had the energy to think of Caitlin at all. Being a dad of three was hard work. Babies were the most demanding, yet adorable, things he had ever been in contact with. He knew he should not really think of them as *things*, but at the moment he didn't know what else he should call them.

He had to admit he had a newfound respect for his father, in raising him without Emily. He was glad his dad had met Clara. His throat constricted as he remembered Clara was dead. He still found it hard to come to terms with.

Ever since he had met Caitlin so much had happened. His life had spun out of control. It was hard to believe that two years earlier he had been a student like any other. And now, he was a hybrid, *single* father of three, living in the Amazon jungle. It beggared belief.

No Caitlin. No degree.

Yet, he knew he had done the right thing, he could not let Lucy raise the children without him.

There was a meeting to attend, so he forced himself into action. He got the feeling it was a big deal, but he was too tired to care.

He made his way over to the breakfast hall, loaded up his plate and took a seat next to Gideon. He had avoided Jenson and Susanna recently – they were too loved up for words.

He tucked in and tuned out the mindless chatter going on around him. A touch of auburn caught the corner of his eye, and he glanced up momentarily to see Caitlin walk past next to

Ingrid. They seemed to be thick as thieves recently. She caught his eye for a moment and gave a sad smile. His gaze lingered on hers for a second as he gave a tired smile back. Then he sighed and returned to his meal. He did not have the energy to even try to bridge that gap at the moment.

Eventually, everyone started to make their way over to the great hall and he followed, whilst trying to keep away from conversation. Over the last few days, he had talked so little that everyone realised he wanted to be left alone. It suited him just fine.

After ten minutes of standing around, he saw Ian and Catherine assembled on the podium. The rest of the originals stood near the front. The atmosphere was tense as people whispered. None of the children were there. Someone must have got the lucky job of looking after them. Come to think of it, Caitlin was nowhere to be seen. He wondered if she was looking after the older children.

Finally, Ian began, 'Thank you for coming along this morning to yet another gathering. A lot has happened over the last two years. First, we found out that we had a new member of the community no-one knew about for nearly twenty years. Steven, we hope we made you welcome.' Ian turned to Steven.

Steven kept a straight face.

Ian continued, 'I know for a lot of you the idea that our kind should breed with ordinary humans is repulsive. And yet when Emily did, the outcome, Steven, is really no different to us, I'm sure you all agree.

A few people frowned.

'Second, we lost our leader and his wife, my father and mother – they are missed every day, and then my sister, Emily,' Ian coughed, then carried on, 'a lot of fallacies have been revealed to us. For years we have kept away from normal society, but not because we were ashamed, because of what we thought we could do. And yet, we *can* die, we are *not* immortal. We also know, since Caitlin joined our community, that a human can become one of us. We have not talked extensively to you about this, but even though Caitlin has familiar traits she is not like the rest of us. Some of you know this already but the truth is Judith was also like Caitlin.'

A series of gasps escaped, and a muffled chatter erupted.

'Settle down everyone,' Isaac said, 'let Ian speak.'

As people quietened down, Ian continued, 'My mother was changed by my father. It is clear now that the reason my father sought to protect us was because he was aware that we could do things that could be construed to be of a vampiric nature, including changing a human being. The question remains and is unspoken... how do we change a human, and more importantly why would we want to?'

Ian took the time to slowly look around the room for moment, before he explained, 'The reason for the why is easy in the case of both my mother and Caitlin – they were both changed in the name of love. But, and this is a big but, it came at a price. I have to tell you all that Caitlin will never have children.'

More looks of horror resulted, and people glanced at Steven in disgust.

'But,' Ian continued, raising his voice, 'Steven did not know this would happen when he changed Caitlin. At least now we know. As to the how – there's no point going there. Why would anyone want to change a human after what we have discovered? We cherish life here, and being able to give new life is the right of any woman. None of us have the right to take it away. I admit we do not know what would happen if a man was changed. Saying that, why would we want to find out?'

Ian glanced at Catherine and she gave him a reassuring smile.

'The truth is, we don't know whether Caitlin will age but, since Judith didn't, we assume she won't.'

He attempted to sound optimistic as he added, 'However, every cloud has a silver lining. Her blood is different to ours, and as luck would have it whilst working with a sample of her blood and that of monkeys we have found a way to make a new, improved, synthetic blood. We don't know if it'll enable the change, but we suspect it will since Tobias survived. And so, another discovery. We don't have to feed off humans for blood – we can make it ourselves.'

He nodded towards Eilif, and held his head high, 'This leads me to the final point,' he paused and coughed, 'we know that the community is too big. We have to start again, or some of us do, on the island of Borneo. The thing is, based on everything I have just said, should we remain hidden away from humanity? Should we shy away from the outside world? Or, should we actually consider joining it? Trust me, the originals have discussed this at length and personally, I have reached a conclusion.'

The atmosphere in the room was intense. Steven had no idea what he could reveal next.

'I'm not your leader, I never was. I'm one of you, and as one of you I am not in a position to tell you what to do anymore. I think we are all entitled to free will, to decide our own destiny. The gates are open, the heads of each family have the exit codes. You can all do as you wish.'

A loud, unsettled chatter erupted, so Ian lifted his hands up. 'I do warn you that if you choose to leave here without the ability to create synthetic blood, you'll become a murderer. At some point you will need blood, and you all take full responsibility for your young. I believe that only those who have changed, and have parental consent, should go. But, that's just my opinion. I choose to stay here for now, this is my home, but I will not tell you what to do from now on. Thank you for being so patient.'

Ian moved to the side with the rest of the originals.

Catherine faced a silent, speechless crowd. 'Isaac, my family and I are still going to Borneo to start again. Anyone wishing to join us is welcome.' Catherine moved next to Ian.

Morten moved into position. 'I'm taking my family back to Sweden. We will start anew there.'

Franco stood next to him. 'And I'm returning to my homeland, Spain. We will start again, we will help my country regain its former power. This is not the end, it is the beginning.'

Steven could not believe what they were saying. The community was falling apart.

He watched as everyone started to talk at once and ask questions. Within a series of minutes, groups had formed around the originals. It seemed that family loyalties were having a swing on people's decisions.

Steven made his way over to Catherine. She caught his eye and made her way towards him and excused herself from her husband, Isaac.

They walked away from the room together.

Once they were alone, Catherine said, 'You will come with us?'

'Right,' Steven nodded, 'and anyone who wants to go just leaves? Just like that.'

'Pretty much.'

'Madness,' Steven said, his eyes narrowed.

'No, it gives everyone a chance at a life. It give those *you* love a chance,' Catherine stressed.

'Caitlin?' Steven felt his chest constrict. 'Has she left? Has she gone?'

'Yes, it's for the best,' Catherine nodded. 'You'll see her again one day, I'm sure. But, now you must let her go.'

Steven fought to keep it together. She could not have left, she could not have abandoned him. This was not the way it was meant to end. He choked out the words, 'Who went with her?'

'I think you know. The only person who can make what they need, the only other person she trusts.'

'Not Ingrid, please not Ingrid,' Steven said, his hands in fists.

'You never understood that Ingrid never meant you any harm. You never realised that all along she only wanted the best for you. And now she's looking after someone you care about. She is a true friend and you should be grateful she has chosen to help Caitlin.'

Steven relaxed his hands, and spoke through gritted teeth, 'And there's nothing I can do.'

Catherine put her hand on his shoulder. 'You cannot perform your duty as a father *and* leave with Caitlin. Besides, I think she's looking forward to finding out who she really is.

You want the best for her and this is it.'

'This is it. Everything I have gone through, the deception, the death, the confusion, all for this. Free will.'

Catherine smiled. 'Do not mock it. Free will is something man has fought for, and we seek to give it back to our kind. We will hide what we are, we will mix within society, and we will have to adapt and find ways to avoid suspicion. It should be easy to do. And if any of us are ever caught, there's no way they'll be able to prove that we're different. If we don't feed we will simply die. Life repeats itself again through our children. We will learn from our mistakes, from our past, just like every other human before us.'

'Okay,' Steven took a deep breath and composed himself. 'I've got to go.'

He walked away in a trance barely hearing Catherine ask him to go see her if he needed help.

When he arrived it amazed him that nothing had changed, life continued.

He did not know what he expected. Somehow, he had the impression loads of them would run for the exits, but it did not appear to be happening. He kept his head low and listened as the others discussed their options. They sounded excited, but not overly bothered. The majority wanted to stay as they were – it seemed the unknown did not appeal to everyone.

'What about you, Steven?' Susanna asked, as she broke away from the others.

'What about me?' Steven smiled.

'What are you going to do?'

'I'll go with my aunt Catherine to Borneo.'

'Hey,' she paused, 'sorry about what happened to Caitlin. It must be tough.'

'Caitlin will be just fine. Don't be sorry, she has always been stronger than the rest of us. She was never fussed about having a family.' He did not know it for sure, but it felt right to say it aloud.

'Of course,' Susanna spluttered, 'I just…'

'Don't worry about it.' Steven lowered his head and swallowed. He did not want to talk about her anymore.

He had a job to do. Deciding how Borneo would be organised had never been so important. It would be easier to accept the fact that Caitlin no longer wanted him in her life if he just concentrated on work, his children and survival.

Love had always been far too over-rated and it was obvious his mind and heart had different agendas.

He would not let his children down – ever.

EPILOGUE

Return

Caitlin giggled nervously as she made her way through the thick trees and undergrowth. 'Are we nearly there?'

Ingrid turned to face her and rolled her eyes. 'After everything we've seen over the past five years, you should have got over your nerves.'

'Oh, it's just that...'

'I know,' Ingrid smiled, 'even I am wary about seeing Steven again, although I look forward to seeing Tobias more.'

Caitlin shook her head. 'Just because Tobias is the eternal romantic. I'm amazed you managed to have a long distance relationship with him after all this time.'

Ingrid raised an eyebrow. 'Hey, don't dismiss it. Love can work its magic via email, telephone and messaging.'

'We'll see if he's as good in the flesh as he has led you to believe. Truly, I hope it works out for you. But, seriously, stop teasing me. Steven and I are history. I left without saying goodbye and he has children with another woman, why would he even remember me?' Her stomach whirled slightly at the thought. It was stupid to go there even though she had put off a visit to Borneo for a long time.

'Yeah, why would he...' Ingrid chuckled, then gasped as she pointed ahead, 'there it is!'

An open community had been created in the middle of the jungle. It was not a hidden world inside a volcano. It was out in the open. If any human stumbled upon it they would simply have their memory erased, or so she'd been told.

There were a lot of things she'd had to do to survive with Ingrid. It was just life.

As they made their way in, a range of familiar faces came into view. Ingrid started to hug a lot of the adults and Caitlin embraced some of the now much older children she had worked with.

Everyone fired questions at them.

Eventually, they took a seat by the fire. Caitlin was given some stew and water. She was ravenous, and did not care what it was. All the time she was eating, her eyes surveyed the area. It was ridiculous and a part of her wanted to get up and run away. It was a mistake to be here.

A little girl came up to her and handed her a wooden doll, with intricate details cut into the wood for a face, and a simple dress made from a green fabric. As Caitlin went to say thank you she saw the girl's eyes were the deepest amber, streaked with gold strands – just like her father. She smiled, and swallowed hard to keep calm. 'Thank you.'

'Will you tell me a story?' the little girl asked, as she twirled a strand of raven hair in her finger.

'Sure,' Caitlin said, 'what's your name?'

'Cara.'

Caitlin nodded, and resisted the urge to smile. 'So, Cara, what stories do you like?'

Cara took a seat on the floor and licked her lower lip, nose scrunched in concentration. After a minute, she replied, 'Where've you been?'

'Well,' Caitlin replied, 'that would take a long time.'

'That's okay,' the girl settled back onto her hands.

Caitlin glanced at Ingrid, but she was still talking to the others. 'Okay. Well, I went to see the world.'

'*Where* did you go?' Her innocent expression and large eyes made Caitlin's heart melt.

'Hmmm… First, we saw a lot of South America. Have you seen a world map?'

'Yes, my mummy showed me, but I don't remember Sou' 'Merica.' She frowned.

The fact she found the words hard to say forced a smile. 'Okay, well, I'll draw you a picture on the ground.' Caitlin took a stick and drew a rough sketch of the world on the ground. Then she pointed at South America. 'This is where we started.' She trailed the stick along the route as she spoke, 'Then we moved to North America, then Canada, then we sailed across the ocean and landed in Ireland, then moved to the rest of Europe, before we crossed into Africa via a tiny place called Gibraltar – the place I was born.'

The girl was enraptured. 'Did you see any animals?'

'Yes,' Caitlin nodded, 'we saw lots and lots of animals.'

'Wow…' Cara stared with an open mouth. 'Can I come with you?'

'I just got here,' she laughed, 'maybe one day.'

'Were they scary?'

Caitlin nearly said "not as scary as us" instead she replied, 'They're just animals. Some are more dangerous than others.'

'When I'm bigger, like you, I can go,' Cara smiled.

'Maybe you will,' a deep voice said behind Caitlin.

'Daddy,' the girl screamed, as she got off the floor and ran into his arms.

Caitlin turned around, her insides falling to pieces. She glanced up at a bearded face, with the same amber eyes. 'Steven, nice to see you again.'

'Caitlin,' he nodded.

Just the sound of her name off his lips make her quiver.

'Do you know Caitlin, Daddy?' Cara asked.

Steven put his daughter down. 'Yes, I know Caitlin. Now, run along and go find your mum. I'm sure Caitlin will tell you more stories later.'

'Will you, will you?' Cara jumped on the spot.

'I promise,' Caitlin smiled.

When Cara was gone Steven sat next to her. 'It's been a long time.'

'It has,' Caitlin said.

'You finally cut your hair,' he gave a half-smile.

'Oh, yeah,' Caitlin said, as she absentmindedly ran her hand over her short cropped hair. 'I said I would cut it all off one day.'

'It's nice,' he said, his eyes fixed on hers, 'it suits you.'

To break eye contact, she asked, 'How's Lucy?' and then glanced towards Ingrid.

Ingrid caught her eye, smiled, and then continued her conversation.

'Lucy's great, she's a good mother,' Steven replied.

Caitlin hated the way the conversation sounded forced, as if neither of them dared say what they really thought. She continued the façade, and asked, 'How are you?'

'As you see,' Steven said.

She could tell he had faced her again and she looked towards him and smiled.

One moment he maintained a stiff posture and intense expression, and the next he relaxed as he saw her more at ease. 'I'm glad you're here now. Are you planning to stay long?'

'We don't know,' she replied.

'Look, I don't want to bring up the past,' he faltered for a moment, 'it's obvious you are doing well. I'm happy for you. Can I just ask, can we be friends?' He held out his hand.

'Of course,' Caitlin gave a cheeky grin and held out her hand. As they touched an electric current raced down her arm. She jolted it away and gave an awkward laugh. 'Sorry.'

Steven gave an amused laugh and stood up. 'It's nothing you could control. I hope we get the chance to catch up again later. Either way, Cara will get you first. She has a way of getting what she wants.'

'Clever girl,' Caitlin stood up next to him.

Steven took a step away, but then he turned back and said, 'Can I say something else?'

'Sure,' Caitlin spluttered, annoyed she felt like a stupid teenager.

'I never forgot you.' His gaze lingered for an eternity before he turned to leave.

Caitlin gulped. 'Okay.'

Steven walked off and left her in an abyss of emotions and confusion. She wondered if that had been his way of telling her he still loved her.

She could not regret having left the community, she was not meant for this life of isolation. She did regret leaving without saying goodbye, there were things that should have been said. She whispered into the breeze, '*I never forgot you either.*'

In the distance, she saw him turn around and smile. His distant reply surprised her, 'Well that's a start.'

Acknowledgements

I have found a lot of inspiration through music for this entire Trilogy, and I have to mention my favourite radio station and soundtracks. I have to admit that, to my family's despair at times, I have an obsession with all of The Twilight Saga soundtracks. For this book, I splashed out and also got a copy of the Carter Burwell Soundtrack for Breaking Dawn, Part Two, and the music from the Twilight Saga (by the City of Prague Philharmonic Orchestra). My favourite radio station is CINEMIX, found via Classical music in iTunes – I have listened to this station a LOT.

As I have mentioned on my blogs, I was inspired to start writing after watching an interview with Stephenie Meyer in the Twilight DVD back in 2010. I figured if she could do it, then so could I. Being a stay at home mum can be a very lonely and soul searching job.

Writing has liberated me and through social media I have made many friends from all over the world. I find it hard to look back now and remember a time when I did not write books, short stories, blog and use social media.

To anyone with the desire to write – DO IT, and if you want to self-publish, then go for it! A warning though, if you are not prepared to do the groundwork then use a formatter, or hire someone to do your covers. I have chosen to do it all myself, and have had some excellent help from friends, fellow social media users, and family. This was a self-imposed challenge and I have always been a bit of a computer geek so I enjoyed figuring it all out, whilst using the helpful advice on the web. I thank Mark Coker, for his free guidelines when I first started, and the writing community on The Word Cloud for their support, advice and encouragement.

Some people express anger at authors like me, who choose to self-publish, but I think I have climbed the mountain and flown my flag at the top. I am proud of what I have achieved. I hope you see the merit in my story, formatting, cover, and editing.

A special thank you has to go to my friend and main editor, Adam, who found my story via Facebook when I first published. Even though he had not been in contact with me in fifteen years, he took a chance and read Hybrid. Two other supportive friends are Lynn and Julie, who I met via the school run. Their advice, feedback and support have helped me with Complications and Return – I am too grateful for words.

In my opinion, the most important thing is to enjoy the story – I sincerely hope you do. In my opinion, without a good story you have nothing, no matter how beautiful your prose is.

Another thank you has to go to my daughter, Elsa, who read my story with vigour and challenged my decisions. She helped me soundboard a lot of ideas in the final chapter (and even tried to write it herself). She believes there should be another book, but, as I explained to her, sometimes the end is meant to be the beginning. This works for me anyway.

Finally, I have to thank my sister-in-law, Minka, for allowing me to use her picture for my cover.

To all of my "fans" online – you are the best. I did start to write a list but realised there was not enough space… you know who you are.

I guess it's time to come up with something new.

Keep reading and writing,
Vanessa Wester

ABOUT THE AUTHOR

Vanessa Wester is bilingual in English and Spanish, since she was born and raised in Gibraltar. She has a degree in Accounting and Law from the University of Southampton, UK. Initially, she embarked on a career in Chartered Accountancy. After a couple of years it became obvious she was not cut out to work in an office.

A change in vocation led her to become a Secondary School Mathematics Teacher, which she loved. For many years, she has been a stay at home mum and gives up a lot of her time towards voluntary organisations. She still teaches maths as a private tutor and has many hobbies which include swimming, walking and reading. She is also a qualified A.S.A. Swimming Teacher and volunteers on weekends at her local swimming club.

Writing is her passion. The day she decided to start writing was the day she found an outlet for her imagination. It is the best way she can think of to express herself and escape from everyday life.

Her debut novel, **HYBRID** (The Evolution Trilogy) was released in March 2012 via Smashwords and May 2012 on Amazon. Since then she has published **COMPLICATIONS**, the second book in the Trilogy, and has also released another short story called **FIRST DATE**, which is based on her true story.

In addition, she co-founded the SHORT STORIES GROUP, and publishes adult anthologies to raise funds for a range of charities. She has also compiled two children's anthologies, again in aid of good causes.

She now lives on the Isle of Wight, UK.

CONNECT ONLINE

Whatever you thought of RETURN, I would love to know. Please leave a review or connect with me online. Thank you.

Twitter
http://twitter.com/vanessa_wester/

Personal Blog
http://vanessawesterwriter.blogspot.co.uk/
http://vanessawesterwriter.wordpress.com/

The Evolution Trilogy Blog
http://theevolutiontrilogy.blogspot.co.uk/

Facebook
http://www.facebook.com/TheEvolutionSeries

Adult Anthologies
http://shortstoriesgroup.blogspot.co.uk/

Children's Anthologies
http://kids4books.blogspot.co.uk/

A Reader's Perspective
http://vanessawester.blogspot.co.uk/

Goodreads
http://www.goodreads.com/author/show/6421055.
Vanessa_Wester

REFERENCES

The power of the internet! Thank you again for divulging many facts I could use in my book!

http://www.borneo.com.au/
http://en.wikipedia.org/wiki/Multiple_birth
http://www.ivillage.co.uk/vaginal-triplet-birth/81859?field_pages=2
http://www.allaboutwildlife.com/amazon-rainforest-monkeys
http://en.wikipedia.org/wiki/Howler_monkey
http://wiki.answers.com/Q/Can_anyone_please_tell_me_what_monkey_meat_tastes_like_specifically_as_I'm_researching_for_a_short_story

Made in the USA
Charleston, SC
10 November 2013